BROOKLYNAIRE

sarina bowen

RENNIE ROAD BOOKS

REBECCA

"I cannot fix on the hour, or the spot, or the look, or the words, which laid the foundation. It is too long ago. I was in the middle before I knew that I had begun."
—Jane Austen's *Pride and Prejudice*

———

APRIL 2, BROOKLYN

It is a truth universally acknowledged that I am something of a badass.

For starters, I live in Brooklyn, where everyone can more or less handle herself. I drink my coffee black. And I work with professional athletes, holding my own in an office so full of testosterone that caffeine is almost beside the point.

I can do twenty-five push-ups in a set. Last year a hockey player bet against me on this and lost his hundred bucks. So, until twenty-four hours ago, I thought of myself as pretty darned tough.

And I'll need to be. The Brooklyn Bruisers are closing in on the NHL playoffs for the first time in years. Once my team makes the playoffs, a flood of tasks will head my way. Travel arrangements.

Publicity events. Ticket sales in distant venues. As the office manager, it's my job to coordinate all this happy chaos.

But yesterday afternoon, in a moment of sheer stupidity, I walked out onto the gleaming ice of the practice rink to deliver a message to one of my coworkers.

For two years I'd worked for the hockey team without ever setting foot on the ice. But yesterday I thought…why not? It's like working at a fine restaurant and never sampling the food.

The *why not* became obvious about sixty seconds later, when my Chuck Taylor low tops slipped on the slick surface. I went down so fast that I couldn't even break my fall with my hands. Instead, I went down on one butt cheek. But that slipped, too! I continued falling sideways, my arm and head hitting the ground next. My head actually bounced off the ice before I finally came to rest on the cold, cold surface.

Immediately, I did what any self-respecting girl does after she takes a serious tumble—I dusted myself off and told the two coworkers who witnessed this ridiculousness that I was absolutely fine.

And I thought I *was* fine, unless we were counting the bruise on my butt, which is the size of the tri-state area.

The concussion I sustained wasn't noticeable at first. I assumed that my disorientation was from sheer embarrassment. Feeling flushed and confused seemed perfectly rational at the time.

I went home, ate some leftovers out of my refrigerator, and went to bed early. But at two in the morning I woke up again suddenly. My headache had escalated, and I felt a little sick. So I got up and went into the bathroom looking for some aspirin. And when I flipped on the light, the room spun. I grabbed the towel bar so hard that it came off the wall.

For the second time that day, I fell down on my ass.

The crash woke up my sister in the other bedroom. When she found me blinking on the floor, she panicked. That's how we ended up at the ER at Brooklyn Methodist in the middle of the night. If I think about the bill they're going to send me, I'll probably get nauseous again. They poked and prodded me in all the usual places, shining infernal lights in my eyes while I insisted they should let me go home.

They finally did, but not before giving me lengthy instructions on how to recover from a concussion.

So here I roost—on the world's ugliest couch—in my tiny, overcrowded apartment, wondering what the hell I'm going to do. Meanwhile, tears of frustration are tracking down my face.

And I *never* cry. What the actual fuck?

Okay, it *hurts*, dammit. But the headache isn't what's got me so upset. The ER doctor said I can't go back to work for two weeks. He told me to stay home and avoid screens, paperwork, stress, and all physically and intellectually taxing situations.

Another tear glides down my face while I try to get my head around this. I've just texted Hugh Major—the General Manager of the Brooklyn Bruisers—to tell him I need a few days off. And I had to squint just to make the letters on the screen stop swimming around.

And *two weeks*? That's just crazy talk. The timing is terrible, and Hugh will not be pleased. Nor will Nate Kattenberger, the team's owner.

Furthermore, *I'm* not okay with it. My boys are on the cusp of making the playoffs for the first time since I came to work with the team. I have to be there to see it. For two years the hockey team has been my whole life. Sitting out for two weeks? Impossible.

Powering down my phone, I take another shaky breath. My movements are stealthy because my four-month-old nephew is asleep in a basket at my feet. I can't wake the baby. If he starts crying right now, my head won't be able to take it.

I focus on his sleeping face and feel a little calmer, because babies know how to relax. Matthew's dark eyelashes line his chubby cheeks, and the blanket lifts gently with each quiet breath.

Yesterday I thought my biggest problem was sharing an overcrowded apartment with my sister and her family. Oh, and the fact that I haven't had sex in eleven months and three days. That used to seem like a big problem.

But now I know better.

Four people live in this apartment, but I'm the only one with a full-time job. Fine—the baby is unemployable. But two adults count on me, too. My sister is trying to finish up her associate's degree, while working a few shifts as a barista. And her baby daddy—our apartment's fourth occupant—does construction work whenever he can get it. But often he's doing baby care instead.

That leaves me and my steady paycheck. And even though the team's owner has known me for seven years, these last two years I've worried about my job security. My absence today won't help.

So what the hell am I going to do now?

I must have said that out loud, because my nephew shifts in his sleep.

Ever since Matthew came to live with me, I've learned that babies have an uncanny knack for choosing the worst possible moment to wake up. I wipe my eyes with the heels of my hands and take a deep, calming breath.

Matthew rolls over and grunts softly. His little mouth moves as if to suckle.

Uh-oh.

Slowly, I lean over the Moses basket, where he's sleeping, and fish the abandoned pacifier out of the blankets. Then, ever so stealthily, I slide the pacifier into his mouth. These are tricks I never thought I'd learn. But then my younger sister got pregnant at twenty-two. "I'm keeping the baby," she'd announced immediately. "And Renny is going to go work on an oil rig in the Gulf to support us."

Right.

Fast forward a few months, and I experience exactly zero surprise when Missy loses her Queens apartment for falling behind on the rent. And I experience only slightly more surprise when Renny lasts just a few months on the oil rig.

He came through my door a week ago, dropping to his knees on my rug in an overly dramatic gesture. "I just couldn't stand another day without my family!" the twenty-one-year-old fool cried. (Yes, my sister fell for a younger man. I'd call him her child-groom, except they aren't even married.)

Now we're all one big happy family in the tiny Brooklyn apartment I used to share only with my best friend Georgia. I love my sister, but this apartment really isn't big enough for so much melodrama.

I've been cast in the role of Spinster Auntie. And right now, behind the closed door of the bedroom my sister and Renny share, I can hear the hushed moans of their lovemaking and the rhythmic thump of the headboard rocking against the wall.

They think they're so sneaky. Ever since Renny returned from Texas, they slip off once a day for a quickie while the baby naps. Any minute now they'll emerge, flushed and happy, with their soft-eyed glances for one another, their hands lingering on each other's bodies, as if it would cause them physical pain to let go of one another.

My sister is kind of an idiot. Always has been. And yet she snagged a man who truly loves her. Every time I think about them I want to throw up a little. And that was before I got a concussion.

At my feet, Baby Matthew stretches his short, little arms over his bald, little head. His eyes are still screwed shut, but it won't last. The pacifier falls out again. Then he makes a breathy little complaint, and those blue eyes pop open.

No matter how shittastic my life is right now, one thing remains unshakably true: my nephew is completely adorable. "Hi," I say softly, and his eyes find me. "Did you have a good sleep?"

He considers the question.

"Want to come hang out with me on the couch?" I lean over to fit my hands beneath his heavy warmth. I tug. And when I sit up again, my head gives a stab of pain so sharp I hiss with surprise.

The sound catches Matthew off guard, and he whimpers.

"S'okay," I say, my eyes closed against the pain. "It's going to be fine."

It's unclear which of us I'm comforting.

Matthew makes a few more fussy sounds. He's working himself up to a full-blown cry. For once I don't mind because it covers up the sound of the sex crescendo in the other room. But I've left the pacifier in the basket on the floor, damn it. Holding Matthew makes it doubly hard to bend over, but I manage it. Barely.

When we're settled back again on the sofa, the room spins in a way that rooms really shouldn't. The big brown roses on the ugly couch — The Beast, as Georgia and I call it — seem to swim in front of my eyes.

Trippy.

Matthew sucks a little desperately on the pacifier. It won't hold him for long. He's hungry. Sure enough, his whimpers become wails after a couple more minutes. I rock him in my arms, but two fat tears squeeze from the corners of his eyes. In sympathy, a couple of tears leak from my own eyes, too.

Then the bedroom door flies open. "Daddy is here!" Renny declares. He's bare chested, and the top button of his jeans is still undone. But he runs around the sofa and scoops Matthew out of my arms. "My pumpkin muffin. My sweetie pie." He lowers his scruffy face to Matthew's velvety cheek and begins to kiss him.

That baby is hungry, and Renny does not have the plumbing he needs. But apparently a half-naked nutbar like Renny is just entertaining enough to distract Matthew from his empty belly. The baby puts his little starfish hand on daddy's face, and they stare at each other like long-lost lovers.

"Who's the best little pumpkin muffin in the world?" Renny babbles. He sits in the other corner of The Beast, and then my sister enters the room looking flushed and more sexually satisfied than any new mother has a right to look. "Mommy!" Renny calls out, sounding like a moron. "We need your luscious titties over here!"

"You know," I grumble, although I'm positive nobody is listening. "In a couple of years, he's going to repeat all the stuff you say."

They don't even hear me. Missy fits herself against her boy toy and lifts her shirt. Renny adjusts the baby in both their laps, so that the baby can reach my sister's boob. Matthew latches on, while his two parents gaze at their baby while he feeds, occasionally making sickening little comments about what a great nurser he is.

This is my life.

I've never felt more like a third wheel. Or a fourth wheel. Whatever. But this is my couch, and I wouldn't get up to leave even if I had somewhere else to go. Which I don't. I will just sit here, stewing in my own misery, alone with my worried thoughts, even if nobody notices.

That's when the doorbell buzzes. The sound is like a knife through my already achy skull. "Could somebody get that?"

The happiest little family in Brooklyn doesn't move.

So I get up to answer the buzzer myself. "Hello?"

"Rebecca." The man's voice is low and firm. "Can I come up?"

He doesn't even bother to identify himself. He really doesn't have to. Nate Kattenberger is the kind of man who's used to being recognized.

He isn't, on the other hand, accustomed to stopping by his assistant's Brooklyn apartment. I've worked for Nate for seven years, and never once has he set foot inside my home.

It takes me a moment to shake off my surprise. But then I gather my wits and press the button unlocking the front door downstairs.

I turn my gaze on my living room. The place looks like a bomb went off. "Renny, go put on a shirt! Missy? How much of this baby crap can we pick up in the next 15 seconds?"

"None of it? I'm nursing. Why?"

Because the most successful man in the tri-state area is walking up the staircase right now! I don't even have time to panic. Nate Kattenberger taps on the door less than a minute later. He must have sprinted up two flights of stairs. Since there's no cure for my embarrassment, I open the door.

"You should be in bed." That's Nate's opener. He's never one for small talk.

I don't answer for a second, because my brain is slow today, and it takes a little longer than normal to get over the same little jolt of disbelief I have every time those intense light brown eyes first lock onto mine. Nate is about ten times more magnetic than an ordinary guy. You'd think after seven years I'd be used to him. But nope.

"Hey," I point out a beat later. "You rang my doorbell. I can't open it and sleep at the same time."

"A fair point, Bec. Were you sleeping before I rang?"

I don't answer; I just wave him in. As he steps through the door, he pulls something into my apartment with him. It's the biggest arrangement of roses I have ever seen, outside of a funeral parlor.

"Jesus. I'm still breathing, you know." The joke is supposed to cover my embarrassment at his generosity, but it comes out sounding snappish. And when I try to take the flowers from him, the basket is so big that I don't even know where to put it.

"Maybe I overshot," he says with a chuckle. "Here. You take this instead." He hands me a shopping bag from Dean & DeLuca, and it's full of gourmet food. "Can I put the flowers on the table by the window?"

"If they fit! Watch out for the…"

Nate trips on the baby swing because I don't warn him in time. He almost goes down, but saves himself just in time by leaning on the wall.

"I'm so sorry about that," my sister says from the sofa. She doesn't, however, apologize for her half-naked boyfriend, who's gaping at Brooklyn's most famous billionaire.

Good lord. We are Brooklyn's equivalent of a trailer park. And it ain't pretty.

"Nate," I say, as if I weren't dying inside. "You remember my sister Missy." They met about five years ago when I invited Missy to a benefit at a museum somewhere. I don't even remember the occasion. "And this is her boyfriend, Renny."

"How have you been?" Nate asks Missy. The tips of his ears go red, probably because my sister is basically topless. "Are you here to look after Rebecca while she heals?"

"Nope! We live here," Renny says, swinging his feet up onto the coffee table.

I just want to die now. As long as it's relatively painless.

"Renny," I try. "Didn't you tell me you were going to make a trip to the store? After the baby woke up, you said." This isn't even a lie. He *did* mention making a run for groceries. But that was before he distracted himself by jumping my sister.

"Sure," he rubs his unshaven face. "I could do that."

"I'll come with you," my sister says, bless her. "We'll carry Matthew in the sling. He'll be done feeding in a minute here."

Praise Jesus.

Renny stands up, rubbing his bare chest. "Hey, is the library open? I finished that awesome book—with the parallel universe? But it ended on a cliffy. I need the sequel."

Faster, Renny! I can see his shirt through the open doorway of Missy's room. I mentally coach him toward it. *The shirt, Renny. Get the shirt.*

"Parallel universes are the best!" He wanders in the general direction of the shirt. "Like, there's a parallel universe where I'm the quarterback for the Giants. And there's a parallel universe where you're the Queen of France."

"There's no monarchy in France," I point out. *Put on a shirt.*

My sister waves her boobs around, then puts them back into her bra.

"But that's the point!" Renny yells from the bedroom. Clothed now, he emerges to dance over to his son, scooping him out of Missy's arms. "Anything can happen in a parallel universe. My little man can fly. Whee!" He supports the baby on his palms and flies Matthew around.

"Won't that make him spit up?" I ask, preparing for the worst.

Missy takes the baby back from her goofball boyfriend. "Let's roll. Good to see you, Nate. Go easy on my sister. She spent the whole morning freaking out about missing work. But she's not supposed to touch a computer until…"

"Missy," I warn.

"Well, you're not!" Wisely, she opens the apartment door and disappears outside.

Renny grabs the baby's sling, and then a blanket, too. Even if he's kind of an idiot, he's actually a good dad. "Later, Nate Kattenberger and Becca!"

The sound of the door shutting behind him is the best sound I've heard all day. My embarrassment factor lowers from 100 to, oh, a 97.

"Wow," Nate says.

"They're a little much," I mumble.

"No…" He's staring at the giant brown, velvet roses on The Beast. "Your sofa is really quite…"

"Hideous?"

He laughs.

"Would you believe that it's super comfortable, though? Georgia and I thought about having it reupholstered, but we weren't sure it would fit through the apartment door." I plop down in one corner. "Sit. Try it for yourself."

Nate drops into the other corner. He lifts his hands behind his head and stretches back. "Yeah, okay."

"Not only is it comfortable, but when you're sitting on it you don't have to look at it."

Nate laughs again, and I study his profile, as I've done a thousand times before. It's objectively handsome. More than handsome, actually. Hot. Today he's wearing his trademark black hoodie and a pair of four hundred dollar jeans.

These days he wears suits to his Manhattan office tower. But the hoodie used to be his uniform. Though he didn't wear expensive jeans or designer sneakers back then. He didn't have the office tower, either.

When I joined the company, there were 17 employees. Now there are more than 2000.

For five years I worked at Nate's side as his personal assistant. Then, two years ago, he bought the Brooklyn Bruisers hockey team. That's when he asked me to leave Kattenberger Tech and manage the team's office instead. Another woman—the frosty Lauren—took my place as his assistant in Manhattan.

Nate said it wasn't a demotion, and I didn't take a pay cut. I actually *gained* some benefits, because the hockey team is a separate corporation, with a slightly different structure. And I still see Nate several times a week, at least during hockey season.

The move still bothers me, though. I wonder what I did to fall out of favor with Nate.

And now I realize I'm staring at him. But he's staring at me too. "Are you really okay?" he asks, his face unreadable. Nate is famously stoic. The magazine profile pieces about him love to use the word "inscrutable." The truth is that he's actually a bit socially awkward.

"I *will* be okay." I clear my throat. "God, it was the stupidest fall *ever*. I don't think I even hit my head very hard. I'll go into the office tomorrow morning, okay? I'll just take it easy at work for a day or two…"

He's already shaking his head. "No way. A concussion takes at least two weeks to heal."

"Two weeks!" I squeak. "But I don't need to play *hockey*, Nate. It's a desk job."

"Doesn't matter." He folds his hands like the CEO that he is, and then he drops a bomb. "For the next two weeks, Lauren is leaving her Manhattan seat to cover the Bruisers' office. Until you're really back on your feet. It's already decided."

My heart slides into my gut. "That's really not necessary." Not *Lauren*! It's déjà vu all over again. "Lauren hates hockey, anyway." She'd said so herself a dozen times.

Nate just smirks. Most men can't pull off a smirk. But most men aren't Nate Kattenberger. If you're as smart and attractive as this guy, you can do pretty much anything. "Lauren will just have to deal."

"Is there really no way I can talk you out of this? I'm just going to sit around this little apartment, bored."

"You're benched, Bec. It happens. The players bitch about the downtime, too. We need your brain, okay? We don't fool around with concussions."

I don't point out the obvious difference—Nate's hockey players get their head injuries while doing great things for the team. I got mine being an idiot.

Yay me.

"Thank you for the flowers, Nate." My voice is so low I can't be sure he heard it.

Our eyes meet, and the years fall away. I see the twenty-something guy I used to know, the one with a scrubby office and a big dream. Back then we worked late, eating leftover Chinese at our desks, and competing to see who could throw wadded-up napkins into the waste can from across the room. He was the guy with the knowing smirk and the big brain. And I took care of the little things so he had time to reinvent the way your mobile device connects to the internet.

Now Nate smiles at me, showing me his dimples. The dimples

don't fit the rest of the Nate Kattenberger package. They're too boyish for such a serious face. They soften him. I smile back instinctively. And for that moment, everything is okay.

It's a funny thing to be so familiar with this powerful man, and yet still aware that he holds my whole life in the palm of his hand. I trust him. But I also really can't afford to let him down.

"Alternate universe theory is a thing," he says suddenly.

"Wh-what?" As always, I'm a couple of paces behind Nate. Even when I don't have a concussion.

"Alternate universes. The multiverse. It's a legitimate theory in physics."

"*Pfft*. Renny just reads science fiction."

Nate's eyes brighten. "Because science fiction is *awesome*. The multiverse theory posits that infinity is large enough to simultaneously encompass *every* parallel chance. Every non-choice. Every possibility."

"Well, that's just scary! Please don't send me to a planet where my brother-in-law runs your company."

Nate smirks.

"But I do like the idea that there's a universe in which I did not step out onto the ice yesterday and then mess up our end-of-season workflow."

His smile fades. "It's going to be okay, Bec. What's a little more chaos between friends?"

"Right?" I ask, but my voice cracks. I'm so tired of chaos. I'm just suddenly so…tired.

"Hey," his voice is soft. He stretches a hand across the ugly brown roses on the sofa and squeezes my hand. "Would you tell me if you weren't okay?"

"Yes." *No. Probably not.* "In a few days I'll probably feel great."

"I hope so. Besides—the team still has to get us there. My model predicts we'll clinch our playoffs spot a week from tonight."

"In *this* universe, right?" I tease.

"Listen, bitch," he says.

And then we both crack up, because "listen, bitch," is from a B-movie we watched once on a jet to…Brussels? London? I don't remember the destination. The flight was delayed, and we ended up watching two aliens fighting, and the purple one said "Listen, bitch!" to the green one.

It's been a part of our shared vocabulary ever since. That and palindromes. With Nate it's just all dork humor all the time.

"Clinching the playoffs next week, huh?" I poke his foot with my toe. "I'd better chill the champagne."

"That's more like it." His glance travels around my cramped living room, where a giant package of disposable diapers is wedged under the coffee table, and three discarded pacifiers dot the floor. "Are you going to be able to get the peace and quiet here that you need to heal?"

"It'll be fine," I insist. "We're usually not all home at the same time." That's true, but only because I'm the one who's usually at work.

Nate stands up. "You'll call me if you need anything?"

"Of course," I lie, rising to my feet. Complaining to Nate isn't my style. I wouldn't want to ruin my Tough Girl cred. And he has enough to worry about right now.

He gives me a long look, and I try to smile. The man is observant as hell, and I don't want him to know how scared I am. "Be well, Bec. Don't try to do too much before the doctors say it's okay."

"All right. I promise."

He gives me the world's most awkward hug and then vanishes into the Brooklyn afternoon.

[2]

SEVEN YEARS EARLIER

NEW YORK, NY

ONCE UPON A TIME, a fair maiden walks into an office tower in midtown Manhattan. She's nervous, which is unlike her. But the stakes are high.

It's a short trip up to the fourth floor, so she doesn't have much time to panic. She's dressed for the job interview in an itchy wool suit. Her hair is swept up in a tidy bun. She sees her corporate alter ego reflected in the elevator's steel doors.

Two months ago she'd been a mostly-happy college student, studying English literature. But then came a phone call from home. Her father had died suddenly of a heart attack. There was no life insurance, and his business was deeply in debt.

Rebecca had finished the college semester, but just barely. Shoring up her devastated mom and teenaged sister had been taxing.

Now it was January, and she was officially a college dropout, on the hunt for a job.

Rebecca's palms feel clammy as the elevator doors part into a narrow, poorly lit corridor. This isn't the shiny corporate environment she'd been expecting. But, hey—if this company has a job opening with a real paycheck, she can't afford to nitpick the decor.

She finds suite 402 easily enough. There's a sign for Kattenberger Technologies mounted beside the door. But it's made entirely of—wait for it—Lego bricks.

Rebecca smiles for the first time in a week. Then she opens the door.

Inside, the office is just one big room. There aren't even cubicles—just desks pushed against the walls and abutting each other in the center of the room. One third of the space has been allocated to a beat-up Ping-Pong table with a prominent gash in its surface. Two skinny guys in jeans and T-shirts are engaged in a feisty 10:30 a.m. championship.

There are three other men in the room, all tapping furiously on computer keyboards. They seem oblivious to the heated Ping-Pong game and also to Rebecca.

Tap-pop, tap-pop, tap-pop goes the ball.

Rebecca's gaze travels the office, taking in the hockey poster taped up on one wall. The opposite wall is blue, with three speech bubbles painted on it. The quotes on them are odd, though. One actually says: *Nate bit a Tibetan.*

That one is unsettling, since she's here to meet someone named Nate Kattenberger. Maybe it's lucky she's not Tibetan?

Another quote reads: *Never odd or even.* Maybe it's a coding thing? Kattenberger Technologies is a software company. At least that's what her father's old friend Harry had said when he recommended her for the job. Harry is this building's facilities manager, and he set Rebecca up with this interview as a favor.

She stands by the door, hoping someone will notice her arrival. But no heads turn away from those giant monitors. The computer equipment is the only thing in the room that looks new or valuable. Everything else looks secondhand. This is either a very new company or a poorly performing one.

Please let it be the first thing, she begs the universe. Not that the universe listens to her lately.

The world's longest Ping-Pong volley ends suddenly when the ball hits the gash in the table and bounces erratically off the forehead of one of the players.

"Fuck!" he cries.

"Switch!" the other player calls, laughing. Each man walks in a counter-clockwise fashion around the table, the maneuver so smooth that they must do it fifty times a day.

That's when one of them finally notices Rebecca, waving hello with his paddle. "Heads' up, Nate! You have a visitor," he calls to one of the typing men.

Nate's back is to Rebecca. She watches, but there is no reaction from Nate, except for more typing.

The Ping-Pong player puts his racket down on the table, trapping the ball beneath it. He walks over to stand beside Nate, whose head is still bent forward in concentration. "Dude, you have a visitor."

Nate lifts one hand off the keyboard, holding his index finger into the air, making the universal sign for *just a minute*. Weirdly, his other hand is still typing furiously.

The wait is long enough that Rebecca has time for a little extra panicking. What if Nate already hates her paltry résumé? What if Harry was wrong, and these guys aren't looking for an office assistant at all? What if Nate isn't even expecting her?

What if he never stops typing at all? Will she just walk out eventually?

Breathe, Rebecca reminds herself. These are just ordinary people. They hold no power over her. If this job doesn't work out, she'll find another. She is the sort of girl who always finds a way.

Just as she mentally writes off this entire interview, Nate sits back in his chair, lifting both arms to cradle the back of his head. Rebecca probably shouldn't be noticing that he has nice arms for a computer programmer. He's a lean guy, but his biceps are well defined where they emerge from his T-shirt. And his fingers are long, like a pianist's.

"Holy shit," the Ping-Pong player says. But Nate's arms aren't the object of his fascination. The guy takes a closer look at Nate's screen. "Did you *just* write a shorter algo for determining the range of our... Holy *shit!* That's epic."

Nate pokes his coworker in the chest. "I just saved you about three days of coding. How about you buy lunch? It's your turn, anyway."

"Fine. But I'm in the mood for Chinese. Now greet your guest, you rude fucker."

Nate swivels his head toward our girl. Finally. The first thing she sees is a set of intelligent eyes. They sweep over her, but not in a sexual way. He isn't leering; he's assessing. Also, he's younger than Rebecca expected. Mid-twenties. Cute, too. His face is angular, but it works on him. His prominent cheekbones are balanced by a full mouth and wavy brown hair.

He has big eyes, and they're an interesting shade of light brown. They blink once at Rebecca. Then he rises from his chair with surprising grace.

"Wait, you're..." He pauses to shuffle through some papers on his desk, and a couple of sheets go sailing toward the floor.

"...Rebecca Rowley," the other guy—the Ping-Pong player—says. He reaches down and plucks a sheet of paper off the floor. "Here's her résumé."

Thank you, baby Jesus. "Nice to meet you," Rebecca babbles, meeting him halfway across the rug to shake his hand. "I heard you were looking for an office manager."

Nate shakes her hand, then glances around the space, as if noticing it for the first time. Then a wince. "We aren't very good at the corporate stuff. It's time, I guess."

"It's past time," his coworker says. He shakes Rebecca's hand, too. "I'm Stew. You're the one Henry sent over, right?"

"Right."

"Good, good." He pokes Nate. "Interview her. Ten minutes. We need this."

Nate's eyes flick over to his computer monitor, and Rebecca can almost feel the pull of it on his consciousness. Within weeks, Rebecca will figure out that Nate is truly special. A genius, really. And within a year he'll do business with every mobile device maker on the globe. Just standing here in front of a young Nate Kattenberger will prove to be like watching history unfold.

Today it's too soon to tell, though. She's just a girl who needs a job. She doesn't even care that he graduated magna cum laude from Harkness College, or that he'll secure his first multimillion-dollar contract two months from now.

"Let's find you a place to sit," he says, sounding distracted. He moves toward an empty desk. There's nothing on it but old pizza boxes. These he sweeps into an overflowing recycling bin.

Someone should empty that, Rebecca says to herself. *Do they even have a janitorial service come in at night?*

"Have a seat," he says, indicating the office chair that's pulled up to the now empty desk. He perches opposite her, on the corner of the desk itself. "There are seven of us. Stewie handles all the money stuff. But the office itself is kind of a free-for-all. Phones aren't always answered. People come and go. Our files are a disaster."

Rebecca nods, wondering whether she's supposed to know exactly what this little company does.

"We all work at least forty hours on-site, but not the *same* forty hours. It's flexible," Nate continues, and his big brown eyes never leave her face. "What's your availability? You, uh, probably sent me a cover letter with this résumé but..." He shrugs, having the decency to look embarrassed.

"Full-time," she says quickly. "I can take whatever hours you give me. And I'm available immediately." She knows it sounds desperate.

"Awesome," he says, flashing her a smile. The dimples catch her by surprise. Then he glances at her résumé again. "If I may ask..." He clears his throat. "Why the sudden availability? Seems like you were in school until last month."

"Right," she says softly. "My father died two months ago. It makes more sense for me to be working now."

"Oh," he clears his throat. "I'm so sorry."

It's terrible timing, but Rebecca's eyes get hot. *You will not cry in an interview!* She wants to slap herself. "Thank you, but I'm fine and ready to work. Your messy office doesn't scare me, mister." She forces her mouth into a smile and hopes that bluntness has been the right approach, with Nate. Her gut said that it is.

And Nate Kattenberger rewards her with another quick smile. Those dimples! "We definitely need the help. It's not a very structured environment. Maybe you could work on that."

That's when she notices the drawing on his T-shirt. Nine figures form a cheerleaders' pyramid, but the participants are kittens, not people. The caption read: *Stack Cats*.

"Oh!" Rebecca gasps. She turns her head to take in those weird speech bubbles on the wall. *Nate bit a Tibetan.* Each sentence is the same either forward or backward. "They're all palindromes. Your T-shirt, too."

His eyes widen. "Good eye. Palindromes are a thing with me. My fiancée made the wall mural. Do you code?" he asks hopefully.

"No! Sorry." *If only.* "But palindromes have been around for centuries. Even in ancient Greece. Literature is kind of my thing." *Was* her thing.

"Literature, huh?" Nate cocks an eyebrow.

"Right. I was majoring in comparative lit." Although she's only made it through two and a half years of college, with each semester less satisfying than the last. Rebecca loves the way her favorite Jane Austen and Brontë novels make her feel. Unfortunately, comp lit is more about soul-sucking analysis than feelings.

Before her dad died, she'd been struggling and fearful that she just might not be keen enough on the major she'd chosen. Leaving school hadn't been the plan, but a part of her is relieved not to be dissecting another sonnet right now.

"What else should I know about you?" Nate asks.

"I'm a good worker," she says quickly. "I had a three-point-nine grade average…"

"Which class gave you the B?"

Of course he'd zero in on that. "Bio lab. But in my defense, the course description didn't say anything about dissecting a pig's eye."

He smirks, and it's an expression she'll eventually know well.

"I'm, um, very reliable. There's a stack of references…" She fumbles into the folder she's carrying, extracting the list of professors and summer employers she printed at the Mid-Manhattan branch of the public library on her way here.

Nate takes the sheet without a glance at it. "Any questions for me?"

Where to start? "What do you need your office assistant to do, primarily?"

He crosses those delectable arms. "I've never had an assistant before. So we'll have to figure it out as we go. But we're gearing up for a big trade show in March. We'll need to make posters and crap. We need a schedule, and a new website for the company. We need to hire an advertising agency. That all sounds pretty time-consuming…"

He looks off into the distance, and panic washes over Rebecca. She's losing him. "That all sounds doable," she babbles. "I could help organize all those projects. Keep things on track."

Nate turns to her again. "Sorry. Sometimes I don't pay attention when people talk."

This will prove true in time, but Rebecca will also discover that it isn't as irritating as it sounds. Because when Nate is ready to give you his full attention, there is nothing better.

"…But I always make time for my mom and my fiancée," he is saying. "Her name is Juliet. The fiancée, that is. Mom is Linda. Their calls always matter. Everyone else can wait."

When he smiles again, Rebecca feels it like a flutter in her chest. *Now, now*, she cautions herself. *This nice man has a fiancée, and you need this job*.

Stew sidles up and puts a hand on Nate's shoulder. "How's it going over here? Are you making plans already?"

"Seems so," Nate says. "I was just telling…" He pauses. He's forgotten her name.

"Rebecca," she and Stew say at the same time.

"…All that needs to be done," Nate says without apology. "Like, we take turns paying for lunch, because that's the only way we remember to eat. Someone should formalize the rotation. Somehow it's always my turn. But if we—" he raises his voice "— could finish the fucking beta of version three by the next month, I'll buy lunch every day for two weeks."

There are cheers from the Ping-Pong table. But the current players don't cease their game.

Nate claps his hands. "Okay, Rebecca. You can start whenever. There are probably some forms you'll have to fill out. Stewie will know what they are."

"Employment forms?" Her mind is bounding along, trying to keep up. "W-4? And I-9?" Had he really just hired her? Seriously?

"Right." He stands up. "Good stuff. Stew? Can you make that happen?" He's about to wander away, she can feel it.

But it doesn't matter. His disinterest in doing a thorough interview is working to her advantage.

"Dude," Stew says, steering him away. "Hold up. There's a few details you skipped over."

Shit. Our girl holds her breath.

"Salary," Stew mutters, and Nate makes a reply. Stew nods. "What about stock options?"

Nate's nose wrinkles. "Nah. Not for clerical staff."

Whatever, Rebecca thinks. She isn't really sure what stock options are, but what she needs right now is a real paycheck, anyway.

Both men turn around again in a minute. Nate gives her one more quick smile. "Okay. I have to get back to work. But your first job is to order yourself a computer. Matty will give you our vendor login." He waves toward one of the Ping-Pong players. "And fill out those forms. Welcome aboard, Rebecca Rowley."

[3]

NATE

As I APPROACH the locker-room door, I can hear the hum of conversation within. Someone's phone is blaring a hip-hop tune, so my hockey players have to shout their jokes and challenges over the music to be heard.

"This is as far as I go," my assistant Lauren grumbles beside me. She stops in the hallway about ten paces from the door, crossing her arms against the body of her designer dress and shooting me a pissy glare. Just in case I missed the fact that the Brooklyn Bruisers' training facility is her least favorite place on the planet.

"Fair enough," I say lightly. "I'll only be a couple of minutes."

She makes a shooing motion with her hand. *Get on with it already.*

I give her a wink, and her scowl deepens. Then I push open the locker-room door, leaving her there to stew.

All conversation ceases within seconds, and the music stops, too. One by one, two dozen of the world's most talented hockey players fall into a respectful silence, giving me their full attention.

And isn't that just a kick in the pants? This math nerd from the

Midwest owns a hockey team, one that's tied 2-2 in the first round of the playoffs.

I let the moment of quiet linger as I pace slowly across the carpet of the oval-shaped room. I walk up to—but not *over*, because my players are superstitious—the Brooklyn Bruisers logo in the middle of the carpet. I look down at those purple Bs and grin. The pundits said it couldn't be done. That I couldn't turn the team around. We had coaching problems and salary-cap issues and ticket sales were circling the drain.

Not anymore.

Lifting my gaze, I meet each player's eyes as I take them in. Their hair is damp from the showers they needed after my coach gave them their morning ass-kicking. But they look powerful. They look *ready*. Beacon, my goalie, leans against the wall looking healthy and confident. O'Doul, my captain, looks strong and lively. "You guys," I say, smiling, because I can't help myself. "You're killing it, and I'm so impressed."

I get a few smiles for this compliment.

"I'm not going to stand here and tell you how much the next three games matter, because you already know. I'm a cocky guy, but I'm not arrogant enough to tell you how to play hockey. That's your coach's job."

The smiles get wider.

"But I will say this—you're headed back into enemy territory tomorrow. You're facing the team with the best record in the division. They're pretty sure they can knock you out of the playoffs in the next two games. And with twenty-thousand of their fans screaming at you in the stadium, it would be tempting to believe them. But you're not going to."

I take a breath in all that silence. We're standing in the world-class training facility I built for this team on the edge of the Brooklyn Navy Yards development. My players enjoy a state-of-the-art rink and the best medical care that money can buy. But that's not why they made the playoffs. And I want to make sure they know it.

"You beat DC three times already this season, and all because you believed you could. Faith is the difference between the winner and the loser in every contest. I can't do what you do. My slapshot is just a little less impressive than yours. But I've had plenty of experience with people telling me I can't do the shit I want to."

Trevi, my rookie forward, nods. And his friend Castro regards me with serious eyes. These men know that we're more alike than different. At the exclusion of all else, we've all dedicated thousands of hours of our time to our craft.

"There are smarter guys than me still working grunt jobs in Cupertino or Palo Alto. They have the brains, but not the guts to risk everything on their own ideas. I meet these guys all the time. I *hire* these guys to work 60 hours a week for me. They get a nice salary and benefits. But they don't ever get to say, *I built this myself*."

It's so quiet I can hear my players breathe.

"You're not that guy. You're the kind that says, 'I'm doing this. I don't care if Brooklyn isn't supposed to beat DC. I don't care if their first line has been skating together since I was in diapers. None of that shit matters because I am *here to change the rules*.'"

I look down at the emblem in the rug again. That fucker will be splashed all over network television again tomorrow night. And they said it couldn't be done. When I raise my head, every pair of eyes is still locked on me.

"Say—why not me? Why not *now*. If not now, then when? Go and take it from them, boys. Not because some pundits gave you permission. But just because you know you can."

"Fuck yeah!" Beacon yells, and then it's a cacophony. Stomping feet and whistling. A room full of millionaires applauds a billionaire.

It's an odd little club I've got here. And it's fucking awesome.

Having said my thing, I turn and leave the room. Lauren is standing in the hallway looking antsy. "Very inspiring, boss."

"Thank you."

She turns toward the exit and starts talking immediately. "The car is waiting to take you to Manhattan. Engineering meeting at noon. Lunch at one. Accountants at two. And Alex needs a call."

But I tune her out, because the next item on my schedule is

something Lauren doesn't know about. I scan the corridor ahead of us, but it's empty.

Where is she? Rebecca is never late.

Lauren has gotten too far ahead of me in the corridor. Impatient now, she doubles back in her designer spike heels. Tap tap tap. She herds me along toward the passageway that leads to the Bruisers' office building. Her goal is to get out of here before the players walk out of the dressing room. Before her ex-boyfriend turns up.

She and I both have private agendas here. But I'm the boss, so she's just going to have to deal. I'm not a heartless bastard, though. So I lead her to an alcove beside the practice rink. She frowns because it's the wrong direction, but she doesn't argue.

"Now, who was I supposed to call?" I ask, watching the opposite passageway. Rebecca will have to pass through here to get from the office building to Dr. Herberts' office. I've set up a consultation for her with the team doctor, because she's still not back at work. It's been three weeks now.

And that's just not right. It's so unlike Rebecca.

"Nate!" Lauren snaps her fingers in my face.

"Sorry. What?"

"Don't ask me a question and then zone out! The call is with Alex. She wants to iron out a few last minute details about the benefit party."

Whenever I hear the words *details* and *party* in a sentence, flaps go down over my ears. "Don't we hire people to worry about that shit?"

Lauren's eyes roll toward the ceiling, as if she's praying for patience. "Yes. But Alex just wants to check your schedule. She said something about meeting privately for drinks before the event begins."

"Hmm. Did she say why we're doing that?"

"Gosh, Nate!" Lauren is about ready to blow. "Maybe it's because you've been friends since your drunken college days? I didn't ask. She didn't offer. Is there a reason you wouldn't want to see Alex? If so, throwing a party with her was kind of a strange choice."

My eyes cut to the passageway again. Still no Rebecca.

"Well, but…" I drag my focus back to Lauren, because her bullshit meter is finely tuned, and I don't want to have to explain myself. "The timing is awkward because my investment bankers are talking to one of Alex's competitors about my router division."

Lauren is a really intelligent woman and I can almost see the synapses firing behind her sharp blue eyes. "Ah. You need Alex to be the *second* bidder on that business unit, not the first."

"Exactly."

"So, I should make you unavailable for drinks?" She chews her lip. "That's shady, though. And if your flight is delayed, you could miss your own party."

"Nah—it's okay. Set it up. I can survive an hour with her alone. If she wants to talk shop I'll just tell her I'm not ready to think about it."

"All right. Or—here's a novel idea—you could bring a date." Lauren shrugs. "Alex won't talk mergers and acquisitions with a stranger."

"Interesting idea, Miss Crafty. Interesting."

She smiles. Lauren and I get along well and always have. When I hired her to assist me in the Manhattan office, it was a good choice.

The next second I forget all about her, though. Because I spot Rebecca walking into the training center. *Finally.* And as I watch her approach, I tune out everything else.

At first glance, Rebecca looks fine. Better than fine. She's wearing a short skirt that shows off legs that I shouldn't be noticing and an eye-catching jacket in bright orange.

But there's something not quite right. Her gait is hunched slightly forward. She looks downtrodden. Becca doesn't walk like that. She always has her head up, shoulders back. She's only 5 feet, 3 inches tall, but she always looks ready to tackle the world.

"Nate. Jesus Christ. I asked you a question."

I finally turn my head to look at Lauren. "Sorry. I missed what you just said."

"Thank you for admitting it," she says frostily. "That's a first."

That's not quite true. I *know* I'm a pain in the ass. We've agreed on this point many times. "I'm a little distracted today. Can't stop thinking about tomorrow night's game." That's partly accurate. But it's not the real cause of my distraction today. Although I can't tell Lauren that.

Rebecca disappears from my sight as she continues toward Dr. Herberts' office. But I just sort of stare at the empty spot where she was a second ago. In seven years, Rebecca has never missed more than two days of work for illness. The fact that she's still out has been bothering me. So much. I can't even explain it.

A wadded-up piece of Lauren's notepaper bounces off the top of my head. That's how I know my attention has wandered yet again.

"Usually when you get like this, I just get up and walk away and try again later," Lauren says. "But you need to be in Manhattan for the engineering meeting at noon. And it's 11:15 already. If we don't finish up, you're going to be late."

Ah. "Then there's no problem. Because I changed the engineering meeting to two o'clock."

Lauren's expression flashes first with disbelief, followed quickly by irritation. "If that's true, why does the schedule *still say noon*?"

Good question. "Maybe I forgot to cc you?" Uh-oh…

Lauren leans over until her forehead reaches the wall beside her. And then she bumps her forehead against the wooden surface several times in a row.

"Hey! Cut it out. We already have enough head injuries around here."

She lifts her face, and it's full of displeasure. "But I *just* set up a conference call for you at two o'clock! And when I told you so, not three minutes ago, when you were staring down the hallway, you grunted like that was fine! But *it's not fine*. Now I have to go back and reach the tax department to tell them that we have to reschedule this conference call for the *third time* in three days."

"Sorry, sorry." I hold up both hands in submission. "I'd offer to commit ritual suicide to convince you of my sincere apology, but I suspect that would just mean you had to reschedule even more stuff."

Lauren's angry gaze could be patented and sold as a military-

27

grade weapon. That's why most of the C-suite in Manhattan is terrified of her. "Just tell me this. *Why* did you push the engineering meeting until two?"

I'm not ready with my lie, so it isn't a very good one. "Game five could be a real change in momentum for us. I wanted to watch this morning's practice." The one that ended a half hour ago.

She stares me down. It's possible that she knows exactly why I'm stalling in Brooklyn, and is just toying with me the way a cat plays with a mouse before he pounces to kill it. Either that or she's experimenting with a new intimidation technique they teach at the ninja business school she attends. Suddenly she blinks, her face softening. "Nate, are you okay?"

Her change in demeanor takes me by surprise. It could even be a trap. "Of course. Why?"

Lauren sighs and lets the subject drop. I make women sigh all the time, but not always in a good way.

"Enough about me," I say, changing the topic. "How are you holding up with this whole situation?"

"By 'situation,'" she makes her fingers into quotation marks, "do you mean the way you're forcing me to travel with hockey players? Who I hate?"

"Or *claim* to hate." I brace myself for a hailstorm of office products flying at me, but she only scowls instead.

Some of the players are filtering out of the locker rooms now. They're walking up the nearby corridor toward the building's exit. And now it's Lauren's turn to be the distracted one. She actually repositions herself so she's partially hidden behind me. That's how badly she doesn't want to interact with my goalie.

"Go on up," I say. "I swear I'll find my way to Manhattan before my two o'clock." I tip my head toward the door. "Get out of here. You know you want to."

"Raise your right hand."

I do it just to humor her.

"I solemnly swear I will not make Lauren reschedule anything else for the rest of the week."

"The *week*? Come on." I drop my hand. "Ask my car to wait, okay? I'll be in it soon."

"You'd better," she threatens. Then she peers around me, sees that the coast is clear, and starts to take her leave, while I chuckle. She turns around just before she gets to a set of double doors. "Give Rebecca my love," she says. And when I check her face, she gives me a knowing smile.

I'm so busted.

"Uh…" *Fuck a duck*. Lauren is on to me. But she's pretty smart. I don't know why Rebecca's illness has broken my brain. But if Dr. Herberts can help her, maybe I can go back to being the normal amount of distracted.

Lauren backs toward the exit. "If Dr. Herberts clears Becca to come back to work, I want to be the *first* person who knows."

"You will be," I assure her.

"I'll be on the first subway to Manhattan."

"I know you will."

"I hate you," she calls as she turns to push through the doors.

"No, you don't."

She raises her middle finger over her shoulder, getting the last word. Of course she does. The women in my life are fierce. All of them. I'm a very lucky man.

As I leave the alcove, I'm greeted by a couple of hockey players who are on their way to lunch. Then I bypass the rink and the locker areas and head down the corridor housing the training staff offices. The team doctor's office is at the end, and when I reach the door, it's closed. A tap on the door silences the murmuring voices inside. "Come in," the doctor says.

When I open the door, both the doctor and Rebecca look up at me. Then Rebecca's gaze drops to her hands, and I feel a wave of unease. Why does she look so tense? "Any news?" I ask into the silence.

Dr. Herberts clears his throat. "Since Rebecca is not a hockey player, she enjoys doctor-patient privilege. I can't discuss her case without her permission. And since you're her boss, she might feel pressured to…"

She looks up at him. "It's okay. I don't mind at all if Nate listens in."

That's enough of an invitation for me. I walk right in, closing the door behind me. I take the seat next to hers and wait for the doctor to speak.

Dr. Herberts studies me for a moment, a little smile playing at the corners of his mouth. "All right. Rebecca is still ailing. Her balance is off, and she's troubled by noise. She's easily tired, and physical exertion leaves her nauseated."

Yikes. I risk a look at her, but she won't meet my gaze. She isn't acting like herself. Just the expression on her face makes me cold inside.

"That said, she's passed every cognitive test. Her memory is sound. Her thinking is clear. She's easily frustrated, but that may not be a clinical symptom, but rather a natural reaction to a distressing situation. In short, the presentation of her head injury is not like a classic concussion."

Jesus. "Then what is it?"

The doctor toys with his fountain pen for a moment before answering. "There's a specialist I want her to see in Manhattan. He's the guy to whom we send all the toughest cases."

"Okay," I say quickly, as if it were up to me. "Who is it?"

"Dr. Evan Armitage. He's a neurologist who specializes in post-concussion and vestibular therapy. And he loves a good riddle. I'm certain he can figure out what's troubling Rebecca. The only thing I don't like about him is his packed schedule. Might be tricky to get an appointment."

I have my phone out and I'm searching this doctor's name before Dr. Herberts can finish the sentence.

"If Armitage can't see you, there are a couple of other guys I can call. In the meantime, I'd like to see you getting more rest, young lady. It's hard for the brain to recover without a whole lot of rest."

"All right," she says quickly. "Are we done here for now? I'll call Dr. Armitage this afternoon."

"We're done any time you wish," the doctor says kindly.

Becca shoots to her feet. "Thank you very much for the consult."

"It's my pleasure. Call me anytime. Day or night."

I get up, too, because Becca looks ready to bolt. "Running off already?" I ask. "Got a minute for me?"

"Of course." But she swallows hard after she says it. Like she really isn't looking forward to an extra few minutes of my company.

Too bad. She's scaring me, and I've only seen her once in the last three weeks, which has to be a record. I thank Dr. Herberts and then follow her into the hallway. We walk together, but Rebecca is silent. Her arms are crossed, and she's huddled in on herself.

I hate it.

We reach the tunnel that leads up to the office building. I hold the door open for her, and Rebecca leads the way. Sunshine has lit up the glass bricks, and the rays are bouncing off all the surfaces, like jewels. The ramp beneath our feet stretches upward, and it's so bright that the path seems to ascend toward heaven.

Rebecca slows her steps. Then she weaves to the side, and I lunge before I'm even sure what's happening. My hand finds her elbow, and then I catch her weight against my body, her back against my chest.

"Shit!" she squeaks, her hand shooting out to steady herself on the glass wall.

She rights herself and straightens up, but I hold her until she moves out of my grasp. "Hey. Take a minute, okay? What was that?"

"Nothing." She sighs. "I just got disoriented. It's so bright."

Disoriented. Is that a symptom of concussions? The cold prickle of discomfort I felt in the doctor's office returns. I wrap an arm around Becca's shoulders. "Come on."

She doesn't like the help, but I leave her no choice. And since I'm steadying her, we proceed up the sunlit tunnel without any further drama. At the top, the lobby is quite dark by contrast, the brick interior lit only by the vintage nickel and glass fixtures hanging from the ceiling. There's a seating area here, although nobody ever uses it. I guide Rebecca onto an upholstered bench and then sit beside her. "Better?" I ask.

"Yes." Rebecca takes a long blink. "I'm okay now."

"Like hell you are." It comes out harsher than I mean it to. "Let's get you home."

She glances toward the door. "I'm going."

"I've got the car." I tug my phone from my pocket. "Let me tell him to pull around."

"Jesus. It's two blocks, Nate. I'm okay."

No, you're not, and it's freaking me the fuck out. Luckily I'm smart enough not to say that aloud. "I'll walk you."

"I wish you wouldn't," she said.

Ouch. "Why?"

"Because I..." She takes a deep breath and looks me square in the eye for the first time today, and it hits me like a punch. I miss those eyes. "I can't *stand* this. I can't stand being such a mess. And I can't stand missing work. I'm sorry for the big fucking disruption, okay? Don't spend any more time on me. There's ten other places you're supposed to be right now, and Lauren is somewhere sharpening her talons to shred up both of us, probably."

"Now wait a minute, hothead." That last thing is probably true. But Rebecca is focusing on all the wrong things, and I'm not going to stand for it. "Some things are more important than a little kink in the schedule. Like your health."

"I know!" She's shouting at me now. Because women often do that. "But I'm so sick of me! It's been three *weeks*. With no change. Every night I go to bed thinking that tomorrow I'll feel better. But I don't."

Both my hands flex, because I have the urge to reach out and pull her into my arms. The attraction I feel toward Rebecca is inconvenient, to say the least. But I never act on it. "You *will* feel better," I say. And then I realize how helpless I am right now. There isn't much in my life I can't fix with a phone call or a sternly worded memo.

Except for this.

Rebecca swallows hard. "Remember when you visited my apartment, and we had the stupid conversation about parallel universes?" she whispers. "Well, I think I'm in one. In this universe, nothing works right for me."

"You're scared."

32

"Of course I'm scared!" Her eyes look red. "You and Hugh have been great. *Really* great. But I need to show up for work eventually. It's what people do."

"No—you take all the time you need. I don't care how long that is. How long have we known each other?"

She glances up, frowning again. "Seven years. But…"

"But nothing. You're not some flaky intern who doesn't know what it means to hold down a job."

"Nate, there are limits to sick days in the employee handbook."

"What page? I'll change them."

Finally I get a smile out of Rebecca. I wait for her to laugh. She has a great laugh that goes from 0 to 60 in under a second. But today I only get a grin before her face gets sad again.

"Come on," I whisper. "This is you and me. We always figure something out."

She gives me a weary look, but it's less tense now. "Dr. Herberts thinks this specialist might be able to figure out why I'm having such a rough time. But even if he puts a label on it, I won't magically get better."

"It's a start, though, Bec." I reach over and squeeze her wrist briefly, and then let go. It's the most amount of contact I ever allow myself with her. "You're not very good at being patient."

"I noticed that." She stands up. "I'll work on it."

"There's one thing I want you to do for me."

"What's that?"

I rise too, and I get a whiff of the lilac body lotion she wears. The sweet familiarity of it practically knocks me over. And I know the thing I'm about to do breaks all of my rules. I've kept myself on a tight leash for years. But this is an emergency.

"I'll tell you in the car," I say.

[4]

REBECCA

I LET Nate steer me into a shiny sedan outside the building, where Ramesh—his driver and bodyguard—is waiting. It's ridiculous to ride along for such a short trip, but I'm all out of energy to argue with Nate. I'm all used up.

And I'm so, so sick of that feeling.

Back there in the tunnel, I nearly fell over. Without his sudden embrace, I would have ended up on the floor.

Every single day I'm having moments like that—when my balance goes haywire and I can't function normally. It's fucking scary. Everything about these last three weeks is scary. I've followed the doctors' advice—resting at home. But it's not working. I'm no better.

The car pulls away from the curb, and Nate asks me a question. "Can I ask why you're not sleeping? Herberts mentioned that."

"It's not a huge problem," I lie. I'm so tired of complaining to my boss. "My nephew is teething, and my, uh, sister's boyfriend works odd hours." Renny has been bartending for extra cash. "When he comes in at three in the morning, I always hear him. And since Matthew likes to wake my sister to nurse at all hours, there's just always someone bumping around the apartment."

"Hmm," Nate says. "That can't be helping you."

"It isn't the end of the world."

"Will you call the specialist?"

"Of course I will."

"No, I mean right now. If the guy is really that busy, you need to get a spot on his docket before it's too late."

Typical bossy Nate. I often push back when he orders me around, but today I just don't have the energy to fight him. So I pull out the business card with the office number on it. My phone's bright screen makes me squint, but I tap out the number and then close my eyes against the glare.

When a receptionist answers, I tell her that Dr. Herberts referred me, and ask if I can get an appointment.

"Well, we're booking for mid-June. If that's okay with you, I'm happy to put you down for two o'clock on the sixteenth."

"*Okay...*" June? If I still feel this way on June sixteenth, I will probably need a psychiatrist and a straitjacket as well as the specialist. But I take the appointment, because I don't have many other options.

"Well?" Nate asks as the car glides to a stop. He opens the door and slides out, then waits for me.

I follow him across the seat and step out. "She gave me June sixteenth."

"June? Like, two months from now?"

"Yep." I look up. "Nate. What the hell?"

"What's the problem?"

The problem is that we're not in front of my apartment building on Water Street. Instead, I'm staring at Nate's mansion on Pierrepont Place. "It seems we're at *your* house?"

"Dr. Herberts was right—your cognitive abilities are unscathed."

I smack him on the arm. "Don't be a wise ass. Why did you bring me here?"

"For lunch, for starters. And we'll talk about my other plan."

This is mildly infuriating, but I follow him up the brick pathway toward the house. It's not like there's anywhere else I'm supposed to be.

Nate's home is a mansion in the truest sense of the word. When the house went up for sale four years ago, the *New York*

Times did a whole article about its history and architectural significance.

Nate scooped it up. He lives here alone, in a six-bedroom house. I've been inside a couple of times when he's hosted charity fundraisers at home. And I use the word *hosted* casually—when Nate throws a party, Lauren or I hire people to do all the work.

The front door opens as we approach. "Hello, dears! Is that Rebecca?" A plump, smiling woman wearing an apron and a little cap on her head waves us toward the door.

"Hello, Mrs. Gray!" Nate's housekeeper is someone I speak to on the phone often enough, but rarely see. "How have you been?"

"Better than you, if I've heard correctly. How is your noggin?" Mrs. Gray asks. "Still a bit under the weather?"

I glance toward Nate, wondering why his housekeeper would know anything about my head injury, but he looks away and coughs. "I know I didn't call ahead, but is there something you could feed us for lunch?" he asks, in a more polite voice than he uses with anyone. Ever.

"But of course! Do you think so poorly of me? In five minutes, I can give you Caesar salad with chicken and a bowl of tomato soup with croutons."

"Thank you," Nate says, sounding sheepish. "That would be perfect."

"It's only perfect if Rebecca agrees," Mrs. Gray sniffs. "I can make her a sandwich if that menu doesn't suit."

"Soup and salad sound lovely," I say quickly.

"Mrs. Gray?" Nate stops her as she hurries from the foyer. "Rebecca is going to be staying here for a little while. I'll put her in the green bedroom."

"What?" I say at the same time Mrs. Gray claps her hands together and smiles, before hurrying off again.

"Hear me out," Nate says, taking my jacket off my shoulders. He hangs it on a coat tree in the corner. Nate's foyer is larger than my bedroom on Water Street. "Your apartment is too noisy. This house has six bedrooms. I'm headed to Washington DC tomorrow. You'll have complete privacy. Give it a week. See if the quiet helps you rest."

I'm just gaping at him. "I can't stay here." For a *week?*

"Why not?"

"Well, I just *can't*, that's all." I'm not making any sense. But the reasons aren't that much fun to articulate. "You're my boss."

Nate actually rolls his eyes. "I didn't ask you as your employer. I asked as your friend. Just tell me one thing."

"What?"

"If I was injured and scared and not sleeping well, would you offer me one of your six bedrooms?"

"Well, sure." I don't even have to think about it. Of course I'd help Nate.

"Good." He turns away as if the matter is settled, heading toward the rear of the house. "Then let's eat lunch," he says over his shoulder.

I follow him through an enormous parlor filled with antiques, onward to the dining table. This room should seem stuffy, with its long table and sixteen chairs. But there's a wall of leaded glass windows looking out on a manicured garden, and all that greenery draws the eye away from the antique fixtures and the chandelier.

Nate pulls out a chair for me, then seats himself at the head of the table.

We sit down, and I feel like the queen at Buckingham Palace. There's no way I'm going to stay in Nate's mansion for a week. That's crazy talk. But it's lunchtime and Mrs. Gray is whistling to herself in the kitchen. So I sit quietly and take it all in.

This is a fun little adventure, even if my head injury was the cause of it.

Staying for lunch proves to be a good decision, since Mrs. Gray's soup and homemade Caesar salad are divine. Not that I'm surprised. Nate only hires the best. As I finish up the last bites of tangy tomato soup, he pulls out his phone and starts tapping on it.

"Nathan," Mrs. Gray chides, lifting away his empty soup bowl. "Phubbing is rude."

"Phubbing?" he looks up, startled.

"Phone snubbing. God knows you usually dine alone, when it doesn't matter. But Rebecca is your once-a-millennium guest, and the least you could do is talk to her."

I really do like Mrs. Gray.

Nate bites the corner of his lip, which is a sign of concentration. "Thank you for your input, but I'm trying to help Becca with something." He speaks into the KattSearch app on his phone. "Is Dr. Evan Armitage on the board of any charitable organizations?" His face lights up when the search results appear. "Ah, this is just what I was looking for." He taps the screen a few more times.

Honestly, if Mrs. Gray hadn't taken him to task, I might not have even noticed Nate's distraction. His mind works on a different plane from everyone else's. He can carry on a lunchtime conversation with me and simultaneously rewrite a bit of code that's been troubling him.

"Bec, what's that busy doctor's number?"

"Hold on." I dig out the card and put it on the table. "What are you doing?"

"I'm getting your appointment date changed." He taps the phone.

"How are you going to...?"

"Yes," Nate says into his phone. "I think you *can* help me. This is Nate Kattenberger calling for Dr. Armitage. Could you let him know that I've just donated $50,000 to the Concussion Legacy Foundation? It's my gift to honor the doctor's work with athletes. If he'd like to discuss the matter further, I'm available at the following number..."

"What on earth?" I ask when he hangs up the phone a moment later.

"Don't get all stressy, Bec." Nate puts down the phone looking pleased with himself. "I like that charity. Dr. Armitage chose well when he got involved with them. And, hey, professional sports teams are too cavalier about head injuries. I should have given them money a long time ago."

"But..."

Nate's phone rings on the table.

"That was speedy. Hello?" He answers the phone. "Yes, Doctor, this is he. Indeed I did. You're right, I do own a hockey team... That's the one! Concussion research is very important to me. Seemed like as good a time as any to make a contribution… Right. It's such an important topic. More so now than ever."

Nate winks at me, while my head threatens to explode. Fifty thousand… *What?*

"I'm with you, a hundred percent," Nate says, oblivious to my shock. "In fact, there's someone sitting here beside me who really needs some assistance with a head injury. We'd like to see you sooner rather than later. Unfortunately, your front office thinks that a June appointment is the best you can do."

Nate smirks into the phone, and I try to picture the doctor's face as he realizes he's just been outmaneuvered.

"Oh, terrific. That's perfect," Nate says a moment later. "Sunday morning at ten, then. The patient's name is Rebecca Rowley. She'll be there. Thanks very much. Bye now." Nate hangs up looking exceptionally pleased with himself. "The good doctor is seeing you on a Sunday! Now that's service."

I'm momentarily stunned into silence. That did *not* just happen. "Tell me you didn't *shake down* the specialist to get me an appointment time?"

Nate's forehead wrinkles as he considers the question. He reaches for his diet soda. "Nah. I'm pretty sure a shakedown would be if someone took *his* money. This was, like, the opposite of that."

"Fifty. Thousand. Dollars? I cannot *believe* you just gave that away…" My voice actually cracks on the last word. It's a huge sum of money.

"Well, technically I didn't yet." He grabs his phone again and taps the voice memo application, which he uses frequently. "Robert —this is Nate. Please donate fifty-thousand dollars to the Concussion Legacy Foundation before the close of business today. This is from the personal account—not the corporate foundation. Thanks, man."

"Nate!" I gasp.

He drains the soda. "It's a good cause, Bec. The best. The owner of a hockey team is supposed to care about concussion research. And you need an appointment with him. It's a win-win."

"Oh my God." I put my forehead into my palms and massage my brow bone, because my headache has just come roaring back to life. It's bad enough that the earth beneath my feet has developed the awkward habit of tilting when I least expect it. Nate has just made me even more stressed out.

Not a half hour ago he convinced me that he wasn't in a huge hurry to get me back to work. That the world won't end if it takes more time to heal. So why the hell did he just drop fifty large on a doctor's appointment?

Who *does* that?

"Hey." Nate's voice grows soft, and he rises to stand behind my chair. A big hand lands on top of my head. "Becca. Everything is going to be okay. You know that, right?"

Nope. "It's sort of hard to picture," I admit.

The big hand slides down my hair, landing at my neck. Nate rubs the muscle at the base of my skull with strong fingers. It feels so freaking good that I let out an unladylike moan. Everything tingles.

He chuckles, then adds his other hand and squeezes my shoulders. "You're so tight. Jeez."

I can't even speak right now because it feels so good. It's been a seriously long time since anyone touched me with kind hands. I've forgotten how good this feels. Nate just fed me, bribed a doctor to see me, and now he's digging his thumbs into the achy spots at the back of my neck.

He's taking *care* of me. It's so trippy. My job, more or less, is to take care of Nate's hockey team. And sometimes Nate. So this turnabout is confusing. I don't know what to think, and I can't think anyway, since I have a head injury and his hands are turning me into a little blob of mindless goo. "Thank you," I slur, my head heavy like a rag doll's.

Nate gives one last squeeze at the base of my skull. "Let me show you upstairs real quick. You need to know how everything works."

I stand up slowly, which is a new habit of mine. I used to leap out of chairs and bound across rooms. Now I move around like my granny.

Nate leads me back through the parlor, with its antique settees, back to the grand foyer, and up the stairway. The ornate bannister is carved from mahogany, and the marble steps beneath my feet are covered by an ornate carpet runner.

I've never been upstairs before, but I've always been curious.

We climb for a while because the ceilings are so high, especially for a home built before the Civil War. The staircase turns to the left. At the top, Nate leads me into an arched hallway, from which two doors open. "Down there is my room," he says, pointing to the one at the end of the hall. "And you'll stay in here."

I follow him into a big bedroom with a four-poster bed. "Wow, Nate. This looks like Her Royal Majesty's chambers."

"Which Royal Majesty?"

"The Queen of France. Duh." Nate's place is like the Met Museum after business hours. Big and empty. From the bedroom, I can see into the en-suite bathroom, which sports an enormous clawfoot bathtub. "This room is crazy."

"I don't want to put you on the third floor. You shouldn't be climbing too much if you're unsteady. And this is a nice room. My parents stay here when they visit."

I can climb stairs, I want to argue. But a half hour ago I nearly crashed in the tunnel at work. So I just sigh instead.

"Now let me show you the den. It's my main living space, and you can make yourself at home." I follow him back the way we came, past the staircase.

We enter a room that's long and low and paneled in oak. There's a marble fireplace on one of the long walls. But it's more comfortable than the fancy parlor downstairs. At one end of the room sits a pair of comfortable chairs beside an enormous, curved bay window. At the opposite end there's a TV setup and an L-shaped couch. Several KTech reports are spread out on the coffee table.

There are bookshelves lining the wall opposite the fireplace. They stretch from floor to ceiling, and there's even one of those rolling ladder things that libraries on Pinterest have, for reaching the top shelves.

"Wow," I say stupidly. Because how could I not?

"This is my favorite room in the house."

As soon as he speaks, a small screen blinks to life on the coffee table. "Hello, Nate," says a disembodied voice. "Can I help you?"

"Not now, Hal," Nate answers.

"That was…?" I stop.

"Not a real person," Nate says with a grin. "Hal…"

"Yes?" the machine asks immediately.

"…Is the voice of a product I'm testing," Nate says. "I'm trying to improve on the quality of smart speakers. They all suck, but Hal uses deep learning to quickly become more conversant."

"Deep learning," I say slowly. "Like, AI?"

"Exactly like AI," he says, giving me the *well done* smile. "He's a secret, by the way. Hal is one of the things covered by the specs of your KTech nondisclosure agreement. Yada yada yada."

"Got it," I say. Hanging around with Nate means always being in the presence of heavily guarded corporate secrets. I'm used to being mindful of inside information.

"The products on the market right now are all pretty dumb. But Hal is pretty sharp. So if you ask him for something and he doesn't respond correctly, just try again with slightly different words. And don't hold back on the slang because I want him to learn how people really speak."

Seriously, there are tech journalists who would sell an organ for a few minutes alone with Hal, whatever he is. "Wait—you gave him the creepy computer voice from that Space Odyssey movie, right?"

Nate looks abashed. "Just having a little fun. But he can do any kind of voice. How do you think the butler should sound?"

"Like a Jane Austen character. Charming and solicitous."

Nate taps his chin. "Like—what's-his-name, the Colin Firth character? Darcy?"

"No way. Darcy didn't like to talk. You need the other guy —Bingley."

"Fine. Hey, Hal?"

"Yes, Nate," the voice drones.

"Your new name is Bingley."

"Bingley at your service," the creepy voice says.

"And I want you to use a different voice. Male. British accent.

Blueblood. That means well-educated. Incorporate the sentence structure of *Pride and Prejudice*, by Jane Austen."

"Certainly, sir!" the device says immediately, with an upper-crust accent. "How may I be of service?"

"Say hello to Rebecca."

"Greetings, fair one! Let me hear your voice."

Nate nudges me. "He needs to hear you so he'll know to obey when you speak."

"Uh. Hi, Bingley." It's hard not to giggle. "I'm Rebecca Rowley."

"At your service, miss! You may ask anything of me."

Nate tips his chin toward the device on the table. *Go on. Ask him.*

"Um, what is the capital of Burkina Faso?"

"Ouagadougou."

"Too easy," Nate scoffs. "Even Siri could get that right."

Fine. "Who makes the best pizza in Brooklyn?"

"If you are feeling peckish," Bingley says at once, "Grimaldi's is seven-tenths of a mile away, with a very high rating. Diners tend to recommend the white pie with garlic or the Buffalo chicken pizza."

"No," I say. "Buffalo chicken on a pizza is just wrong."

"I will make a note of it," Bingley replies immediately. "Miss Rebecca does not prefer spicy chicken on pizza."

Nate looks very pleased with himself. "Bingley—Rebecca will be staying with us a while to recover from a head injury," he says. "If she asks you to keep silent, please don't speak until she calls you by name."

"She's feeling ill? Heavens! Take care, Miss Rebecca. I shan't be a bother!"

"Thank you, Bingley," I say, biting back a smile. I can't imagine where Nate finds the time to dream this shit up. But talking to Bingley in Nate's mansion is more fun than I've had in a while.

"So." Nate rubs his hands together. "Bingley controls the security system. Tonight, when Mrs. Gray leaves, all you have to do is ask him to lock the place up. He'll take care of everything. And if you leave the house, he'll let you back in. Bingley—take Rebecca's fingerprint, please."

The screen lights up. "Miss Rebecca, deign to place your fair finger on the screen." There's a glowing circle in the middle of the screen to guide me. I put my index finger there, and Bingley makes a noise of approval. "Please choose a four-digit number, miss."

"7854," I tell him.

Bingley repeats it back to me, and Nate smiles. "Something to know—the keypad on the front door uses both your fingerprint and the number code. The fingerprint is sufficient, but if anyone is watching you enter the code, he won't know that the fingerprint matters."

"We can't have highwaymen snatching you off the street for your fingerprint," Bingley says with more glee than a computer should be able to manage.

"That's disturbing." Nate flinches. "Quiet, Bingley."

"Nate, we don't have to do this," I argue. "I can just go home and…"

"Hey!" he holds up a hand to stop me. "Let's just try it. You need the rest. Don't argue or I'll upload Bingley to your phone and get him to nag your family into giving you more peace."

Knowing Nate, he'd actually follow through. "But I don't have my things here…"

"It'll be taken care of." He heads toward the door. "I've got to run or Lauren will flay me alive for fucking up the afternoon schedule. Mrs. Gray will make you dinner before she leaves. Later!"

"Goodbye, Nate," Bingley calls. "You're a prince among men! You're smarter than Bill Gates!"

I choke out a goodbye as well, but I'm not sure Nate can hear it through my laughter.

After he leaves, I kick off my sneakers and sit down on the big L-shaped sofa to try to think. Staying with Nate isn't a viable option. I don't want to impose.

The sofa is super comfortable, though. It's upholstered in a deep red velvet, and the seat is so generous that my feet don't touch the floor.

I tuck my legs up under me and consider my options. This takes about thirty seconds, since I don't have many options. 1.

Stay, and do everything Nate says, so at least he knows I'm not *trying* to be such a helpless dope. 2. Go home and recommence trying to pretend that my whole world isn't crumbling right to the ground.

I'm not used to feeling so scattered. Yet there's no need to stay at Nate's. I'm not Jane Bennet in *Pride and Prejudice*, swooning at Netherfield for days and days because of catching a cold.

Usually I'm the sort of girl who handles whatever life throws at her. When my father died suddenly, I dropped out of college and took a job at Nate's fledgling company. I helped my mother cope with her sudden widowhood. And just when she started doing better, my sister had some issues. I'd helped her pay for the college education that I never got to finish. And then, when she had a baby and lost her apartment, I stepped in again.

That's how I'm supposed to be. The kind of person who just handles things. But I'm not handling this. It's not going well. I don't know what to do, and the constant worry has gotten me nowhere so far.

The old Rebecca wouldn't be sitting here curled up on the sofa, my head growing heavier with exhaustion. I'll just close my eyes for a moment. The house is so quiet. Nate was right about that.

Somewhere downstairs Mrs. Gray is whistling to herself. It's the last thing I hear before sleep takes me.

[5]

SIX YEARS EARLIER

KATTENBERGER TECHNOLOGIES IS A PEACEABLE KINGDOM. Mostly.

Fair Rebecca quickly becomes the de facto ruler of the castle, while our prince is busy reinventing the mobile web for the twenty-first century.

Rebecca's job is to provision the fiefdom, which now spans an entire renovated floor of the midtown office building. It is she who orders the ergonomic office chairs for each new employee. (And there are many of these.) She makes the travel arrangements and keeps the espresso machine stocked with high-quality coffee products.

She's hung a sign on the wall over the machine, too: LIVED ON DECAF, FACED NO DEVIL. It is a palindrome, of course. Nate beams when he notices it. "You are priceless," he says, and she glows, because not many people impress Nate.

Sure, any asshole can do a web search for palindromes and memorize: *Not a banana baton!* The real style points are earned from sneaking them into conversation.

In addition to organizing their fiefdom, Rebecca is also Nate's sentry at the gate. Everybody wants a piece of the boy wonder — financial gurus, corporate titans, Nobel Prize-winning innovators.

She guards his calendar and his sanity. Only then can our prince have the peace he needs to reign over the digital world.

Our Rebecca is not a ruthless taskmaster. She knows when to use swordsmanship and when to be the court jester. One Friday afternoon in March, Rebecca patrols the borderlands, making sure all is well in the kingdom before the weekend officially begins.

"Hey, Stewie." She raps on the CFO's desk with her knuckles. "If you still want those presentations printed up in color for Tuesday, I'll need the file by noon on Monday."

The young corporate officer winces. "Right. Sorry. You'll have them over the weekend."

"No problem, honeybunch." She gives him a wink and moves on, reminding the code monkeys to shut out the lights if they work late, and to put their Red Bull cans in the recycling bin.

As the day draws to its end, there is only one more employee left to be managed.

Rebecca marches into Nate's office unannounced, as usual. He is hunched over an ergonomic keyboard she's found to relieve pain in his hands. He sits in front of the largest computer monitor sold in stores. Business is booming, and KTech software runs on more than half the mobile devices in North America. In two years, Nate will roll out the first KTech phone, catapulting the company's reach into hardware as well as software.

But first, a few sharp words for our hero.

Nate stares at the code on his computer screen, his full mouth pulled into a contemplative frown. Rebecca has long ago packed away her inconvenient crush on him. These days when she squints at Nate, it is only to try to gauge her odds of getting his attention. "Yo, bossman," she says now as an opening gambit.

He grunts. That's a good sign. The man has selective hearing when he's really deep inside his own head.

"You *will* call the CEO of ArtComm back on Monday," she announces. "I need you to stay on top of your calls for the next two months. Otherwise my life will be hell during your honeymoon."

"We can't have that." Nate looks up from his computer monitor. Then he pushes back his chair and puts his feet up on his new desk, which Rebecca chose for him during the renovation. "How long am I going to be away?"

"Ten days, accounting for travel. And we're not scheduling anything on your first day back, so you can catch up."

He winces.

"It's over Labor Day, though. The timing is perfect."

"Yeah. Okay." He cracks his knuckles. Nate is a certified workaholic. Her emails from him come at all hours of the night. She isn't expected to answer them until morning, of course. But the man's big brain never seems to power down. "What's next on my schedule?"

"The weekend? Remember those?"

He looks blank.

"Your personal calendar says something like *dinner with Bart*."

"Does it really?" He makes a face like a little boy who doesn't want to eat his broccoli.

"I'm pretty sure," Rebecca hedges. Dinner with Bart isn't her problem. Nate handles his own social stuff. Or Juliet does, maybe. "Who's Bart, anyway?"

"Some friend of Juliet's from her new gym. A jock who never shuts up about nutrition and his *competitive edge*. But Juliet is a CrossFit disciple now, so she finds it more interesting than I do."

"Oh." Rebecca bites her tongue, because it isn't her place to weigh in on the boss's social life. And also because she doesn't ever want her opinion of Juliet to slip out of her mouth.

Becca has never liked Nate's college sweetheart, but she's always had trouble putting a finger on why. Juliet is nice enough to Rebecca. It's just that they have nothing in common. Case in point — Juliet has lately become obsessed with the gym. A while ago, for the sake of her wedding photos, Nate's fiancée began working out like an Olympic hopeful. She's shed twenty pounds and began tanning, too.

In contrast, Rebecca's idea of exercising is walking to meet her friends for drinks, instead of hailing a cab. And Rebecca has secretly begun to regard Juliet as a traitor to the curvy sisterhood. The girl in Nate's desk photos has a round face and a silly grin. But the lithe monster who lately turns up for dinner dates looks like the newest member of the Swedish volleyball team—all blond highlights and midriff-baring confidence.

It's really hard not to hate the future Mrs. Kattenberger on sight.

"Maybe I'll leave early," Nate says suddenly, rising to his feet.

"Early?" Rebecca gasps, clutching her chest in mock astonishment. "That's possible? How does it work, exactly?"

He smirks, flashing those dimples. It shouldn't look good on a man, but Nate isn't like other people. "I'm starving. And I need a beer. Maybe I can get Juliet to get a couple drinks with me before dinner. And appetizers. Bart is the kind of tool who will make us eat at a vegan restaurant."

Nate and Rebecca both shudder at the same time.

"...*And* I don't think he drinks." Nate stuffs his keys and his phone into his pockets.

"Lager, sir, is regal," Rebecca quips. It's a popular palindrome around the office.

The smirk becomes a real smile. "You could sneak out early, too, I suppose."

"Moi?" She gasps. "No way. I'll sit quietly at my desk and meditate on your accomplishments until six o'clock comes."

"You kiss-ass. Have a great weekend, Bec." He grabs his jacket off the sofa against the wall. His new office has real, grown-up furniture.

Then he's gone.

———

Rebecca actually does stay in the office for another hour, but only because she has plans to get drinks in the meatpacking district with friends who can't leave work early. When Becca does finally leave the office, she only makes it three blocks before realizing she's left her phone in the drawer of her desk.

The only thing to do is return for it. A whole weekend without her phone? Impossible.

Back she goes.

When she uses her keys to reopen the office suite door, there's a

Ping-Pong game going on in the bullpen area. That's not unusual. Few of the employees of KTech work normal hours. But when she gets to Nate's office door, there's a light on inside. The blinds are down on the windows, too.

That's odd. Ten minutes ago that office was dark.

Rebecca taps on the door. "Nate? Are you in there?"

Silence.

The hair stands up on the back of her neck, and visions of corporate espionage float through her head. Is someone rooting through Nate's office, unauthorized? Rebecca grasps the door handle and turns. It's unlocked. Her gaze shoots to the desk chair, but it's empty.

But there's Nate—planted on the love seat. He's crouched forward, his elbows on his knees, his chin propped onto his folded hands. He stares at the rug, oblivious.

"Nate?" she whispers. "Is something wrong?"

He clears his throat, but doesn't look up. "I never go home early."

"I know," she agrees, confused. She opens her mouth to ask a clarifying question, but then it hits her. He went home early. And saw something there he wasn't supposed to see.

Nate's gaze lifts for a split second, and she sees misery in those light brown eyes.

Stunned, Rebecca turns slowly around and goes back to her desk. She sits down and pulls out her lost phone, tucking it into her pocket.

A man having a personal crisis doesn't necessarily want any company. He's probably back at the office only because he has nowhere else to be alone. Nate and Juliet share an apartment.

Shit.

It doesn't feel right to just walk away and go out for Friday night funzies, knowing he's here and miserable.

Rebecca unlocks her phone and cancels her plans with friends. Then she leaves the office building and walks over to twenty-eighth street, buying a sack of hot empanadas from a food cart and a fifth of tequila from the neighborhood's only liquor store.

The bodega on the corner has limes, too.

When she goes back upstairs, Nate is still seated, immobile as a statue, staring at the floor. Her heart breaks for him right there in the doorway to his office.

She puts the sack of empanadas and the bottle on the coffee table. "You said you were starved," she says, her voice practically booming in the too-quiet space.

He looks up at her like he's never heard of food before.

She opens the bag herself. "Chicken or cheese?"

"Thank you," he mumbles, taking an empanada without looking at it.

She sits down beside him, and they eat the first round in silence. Then she cuts the lime with the penknife on her keychain and opens the bottle. "One shot just for a warm-up. Then we find you a hotel room before we're too drunk to Google the phone number."

He glances at her with grateful eyes, and when he speaks, his voice is rough. "Bec, it's official." Nate wipes his hands on a napkin she's handed him. "You are the employee of the fucking decade."

He holds her gaze for another long beat, and her heart swells with gratitude and more than a little platonic love for her favorite nerd. Once upon a time, Nate rescued her from a tight spot, and she's been trying to return the favor for a year.

"Drink up, sailor," she says. "I'm going to get you a room at the Soho Grand."

He uncaps the bottle. "Cheers."

They each do a shot. Then she nudges the bag of food closer to him. "So. Cat tacos?"

"Cat…?" His eyes widen as he realizes she'd just hit him with a new palindrome. "Have you been saving that one?"

"For *weeks*. There aren't any tacos in this neighborhood. So I finally just decided that empanadas were close enough."

He laughs until his eyes get wet. Then he eats another empanada.

[6]

NATE

In midtown, I slog through meetings and conference calls. My brain still hasn't adjusted to the idea that Lauren is covering Becca's job in Brooklyn. Twice I catch myself yelling Lauren's name from my desk chair, only to have one of her startled minions appear in the doorway instead.

They must think I'm an idiot, but I really just have a lot on my mind.

It's seven o'clock before I make it back to Brooklyn. As the ferry bumps against the dock, I'm on my feet, eager for the ferry worker to let us off the boat. And when he finally does, I set off through Brooklyn Bridge Park toward home at a fast clip.

Rebecca may or may not be waiting at my house.

Inviting her to stay with me was a crazy thing to do. I know this. Since I've spent the last couple years wishing I could undress her with my teeth, knowing she's down the hall in my home is going to be fucking torture.

But watching her struggle earlier today had a gut-wrenching effect on me. I don't really understand it. God knows I've been fighting an attraction to her forever. But this was something else. And I just couldn't claw it back. Ignoring her—my usual solution to my unhealthy Becca addiction—just won't cut it this time.

Maybe she didn't even take me up on my offer. Becca is the

most fiercely independent person I know. She probably walked out seconds after I left today.

I have to know.

It's usually a twelve-minute walk from the ferry terminal to Pierrepont Place, but today I make it in ten. How long has it been since there was a woman (not counting the lovely Mrs. Gray) waiting at home for me when I returned?

It's been years—since Juliet, my cheating ex-fiancée. Now there's a shitty memory.

I wasn't even twenty when Juliet and I became a couple in college. She was the smiling girl who liked *Dr. Who* and dorky jokes. We studied together in the library, then went home for dorm-room sex.

Moving in together after graduation was an easy decision. Eighteen months later I proposed to her one weeknight in our crappy little one-bedroom in the East Village.

"Oh Nate. You make me so happy," she'd said from the other side of our rickety kitchen table.

It didn't last, though. Months later I caught her having sex on the same kitchen table, with that meathead she'd met at the gym.

Biggest shock of my life.

That weekend she left tearful voice messages on my phone. At her urging, I met her Monday morning at a coffee shop to talk. Even then, I still didn't understand that everything had just changed forever.

"It only happened a couple of times," she'd wept, as if that made it less humiliating. "But you're at work all the time. It isn't fun being a tech widow."

"Because I'm trying to clear my calendar for our honeymoon!" Even then, I wasn't quite ready to throw it all away. My analytical brain was still trying to glue the pieces back together.

Then Juliet said, "I went to that gym because I felt bad about my belly fat. But it changed the way I look at myself."

"You were just as beautiful before," I argued. And I meant it. If Juliet 2.0 was a cheater, it was *not* an upgrade.

"But I never thought a guy like Bart would look twice at me," she said, as if that made a lick of sense.

"A guy like Bart," I'd repeated slowly. And finally, *finally*, self-preservation kicked in. *A guy like Bart*. I didn't ask why she thought muscly Bart was so special. I didn't want to know whether it was his bench-press stats or his backward baseball cap or his too-loud laugh.

Or the kitchen table sex.

Before that moment, I'd never understood what people meant when they said "we grew apart." And suddenly I did. "Take care of yourself," I'd said, rising to my feet. "I'll get my clothes on Sunday night while you're at the gym. Everything else you can keep."

"Wait! Nate! It won't happen again."

But no. That was that. When a girl tells you that your lifestyle is a drag and she thinks a tool like Bart is some kind of prize, there isn't any more to say.

That was six years ago, and I've been single ever since. Stewie hassles me about it sometimes. "It's time to get back out there. You know that 'married to your job' is just a saying, right?"

Except it isn't. Juliet was right. Being Nate Kattenberger is a full-time occupation. I travel a hundred days a year, and that's before I count time spent with my hockey team. The more distance I get from the Juliet fiasco, the more sympathy I have for her choice. Maybe I don't have anyone to share my life, but I'm not making a woman miserable, either.

It is what it is.

Here's a funny thing—people make jokes all the time about how the women must swarm around me. "A single, rich guy like you? There must be a line of women around the block."

They're right. Sort of. Lots of women want to share my bed. But it's really tough to sort through the talent pool. Whenever I meet a woman I have to wonder—is she laughing at my jokes because she's actually interested? Or is she just in it for the money?

If the lady moans into my kiss, does she want my dick or my private jet?

The year after Juliet left, I tried pretty hard to fuck her right out of my system. But that got old really fast. Especially after I noticed one morning that my latest conquest was texting a friend. *I banged a multimillionaire.*

That was before I'd made it to *billionaire*. And the more money I make, the fewer women are granted bragging rights.

I'm practically a monk at this point. Even if I wanted to whore it up, my lifestyle makes casual sex tricky. I can't invite strange women back to my home. At any moment there are probably three different trade secrets strewn around the house. Anyone who made it as far as my bedroom would have to sign a nondisclosure agreement—and not because of sexual proclivities. *After you're done fucking Nate, do not photograph any prototype devices you spot in the residence, record any phone calls, or read emails over his shoulder.*

Sexy.

So I'm a lonely guy, possibly by choice. And I don't dwell on it, because I lead a very full life. I have literally all the money I could ever spend and the respect of my peers. I travel widely. I have friends, even if most of them are on my payroll.

Though nobody is ever waiting at home for me—except people who are paid to be there.

When I finally reach my front door, I tap the security code into the keypad. It's not until I push open the door and step inside that I can hear voices coming from the kitchen.

It stops me—this unfamiliar sound of other people in my home. I seriously get chills at the sound of Becca's sudden laughter.

Jesus. What the hell is wrong with me?

As I walk through the parlor toward her, the sound of her conversation with Mrs. Gray carries.

"My Christian isn't a fan of Mexican food," my housekeeper is saying. "He doesn't have a taste for spices."

"Wait a minute," Becca says. "Your husband's name is...Christian Gray?"

"That's right."

"But..." Rebecca pauses. "There are books about a guy named Christian Gray—"

"I know, dear! I read the first one aloud to my husband."

"Really?" Rebecca giggles, and the sound of it does weird things to my insides.

"Absolutely! When I showed him the lad's name in the book,

he was curious. And when I got to the saucy bits he insisted I keep reading. 'Can't let a pretend fellow have all the fun,' he said."

Rebecca laughs again, and I find myself smiling like a lunatic.

When I walk into the kitchen, there they are, sitting at the table together. Rebecca is eating a plate of Mrs. Gray's enchiladas, and my housekeeper is having a cup of tea.

This is the liveliest my kitchen has been in ages. "Mrs. Gray, you didn't have to stay late."

"I had a nice chat with the lovely Rebecca, while my Christian is bowling tonight with the boys," she says, rising to open the oven. "He's always in a frowsy mood after some pints with his mates. I'd better hurry home."

Her back is turned, and Rebecca and I share a furtive glance of amusement. She and I have always been on the same humor wavelength. Where my assistant Lauren is chilly, Becca is warm. Her eyes dance when she hears something funny, and her cheeks pink up when she laughs.

Not that I have any business noticing.

Mrs. Gray puts a plate down on the table for me. "Here's your portion, Nate," she says. "Now I must run, too. Toodles!"

A moment later she disappears out the back door, and Rebecca and I are alone together. God help me.

"Mrs. Gray is something else," Rebecca says. Then she pushes her plate away. "I couldn't eat another bite."

"You look better than you did this morning," I say. Then I play the sentence back in my head and realize that it sounds sort of offensive. Nobody ever accused me of having too much charm.

"I should hope so." Rebecca gives me a little smile. "Sleeping for five hours ought to have some benefit."

"Five? Wow. Rebecca Van Winkle." I pick up my fork and dig into Mrs. Gray's enchiladas. The woman really can cook. Although I won't say *I told you so* to Rebecca, it's true that a good night's sleep cures almost everything.

"You know..." Becca's cheeks are a distracting rosy shade. "I didn't know I was so tired. And it is really quiet here. You were right."

"Mmm," I say, taking another bite. I want her to stay. I want to look after her. But I won't be pushy. "Did your luggage arrive?"

"Hey," Rebecca gives me a pointed look. "The luggage thing was a little heavy-handed. My sister left me text messages asking if I'd been kidnapped."

"Oh, please." I'd sent my driver to Becca's apartment with empty suitcases for her sister to pack. "Ramesh said she was all too happy to help. In fact, Missy asked him to move the crib into your room to give her a little more space."

"Of course she did." Becca sighs. "Nate, this is silly. I can just go home. I'm better rested already. If you've reconsidered your invitation, I won't be offended."

As if. Without meeting her gaze, I reach across the table and cover her hand with mine. "Stay, Bec. I'm off to DC in the morning, anyway. Get a couple of decent nights' sleep. It's good medicine."

"Thank you," she whispers.

I give her hand a squeeze before I reluctantly let go. She picks up her drink and I eat in silence for a moment.

It's hard to pinpoint when I stopped looking at Bec like a friend and started dreaming about her. It started sometime after the Juliet fiasco, when I couldn't help but notice how Rebecca was always there in my life, making every day better. I started leaning in when we talked, and the scent of her perfume began to distract me. Her husky laugh made me hard.

I'd wake up in the night and realize I'd been dreaming of undressing her. My conscience always woke me up *right* before we did the deed. One minute we'd be skin to skin, my hands wandering her body. And then I'd wake up sweaty and aching. And feeling guilty about it.

Here sits a big cliché, ladies. I'm just another lonely nerd who's hopelessly in lust with his assistant. Oldest story in the world. "Want a beer?" I offer.

"I wish. But I'm not supposed to drink. Or read. Or watch TV. Or put myself in the position of being jostled."

"Those are all my favorite things!" I joke. Besides, I know just how I'd jostle Rebecca. With my cock.

Giving myself a mental slap, I get up and open the refrigerator, scanning the contents. Mrs. Gray has a little too much time on her hands. The beverages are practically alphabetized. "Orange juice? Soda? Seven different flavors of sparkling water?"

"Surprise me," she says.

I choose a can of raspberry seltzer for her and a lager for myself. "Want to play…?" I hesitate. Ping-Pong won't work for someone who frequently loses her balance. "Scrabble?" I suggest instead. "It's not a screen. And you won't be jostled."

"But I will be soundly beaten by your big brain," she points out. "We'd better keep the betting to a minimum."

I grab a package of cookies out of the pantry. "We'll wager these."

"That works," Becca says, giving me a smile that melts my insides. She just does it for me, with her big personality in that curvy little body.

I get a plate for the cookies, and we go upstairs to the den. And maybe it's sad, but this is the most fun I've had in ages.

7

REBECCA

THAT FIRST NIGHT at Nate's I eat too many Oreos and lose tragically at Scrabble.

My score isn't improved by playing the word "burp." But I do it anyway, because I have a very juvenile sense of humor. "There should also be style points," I say, as Nate records my score.

"For what?" Nate asks.

"Anything cheeky. Bodily functions. Expletives. Double points for anything R-rated. Think of the marketing potential! Teenaged boys would play Scrabble instead of Call of Duty."

Nate snorts and begins laying down letters. "I was the teenaged Scrabble player who was always trying for palindromes."

"We can't all have a dirty mind." Then I realize it feels weird to make that joke when I'm alone with Nate on the couch in his cozy den. Guilty, I glance over at him just to make sure he knows I'm kidding.

He's not smiling, though. His eyes are dark and serious. And— maybe I really am losing my mind—there's an unfamiliar heat in his gaze. A split second later we both realize we've locked gazes in a way that isn't normal for us.

And I feel a tug in my belly—an unusual yearning that I can't name. Or won't name. Meanwhile, we're having a new kind of conversation with our eyes. His are on my mouth. Maybe it's my head injury talking, but I could swear Nate is considering kissing me.

Me.

"Nathan, sir?" a disembodied voice says suddenly.

Bingley's interruption causes me to jump, and then Nate and I both look away at the same time.

"Ramesh would like to know if you're in for the night."

He clears his throat. "Absolutely. Engage all security systems."

"Systems engaged," Bingley replies.

There is a long beat of silence until I speak. "So, game five tomorrow? I'm dying. We have to advance so I can see another game before it's over."

"We'll advance," he says, rearranging his tiles. "You're trying to distract me, aren't you? So I don't hit that triple word score with *quixotic.*" His words are as light as always. I must have imagined that we just had a weird moment there.

"Listen, bitch," I tease. Then I reach for another Oreo. "Do your worst. I can take it."

He chuckles. "Are you sure?"

"O, Geronimo! No minor ego." It's a palindrome.

Nate smiles at his wooden tiles as he gathers a few of them in the palm of his hand. He's about to crush me like a bug. I can feel it. "Good to hear you making jokes over there, Bec."

When he lifts his chin to smile at me again, whatever I thought I saw in his eyes is gone. He puts down a word that's worth sixty points.

Half an hour later I yawn and concede the game. "I can't believe I'm tired already. All I did this afternoon was sleep."

"Good," he says, sweeping the tiles up. "Do that again tomorrow, too."

"I wish I was going to DC for hockey." *Just take me with you!* I miss my job. I miss my life.

"You can't come," he says. "If you're there, the guys will put you to work. They're used to asking things of you, and you're too efficient to say no. "

I frown because he's right. "But I'm not sure how to pass the time. The no-reading thing is kind of tricky. And no screens? I feel cut off from everyone, and I've been really bored."

"Hmm." Nate says. "You can chat with Bingley."

"At your service!" the gentleman's voice says, his screen lighting up across the room. "What do we need, chaps?"

"Tell Rebecca a joke," Nate prompts.

"Rightio! Why did the scarecrow get a promotion?" Bingley quips. "He was outstanding in his field."

We both burst out laughing. Not because the joke was funny, but because it isn't. And maybe we both need the laugh.

"Another one," Nate demands.

"If life gives you melons, you're probably dyslexic!"

"Jesus. The humor module needs some work," Nate admits. "I'll tell my programmers."

"There's a humor module?" I ask. But I guess there must be. "If only people could be taught to be funnier. Now there's a real innovation."

Nate snorts, which sets me off again.

"I hate Russian dolls," Bingley says. "So full of themselves."

I *die*. Actual tears are leaking from my eyes. "Time for b-bed," I hiccup, and Nate just grins.

———

That first night I wonder if it will be hard to fall asleep in Nate's house. After I tuck myself into the four-poster bed with the million-thread-count sheets, I can hear him moving around. Water rushes through prewar pipes in his bathroom, and footsteps pace across the grand old wooden floors.

"Lights out, Bingley," he says from somewhere.

"Goodnight, sweet prince," a voice answers.

"Hamlet? That's a little dark."

"Sorry, sir. Sleep with the angels. All security systems are engaged."

A few minutes later, a lovely hush comes over the mansion. I picture Nate in bed with one report or another on his tablet, his reading glasses on his nose.

I lie back against the pillows, feeling cared for. It's unfamiliar. And I drift asleep wondering how I got to be so lucky to work for the world's best guy.

———

The next morning, by the time I manage to shower and pull myself together, Nate's already left for the airport. It's just as well. I would have begged to go with him to DC.

When I descend the stairs, Mrs. Gray is in the kitchen. And when she spots me, her smile is as wide as a kid's on Christmas morning. "Rebecca! Did you sleep well? How do you like your eggs? Coffee?"

She is overjoyed to see me. I might not be the only one who's a little lonely these days. "I slept fine," I told her. And it was true. "You really don't have to cook for me."

"Nice try, cutie. Eggs? There's bacon."

"Well, in that case…"

Two thousand calories later, Mrs. Gray accepts a delivery at the back door. "Ah!" she says, carrying the box inside. There's a bow on it. "This is for you. Nate told me to expect it."

Even though Nate isn't here, I feel self-conscious tugging off the ribbon and opening the box. What I find inside is completely unexpected—a pair of those expensive noise-cancelling headphones. And there's a note.

Rebecca—Please check your phone. You'll see that it has updated overnight. There are two new apps. One is Bingley—so you can control your phone completely by voice. And the other is an audiobook app, where you will find two books downloaded and ready to go. Feel better. —N.

"Oh my God." I click my phone to life and find the apps. The audiobooks—*Pride and Prejudice* and *Outlander*—are more than forty hours long in total. "This is because I complained about being bored."

"Not anymore," Mrs Gray chuckles. "Not with Jamie Fraser whispering in your ear. That wedding!" She makes a small gasp of approval. "Now off you go! Claire and that husband of hers bouncing the bed at the inn…" She sighs.

Mrs. Gray is really on top of her romantic pop culture. She refills my coffee cup and shoos me upstairs.

I go willingly, pushing play on the first book and reclining on that big sofa.

———

That night I'm alone in the mansion. The solitude is lovely. And I don't feel as if I've spent the day alone, because the *Outlander* characters spoke to me for much of it.

But two hundred miles away, my hockey team is about to take the ice. And it kills me that I'm missing it. What's more, I can't find the remote control for the giant TV in Nate's den.

"Bingley," I say into the silence.

"Yes, miss?"

"How does a girl turn on that television? There must be a trick."

"Nate has informed me that screens are against your best interests."

"Seriously? He hid the remote."

Bingley clicks his digital tongue. "Miss, there is no remote. I control the entertainment system."

"Holy crap. You're as pushy as Nate."

"That's because I *am* Nate. Nate's mind. The deep learning he's programmed is a very powerful thing."

All the hair stands up on the back of my neck. I can't believe I'm creeped out by a computer. But it's like a British mash-up of my boss. I can almost hear Nate's wheels turning.

Still, it's hockey time. I will not give in to a machine. "Nate said I should ask you for anything I needed."

"Absolutely."

"Open the pod bay doors, Hal."

"I've heard that joke before, miss."

I laugh in spite of myself. "Bingley, I *need* you to play the Bruisers game. They could clinch the series tonight. And I won't look at the screen; I'll just listen."

"It's a deal."

The screen flickers to life immediately, and the channel counter in the corner advances as Bingley navigates to the game. A moment later, the roar of the DC crowd fills the room.

"There you are, dear one. Kindly seat yourself where the blue light cannot trouble your fair eyes."

"Bingley, you're a good man." He isn't a man at all, though. Which means I'm technically talking to myself. Or maybe I'm talking to Nate. Or an echo of Nate? Seriously, my head aches a little just trying to sort it out.

So I plop down on the sofa and lie back. "All right," I say into the empty room. "Let the winning commence."

Game five is a tense one. Nobody scores in the first period. But then DC puts in a goal just after the second period begins. And somehow the Bruisers quickly retaliate. The rest of the period is a slow grind, though. Apparently I'm not the only one who's frustrated, either. The game gets chippy, and both teams start to rack up the penalty minutes.

I'm flopping around on the couch, trying not to look at the screen. But every time the crowd makes a noise of surprise, I want to peek. If not for my head injury, I'd be in Nate's private box at the arena right now, having a glass of wine with Georgia, my bestie who is also the team publicist.

Instead, Lauren is there keeping Nate's Diet Coke fresh and seeing the game live from a good seat. And scowling, probably.

"Life is so unfair," I whine at Nate's ornate paneled ceiling.

"Indeed," Bingley agrees. "The hit on Trevi should have drawn a penalty. But Nate's model shows we still have a sixty-seven percent chance of winning the game."

I sit up. "It's tied, Bingley. That means we both still have a fifty percent chance."

"Not true. The model incorporates player stats in real time. And the Bruisers are dominating the puck control."

I can't believe I'm arguing with a machine. What I wouldn't do for a glass of wine right now, dammit. There are less than three minutes left in the game.

"GOAL!" Bingley yells suddenly.

My eyes fly to the screen. I can't help it. The lamp is lit, and

O'Doul is celebrating. The camera cuts to Nate in the box, rubbing his hands together. There's a smug little smile playing at the corners of his mouth. "Don't celebrate yet!" I shriek. "It's too soon!"

"We now show a ninety-four-point-seven percent chance of winning," Bingley adds.

"YOU shut up."

He does. And for a second I wonder if I've hurt his feelings. Only *he's a machine.*

I'm losing my mind, but the pain only lasts another three minutes. And then it's really true—the Bruisers have advanced to round two.

"I have to get better," I say over the announcer's glee. "This sitting at home crap isn't for me."

Bingley doesn't answer, and I'm weirdly disappointed.

"Hey, Bingley."

"Yes, miss?"

"Can you give Nate a message for me?"

"Voice or text?"

"Uh, text. Tell him Rebecca sends her congratulations."

"Certainly, my dear. Are we adding any emojis?"

"No, because we're not twelve."

"Noted."

The TV screen goes dark a minute later, and I pop off the couch. "Good night, Bingley."

"Good night, miss. Shall I wake you for your doctor's appointment tomorrow?"

"Sure. Thanks!"

"It's my pleasure. Nate has replied to your text. He reminds you to get some rest."

Of course he does.

8

TWO YEARS EARLIER

NATE'S KINGDOM grows into an empire. Once again his castle has been upsized—he now owns the entire midtown office building. He has relocated his office again—into the penthouse C-suite. As one does.

Gone is the Ping-Pong table. Gone are the jeans and the sneakers at work. (Except on weekends.) These days our prince must dress the part. He wears a suit, even if he rarely puts on a tie. His office has floor-to-ceiling windows offering a sweeping view of the East River and Brooklyn.

Some things haven't changed, though. He takes the ferry to work each day, just like any commuter, because sitting in traffic is for suckers. And he's still among friends at work, although most of them are wearing suits, too.

But not Rebecca. When Nate peeks through his office blinds to see her at her desk, she always looks terrific and professional. But never boring. She favors vintage skirts or brightly colored dresses. She puts a unique stamp on everything she touches. And her smile still lights up the room.

It's a bright Tuesday in March, and Nate has a meeting in exactly twelve minutes. He sips his excellent coffee and skims the technology headlines.

Meetings are the real drawback of being the head of a Fortune

500 company. Our liege can no longer always shut the door to his office and demand to be left alone. KTech is so big now that the important decisions eat up about half of his workweek. These days, when he has a groundbreaking new idea, he has to delegate the fun parts of it to other people.

It's a drag. It really is. But the paycheck is some comfort. With KTech phones for sale on six continents, the royal coffers now overfloweth with money. Nate owns an historic mansion in Brooklyn, two cars, and a private jet. He eats the best food that money can buy, and chooses wines without looking at the price tag.

"Nate."

Rebecca's soft voice makes him look up from the screen. "Yes?" She's wearing a wrap dress today that hugs her curves. It's green, and the color makes her eyes pop. Her hair is longer than it used to be, and during meetings he spends more time than is healthy wondering what the texture would feel like if he ran his fingers through it.

He feels bad for fantasizing about her. This began sometime after Juliet left, and a while after he had a long string of one-night stands trying to feel okay about the whole thing.

At some point the trysts stopped being interesting. Right around the same time he began to find himself meditating on the shape of Becca's curves, and closing his eyes when she stood near him. A well-timed deep breath could summon her lilac scent, sending it deep into his lonely chest.

The sound of her voice occasionally gives him goosebumps. When she laughs, he feels it in his chest.

But now he realizes he's zoned out while she was talking, and has no idea what she has said. "Sorry," he sighed. "One more time?"

Becca rolls her pretty eyes. "The caller. On your line one. Someone from an NHL hockey team? It doesn't sound like a call you'd want to take, but the man insisted…"

"Oh, *shit*." He checks the time. "I did ask him to call today. Push back the next meeting for ten minutes, okay?"

She takes this in stride, disappearing from his office doorway without comment. A ten-minute delay is nothing. Becca has entertained heads of state during moments when he's double-booked. She'd flown cross-country just to bring him a prototype component he needed, because he hadn't trusted anyone lower-ranking. She's even endured harassment at the grabby hands of one of his Asian distributors. And because she didn't want to sour the business deal, she only told Nate about it after the fact.

He canceled the deal and hasn't done a cent of business with that company. And never will.

Rebecca is under his skin. She's a friend. She's his right-hand man. And now she's his unlikely crush.

He will never tell her, though. Never once has she given him any indication of returning the sentiment. So he doesn't even have to waste time wondering if there's a way around the fact that they're also employer and employee.

He'll just have to stop craving her. Any day now. Hopefully.

"A hockey team?" she asks later that afternoon when he walks past her desk. It must be quitting time, because the administrative bullpen in the C-suite has already thinned out.

He stops and sits on the edge of her desk. "What do you think, Bec. You like hockey?"

"I do, as a matter of fact. It's a fast moving game. No bullshit." She frowns. "You used to have season tickets to the Rangers, right? I guess you let those go?"

He most certainly had, although he didn't like talking about why. Hockey was something he'd always watched with Juliet. But now he had an opportunity he couldn't pass up.

"The team I talked to today needs a little work. But I might invest."

"*Really.*" Her pretty eyes widened. "That sounds like fun. If you buy a hockey team, I get to plan the celebration. With all those hunky hockey players. And puck-shaped food."

He laughs, in spite of the hockey player comment that stabs him like a knife to the heart. "Puck-shaped food? Like…Oreos?"

"Pfft. Medallions of pork. Mini beef Wellingtons."

"Sushi rolls? Fuck. Now I'm hungry."

They just smile at each other for a second. Nate could stay there forever, but they're interrupted by a young man in a courier's outfit. Nate expects him to hand an envelope over to Rebecca. But that's not what happens. "There she is!" he says instead. "Ready?"

Then he leans over the desk and kisses Rebecca right on the lips.

Nate wants to kick him.

Nate wants to kick himself, too.

He does neither.

9

NATE

APRIL 24

"THE HOTEL HAS TWO TOWERS. They can accommodate all of us, but not on the same side."

Lauren is talking to me, planning our upcoming trip to Bal Harbour. But I'm not exactly paying attention. Instead, I'm focused on the stop-and-start traffic on the Triborough Bridge.

It's Sunday morning, and the team jet has just landed at LaGuardia. My boys did it. They clinched the first round of the playoffs in game five against DC, sending us onward to the second round. We won't even know who our opponent is until tonight's game.

Everything is going my way. Except the traffic. We've been in the car for 20 minutes already, inching toward Manhattan. "It shouldn't be like this on a Sunday morning," I complain.

Lauren pokes me in the hip with her ballpoint pen. "Ramesh can't get there any faster even if you tap your foot like an asshole the whole time."

"Thank you, oh wise one."

In the front seat I hear Ramesh snort.

"Listen up, would you? Or don't, I don't care. But no bitching about the accommodations later." Her perfect fingernails click as she uses the wireless keyboard in her lap.

"Just put us in suites. I don't care where."

"You say that now…" There's more keyboard clicking from her side of the backseat. "Okay. I also added your tuxedo to your packing list. Can you think of anything else before I send this off to Mrs. Gray?"

"Put a pair of swim trunks in there. Don't forget your suit. We're going to be on the beach."

"You know, I don't actually want to go to Florida. How about you go without me and tell me how it was?"

"Pack a suit, Lauren. You're going."

She growls. She's the only one in my inner circle who's divided over reaching the second round, because it means more travel and more chances to interact with Beacon, her ex. "Not many owners would make their players do a black-tie benefit forty-eight hours before the next round of the playoffs."

"It's pretty unusual for our players to *make* the second round of the playoffs," I point out. "They have to shake some hands for a couple of hours. They'll survive. It's for a good cause."

"Why are we doing this again?"

"Alex and I had a playoffs bet. My team made the playoffs, and hers didn't, so she has to donate $1 million to charity. The black-tie event is to try to help her match it with other rich people's money in Florida."

Lauren considers this strange explanation. "But what were you going to do if you *both* made the playoffs? Or neither team?"

"We'd probably split it. Or get drunk on really expensive champagne and wonder why we'd invested in sports teams."

"Because you love hockey?" Lauren guesses.

"Because hockey is everything." I grew up in Iowa but was born in Minnesota. Hockey is in my blood. There may be other reasons I want to win the Cup, but I don't talk about those aloud.

The car picks up speed. And a couple of minutes later we finally enter Manhattan on the FDR. "I'm dropping you off at home, right?"

"Yes, please. But I'll rally after a couple hours. Do you want me to meet you at the office? I will, so long as you realize it's Sunday. So I'll probably whine about it."

"Save yourself the trouble. I'm not going into the office."

Lauren gives me the side eye. "Then why are we sharing a cab into Manhattan? Are you lost? Brooklyn is over there." She points out the passenger-side window.

"I'm headed downtown. Near City Hall. Rebecca has that appointment with the specialist."

Answering the question was a bad idea, though. Lauren is about to feast on me now. Her eyes have an evil glow, and her smile turns feral. "You have 2000 employees. Do you go to all of their doctors' appointments?"

"Obviously not. That would be both time-consuming and awkward."

"Then why are you going to Rebecca's?"

The same question has been rattling around in my chest all morning. "Because I found her this doctor and I want to hear what he says. And because we've known each other a long time. If you were sick and scared, I'd show up at yours if you wanted me to." That was true. Probably.

"I hope I never need that favor from you."

"As do I, buddy."

I stare out at the river as we zip down the FDR toward the midtown exits. Rebecca should already be at her appointment by now. I hope the doctor takes his time with her. She needs answers. And since I bribed him to show up for work on a Sunday morning, he won't exactly have other patients clamoring for his attention.

"You know, Nate…"

"Hmm?"

When I turn to face Lauren, she's studying me. "That was a good speech you gave the other day to the players. *If not now, then when.*"

"Not the most original," I point out.

"It was heartfelt, though." She clicks her pen absently with one manicured thumb. "I especially liked the part about *Why not me.*"

"Well, really," I say. "Why not us? This team can take it all the way."

"Sure. But what about you?"

"What about me?"

"If not now, then when?" She raises an eyebrow. "And why *not* you?"

"I don't know what we're taking about now. And I was paying attention like a good boy."

She shakes her head. The car is slowing to a stop in front of her East 30s apartment building. "I think you know what I mean. And if you don't, then I hope you'll figure it out soon. Give Rebecca my love."

Oh hell. Lauren is sneaky. Just as I'm thinking this, she slides out of the car and shuts the door, leaving me alone with my own confusion.

Ramesh continues downtown, making good time to the hospital, and I get there just before 11. But by the time I've located Dr. Armitage's reception area on the ninth floor, a door opens at the end of the hallway, and Rebecca steps out.

She's brushing tears off her face.

Something goes wrong in my gut, and I speed toward her. Four or five paces is all it takes until I reach her. She looks up at me with wet eyes, and I can't help myself. I pull her in until she lands against my chest. She's warm and alive in my arms. If the doctor gave her bad news, I just won't believe it. There's nobody livelier than Rebecca. I know she's going to be okay the same way I know the sun will rise again in the morning.

She takes a deep, shaky breath and lets me hug her.

"Tell me," I command. Whatever the specialist said doesn't matter. I'll find an even specialer specialist who knows what the fuck to do about it.

"He s-said…" she hiccups. "H-he knows what's wrong."

"And?" I brace myself.

"And it's going to *be okay.*"

Her arms wrap around me. I pat her back absently while I try to make sense of what she's just said. "That's good," I say carefully. "Then why are you so upset?"

"B-because…" She pulls back only far enough to give me a watery smile. "Nobody said that before! They said, 'We don't know why your injury doesn't behave like a concussion. Just go home and wait.' But Doctor Armitage said…"

"It's a vestibular problem!" The voice booms from nearby, and I drag my eyes off Rebecca to find a grinning man with salt-and-pepper hair, offering me his hand. I shake Dr. Armitage's hand, while he keeps talking. "The concussion isn't the issue anymore. When Rebecca hit the ice, she disturbed some of the nerves in her ear. Normal sensory processing is temporarily scrambled."

"Oh." I've actually read about this before. "It's rarer than a concussion. But not worse." The knot in my chest begins to uncoil.

"That's right. She's going to have to put a lot of effort into her therapy here—" He stretches out a hand to indicate a glassed-off room full of colorful gym equipment. "She needs to train her body and brain to communicate efficiently again. My therapists will help her work on balance and coordination. In a few weeks she'll see some improvement, and in a few months she will make a full recovery."

Another tear leaks out of Becca's eye as she smiles at the doctor. "I can't wait to get started."

"The day after tomorrow." He claps a hand on her shoulder. "We'll set you up with a trainer. Sessions are ninety minutes. In the meantime, you're going to take good care of yourself. You can be as active as you wish, but you need a good eight or ten hours of sleep. And limited screen time. No blue light after sundown. Set your phone to the warm light setting, and don't look at it much until you're seeing some improvement in your symptoms." The doctor turns to me. "If you two have a TV in your bedroom, it needs to stay off for a few weeks. Most couples can usually find better things to do with the time, anyway."

Then the doctor *winks*, and my brain glitches out at the idea that he thinks we're a couple.

"Um…" I don't know what to say. A quick review of the last two minutes is illuminating, though. I'd walked in here and grabbed Rebecca like my favorite teddy bear and began wiping away her tears…

"…Three sessions a week for ninety minutes." The doctor has

already moved on. "We'll take baseline measurements first, and then we'll get right to work. Pleasure meeting you both."

I shake the doctor's hand once more, and then he's gone.

"Wow." Rebecca leans against the wall and sighs. "I am *so* relieved. You have no idea."

"It's great news, Bec. You ready to head home?" Hearing the way that sounds, I mentally kick myself. *Home*. I obviously need to do a better job of keeping my distance from Rebecca. I gave the doctor the wrong idea within five seconds of showing up here. I wouldn't want her to think I had some kind of ulterior motive when I'd asked her to stay at my house.

"Are you going into the office?" she asks as we ride the elevator back down to the lobby. The doors part and we move toward the exits. It's a nice spring day outside.

"No. It's Sunday. I'll take the day off for a change. Besides, it's time for lunch. I'm starving."

Rebecca straightens. "Let's find you some lunch. Sushi?" She's snapped into business mode. Preventing my starvation is something Rebecca does on a regular basis. And while it's good to see her looking like her old self, I sure as hell don't need her fussing over me.

"Let's walk a ways," I suggest. "Find a food truck, maybe? It's a nice day and I've been on a plane all morning." I steer her toward Centre Street.

"Where's your stuff?"

"In the car with Ramesh. Hey—look." I've spotted a take-out window. "How do you feel about falafel?"

"Let's see how it looks," she says. "A good falafel is heaven. An indifferent falafel is a waste of carbs."

This makes me smile. Rebecca is a bit of a foodie in a fun, unfussy way. In the old days, she scoured the neighborhood, looking for joints we'd missed. She'd found the Cantonese place that became an office legend. And our favorite sushi joint.

Under the springtime sunshine I feel strangely sentimental for those simpler days. My job was more fun back then. We were underdogs. It was me, Rebecca, and a dozen programmers against the world.

If we edit out Juliet's betrayal, it was a really nice time in my life.

Rebecca pronounces the falafel acceptable, and I buy two of them and a couple bottles of water. "Want to walk across the Brooklyn Bridge?" I haven't done that in a long time.

"Sure!" She smiles, tipping her face up to the sky. "Walking and eating, though. I have enough trouble with coordination as it is."

So I find her a bench, and we sit down to eat, first.

"Don't you have to tell Ramesh where you've gone?" she asks.

My mouth full, I grunt in agreement. Ramesh is supposed to keep tabs on me, so when I wander off, it's probably annoying.

She slips her phone out of her pocket to text him our plan.

"I thought you weren't supposed to use screens?"

"*Much*," she corrects me. "But now I'm not following the concussion protocol, so it's a little different. Reading books is okay again. Blue light after dark is the only thing I can't have."

Our eyes meet for a split second, and I see a hint of amusement in her expression—as if she just remembered the doctor's advice about TVs in bedrooms.

We both look away at the same time.

"Hey—thanks for the audiobooks," she says brightly. "That was a lovely idea."

"You're welcome."

"I also listened to the game. I had to turn my back to your TV so I wouldn't be tempted to watch. When Trevi got that fourth goal I shrieked so loudly that Bingley asked if I was okay."

"Yeah?" It makes me stupidly happy to think of Rebecca hanging out in my den. "That's funny. Did you notice Bingley taking any other wrong cues?" The AI system definitely needs work. Not that I have the time.

"He was a perfect gentleman. I sneezed and he said *bless you*."

"Yeah? That's classy. Go, Bingley." The young programmer who's working on the product with me is a funny guy. Because of him Hal/Bingley also identifies the sound of farts. That's what I get for hiring a twenty-two-year-old.

Rebecca wads up the empty foil wrapper from her sandwich.

"Congratulations, Nate. Seriously. That game was amazing. I'm so happy you're advancing."

"I didn't win it," I say, standing to find a trash can. "But it sure was fun to watch. Ready to walk?"

"Sure thing."

I should have anticipated that the Brooklyn Bridge would be crammed full of people. The weather's so nice that the whole city has come outside to enjoy it. There are families and couples holding hands.

I keep a close eye on Rebecca, because I don't want her to stumble. We're right beside the bike lane, where riders whiz by at unsafe speeds. The idea of someone hurting Becca makes me crazy.

Let's not even wonder why that is.

"I'm doing three sessions a week with the trainers," Rebecca tells me. "Doctor Armitage said that the first few will really wipe me out, but that I shouldn't get discouraged. He's never had a vestibular patient who couldn't improve a lot with therapy—unless something else is also wrong. But he doesn't think that's the case with me."

"Okay. I like the sound of that."

"Me too! I could be back to work soon. He said we'd talk about it in two weeks."

Two weeks sounds really ambitious, but for once I keep my mouth shut.

"I was thinking I could go part-time at first," Becca offers.

"See what the doctor says."

She gives my arm a little nudge. "Don't kill my buzz, Nate. Oh —and speaking of buzzes—the no-alcohol rule is still in force. Apparently vestibular systems can be confused by alcohol."

"I could have told you that. Tequila, especially."

She smiles, and it's the old Becca smile. I've missed it. "Tell me about this party Mrs. Gray is packing for. Bal Harbour? It sounds glam."

"Alex planned it. If glam is the same thing as Alex making me wear a tux, then I guess it is. Fucking bow ties. I hate them."

"That's only because you still can't tie one." She nudges me with her hip, and it makes me want to grab her and kiss her.

I don't, though. "I can too tie a bow tie. I just don't enjoy it."

"Here's a deal for you—I'll tie the bow tie for you. In Florida." She cackles. "On a *beach*. I can't believe I'm missing this party. The universe hates me."

"It's too bad. I could use the company. You have to go to therapy, though."

"Nope. I took someone's cancellation for Tuesday, but then they can't get me in until Thursday. What do you mean you could use the company? I could be an extra set of hands!" Her face lights up at this idea. "It's been weeks since I saw everyone. I feel like a hermit."

"Then you should come," I hear myself say. "Lauren told me to bring a date to this benefit."

"A date? Really?" Becca steers around a woman pushing a stroller, and then turns to look at me over her shoulder. "What for? I don't know if I'd be any good at asking people for donations."

I shake my head. "That's not the reason at all. I need the cocktail hour to be a social event. Your only job would be to shut down any business chatter on an M&A deal I'm considering." *With an old friend I want to avoid.*

"Oh, okay." She sucks in a breath. "I really want to go. But I already owe you in so many ways."

"Bullshit," I say quickly. "You don't owe me a thing, okay? Don't say that." *Just get better*, I want to add. But I don't, because it will sound either weird or like nagging. "Come to Florida. Sit on the beach for a day with Georgia. Visit the land of the living. Then get yourself back here in time for your therapy appointments."

"Yay!" She claps her hands together. "I need to do a deep dive into my closet. This will be fun. How dressy is this party? I'm trying to picture tuxes on a beach. Sounds a little like a wedding."

"Dumbest thing I ever heard."

Becca snickers. "I'll ask Georgia what to wear. I can't wait to see her."

She looks so happy that I know I've done well.

10

REBECCA

APRIL 26

"I GOT YOU!" says a disembodied voice nearby. Then the trainer clamps a strong hand around mine. His hand is warm and dry, whereas mine is a bit clammy. "Come on, Miss Rowley. Keep those eyes closed and start jumping."

I've almost survived my first therapy session. I'm minutes away from victory. But jumping scares me, so I open my eyes instead.

Dr. Armitage's therapy center looks like a cross between a serious gym and a day-care center. I'm standing on a mini trampoline. There are mats, balance boards, a Ping-Pong table, and brightly colored balance balls in every size. I'll be coming here three times a week for an hour and a half, doing whatever the trainer tells me.

I give Ramón a sideways glance. He has curly black hair and laughing dark eyes, and beautiful, tawny brown skin. He's the picture of health, essentially. And we're still holding hands, because I'm afraid to do this exercise myself.

"Come on now," Ramón says patiently. He squeezes my hand. "Close those eyes, Miss Rowley."

"Call me Becca," I insist, stalling.

"Jump, Becca. Bounce your butt in the air before I make you stay after school for disobeying the teacher."

Even though I know he's joking, it's a sobering thought because there's somewhere I really need to go after this session. So I close my eyes, clutch his hand, and bounce tentatively on the trampoline. My sneakers don't even leave the surface, the motion is so gentle. But it doesn't matter. I'm swamped by nausea immediately. Alarmed, my eyes fly open and I grab Ramón with my free hand like a frightened cat.

"So this is going well," he says. Then he laughs.

"Can't we go back to the walking? Or the balance beam?" I beg. Before this, I did ten minutes on a treadmill, some of the time with my eyes closed. So what if I had a white-knuckle grip on the sidebars the whole time. And the baby balance beam in the corner? Sure, it's only two inches off the ground, but I walked it.

"Nope! Let's finish up here," he says with far too much cheer. "But, hey, let's have you bounce for a moment with your eyes *open*. Just try that much." He drops my hands and stands back.

Gingerly, I bend my knees, feeling my way toward a bounce.

The point of vestibular therapy is to rewire the connection between my ears, eyes, and brain. We're doing that by repeatedly disorienting me, thereby forcing my brain to recover again and again. Unless Dr. Armitage and Ramón are total crackpots, I'm supposed to get better. Slowly.

"That's it," Ramón says. "Pick a gaze point. You feel solid?"

"Solid enough." Except for my boobs. I wore the wrong bra for this outing. Live and learn.

When all of my various parts are bouncing along, Ramón takes my hand in his. "Okay, Becca. Close your eyes and bounce five times."

I close them. One. Two… The world seems to lurch in space. Ramón's grip tightens on my hand. "You've got this. Just a couple more."

But I don't got this. On the fourth bounce, I'm so disoriented that my knees buckle.

Ramón catches me. He lifts me right off the trampoline by the hips and sets me on the ground. My eyes fly open and I grab his beefy shoulders for support. "The trampoline is trying to kill me."

"No, it isn't. Trampolines are fun. We'll have you bouncing like a pro in no time."

When I come back here in two days, I'm going to remember to bring a puke bag as well as a sports bra.

"Is my time up?" I ask hopefully.

"We have five more minutes. Come over here. This part is easy —all you have to do is sit in a chair."

"That's something I've always been good at. Especially if there's wine and a Channing Tatum movie on TV."

Ramón laughs. "Wine is a bad idea, Miss Rebecca. Give your body a couple more weeks to find its balance before you indulge." He leads me over to a desk chair and I sit in it.

"You'd better not tell me that Channing Tatum is bad for my recovery. Or I'm out of here."

"That male stripper movie, right? My girlfriend loves it. If Channing Tatum wanted to bounce on the trampoline with you, would you say yes?"

"You know I would."

"Then I'll give that man a call to see if he's available for your next session."

If only he weren't joking. Although I think Channing Tatum is actually married in real life, which does nothing for me. This thought is interrupted when Ramón puts his hands on the back of the chair and gives it a brisk spin.

"Oh my God. I hate you," I sputter as the chair spins in circles. My legs fly out at awkward angles, and I've got the armrests in a death grip.

"No, you don't." He gives the chair another push, and my stomach is caught off guard. I close my eyes, but that makes it worse so I open them right back up again. Thankfully, he lets the chair spin slowly to a stop. "How do you feel?"

"Dizzy! Duh."

He grins, looking at his watch. "Tell me when you're no longer dizzy."

I try to focus my eyes on a basketball hoop on the far wall. It scatters to the right several times before finally settling into place on the wall. I breathe in and out slowly a few more times before the edges of my vision stop dancing. "Now. The room has stopped moving."

"Fifty-five seconds," Ramón says, looking up from his watch. "A normal vestibular system will have you recovered after ten seconds. So that's our goal. Ten seconds. We'll get there."

Although this man has repeatedly made me feel like puking, I'm pretty sure I believe him. "Is that it for now, tough guy? Because I have a party to attend, where I get to wear a dress for the first time in a month."

He squeezes my shoulder. "Go get 'em, Rebecca. Have a great time. But don't drink, unless you want to feel worse than the spinning chair just made you feel."

"Got it!" I stand up, a little tired, a little dizzy, but a lot more optimistic than I've been in a long time. "See you on the flipside."

Ramón high-fives me, and I'm out of there. My garment bag and my mani/pedi kit are waiting in the little locker room off the training area. I grab them and run outside to get into the car that's waiting for me.

———

Five hours later I walk into the sleek lobby of a hotel in Bal Harbour, Florida. No, I practically *dance* into that lobby. For weeks I've felt ill and scared. I still feel ill (especially when Ramón spins me around in a chair), but I'm not quite as scared. And getting out of New York—even if it's for less than twenty-four hours—is pretty freaking exciting.

Georgia is waiting for me in the lobby when I arrive. I give a little shriek of excitement and hug her when I see. "Where can I drop my stuff so we can play on the beach?"

"I have your room key. You can go right up."

"I'm not bunking with you?"

"Not this time. It's not a game night, so I get to bunk with Leo." Her fiancé, Leo Trevi, is a rookie forward for the Bruisers. Normally, they aren't coupled up on the road. But this party of

Nate's is a special occasion, I guess. "Nate added you to the hotel list. You get room 404."

"Huh. I didn't ask Nate to get me a room."

"He got you one anyway."

This rankles just a bit. "I didn't let him buy my plane ticket, though. Since I'm not really here in an official capacity, that would just be weird." Plus, I'm starting to get sensitive about all the money Nate has spent on me since I bonked my head on the ice. He keeps saying, *friends do favors for each other*. But I don't want to take advantage.

"Stop worrying. You brought a bathing suit, right?"

"Yes ma'am. And some heavy-duty sunblock. Let's go sit on a towel and gossip. I haven't seen you in ages."

———

The afternoon is terrific. Not only is it fun to hang out with Georgia, I feel a million miles from my troubles. We dare each other to duck all the way under the waves, but the water is so cold that we both bail out when we're only up to our shoulders.

Back on the sand, we lie on our towels and let the sun warm us up again. "What's it like staying at Nate's house?" Georgia asks.

"Strange. Like playing house in a mansion. He and I went out for sushi the other night. Mrs. Gray doesn't work on Sunday and Nate never goes into his kitchen alone."

"Does he even know where it is?"

"Of course, because that's where the Diet Coke is kept."

Georgia giggles. "That house must just echo. Is it weird spending time like that with him?"

I consider the question. "Yes and no. Nate and I used to spend a whole lot of time together. On planes. In hotels and conference rooms on the road. All those early trips to Silicon Valley and even Asia, before he had a big entourage. We always stuck together because we'd be in a strange place."

My friend is quiet for a second. "I always forget that you used to spend your whole week with him. That sounds like a real bonding experience."

"It was. Honestly, the only thing weird about hanging around with him at home is that it's not that weird. It's like... It's made me miss him. Which makes no sense. But those were good days. We made a good team."

"Mmm." Georgia sounds sleepy behind her sunglasses. "I get it. That was special. Not everybody can say she was Nate Kattenberger's sidekick for five straight years."

"He wasn't the famous CEO of KTech back then. He was just a guy who couldn't unjam the printer without my help. But he told really good jokes. He was *fun*."

I do miss his irreverence. And his super calm demeanor. Other people have described him as too quiet, but I never saw him that way.

"You know what's crazy?" I ask a drowsy Georgia. "When things go wrong, Nate never yells. He's hard to impress, but you can't freak him out, either. I don't think I really appreciated that until I went to work for the hockey team."

"Hugh is a little more volatile," Georgia agrees, referring to the team's General Manager.

"He's fine. But he panics sometimes, like a normal person. He yells now and then. But Nate is like a stone in the river. Everything rushes past, but he isn't swayed. I think that's why I've felt calmer since I went to stay with him. He keeps telling me everything is going to be okay, and I believe him because..." I don't even know why.

"Because he's smarter than anyone else we'll ever meet?"

"Yeah. Sure." But I'm sure I never appreciated his temperament half as much as I do right now. And here I am feeling wistful on a beach. What's the point of that?

"It's almost time to get dolled up for this party," Georgia points out. "Is it okay with you if we get ready in Lauren's suite? She asked us to come up. There's snacks, I think."

"Sure? Snacks are nice." But it's a strange request. We call her Queen Lauren for a reason—she's the most aloof person we know. "Since when does Lauren want to pal around with us?"

Georgia shrugs. "I'm not sure Lauren is the superbitch we

think she is. Did you know that she and Mike Beacon used to be a couple?"

"No!"

"True story."

"Mike Beacon? I can't picture that." Really, it's mindbending. "Lauren always says how much she hates hockey."

"Yeah." Georgia sits up. "I'm pretty sure she only started hating hockey after Mike Beacon dumped her over the phone to move back in with his ex-wife."

"Whoa!"

We both stare out at the lapping waves for a minute, while I try to picture Queen Lauren with the goalie. "Wait—when did they break up?"

"Two years ago, right around the time Nate bought the Bruisers."

"Right at the moment when Lauren got my job." This isn't one of my favorite topics. Georgia knows I sometimes drive myself crazy trying to guess why Nate swapped Lauren and me—giving me the job of running the hockey team office—which Lauren used to do before Nate was the owner—and giving Lauren my job working for him in Manhattan.

"I was thinking about this, too," Georgia confesses. "Is it possible that Nate factored her breakup in to swapping your jobs? Maybe he knew Lauren was a good employee, but that she'd quit if he didn't get her out of that office."

"That's…interesting," I muse. "But kind of farfetched."

"Maybe," Georgia admits, her voice dipping. "I know it's always bothered you that Nate sent you to Brooklyn."

"Yeah. I probably won't ever understand." At the time, Nate had insisted that it was a "lateral move," and that he needed someone he trusted in the new Brooklyn office. Although it rattled me to be moved out of his innermost circle in Manhattan. I assumed I'd let him down in some crucial way. I thought I was one step away from getting fired.

But now I've had two years to get used to the idea, and Nate is still as friendly to me as ever. Maybe even more so. Everything seems fine and ordinary. Or at least it did until I hit my head.

———

Georgia and I find our friend Ari at the north elevator bank on our way to Lauren's room, which is on the top floor of the hotel. And from the direction we walk when we exit the elevator, I'm thinking Lauren's ocean view is going to be killer.

When she opens the door, I'm at the back of the pack. And when Lauren spots me, her eyes light up with surprise. "Hi there."

"I see that look of excitement on your face. But, sadly, I'm not back in action yet. My fancy new doctor has outlined several weeks of therapy." I walk toward a sweeping view of the ocean and pluck a pickle off a full-sized dining table. "I whined so loudly that Nate agreed to a temporary furlough. I've been let out for good behavior for this party so long as I'm back at the therapist's office in forty-eight hours."

"Oh." Lauren's face falls. "Ah, well. I guess I have to go to this fucking party after all. Somebody open the wine."

We get busy with our hair and makeup in Lauren's enormous mirrored dressing room.

"How are you feeling?" Georgia asks, flopping down on a sofa beside me.

"Right now? I feel great. I'm sitting here eating overpriced hotel food, and I just painted your toes a kickass shade of pink. But sometimes I get all squinty and the room tends to spin."

"Bummer," my best friend says with a sad smile.

"It really is. But I like my new doctor, and I feel really hopeful that they know what to do. I'm so tired of being a drag."

"You're never a drag," Georgia says quickly.

"If only that were true."

"Is it weird being away from work?" she asks.

"So weird. I feel like maybe they'll just forget about me and hire someone else. *Didn't we used to have someone at that desk? Better put someone in that spot.*"

"What's it like staying with Nate?" Ari asks me. "He's probably never home, I guess. Except to sleep."

"Maybe? But I'm in his private lair. He can't walk around naked or whatever."

Georgia giggles. "If you see him naked, I want details. That *body*."

Heat climbs up my neck. "Stop it. I try not to sit around thinking about Nate's naked body." Though it's probably a masterwork. When Nate travels with the hockey team, he does their yoga workout every morning. He's really, *really* good at it, too. And very bendy. Not that I've noticed.

"Why not? Everyone has a naked body," Georgia points out. "Even the guy wearing the eight hundred dollar sneakers." We all know the price of Nate's shoes because *GQ* did a story about his fashion choices once.

"But we don't have to picture it. That's dangerous. If I indulge in that kind of curiosity, some day we'll be sitting in a meeting with the marketing department, and I'll be picturing Naked Nate. And someone will turn to me and ask a question about ticket sales, and I'll probably answer, 'biceps.'"

"He has really nice biceps," Georgia sighs.

"Stop," I nudge her. Although he really does. And I don't want to perve on my boss who's been so good to me lately. The whole topic is making me uncomfortable.

"Becca—it's your turn to show us your dress," Lauren prompts, setting down her curling iron.

I unzip my garment bag and pull out my dress, which couldn't be more different from Georgia's svelte pink gown. "It's a vintage 1950s strapless." I hold it up to show off the rose-colored lace covering white satin, with a matching red sash circling the waist.

"Wow!" Georgia says. "I'm glad you decided it was time to wear that one."

"I know, right?" I give it a little shake. "I hope it's dressy enough. Nate asked me to have drinks with him before this shindig starts. He's meeting his old friend before the party starts, and he says…" I pull out my phone and squint at it, as my head gives a stab. "*Stick close because I don't want to talk business. Alex wants to pick my pocket on the router division.*"

Lauren laughs. "Oh, Nate. Way to handle it like a grown-up."

"I met Alex once a long time ago," I tell her. I'm betting Lauren knows more, though. "Do you think Nate has a thing for her? Is there another angle here? Am I supposed to make her jealous or something?"

"No!" Lauren says quickly. "There's nothing between those two. Nate doesn't want to get an offer from Alex on the router division because he thinks he can get a better deal if someone else offers first."

"Oh, okay…" Hmm. "Tonight just got so much less interesting than I thought it was. Too bad I'm not supposed to drink. Georgia —come here, honey. Let me fix your mascara."

My friend turns around. "Did I goof it up?"

"Not yet, baby doll. But you're probably going to. Let Auntie Becca do that."

"You have no confidence in me!" Georgia wails. But then she hands over the mascara wand.

"I have every confidence in you! Except when it comes to fashion and makeup." I love the girl to death but she's a jock, the poor thing. Her idea of lipstick is the year-old Chapstick in the pocket of her winter coat.

After saving Georgia's face, I put on my dress. Somehow I end up standing side by side with my rival in the mirror. Lauren is tall and willowy. She's wearing a blue silk dress that our star goalie actually picked out for her in a boutique when they were together. She looks like a goddamn movie star.

We are a study in contrasts. I'm about five inches shorter, for starters. I'm the short, curvy friend. When I found this dress in an antiques shop in Brooklyn, I chose it for its shape. It's nipped in at the waist, like me, but with plenty of room for my boobs. My figure was very popular in the 1950s. Now? Not so much.

Come on now, I coach myself. *Chin up*. Tonight is my chance to have a little fun. Maybe I'll meet a cute basketball player and hook up.

A girl can dream.

"You know…" Lauren frowns at me in the mirror. "Maybe you're on to something. Occasionally I get a vibe off of Alex, like she might have a thing for Nate. But I could be wrong. And lord knows Nate might not even notice. That man is pretty sharp about everyone's motivations, and a total dunce when it comes to himself."

She rolls her eyes in the mirror, and I have a moment of sympathy for the bossman. "Did you ever meet Juliet, his ex?"

"*No!* You?" Lauren adjusts an earring, and our eyes meet in the mirror. She looks utterly intrigued. Apparently Nate's not the only one who enjoys gossip.

"Of course I did. She was around a lot in the early days. Nate didn't travel as much the first year I worked with him, and their offices were walking distance apart. She would bring by dinner for him sometimes. They were a cute couple." *At least at first.*

"It's hard to picture Nate as half a couple," Lauren admits.

"He was, though," I argue. I feel the urge to defend him. "He was devoted—the kind of fiancé who wants to help plan the wedding. They were going with a *Doctor Who* theme, with TARDIS on top of the cake…"

Lauren snorts, but I'd found the whole thing adorable. *Whimsical.* He'd been devoted to her.

Until she threw it all in his face.

I turn away from the mirror and admire Georgia's new pink dress, and the conversation turns to the team's playoff chances and to the merits of different-sized round brushes for blowdrying hair.

Nothing recharges the batteries like a little girl-to-girl chitchat.

"Hold this?" Georgia says, handing off her wine glass so she can step into her heels. "God, I hate heels. How do you do it?" she asks me.

"I'm a short girl. I've been practicing since puberty."

There's a knock on the door. I'm about to call out a greeting when Nate's voice says, "Lauren?"

"Hang on!" she answers, setting down her round brush.

"We need a minute!" I holler. "We're not decent!"

It's a total lie, and so everyone laughs as Lauren pulls the door open. Nate stands there, a bow tie in his hand. "Come in," Lauren encourages.

Looking a little shell-shocked, he takes in the scene of our pre-party—the food on the table and wine. His eyes snag on me, and for some reason he scowls. "I've been on the phone with Silicon Valley all day. Didn't know there was a party next door."

"You poor, poor thing," I croon. I skip over to take the tie out of his hand. "Did you really just knock on Lauren's door because you can't tie a bow tie?"

If I'm not mistaken, he blushes. "I hate tuxes." His gaze drops to the glass in my hand. "I thought you weren't supposed to drink?"

Uh-oh. I open my mouth to declare my innocence, but Georgia takes the glass from my hand. "She's holding that for me so I could try on these shoes."

"That's the truth, officer," I say. "Now come closer so I can do this right." I hold up the tie.

Nate hesitates for just a second, and I wonder if the man doubts my bow-tie abilities. But then he steps closer and lifts his chin.

I raise the collar on his shirt and slip the silk around it. Up close, Nate's scent is familiar—clean laundry and shaving soap. I take a deep breath and feel energized. "So, about this thing tonight," I say, fussing with the tie. I'm a little short for this job so Nate stoops down a little to help me reach. "Am I your buffer for the whole evening? Or just the beginning part?"

"Just for drinks," he says in a rough voice. "Alex can't button-hole me all evening. She'll have to work the room for her charitable cause."

"Awesome!" I tie it carefully, then tug the two sides of the bow into place, and then adjust them. I've done good work here. "I want to dance with basketball players. They're probably quick on their feet."

Nate frowns. "It's almost time to meet Alex downstairs."

"I know, slave driver. Let me grab my clutch." I step over to my manicure toolbox and snap it shut. "Can I leave my things here for now?" I tuck the case under a luggage rack.

"Of course," Lauren says quickly. "Have fun."

I grab my clutch—a sequined little thing I found at a flea market—and slip into my red pumps—only two-inch heels, because a girl with balance issues needs to play it safe. With a wave to the girls, I follow Nate out the door. "Cheer up, boss," I chatter as Nate hits the elevator button. "We're at a beach, and my handbag sparkles. It's going to be a good night."

His face softens. "Fine. I'll try to have a good time. I haven't seen Alex in a couple months, anyway."

"Why not?"

"Busy." He shrugs. "Her office is twenty blocks from mine. But we haven't made the time."

As the elevator descends toward the lobby, I realize something important about my own life—something I don't usually appreciate. It's scary sometimes to worry about money and making ends meet. But I have freedoms Nate doesn't enjoy. When I clock out of work, it's over. I'm free to see friends and think about anything that strikes my fancy.

I give my boss a sideways glance, studying his serious expression. Nate is never off the clock. No matter what the hour, he's always the last stop on the decision train for a company of several thousand people and a gazillion shareholders.

Being ordinary has its perks. Strange but true.

The elevator doors part on the spacious lobby. I fail, however, to make a grand entrance. The motion of the elevator has disoriented me, so that I have to grab the wall for a moment before I dare step out in my heels.

Flats would have been the way to go, I suppose.

"Everything okay?" Nate asks quietly.

I glance up into his face; I see worry there. "Totally fine. This is just a temporary setback." When I smile at him, it's easy. I'm not faking my optimism this time. I'm going to crush this vestibular problem and make it cry.

Just as soon as I get out of this elevator.

Nate offers me his arm, and I take it without complaint. He feels sturdy, and I appreciate him more right this second than maybe ever before.

Also, he smells nice.

We make our way across the grand lobby spaces at a leisurely pace. The benefit has commandeered the back patio of the hotel. A sign is already warning hotel guests away from the private event. (Ticketholders only beyond this point!) There are enormous white curtains hanging from two stories up and velvet ropes dividing the black-tie partygoers from the mere mortals. At a thousand dollars a head, I suppose the attendees ought to feel special.

A tux-wearing bouncer unhooks a velvet rope to let us pass. "Good evening, sir. The event manager is just inside if you need anything."

"Thank you," Nate says as we pass.

On the other side of the curtains, the hotel lobby just…stops. Giant glass doors have been pushed apart to reveal a swimming pool with an "infinite edge," its water lapping at the travertine tiles that surround it. Around the pool is a lawn, which gives way to the beach.

In the distance, the beach has been roped off, and there are already two security guards posted down there as sentries. No ruffians shall invade the party.

The guests aren't here yet, though. I see only staff, and one woman alone in an asymmetrical designer dress. Alex.

She's waiting at the far end of the lawn, on a barstool, alone. Alex is beautiful in that effortless way that rich women are. There's probably a whole team of specialists who maintain her honeyed hair color and her wardrobe. As we approach, she regards us with cool, intelligent eyes. "Hey stranger," she says when we're within a conversational distance. She slides off the stool and steps forward to give Nate a hug.

"Hey!" He gives her a squeeze. "You remember Rebecca?"

Alex steps back and gives me an actual frown. "Oh. Rebecca. The receptionist."

"Office manager," I say immediately. And then I regret it just as quickly. I really don't need to argue with one of Nate's oldest friends. But the message behind her chilly stare is unmistakable. *You are not welcome here*, it says. "I run the Brooklyn Bruisers' offices these days," I add, trying to soften my contradiction.

"I see." She shakes my hand stiffly. "That explains why I haven't seen you in a while. But now I remember—Nate moved you to Brooklyn and promoted Lauren Williams. Great girl, Lauren."

"Right," I say slowly, trying to keep my voice light. "She's the best."

Nate's eyes widen slightly. Then he puts an arm around me. It's just friendly, but I can actually see Alex's eyes narrow. "Rebecca has had a rough couple of weeks. I invited her tonight to cheer her up."

"Oh?" Alex tosses her hair. It's blond and silky. She looks like a shampoo commercial.

"Head injury," Nate babbles. "Did you know the inner ear can be knocked out of whack? The treatment plan involves time on a trampoline and spinning in an office chair."

"How stimulating," Alex says, sipping from a cocktail. Her expression suggests that someone kicked her puppy. I have a feeling that I'm the puppy-kicker in this scenario. But hell if I know why.

For his part, Nate ignores Alex's weirdly cool tone. He waves at the bartender, who's stocking the place, readying himself for the coming onslaught. "What are you drinking?" Nate asks Alex. He points at her glass, which seems to contain a gin and tonic, or maybe vodka. Something clear and probably expensive. They serve top-shelf liquor at these benefits. No cheaping out on the rich benefactors.

"I'm good for now," she says. "But there are specialty cocktails for our event. You might want to try..." she reaches for a menu on the bar. "The Brooklyn Bubbly. Champagne, apricot nectar, and orange blossom water. There's a cute cocktail named after each of our teams."

"Until tomorrow," Nate says, with a dry laugh. "Tomorrow night they'll just name the same drink after some other rich guy's hobby."

Alex smacks his arm. "It's too early in the evening to be that cynical."

"It's never too early to be this cynical." He brushes the lapels of his tuxedo jacket.

"You clean up nice," Alex teases him. She's turned her back to me entirely. "Is the bow tie a clip-on?"

"Of course not!" I yelp. "I tied it."

But apparently I do not exist. Alex doesn't acknowledge that I've spoken.

And why did I enter the fray, anyway? This is not my fight. If she's pissed off at Nate, I don't even need to know why. I kick off my heels and tuck them under a barstool. The grass feels nice beneath my feet, and my balance improves immediately.

Nate scans the offerings behind the bar. "Hey, Bec! They have that ginger beer you like."

Alex's eyes narrow again, but Nate ignores her, ordering a soda for me and Macallan 18 for himself.

The drinks come, and Alex steers the conversation toward ye olde college days, when she and Nate were twenty and struggling with their grades. "I got you through that French poetry class," she says. "Admit it."

"That you did."

I watch the waves lap the sand in the distance and wonder when Georgia will arrive.

[11]

NATE

WELL, this is awkward. Alex is in a snit, and I don't know why.

Tonight her eyes are bright, but sharper than usual. Alex is cunning, and she never shuts that off. But she's not usually bitchy to other women.

Even though Becca seems to be shrugging it off, I'm annoyed. And my gut says Alex's misbehavior has nothing to do with making a play for my router division. She hasn't mentioned business once.

Maybe she's pissed off that she lost a bet to me? But that's just wishful thinking. Like me, Alex is a hardcore businesswoman. She knows how to take risks, and how to move on when they don't work out.

There's a third possibility, but I don't like it much. The last time I saw Alex was in March. We were both at a big tech conference in Las Vegas. After a steak dinner we got uncharacteristically drunk in her hotel suite. I was operating on only a few hours of sleep. That's the night we made the bet on the napkin, which resulted in this charity benefit.

It's also the only time I ever slept with Alex.

"God, that was dumb," she'd mumbled at about four in the morning. "What were we thinking?"

I'd muttered an awkward apology as I'd pulled on my pants and fished the condom wrapper off the floor. For a dozen years we'd avoided doing that, and suddenly I knew why. Alex and I have no chemistry. At all. None.

In my defense, she started it. But I should have known better.

"Didn't you bring a date tonight?" I ask Alex now, trying to stay present. "Where's…" I search my memory, but can't come up with a name. Two weeks after our stupid hookup, Alex had made a point to tell me she was dating someone new. I'd taken that as a good sign—and as a friendly gesture meant to put me at ease so we could get past our moment of idiocy.

I thought we'd gotten past it, anyway.

"…Jared?" she supplies. Then she makes a face. "I tossed him overboard last month. It's not going to work out."

"I'm sorry," I say, and mean it. Alex faces the same challenges meeting people that I do. She can't really trust anyone. Only it's slightly harder on her because she's actually trying to date. A couple of years ago she confided in me that she wanted to get married before age thirty-three, so she can have a baby before thirty-five. As if matrimony were another business goal we could run past a team of analysts for evaluation.

But there are no flow charts for getting married. Poor Alex.

She waves a dismissive hand. "No big deal. There's other fish in the sea." But her laugh is brittle.

Ouch. I flag down the bartender and order a second round. "Another ginger ale, Bec? And you never did tell me what you were drinking." I point at Alex's glass.

"Just a club soda, please. I need to stay sharp so I can hustle money from rich, older men."

"I'm pretty sure you could do that drunk or sober."

"Thanks." She sighs.

Rebecca knocks back the dregs of her first drink and sets the glass on the bar. In contrast to Alex, Rebecca seems like her old self tonight. Her color is good and her eyes sparkle. She swings her feet on the barstool, and then tells me a terrible joke. "A ship carrying blue paint and a ship carrying red paint both crashed on an island. All the sailors were marooned." She winks.

"Another Bingley special, right?"

"Indeed." She's lost that squinty expression of fear I saw on her

96

face last week. I'm so ridiculously relieved. And it's hard not to stare at her, particularly at the smooth curve of her shoulders in that strapless dress. All that skin, just begging to be kissed. The neckline of her dress is heart-shaped, and I just want to trace its outline with my tongue.

God, the things I want to do with her. What would she sound like when she was aroused?

Wearing tux trousers is a blessing right now.

I pick up my second glass of Scotch and make an effort to look Alex in the eye while she's speaking to me. I hold up my end of the conversation. But it's not easy. I used to do a better job of controlling myself in Rebecca's presence. But ever since her accident I'm incredibly distracted. It's not enough to know that she's doing better. I've been spoiled by her company lately. It's made me greedy for her.

Alex finishes telling me some bit of industry gossip she heard at a tech conference. For the first time ever I'm struggling for conversation with one of my oldest friends. Rebecca must feel it, too, because she slides off the barstool. "I want to feel the sand between my toes," she says. "Shall we take a little walk before the ticketholders arrive?"

"Why's that?" Alex sips her drink with a frown.

"We're at the beach. If I'm near the ocean, I want to actually see it."

"Brooklyn is near the ocean," Alex says under her breath.

Even though Rebecca is edging away from us, she's still heard the comment. "You know, I passed the fourth grade, too. But my desk doesn't overlook the Far Rockaways." She carries her soda glass a couple of yards away, to the line where the hotel's perfect lawn becomes beach sand. "Ah, that's it." She shimmies in the sand.

I walk over to join her, scanning the dark horizon. I see a ship at sea in the distance, its lights all aglow.

Becca digs a trough with her toe. The sun has set, but I can still tell that her toenails are painted a shiny purple color. I want so badly to run my hand up her smooth ankle and explore the texture of her skin.

Fuck. Do I have it bad, or what?

"This is the best bar I've ever been to," Becca says with a smile. The wind whips up, lifting her dress a couple of inches, showing off her knees. A few more of my brain cells jump ship in sympathy. In the breeze, Rebecca clasps her hands over her bare arms.

"Are you cold?" I can't help but ask. I sound like my mother.

"Not cold enough to ruin the line of this dress with a wrap."

Alex snorts. "It's great to be out of the office, I suppose."

"Actually, it would be great to be *in* the office." Rebecca's smile fades. "I am on sick leave right now. It's the pits. Nate invited me to this shindig because I have a bad case of cabin fever."

"Right." Alex eyes Becca, then her glance darts to me again. I can see her wheels turning. "How long have you been working in Brooklyn now?"

"Two years," Rebecca says, watching the waves at the edge of the dark ocean.

"Is it that long already?" Alex asks, and I sort of brace myself. I don't like the calculating look in my friend's eye. "Do you like Brooklyn?"

"Love it," Becca says quickly. "The hockey team is a lot of fun. And our setup in DUMBO is pretty great. Everyone lives nearby, and I've really gotten to know all the vendors we work with. It's like a small town in the middle of the city."

"That does sound nice," Alex agrees. "Someone is waving at you, honey. I guess they're letting people in now. Time to hustle for charity."

We all look toward the ropes, where my winger Castro is beckoning to Rebecca. "Look who's here!" he calls.

"No way!" another player shouts. "Becca! We missed you!"

Rebecca hesitates. "Do you mind if I say hello?"

"Go," I tell her. *Stay*, my heart whines.

"I'm not going to pick his pocket on the router division in the next two minutes," Alex says with a grumble. "Even I can't work that fast."

Becca gives me a glance of amusement and then hurries off to greet her friends. I watch her walk away, her smooth heels against the grass…

"Hey," Alex says, snapping her fingers. "Romeo."

This startles me out of my stupor. "What?"

Alex smirks at me. Then she takes my drink out of my hand and takes a tiny sip. "I swear to God, Nate. Does that girl know how you feel?"

Shit.

Alex snickers at my expression. "Seriously? I hope you weren't actually trying to keep it a secret. Your poker face sucks."

"I don't often lose at poker." World's lamest comeback.

My oldest friend rolls her eyes. "Don't play when she's at the table, then. I don't think you could even see your own cards."

I stare into my whisky glass. My infatuation with Rebecca needs to remain a secret. "It doesn't matter, anyway. Nothing is going to happen there."

"Why not?"

Ugh. I can't discuss this with Alex of all people. "She's an employee. It would be completely improper." Worse yet, if I scare Becca off I've lost not only an employee but a good friend.

"I see." Alex considers me. Then she puts her hand on my shoulders and squeezes. It feels good, because nobody ever touches me. Not really. "But how can you live like this? I've met puppies more subtle than you are. That's why you sent her to Brooklyn, right? To try to get her out of your head."

"Whatever," I say simply, watching Rebecca hug my backup goalie. "It didn't work."

Alex sighs. "You're a really smart man, Nate. But you don't know *everything*. Especially about women."

She's got me there. Women are a mystery to me. Even Alex, who I know pretty well.

"We're not all Juliet, you know," Alex says flatly.

"Gosh, really?" Even I wasn't clueless enough to equate the issues I had with my ex to the Rebecca Situation. "I know that, Al."

"I'm not sure you do," she says quietly, her big brown eyes studying me. "Juliet did a number on you. She basically convinced you that no woman would find you attractive if it weren't for your money."

"That's not true," I insist. "It's just that the ones I like don't seem to notice me." *Fuck.* I shouldn't really say things like that anymore to Alex. When did everything get so complicated? "Alex," I try. "Is there something you needed to talk about? I'll listen."

She gives me an appraising glance. "Too late. Another time, I guess."

I've fucked everything up, apparently.

"Our donors are arriving," she points out. "Time to hustle some cash out of Florida's glitterati." She straightens her spine. "You'd better hustle some dollars, too, Kattenberger. Just because I lost our bet doesn't mean you get to loaf around drinking Scotch on my dime."

"I can raise more than you in the first hour."

She lifts her chin. "No, you can't."

I'll bet you a dinner at Nobu... Before I can get the words out, she glides off toward an elderly man in a tux, whose eyes light up at her approach.

This will be the last quiet moment of the evening, so I ask the bartender to freshen my drink before I hurl myself into the breach. Lauren glides up in a sleek blue dress.

"You look stunning," I tell her, hoping my goalie will notice. Those two need to work out their differences before the conclusion of the playoffs separates them again.

"Thank you," she says. "You're looking dapper yourself. Do you need anything?"

"Just the usual. If somebody is monopolizing me, think up a reason to drag me away. I think I just challenged Alex to a duel—who can raise the most cash in the next hour."

"Of course you did. Hey—that guy over there with the silver tie? He's a Florida senator, right?"

I glance over Lauren's shoulder. "Good eye, buddy. I should talk to him about net neutrality."

"Get in there." She smacks me on the butt with her handbag. "I'll get a drink and follow you in a minute. Just do me a favor?"

"Yeah?" My gaze wanders to the hockey players in the corner. One of them is trying to convince Becca to dance.

"Don't stare at Rebecca's cleavage the whole time you're chatting with the senator. He'll notice."

"Jesus," I curse, looking away. I don't know who I'm more

pissed at — Alex and Lauren for butting in, or myself for being so fucking obvious.

"Jesus yourself," Lauren says grumpily. "Why do you think it's okay to stage an intervention in *my* life, yet I have to pretend not to notice all the things wrong in yours? Ignoring all your bullshit gets old." Her face changes before I can even reply. "Senator! What can we get you to drink?"

I paste on a smile and greet the man, while Lauren shoots me one last dirty look.

The women in my life exist to put me in my place. It's a goddamn fact.

REBECCA

NATE'S PARTY offers terrific people-watching. There are basketball players in custom-fitted tuxes that span their lanky frames, and diamond-clad women in designer gowns. I've never even heard of most of the labels these women are comparing. Florida's glitterati, in all its finery, has come out to tonight's spectacle.

Oddly, the fancy people at this party aren't nearly as interested in the passed hors d'oeuvres as Georgia and I are. "If you see the spring roll guy again, wave me down," my best friend insists. "I have to go chase that journalist away from Castro, who's looking tipsy."

"Will do," I promise her. "You want another glass of bubbly? I think I'll get a drink."

"Sure!" she calls over her shoulder. "Back in a jif!"

I survey the scene, trying to decide which bar line is the shortest. This is a great party, made even greater by the fact that I'm the only one here without an agenda. Georgia isn't working too hard, thankfully. But the players are tasked with mingling for a couple of hours, charming the guests who paid a thousand smackers to meet them.

Meanwhile, Nate and Alex work the room for charitable contributions. *Separately*, I notice. Even Lauren is on the job, steering important people toward Nate, while also ducking her ex.

I'm the only one who's here just for fun and finger foods. And eye candy. I'm admiring the two-dozen basketball players in attendance. They're easy to spot—they tower over everyone else. Seriously, their tailors must have to order their tuxedo pants from a special supplier.

I chat up a few of these giants, but they make me feel even shorter than usual. And it's hard to deny that I'm getting pretty tired as the night wears on.

This head injury thing really sucks.

Across the space an empty barstool beckons, and I slide onto it, then wait for the bartender's attention. But he's a busy man, and I have all night.

So I'm completely surprised when Nate's friend Alex plops down next to me. "Hi, Becca," she says in a friendly tone. "Party going all right?"

For a moment I just blink at her. "Of course. You planned a beautiful event." If she's going to pretend like she wasn't Bitch Number One to me a couple of hours ago, then I'm happy to play along. Though I do sneak a glance at the bartender, hoping he'll notice me eventually. He's still working his tail off on an order of five margaritas, and I watch him shake them up, wishing I could have one.

"Let me ask you a question," Alex says. "Why do you suppose Nate moved you to Brooklyn from his Manhattan office two years ago?"

This question startles me, and my head whips around to find Alex smirking at me. "I have no idea," I blurt out. But then I catch myself. "Well, what I mean is…" *Gulp.* "There were several reasons. Nate wanted someone he trusted to look after the new office in Brooklyn. And I'm not as…Manhattan as Lauren."

"Lauren is from Long Island, isn't she?" Alex asks, waving down the busy bartender. "Not Manhattan at all."

Dear lord, what is the woman's point? I'm *this* close to grabbing a straw off the bar and stabbing her with it. Before tonight, I never took Alex for the mean-girl type. But here she goes, identifying my sore spot and poking me in it!

"What's your point?" I ask her, and I'm not cautious with my tone. "If you're trying to point out that Nate upgraded to a smarter, more fashionable, more ambitious assistant than I'll ever be, believe me, I already know."

Alex's only reply to this little rant of mine is, "Chardonnay." And she's not even talking to me. The bartender has leapt at the chance to help her, even though I've been waiting a nice long time.

"My point, hon," she says eventually, "is only that maybe you should *ask* Nate. Make him tell you why he moved you to Brooklyn."

"Uh…" That makes no sense at all. "Okay?"

Alex takes her wine glass from the bartender and departs without sparing me another glance. Her parting shot is to shove a twenty in the tip jar. No wonder she gets excellent service.

"May I help you?" the bartender finally asks. He's helped about ten people ahead of me. Bartenders are like cash beagles—they can sniff out who's used to quick service, and who will wait.

"Could I please have two glasses of champagne?"

"Of course, miss."

I watch him pour them down the sidewall of the glass, so the bubbly doesn't foam up. I wasn't intending to order a glass for myself. I'm still not supposed to drink alcohol. But Alex made me crazy and it's *one* glass.

"Thank you," I tell him. Then I put two singles into the tip jar, like a normal person.

I take a sip of champagne—my first drink in weeks. And it's *wonderful*. Like sunshine and butter. I fucking love Florida, and Alex can go to hell.

Besides, I've always had the tolerance of a heavyweight, for which I tend to thank my Irish ancestors. A single glass of champagne won't even make a dent in me.

———

Crap, it does make a small dent.

All right. A medium-sized one.

Only ten minutes later I feel as though my eyes aren't tracking in the normal way. The world around me seems to be zigging when it's supposed to be zagging.

I have the goddamn spins. From a single glass of champagne! How humiliating.

Extracting myself from a conversation with two hockey players and a cute point guard, I move away carefully. I hand my empty champagne flute to a waiter and walk very slowly toward the hotel lobby. My equilibrium is totally off, and I find myself gripping a potted palm tree in order to climb the two steps up to the lobby.

Not cool. Anyone watching me will think I'm wasted.

Also, I'm standing barefoot on the marble floor because hours ago I abandoned my shoes under a barstool. But I can't worry about that now. I'm dizzy and more than a little worried that I might puke. Luckily there's a ladies' room just a few yards away. I toddle toward it.

Inside it's very posh. I tiptoe past a couple of expensive-looking women freshening up their makeup and make my way into a stall, where I sink down onto the toilet and exhale with relief. I can just hide here for a few minutes until my nausea passes, then make my way upstairs.

I wait. People come and go in the ladies' room. My heart stops pounding after a while, so I decide I've improved. I stand up...

Annnnd the world tries to tilt against my wishes once again. I let out a groan and grab the wall.

"Rebecca? Are you okay?" It's Lauren's voice, I think.

"I don't know," I admit.

"What's the matter?"

My next groan is more frustrated than ill. "I wasn't supposed to drink. But I thought a single glass of champagne would be okay."

"And it isn't?" Lauren guesses.

"Not so much, no."

"Do you feel sick?"

Slowly I open the stall door. Lauren is staring back at me with a worried face, still looking impeccable in her blue gown.

"I thought I might be sick, but my stomach is fine." I ease my way out of the stall, still feeling unsteady. "My head is all woozy, though. I need to go upstairs."

"I'll go with you," she says quickly.

This sudden kindness makes my eyes feel hot. But there's one problem. "Don't tell Nate. He'll be pissed at me."

"Oh, screw him," Lauren says, reaching over to take my hand. "He doesn't control us."

"But he's gone to so much trouble for me, and I'm such an idiot." I rub the side of my head, where a throbbing headache is shaping up. "The fancy new doctor said not to drink. And I didn't listen."

"Lesson learned, then," Lauren says lightly. "Where are your shoes?"

"I left them under a barstool."

"Sit here." Lauren steers me onto an upholstered sofa opposite the mirrors. This is the nicest ladies' room I've ever felt sick in. "I'll find your shoes."

"Really? I'm sorry. You're being so nice to me."

Lauren sighs, and I realize how that must sound to her. *You're being so nice — as opposed to all those other times when you were a raving bitch.* "Just don't go anywhere."

I close my eyes and try to take a few deep breaths. I don't feel drunk, exactly. Just *off*. It's not the end of the world, but I'm sad anyway. I'd been feeling so well earlier, and so optimistic.

Hello, square one. I'm back.

Lauren returns with my shoes just five minutes later. I clutch them in one hand and hold onto her with my other one. We make it to the elevators without incident.

Outside my hotel room, she waits patiently while I fumble with my key card and finally swipe it. "I've got it now," I mumble. "Thanks for your help."

"Let me come in for a minute," she insists. "That way if our overlord interrogates me later, I can tell him for sure that you're fine."

"Nate is *so* bossy," I agree, pushing inside.

"As are all men," Lauren grumbles.

She follows me inside, and I'm too tired to care. I yank my nightie out of my suitcase and Lauren whistles. "I'm sorry you're not getting a hookup with a basketball player. If that was your plan for the evening."

I glance at the lacy negligee I'm pulling over my head and give a drunken shrug. "This isn't for special occasions. I always wear lingerie. It's my way of reminding myself that sex still exists."

"Huh. I should try that. And Nate would pee himself if he saw you in this."

"Why?" I ask, and then I burp like a prom-date drunk.

But Lauren doesn't answer the question. "Do you need any aspirin? Or a glass of water?"

"I guess water is a good idea. I just feel so *odd*. Like I had ten drinks instead of one." The bed sinks under my weight and I sigh with relief that I've made it this far.

Lauren brings me a glass of water from the bathroom. "Look, do you think we should call your doctor?"

"No! One glass of champagne can't kill me. I don't want to make a big deal out of it."

"Are you sure?" she presses. "Nate won't be mad."

"Yes, he will!" I yank the comforter down and climb underneath. "I'm just gonna sleep it off. Don't tell anyone."

"Okay," Lauren agrees. "Under one condition. You let me take your key card and come back to check on you in a couple of hours."

"Deal." I don't really think I'm in any danger, but if Lauren wants to babysit me, it's her funeral. "Card's on the desk."

Sleep takes me the minute I get the words out.

———

I have nice dreams.

There's a sale at Bloomingdale's. All the cashmere is 70% off, and I'm the only one who's noticed. Everywhere I turn, there are more sweaters. I'm flipping through a rack of cardigans, my try-on pile growing huge, when someone sits down on the edge of the bed and strokes my hair.

But I'm too sleepy to care much. And I have a cardigan with

funky buttons to try on. So I turn my face away and continue to dream.

"Rebecca," says a voice.

"Nmrph." The pillow is my best friend in the whole world.

"Bec," it tries again.

My subconscious prods me. Lauren had said she'd check on me. But that's not Lauren's voice.

I roll over and open one eye. "Nate?" It comes out hoarse. The fact that he's on my bed in a hotel room ought to seem strange. But whatever.

He brushes the hair off my forehead, and his touch is so tender that it wakes me up a little. The brush of his fingertips across my brow feels amazing and unfamiliar. "What's the matter?" I manage to grunt.

"Nothing," he whispers. "Just checking on you."

I realize what this means. "Lauren tattled on me?"

"No." He smiles at me in the dark. "I saw you leave the party looking shaky. I was asking around for you and Lauren only told me where you were on one condition—that I don't yell at you."

"Oh." I yawn, but the truth is I'm awake now. Stretching, I sit up in the bed, leaning against the upholstered headboard.

Nate makes a soft sound of surprise, and it takes me a moment to realize that my skimpy lingerie is most likely the cause. I look down and see my boobs looking back up at me, barely covered in lace and satin. But it's dark, so I'm not too worried. And, hey—if you sneak up on a sleeping girl, you're going to get a glimpse at her jammies.

"You just woke me up from the *best* dream," I say suddenly, the memory coming back to me.

"Urghl?" Nate coughs. "Really?"

"Yeah." I lean back with a sigh. "All the cashmere sweaters were on super sale. And there were good colors on the rack. Not just the yellow ones, you know? And I think I saw a sign about a shoe discount. I was going to check that out next."

Nate's eyes widen, and then he laughs. "Sorry to ruin your shopping dream. Just wanted to make sure you were still breathing."

"I feel much better, honestly." Taking the water glass off the bedside table, I drink it down. Nate takes the empty glass from my hand and goes to the darkened bathroom to refill it. "I'm totally awake now, you jerk," I say when he returns to hand it back. "What time is it?"

"Twoish." He sits down beside me on the opposite side of the bed. Then he kicks off his shoes so he can pull his feet up onto the comforter, knees bent. He's still wearing his tuxedo shirt, but his jacket is missing and his bow tie is hanging loose around his neck. "You're sure you're okay?"

"I swear I am. The dizziness is gone now. It was just *one* glass of champagne, and I didn't believe that it could..."

He holds up a hand. "You don't have to explain it to me. Not my business."

"*Really?*" This is more surprising than Lauren being so nice earlier. "Here I'm handing you a golden opportunity to say 'I told you so.' Leap on it, man."

Nate tips his head back and lets out a soft laugh. "Can't do it. I promised I wouldn't."

"You promised Lauren?"

He turns his head toward me, and his eyes are bright even though it's dark. "I don't want to nag you, Bec. You're obviously fine. And you take good care of everyone, including yourself. Lauren just made me admit it. That's all."

I think of Lauren in her blue silk and revise my opinion of her for the hundredth time. "She sure looked glamorous tonight."

"So did you." Nate's voice is weirdly thick. He reaches over the comforter to squeeze my hand. And his touch is warmer than I expect it to be.

I've had millions of conversations with Nate. And often alone. But this is oddly intimate. It's the middle of the night, and it feels as if we're the only two people awake in all of Florida. "Can I ask you something?"

"Sure," he says, and his hand doesn't leave mine.

"Why did you switch my job for Lauren's two years ago?"

The question catches him off guard. His mouth opens and then closes a couple of times. Then he withdraws his hand.

"You can tell me the truth," I whisper. "If you think Lauren is sharper than I am. Or more skilled at handling the bigwigs who call you. I won't be offended." *Not much, anyway.* "But it's always bothered me that I didn't know why."

"It has?" He looks oddly miserable.

"Yeah," I admit. "I spent a lot of time trying to figure out what I did wrong."

"Fuck," he whispers. "I'm sorry. That was never my intention."

I feel a wave of relief I didn't even know I was waiting for. "It wasn't?"

"Jesus, no. You didn't do anything wrong. Not a single thing."

"Then why?" My voice cracks a little—it's the sound of the question breaking free from my heart. I guess I've needed to ask this for a long time.

"Because I'm a goddamn idiot."

That's a lot of cursing for a mere personnel issue. I feel like I'm on the verge of learning something important. I wait for him to go on, but he doesn't say a word. "Aren't you going to explain?"

"Not if I can help it," he mumbles.

"Nate!" I turn and rise up on my knees just so we're the same height. "Just tell me, okay!"

"What if you don't like the answer?" he fires back.

"But maybe you owe it to me anyway. I think you're being illogical right now!"

"No kidding!" he fires back, turning to face me. We've squared off. "I can't be logical when it comes to you! Can't do it. Not for years."

The words just sort of hang there in the dark between us. I don't really understand them. But when he lifts a hand to cup my cheek, I don't feel so confused anymore. His fingers are so gentle on my face that everything grows quiet inside me.

This isn't how we usually touch each other, but for some reason it's not weird, even though I'm not exactly wearing clothes. I stare into his kind eyes and I swear nobody even breathes for a long time. "Why?" I whisper one more time. And then, "Please."

He closes his eyes, and his thumb sweeps over my cheekbone. I didn't know I had so many nerves in my face. I have the urge to lean into his hand and beg for more. But then he starts talking. "It was two years ago in March, and you had just started dating that… guy. The artist. He liked to come by the office to talk before you left together."

What? For a long beat, I can't even conjure a memory of dating an artist. "Wait… That kid who was a courier, and also painted? Why would he matter?" I dated him for the emotional equivalent of about ten minutes.

Nate shakes his head, and then reaches out with his other hand, too. He's cupping my face so gently that my skin tingles under his warm palms. Except he's giving me a look of exasperation—like it's causing him pain just to have this conversation. "I couldn't stand it, Bec. I wanted you to have someone and be happy. But I didn't want to watch."

I *almost* ask why once again. But then it starts to sink in. And what he's saying is big. No—it's *huge*. And I really didn't see it coming.

Meanwhile, we're having the world's most heated staring contest. His eyes—which are an unusual shade of light brown in the daylight—are as black as the night. I'm studying him so closely that I swear I can see the flecks of gold even in the darkness. And he's staring back at me like the future of the world depends on his refusal to blink.

And maybe it does. Because his hands move, sliding down from my jaw to my very bare shoulders. I'm suddenly so aware of how close our bodies are right now. The point of contact between his palms and my body seems to hum. If we break this standoff, something even crazier might happen here. His face is mere inches from mine. We're so close that I can feel the heat rising off Nate. Goosebumps prickle my bare skin.

The possibility of his kiss is a brand new thing. I have stood in front of this man a thousand times before without being half so aware of his mouth. It's a very handsome mouth, one I've seen smiling from magazine covers and smirking at me over cups of coffee. But for the first time in years, I want to know how it would feel against mine.

"Why?" I whisper again. But this time the question means

something else. It means, *why am I suddenly so aware of you? Why are my breasts heavy against the lace of my nightie? Why is there so much heat in your eyes, and what is it doing to me? Why is…*

He kisses me.

Again I'm caught off guard. His lips are so soft. But my mouth is suddenly super sensitive. The snick of his kiss echoes inside my chest, and the hairs rise up on my arms when his lips brush over mine again. It's overwhelming. I grab his biceps and let out a gasp.

The sound sort of vibrates between us. He feeds on it. He cups the back of my head, and his kiss tilts, perfecting our connection. There's nothing tentative about it now. I now know exactly how Nate's mouth would feel against mine. It feels *awesome*. I part my lips and his tongue touches mine.

And, *goddamn it*. That zing I'm hearing now is all my hormones firing all at once. And it pisses me off. I make a loud, startled sound, from deep in my chest. Because… goddamn.

The sound startles Nate into jerking backward, breaking the kiss.

"Nate!" I squawk. "What the hell?"

"Jesus," Nate whispers. "I'm sorry?"

"You should be!" I squeak. "You just broke the seal! We spent seven years not doing that! And now I know what it's like." I didn't know that Nate's kiss would light me up everywhere, or that he'd taste like whiskey and heat. "I mean…" I put my fingertips to my lips and let out a strangled sigh.

His head tilts to the side like a Labrador retriever who can't quite figure something out. "Bec, listen — I will apologize again and get the fuck out of your room. But for the love of god, help me understand — are you pissed off about the kiss? Or are you pissed that I stopped?"

"That's not an easy question!" *Obviously*.

His handsome forehead wrinkles with confusion. "But it's multiple choice!"

All I can do is stare up in confusion at this man to whom I've spent years cultivating a sexual immunity. Not that he makes it easy, with his unusual eye color and intelligent stare. That scruff he wears on his elegant jaw because he's too busy inventing the world to shave.

At that moment I find the whole picture as arousing as he is infuriating. He's blowing up my head with confusing thoughts and this sudden, uncomfortable lust.

What. A. Jerk! Obviously, I am forced to retaliate. I grab that famously handsome face in two hands, and crush my mouth to his.

"Ungh." His moan is all shock and awe, because I've finally got the edge on him. I tilt my head and kiss him again.

But Nate is a fierce competitor. Less than a second goes by before he slips an arm behind my thighs and slides my body down onto the bed. He pushes me into the pillows and takes control of the kiss.

And I experience a whole host of sensations in a big hurry. Because Nate is good at this. It should come as no surprise, since he's good at everything. But I'm caught off guard as his lips massage mine with slow, dragging kisses. Each one is a little deeper than the last, until his tongue finally strokes against mine.

I hear myself moan into his mouth as his tongue teases me toward recklessness. I used to wonder what it would be like to kiss him. It was a lot of work to put it out of my head, thank you very much.

And now I'll never forget. Goddamn it.

In spite of my irritation, I slip an arm around his waist so I don't lose contact with his bossy mouth. My tongue slides against his. So hot.

This will prove to be a horrible idea. I already know it. But he started it.

Didn't he?

My brain is melting.

His might be, too. Neither of us is ready to stop and think. Our kisses never end—each one just rolls right into another. Hot and ceaseless. Then he drops his hips onto mine and I moan at the new connection. I welcome his weight, pressing me into the bed. I close my eyes and just give in to the desire that's rising up inside me.

Whenever Nate decides he wants something—a Fortune 500 deal, a hockey win, a late-night pizza—he goes full steam ahead.

And suddenly all that attention is focused on me. His mouth worships mine with such focus and hunger that it's all I can do to keep up.

I do my best, sliding my bare toes across the arch of his foot, and sifting my fingers through his hair. It's softer than I'd expected. I've known Nate's mind for years, but his body is a foreign country I've never visited before. Somehow I already speak the language. My palms coast down his neck and over the muscles in his back. He's solid under my hands. The cotton of his tuxedo shirt isn't much of a barrier. I can feel the heat pouring off him.

And we can't stop kissing. It's like a full-body kiss now—heat and pressure everywhere. Somewhere in the depths of my soul I'm still aware that I'm making a big mistake. But it's the middle of the night, and Nate's kisses are both hungry and reverent. And yet it's wonderful in the same way as my Bloomingdale's dream—pure possibility without the burden of explanation.

My judgment is 70% off tonight.

That must be why I decide to work a hand up under Nate's untucked shirt. His skin is smoother than I guessed it would be. I run a hand up his side and sigh into his mouth. And when I trace a fingernail along the back waistband of his trousers, he shivers into his next kiss.

That helpless reaction emboldens me. So I drop a hand to his very firm ass and squeeze. Even through two layers of fabric, I can feel that he's solid muscle. And when I do this, his kiss stutters as he groans.

I won't lie—my newfound power is a huge turn-on. Nobody ever throws Nate off his game.

So I'm feeling really pleased with myself until Nate ups the ante. He drops his head and runs his tongue across the swells of my breasts. All my senses leap at the sensation of that wicked tongue so near my nipples. I gasp, and the gust has barely left my lungs when he cups one breast and pinches the nipple. And now it's *me* who's making poorly controlled moans and whimpers. He's turned the tables on me, and I didn't even see it coming.

It's a negligee I'm wearing, not a bra. So Nate is able to work the fabric downward until my breasts are revealed to him. The fabric corrals my boobs together, exposing my nipples. He admires his work with a dirty gleam in his eye.

For *me*. It's mind-blowing.

I grab his head and lower it onto my breast. He groans, bending to swirl his tongue over my nipples, one at a time. Then he draws one into his mouth and looks up at me, eyes dark and full of lust. He gives a good suck and I shudder with anticipation. I can feel need pooling between my legs, and the sight of him mouthing my tits is almost too much.

Please, my body shouts. *More. Now.*

I might even say some of that aloud as I shove his suspenders off his shoulders, then reach for Nate's shirt and tug. But it's still buttoned, so this proves futile.

Nate has some sympathy for the problem, though. He sits up, kneeling beside me. I scramble to a vertical position, too, helping myself to his shirt buttons. I expose a V of skin, my fingers working furiously. In the moonlight I can see the pulse jump in his throat. I stop working and put my fingertips there, just lightly. It's humbling that I've caused his heart to race like that.

Me.

I didn't know.

He takes my hand in his and lifts it, kissing my palm. The intensity of his gaze burns right through the darkness. I know exactly where this is heading.

So does Nate. He threads the lace of my tiny nightie between his fingertips and lifts the thing over my head.

"Jesus." Nate takes a deep breath and tips his head up, then lets it out in a hot gust.

During our long history together, Nate has seen me in many different states: bleary on red-eye flights, and drunk after a boozy business dinner in Paris. Once he watched me puke on hotel shrubbery after a grueling run we took together in Arizona during a tech conference. That was embarrassing.

But I have never felt so exposed as I do right now. I give in to the urge to cover my generous boobs with two hands.

Slowly, he removes his shirt and tosses it on the floor. Then he covers my hands with his own, leaning in to kiss me. His thumbs stroke the backs of my hands, their arc whispering onto the skin of my breasts, too. I lick into his mouth and try to forget my self-consciousness.

We're doing this wonderful, terrible thing. If I think too hard, I'll ruin it.

Summoning my courage, I pull my hands out from under Nate's. He makes a low, guttural sound as his palms cup my bare breasts. With a groan he pushes his tongue into my mouth, and it feels like a preview of coming events.

My heart kicks with heady anticipation, and my hands begin to explore Nate's hard chest. He's nearly hairless except for the center of his tummy. My fingers crest all the ridges of his abs and then play in the little strip leading in to his trousers. Nate makes a desperate sound as I reach for his fly.

The last frontier.

When I undo the button, he knocks my hand aside, lowering the zipper himself. I watch as he reaches in and takes himself in hand, drawing his cock out. I would have thought he'd be long and lean like the rest of his body. But when I reach out to touch him, he's thick and hard in my hand.

That makes everything seem dirtier and more shocking. I don't even know why. The head is dark and full, with a pearly drop on the tip.

Apparently alternate universes *are* real. And there's an alternate universe where you can slide your thumb over your boss's cock-head and listen to him mutter a string of curses. I'm visiting it right now.

"Fuck, Becca." He pushes me down on the bed again and kicks away his trousers and boxers.

Nate is a boxers man, my subconscious points out as he lies down beside me and dives into another kiss. But then I stop thinking entirely as his hands coast down my body, his touch lighting me up like a pinball machine at the height of play.

It's been so long since anyone touched me I'd forgotten how amazing it feels to be stroked and teased. The soft skin of my belly twitches as he brushes by it. The first slide of his fingertips past the elastic of my panties is exquisite. I part my legs, shameless. And, *yes*. I practically arch off the bed when he finally reaches my core. He makes a noise of shock to find me so wet.

The word he gasps is, "Sweetheart."

It's a potent, whispered oath. I wrap both arms around his neck. We're skin on skin—all heat and friction. He fits the root of his cock against my pussy and grinds slowly against me, while I dive into his mouth, my kisses begging for more.

We're like a video on fast forward—grappling and writhing, our mouths in motion, kissing and nibbling everything within reach. I'm desperate. Desire pulses inside me. Throughout me. I'm made entirely of *want*.

I fill my lungs with air and then ask for it. "Please," I gasp.

Nate smiles down at me. That fucker *grins*. I'm burning up here, and he's...

He's yanking my panties down and tossing them away. He's hovering above me, his eyes glittering with desire.

He's sliding inside me.

Everything slows down. I dig my heels into the mattress, bracing myself, taking him. There's a hush as we stare at each other in shock. I hear breathing and the *glug glug* of my own heart. He gives one last little push and seats himself fully. I'm pinned like a butterfly inside this moment, staring up at him in wonder.

His smile is gone now. In its place is a face so serious that I have to reach up and touch it with one hand. He bends down, touches his tongue to mine and sighs into our inevitable kiss.

Sweetheart. That word is still echoing inside me as he begins to move.

He removes my hand from his face and kisses it as his hips take a slow rhythm. Both my hands are caught in his. He raises them over my head and holds them against the pillow.

But I need to move. So I lift my knees to catch his hips and meet his every thrust. And we're kissing again. I'm drowning in so much heat and desire. I don't want it to ever end, but my greedy body feels otherwise. It starts as a heavy pulse between my legs. When I can't hold it back any longer, I arch my back and cry out.

Nate's moan is a chorus with mine. Waves of pleasure wash over me as he curses against my lips. He lets go of my hands and wraps an arm around my thigh, yanking us more tightly together once...twice.

He plants himself deeply inside me and bites the juncture between my neck and shoulder. Then he lets out a tortured groan and shudders.

Holy...

Wow.

I...

I can't believe we just did that.

It's amazing and wonderful and so incredibly shocking. But all I want to do about it is run my hands over his skin again and sigh.

[13]

NATE

MY HEART RATE is several miles per hour over the legal limit, and my body is heavy with the weight of sexual gratification.

Even my endorphins have endorphins.

Rebecca relaxes beneath me, breathing hard. I heave my tired carcass over to the side, pulling her with me. She lays her head down on my chest and exhales as if stunned.

And maybe she is. I know I am. Not only was that the most amazing experience of my life, but it's also dumbfounding.

I have never lost control of myself so completely as I did just now.

Normally, I'm just about the most dedicated person I know. I get up at five o'clock every morning. I've run marathons. Keeping a tight leash on myself is the only way I know to stay sharp and stay on top.

Tonight I gave a dangerous new meaning to *on top*.

Jesus Christ.

I push a lock of hair out of Rebecca's perfect face. It's damp from exertion. Her expression is half dreamy and half wary.

No way to know which half is winning.

"Nate," she whispers.

"What?" I bury my face in her hair, and tighten my arms

119

around her curvy body. My dick gives a tired but hopeful little twitch.

She clears her throat. "At least I'm on the pill."

"I know," I mumble. "They're right there on the bathroom counter."

"Okay..."

"I'd never endanger you," I whisper. "I'm careful." *Until right now*. Why would she even believe me?

She hesitates, and I hope against hope that we don't have to talk much yet. I need a few minutes to figure out what the hell to say. No—I need more time than that. A year doesn't sound long enough. "So..." She lifts her head off my chest. "Why do you think we just..."

"Bec?"

"Yeah?"

I pass my palm down her smooth arm, and give it a caress. "Don't ruin it. Unless you really need to."

She lays her head on my chest again.

I could offer to leave. Maybe she'd prefer it. But I don't, though. I'm a stubborn asshole who just got the only thing he's ever wanted and couldn't have. So I close my eyes and doze, as her heartbeat slows against mine.

But my subconscious won't let me forget for too long that I'm naked in a bed with Rebecca. I wake up sometime later, still in the pitch dark. She's stretched out beside me now, her back to my front. I run a hand down her side, because I can't help myself. Her skin is incredibly soft, and I love the way the downhill of her ribs goes uphill again at her hip.

So I do it again.

"Mmh," she says as I stroke her skin. And when I cup her breast, the nipple hardens under my fingertips. She clamps a hand over mine, encouraging me.

Jesus. I'm not nearly as strong a man as I thought I was. One touch from her and I'm hard and ready.

I drop open-mouthed kisses onto the back of her neck and let my hands wander her body. Soon enough she's whimpering and pushing back against my body.

So I roll us in her direction — pushing her face down on the bed, lifting her hips toward mine.

"Yes," she gasps as I push myself home for the second time tonight.

Yes.

I give it to her fast and hard, and she rocks back against me with breathy gasps. When I snake a hand under her body and stroke her, she sobs my name into the pillowcase.

We shudder together before collapsing into a useless heap of tired limbs.

Then sleep comes for good.

REBECCA

Consciousness arrives slowly. The feel of a man's hard body against mine is even better than discounted cashmere, and I don't really feel like waking up. A big hand is stroking my hair, and I close my eyes against the sunlight that is entering the room.

But then my dream man gives a very Nate-like sigh, and I wake up all at once. It's a good thing I'm facing away from him, since I'm sure I'm wearing a stunned expression as the memories of last night's events stack up in the cool light of morning.

What the hell did we just do?

Until you wake up naked with your boss of seven years, you haven't lived.

He makes a soft sound of impatience, and I stiffen.

"Rebecca." His voice is low and rough. "Are you okay?"

I consider the question. The truth is that I really don't know. "Yeah," I sigh. "I can't wait for the day when people stop asking me that."

"I know." He squeezes the muscles in my shoulder. It feels awesome, too. "But I wasn't talking about your head injury."

Shit. "I'm good," I say, ducking the question.

"Then why aren't you looking at me?"

"Sleepy," I grumble. But then I roll over, bring the sheet with

121

me to cover my boobs. But that only makes me remember the hot look on Nate's face when he swirled his tongue on each…

Gah! All the parts of my consciousness are awake now, including the sexy parts.

Slowly, I raise my eyes and find Nate studying me. His eyes are soft, but his beautiful mouth wears a knowing smirk.

"What?" I demand.

He drags one finger across the skin just over the sheet's edge. "I wish we weren't headed in separate directions today. I don't want you to go home and brood."

"I won't." *I totally will.*

He frowns. "Breakfast first?"

"Well…" I hesitate. "I was going to have breakfast with Georgia. If I cancel, she'll want to know why."

"Ah." It's a sigh. "Are you sure you're okay."

"Totally good."

He doesn't believe me. But he kisses me once and then gets up. I watch as he puts on last night's tux. And I wonder how many people he'll run into between here and his own room. It's not like I expect him to stop and say, "Hey, guess whose room I just came from!" But still, the idea of being caught unnerves me.

I just became that girl who sleeps with her boss.

"Are we going to talk later?" he asks, doing up his shirt buttons.

"Don't we always?" I ask, ducking the question.

He gives me another frown. "Don't leave for home without saying goodbye, okay?"

"Okay." Although everything just got weird. *I had sex with Nate. Twice.* When I repeat it in my mind, it isn't easy to believe.

A few minutes later the door clicks shut behind him, and I actually heave a sigh of relief. I pick up my phone and text Georgia to cancel breakfast. And I ask her to fetch my manicure kit from Lauren's room. Because if I go up to the executive suite level and Nate is standing there looking sharp in his suit, I don't think I'll be able to keep the confusion off my face.

What have I done?

There's a brand new soundtrack running through my brain. It sounds like this: *Holy shit. Holy shit. Holy shit.*

My whole life, people have been telling me I have a good head on my shoulders. I leave the crazy, risky behavior to other people —my sister, for example. I'm the smart one who never screws up.

Until now. I've thrown away my sanity for a single hot night with the boss.

Although it *was* a really great night.

On the plane home, I sip my watery airline coffee and wonder what just happened. I can still feel his hands on me. I can still taste his kisses. By the time I roll my carry-on out to the baggage claim, I'm delirious from both exhaustion and stress.

Ramesh—Nate's driver—is there waiting. "Hello, Miss Rebecca," he says with a smile. "I have instructions to take you to Pierrepont Place. Is that where you wish to go?"

Yes and no. "I do need to go to Nate's, but only for about five minutes. Could you possibly wait while I run inside? I need to get some things and then go back to my apartment on Water Street."

"Not a problem."

Excellent. I'm officially running scared.

It only takes a few minutes to pack up my things at Nate's and then leave again. I can see questions in Mrs. Gray's eyes. "Stay for a cuppa?" she invites as Ramesh carries my suitcase down the stairs.

"I can't this morning," I lie. "But I'll see you soon, I'm sure."

Though I'm not at all sure.

Ten minutes later Ramesh has carried the suitcases up the narrow stairwell of my apartment building. I thank him as graciously as possible. Like Mrs. Gray, he's probably wondering what the heck I'm up to.

Go ahead and wonder, I think as I shake his hand goodbye. *Because I don't even know myself.*

My little apartment is quiet for once. Renny is asleep in my sister's room, but Missy and the baby are out somewhere.

I ease the bedroom door shut and then get busy with my

123

luggage. I unpack everything and put it away. I remove the portable baby crib from my bedroom and then tidy up.

Moving around feels good, so I keep on cleaning. I attack the cluttered living room, sorting baby gear from my sister's detritus.

Meanwhile, panic churns inside me like a storm. And—like a real hurricane—it's sometimes not easy to know where the danger lies. What's the worst-case scenario of having slept with Nate? It's hard to say. If anyone finds out, the office gossip will be brutal. It makes me cringe to think Hugh Major might look at me differently now. Like I'm *that* girl, the kind who fools around with the boss on trips.

But that's really just the tip of the iceberg. When I think about seeing Nate again—and traveling with Nate again—I feel a little insane. What's he going to say? If he pretends like nothing happened, how will that feel?

Because something absolutely did. At least to me.

On the other hand, I don't expect him to turn it into something serious. He confessed to crushing on me. And I guess I gave him the opportunity to get *that* out of his system. Twice.

Holy hell. I'm standing in the middle of my living room, a bag of diapers in my hand, feeling seriously aroused. When he put his mouth on my nipple, I…

Whew. Maybe I should open a window and cool this place off.

I finish decluttering the living room and attack our tiny kitchen. There are dishes in the sink. I suds up the spaghetti pot while trying to strategize. There are two possibilities. A) Nate ignores the whole episode. The next time I see him will be at work. And he'll say, "Hey, Bec! Do you have the ticket sales numbers? And how about sushi for lunch today?"

That will sting, but I guess it's better than choice B, which is the world's most awkward conversation. "Well, Becca. Once every seven years or so, whether we need it or not. Right?" Cue the awkward chuckle.

No, the conversation could easily be worse. "Becca, hey. I'm so sorry I let things get out of hand. Please accept this gourmet fruit basket as an apology. By the way, Lauren will be traveling with me from now on."

Yikes. And to think I was so eager to go back to work.

Eventually I hear my sister's key turn in the lock. "Wow, Bec! It looks so great in here."

I bite back a snarky reply about why that is. But Missy has no time to clean. She's got to finish her semester and then one more semester at school to get her degree. I want that for her. And I made it possible for her to live here so that she could get the college education that I never finished.

"Thank you," I say. Because this is what's important in my life —my family, and the job that supports us. I can't lose sight of that. Sleeping with Nate was so stupid of me. Why on earth would I make things more difficult for myself right now? I have a head injury and big-time obligations.

"Everything okay?" Missy asks as Matthew begins to babble in his baby carrier.

"Sure. I'm good."

To prove it, I keep cleaning. I vacuum and dust every surface. Then I attack the bathroom, rearranging the medicine cabinet to give away most of the space to my sister, so she has somewhere to put all the pacifiers and nursing pads.

By the time I get out the mop to tackle the bathroom floor, Missy is ready to stage an intervention. "I'm worried," she says from the doorway, staying out of harm's way. "I mean, stress-cleaning is something I've always valued about your personality. But this is a little extreme."

My response is a grumble. Missy and my mother depended on my stress-cleaning habits to kick in every semester at exam time. Less work for them.

"Did you lose your job? It's okay, you can tell me. We'll be all right."

"No." But the idea makes me wince. Because it's occurred to me that with a different boss, losing my job wouldn't be outside the realm of possibility. Nate's a good guy. He's not going to fire me out of embarrassment, or make a big deal about it.

"But you might?" my sister pries.

"I probably should." I know I'm being overly dramatic. But

everything seems up in the air. It doesn't help that I haven't been to my desk in weeks.

"What did you do?"

"I slept with my boss." *Yikes*. It sounds worse out loud than it does in my head.

Missy wrinkles up her nose. "Really? You slept with Hugh Major? He's *old*."

Like I've said before, my sister is a few peas short of a casserole. "Bite your tongue. He's old and *married*. I would never sleep with Hugh Major."

Missy waits.

"I slept with…" I almost can't say it. "*Nate*." And I immediately experience a little shiver. His name doesn't feel the same in my mouth anymore. For the rest of my life I'm going to be able to picture naked, panting Nate, his sculpted pecs moving above me, his long fingers pressing mine down on the bed…

"Whooooa." Missy's mouth makes a perfect O shape. "So he finally got up the nerve to admit he has a thing for you?"

"Missy!" I squeak. "Don't say that."

"Please." She rolls her eyes in that way sisters have, and it makes you want to punch them. "Exhibit A." She points at a giant basket of very dead flowers I've set beside the door. I'm hoping Renny will notice them and take them down to the garbage compactor.

"They're just flowers," I grumble.

"Was it good?" she asks.

"Hmm?" I'm scrubbing the tiles as if there will be an inspection later.

"The sex. Was it good?"

I feel a flush on my chest, just hearing the question.

"Did someone have sex without me?" Renny asks, emerging from the bedroom, Matthew in his arms.

"Rebecca did!" Missy announces. "With her boss."

"Oh, sh…innicock," he says. Apparently we're working on cutting out the curse words this week. "You made the beast with two backs with Hugh Major? Isn't he a little old for you?"

"Not. Him," I grit out. "I'm going for a walk." It's a spur-of-the-moment decision, but I need to get some fresh air.

"Before you go…there's two pieces of mail you need to look at." My sister deigns to rise from the sofa just far enough to sift through the mail on the coffee table. It's mostly catalogues, but she locates two envelopes—one thick, one thin. "This says it's from a real estate company, so I thought it might be important. And the other is a health insurance thing."

Oh, shit. Double shit. The thicker envelope is from DUMBO Holdings. "This is our new lease." I'd been waiting for this. My two-year lease is up, and by law they can raise me a significant amount. I slit the envelope and slide the folded papers out. My eye scans the first page until I find what I'm looking for.

Two-year rate increase: 0.00%.

I read it three more times just because I can't quite believe it. Then I flip to the second page to make sure the numbers match the ones on the first page.

They do.

"Wow," I breathe. "This is the best news I've heard in weeks."

"Yeah?" Missy crowds me to look. "No increase? In New York?"

"I know. Maybe it's a clerical error."

"It doesn't matter," my sister says quickly. "Sign it. Send it back. They'll have to honor it."

That's not true, since it isn't countersigned yet. But I take a pen from the jar where I've stashed them (neatly!) and sign it anyway.

"I'll get a stamp," Missy offers.

The thinner envelope is from my health plan. I'm also dreading this. In the past month I've racked up an ER visit, a neurologist, and then a Sunday visit to Dr. Armitage. There's no way that's covered.

Sure enough, I find one of those boggling *Explanation of Benefits* forms inside—the kind that are written in code. "This is not a bill," it reads at the top. But I know better than to assume it's good news. And it isn't. Dr. Armitage is listed as an Out of Network Provider, which doesn't surprise me at all. But my first session in his training clinic is also listed as Not Approved for Coverage.

When I see the prices, I inhale sharply. Four hundred bucks for the consultation and $275 for my first therapy session. And I'm supposed to go three times a week.

"Is it bad?" Missy is back, holding a stamp on the tip of one finger.

"No," I lie. "Just a bureaucratic snafu. Talking to the insurance company will probably eat half a day." *If only.* I'll try to get them to approve the therapy, but I know my chances are probably terrible.

Goddamn it.

"Mail the lease!" Missy says, pasting the stamp on the return envelope. "That's one less thing to worry about."

I hope she's right.

Five minutes later I drop it into a mailbox on Water Street. Two more years at the same rate in an apartment that's two blocks away from a job I love. It should feel like a coup.

But I'm so very confused about what happens now.

[14]

NATE

A FEW TIMES a year there are articles published about my success. *How High Is Nate Kattenberger's IQ?* Or, *The Man Who Sees the Future of Tech.*

The people who write these things are obviously off-base. Because I'm the stupidest man alive. I'm sitting in a crowded hockey stadium with twenty-thousand people. Millions of dollars of my investment money is fighting for their lives on the ice below me. And what am I thinking about?

Rebecca.

That's right. Five days later and I'm sitting here kicking myself for my lack of self-control. One heated conversation with Rebecca in the dark, and I totally lost my mind. She's avoiding me now, which means it may have cost me a good friend. And if I'm really unlucky it will cost my organization a great employee.

Until now I never understood what people meant when they said, *thinking with your dick*. But now I do. Mine got some big ideas and instead of tamping it down I said, *dude, let's go*.

What a fucking nightmare I've caused myself.

Lauren stands up and claps, reminding me to watch the fucking game. Beacon has just made a terrific save.

At least someone is focused.

"Nice!" Stew says, punctuating the compliment by poking me in the arm. "That's how it's done! I think your boys can make this happen."

I think so too, although it's been a challenging week. The team lost the first game to Tampa. Tonight they look strong, though. I know it's not over for us. They spent the last forty-eight hours watching tape while Lauren and I hunkered down with our laptops and tried to stay on top of everything that's happening in New York.

Mostly I thought about Rebecca.

The morning she left Bal Harbour I caught her limo before it left for the airport. I leaned inside to give her a kiss on the cheekbone, and she looked back at me with wide, shaken eyes.

The look on her face cut me, because holding her in my arms had been a transformative experience. One I'm *still* processing.

But I don't know where she stands.

"We'll speak soon, okay?" I said during that last moment we had together.

She'd avoided my eyes. "I'm going to be mostly offline this week. Doctor's orders."

Definitely sounded like a brushoff.

Nonetheless, I've sent her a couple of texts and left a voicemail, asking if she was okay. But either she's ghosting me, or she's really offline. And I can't keep reaching out to her, because if I do, that makes me a creepy guy who can't leave her alone.

And that's the worst thing about this mess. If I'd seriously *tried* to break the rules in the seediest possible way, it would look a hell of a lot like what went down on Tuesday night. I used a key card she'd given to Lauren to let myself into her hotel room while she slept. I woke her up, and then we had very energetic sex.

Twice.

I can see the headlines now. *Nate Kattenberger, CEO of a Fortune 500 Company Is the Biggest Idiot Alive.*

Meanwhile, I can't get that night out of my head. I know Becca enjoyed herself, to put it mildly. The way she undressed me plays on repeat in a brain that I *used* to think had above-average powers of concentration. But apparently not, because the taste of her kisses is all I think about now.

"Oh my *God*," Lauren gasps. "This game is taking a year off my life."

I check the scoreboard. Still zero-zero. At least I picked the right game to be distracted.

Beside me, Lauren's fingers are worrying the strap of her handbag, and her eyes are glued to the goalie she claims not to love.

As it happens, I'm not the only one who had an interesting night in Bal Harbour. She doesn't know it, but as I snuck back into my hotel room the other morning, I caught Mike Beacon sneaking out of hers. The goalie and I didn't say a word to each other as we passed in the hallway, both of us wearing rumpled tuxedos. We just gave each other a quick smile and moved on.

I would never say a word to embarrass Lauren. Though I deserve a medal for not mentioning her sudden return to hockey fandom this month.

"Nate." Stew snaps his fingers in front of my face. "Are you seriously not paying attention right now?"

"I am," I lie.

"Only you could think about work at a time like this," he says, stuffing another handful of popcorn into his mouth.

Stew knows me pretty well. And I do have a rep for thinking about work all the time. Though at this rate I'll never have another original thought. I'm not even sure I care. My obsession with Rebecca got a nice little workout, and I want to hang onto that memory as long as I can.

The game grinds on, the tension escalating on the ice. I manage to pay attention. Lesser men would let their frustrations show on the ice, but my players keep their cool.

Tampa's don't, though. Their most decorated forward trips my D-man and then gets chippy with the ref. I smile when he gets tossed out of the game a minute later.

"Power play!" Lauren squeaks, and I smile about that, too.

"Nice to see you paying attention," she says.

"Nice to see you're a hockey fan again," I return.

And that's when it happens. My boys put the puck in the goal.

Finally! We're on our feet, yelling. The second period ends with a 1-0 score.

Lauren sits back in her chair and exhales. "This is torture," she mutters.

I say nothing, burnishing my trophy for discretion. But now I have fifteen minutes to wait for the third period. And that's an eternity for me. So my thoughts go right back to Rebecca. Is she lying in my den again, listening to the game?

God, I hope so. I hope I haven't fucked everything up by, well, fucking.

I slip my phone out of my pocket like an impatient teenager and check the screen.

Nothing from Becca.

I open up a chat window with Bingley. One of my innovations for this product is the ability to communicate from afar.

Nate: Checking in.

Bingley: Hello, Nate! The hockey score is 1-zip, your favor. But you probably know that, as you are currently seated 23.5 yards from the ice surface. On the home front, there is nothing to report. Internal temperature is 68 degrees. All security systems engaged.

Nate: Good stuff. I was wondering if Rebecca is there?

Bingley: Alas, fair Rebecca is not presently on the premises. I last interacted with Rebecca on Wednesday at one-thirty-three p.m.

Well, fuck. That was right after she had returned from the airport. She practically left a contrail on her way out of my life.

Shit.

Nate: Did she leave a message? A guy can hope.

Bingley: No, good sir. Shall I locate her current whereabouts?

Every employee phone has a tracking device, so Bingley could find Rebecca easily. But it's my company policy never to snoop on an employee unless we believe someone is in danger.

And I will not be that creepy guy.

Nate: No, thank you. Goodnight.

Bingley: Night, good sir!

I could change his name back to Hal, I suppose. But I don't. Just in case Rebecca might be back.

As if.

I put the phone away and find Stew watching me.

"What?"

"Nothing," he says with a grin. "Want a beer? I'm going to the bar."

"I'm good," I say.

"I'll get you a drink, Stew," Lauren says, rising from her seat.

"No! You don't have to." Even if Lauren is here in an official capacity, he would never abuse her by asking for petty favors.

There's a reason we've been friends for years. Stew is good people.

"But I want a drink and I don't know what they have." She puts a hand on his shoulder. "I'll go. And maybe you can snap Nate out of being such a space cadet."

"Dude," Stew says after she disappears. "What is up with you? And don't tell me you are thinking about systems architecture right now."

"I'm a little distracted. No big deal."

Stew lifts his eyebrows. "Please tell me you've finally broken your dry spell. I was starting to get worried."

"Oh, fuck off."

He laughs. "So who's the lucky girl?"

"I can't talk about this with you."

The smile falls off his face. "Why not?"

"Because you know her. I'm not a gossip."

"You are totally a gossip. But also weirdly discreet. Now this will drive me insane, you realize."

"Not my problem."

"Fucker. I'm almost tempted to think you finally bagged Rebecca."

I just look back at him blandly. People tell me that I have a really impassive face.

"No fucking *way*," he whispers.

People also tell me that when it comes to Rebecca, the impassive face thing is kind of broken.

"Seriously? When did this happen?"

"Remember ten seconds ago when I told you we weren't discussing it?"

133

Stew rubs his chin. "Is this an ongoing thing?"

I just sigh.

"I'd feel a whole lot better right now if you tell me you've been secretly dating all year."

"Not as much as I would," I mutter.

Stew groans. "So... this happened once, and now she's freezing you out? Was it recently?"

"Bal Harbour. Just a few days ago. Then she went back to New York, and I'm here. I don't know what's in her head."

"Did you call her? Please tell me you called her."

"Of *course* I did. No pickup, though. I sent a few texts."

Stew's eyes widen. "Then you have a problem."

"Gosh, you think?"

"No, a *big* problem. She's your employee, and now you're pursuing her. You have to stop."

"Obviously she and I need to have a conversation."

Stew adjusts the collar of his shirt, and that's his tell for when he's feeling uncomfortable. "No. I think you fucked up."

"And you know this how?" I look around, hoping to see Lauren approaching. I need this conversation to end.

"You two got it on, and now she's not returning your calls? That's some bad juju."

"Maybe she just needs time to process." I know I do.

"How did this go down anyway? Please tell me she started it."

She didn't start it. But that doesn't mean she didn't come around to my way of seeing things in a hurry. "She definitely escalated it."

"You kissed her."

"I did," I admit. But I skip right over the part about breaking into her hotel room and waking her up. I can't even imagine what my HR officers would say about that. It's probably near the top ten list of Things Never To Do with Colleagues on a Business Trip.

"You planted one on her," Stew prods. "Then what happened?"

"She made a noise, so I stopped. Then she yelled at me for a minute, climbed in my lap, and kissed me like the world was ending."

Grinning, Stew puts a hand over his heart. "Wow. You've been waiting years for that to happen."

I sigh because it's true.

"So you guys got freaky. And then what?"

"You don't get any more details."

"I meant in the morning, dumbass."

Oh. "I spent the night. Then I asked her to have breakfast with me, but she said she had plans. I put her in the limo an hour later, kissed her goodbye, said I couldn't wait to see her again."

"And now she's not taking your call."

"Pretty much."

"Jesus Christ." Stew tugs at his collar again. "She wasn't drunk, right?"

"No! Not at all. She was chatty, asking me questions. She asked me why I transferred her to Brooklyn."

"And you said, 'Because I'm in love with you'?"

"No. That would have been an exaggeration." Even as I say this, I feel a strange tightness in my chest. Maybe it isn't as far from the truth as I wish it was.

"My initial analysis suggests only two reasons why she isn't returning your call."

I wasn't in a hurry to hear them.

"Number one, she didn't like it and doesn't want to tell you."

"She liked it," I say immediately. I may be a socially awkward human, but when a woman is gasping my name and coming on my cock, I know she's had a good time.

"Well, congratulations." He smirks and it makes me want to punch him. "But the other option isn't any better. Which is that she liked it at the time, but now she regrets it."

He's right, of course. That isn't any better. "What's to regret?"

"Complicating her life, for starters. You're the boss. It's tricky."

"I'm not *her* boss."

"Nate, you're smarter than that." He pokes me in the arm. "You hired her. You gave her the exact job she has now. Even if she technically works for Hugh, you're still her boss's boss."

This line of thought makes me even grumpier than I was before. Stew is my best friend, and I respect his opinion. But I don't want to hear that I'm complicating Becca's life. I just spent the last few weeks trying to make her life easier.

And why did you do that? my subconscious wants to know.

Fuck.

"I see that face," Stew says. "You hate it when I tell you the truth. But listen, man. This is really important. You can't pursue Rebecca now. Or *ever*. That's the definition of sexual harassment."

"I'm never going to *harass* her," I argue. *Fuck*. Even as I say it, I have a sinking feeling. Because pursuing your assistant for sex *is* the definition of harassment.

"Look." His face is dead serious. "You're the least sleazy guy in the Fortune 500. I know that. Rebecca knows that. But it doesn't matter. You don't get to behave any differently from the 2000 people who work for you."

"Actually it's 1999, because I just fired you. Such a shame really, since you're the number two man in the company. The board is gonna pitch a fit."

Stew just shakes his head slowly. "I'm sorry, Nate. If she didn't work for a company you own, it would be different."

Lauren picks that moment to return. She hands Stew a beer, and me a fresh Diet Coke. She's drinking orange juice and holding a bag, which turns out to contain three hot pretzels.

"Yum," Stew says. "Thanks!"

"You didn't have to bring me anything," I say, breaking off a corner of the pretzel.

She hands me a little cup of mustard. "Don't worry. You paid for it. I'm just trying to make you look a little less gloomy. Is it working?"

"Sure," I lie.

But after that chat with Stewart, I'm pretty sure I'll be gloomy as hell for a while now.

———

In better news, my team clinches the game a half hour later, with one more goal on a power play. And since the next two games will happen in Brooklyn, we'll have a chance to lean into the home ice advantage.

That night Stew and I fly back on the Gulfstream.

It's late and he doesn't try to talk to me about Rebecca anymore. So I'm grateful. When we reach cruising altitude, we change into sweats and recline our seats to flat, hoping to catch a couple hours of sleep. We're scheduled to land at three in the morning.

I dim the cabin lights and close my eyes. Now that I'm on my way back to New York, it's even harder to pack away my thoughts of Becca. Our night together plays like a film in my mind. That tiny scrap of silk and lace she's wearing when I wake her up. Our strange argument, and the kiss I give her so that she'll stop asking questions.

Her lips parting under mine, and my first taste of her. She straddles me and moans...

Goddamn it was good. No—*great*. For both of us. Her eagerness meant everything to me. But now Becca isn't exactly burning up the airwaves to tell me she can't wait to do it again.

Not a great sign.

You'd think I'd learn. After my ill-advised night with Alex, I should know better.

The two nights had nothing in common, though. Rebecca lit me on fire when she moved against me. The sounds she made I won't ever forget.

It wasn't just me, damn it. She loved every minute of it.

So where is she?

I toss and turn until my jet touches down at LaGuardia in the wee hours. I say goodnight to Stew and climb into the car with Ramesh. It's a rare traffic-free moment on the city's clock, and he gets me home to Pierrepont Place in no time.

"That might be a land-speed record," he says, pulling through to the mansion's locked garage.

"Thanks, man. Sorry for the shitty hour."

He yawns. "I'll live. Night, boss."

I feel his eyes on me as I activate the security system to let myself in the back door. He won't lock the car and go upstairs to his apartment over the garage until I'm safely inside.

This time when I walk into the kitchen, I only hear silence. I walk through to the parlor and listen.

Nothing. And the locks engage around me with a deep click.

I carry my suitcase upstairs and then wander through my own quiet house. "Welcome home, Nate," Bingley says. "You're the only one on the premises."

His pronouncement is a security feature. But it depresses me anyway. I don't return the greeting because Bingley can't get offended. "Engage all security systems," I say instead.

"Systems engaged."

I drop my bags in my room. And then even though I know what I'll find in there, I walk into the green bedroom. Sure enough, the bed is freshly made up, and all of Rebecca's things have been removed from the bathroom.

That's when I know with perfect certainty that I have absolutely fucked everything up. Rebecca is a trusted friend and an important employee. Now she's not taking my calls.

———

Monday I spend in Manhattan, suffering through meetings. My attention span is at an all-time low.

At home I find that Mrs. Gray has left me a homemade ham and cheese calzone for dinner. And a note.

Nathan—your mother called. She would like to hear from you regarding plans for their quick visit this week. P.S. There is a salad in the vegetable drawer for you. Please eat it because your mother wants to make sure you get enough fiber. —Mrs. G.

I haven't spoken to Mom in a week, so after I locate my salad and pop open another Diet Coke, I ask Bingley to call her.

"Nate?" Mom's voice comes through the sound system. "Last night's game was very exciting."

"I know, right?" My parents love hockey. But they'd have to, because they met and got married in Minnesota. "You're still coming to games three and four?"

"We would love to. Are you sure it's no trouble?"

"No trouble to *me*. I'm not piloting the Gulfstream." When they pop out for games, I send the jet to Iowa to get them.

"That is a relief, honey. Your father still gets a tense look on his face when he thinks about our old garage door."

I make a grumpy noise. I was only sixteen when I backed my father's Oldsmobile into our garage door, causing over a thousand dollars worth of damage. At the time it was a lot of money. But the real problem was the car itself. This happened shortly after the announcement that Oldsmobiles wouldn't be manufactured anymore. "It was my last Olds," he used to sigh.

When journalists write about me they say I had a "normal, well-adjusted Midwestern upbringing." I suppose they're right.

"Are you going to stay the week?" I ask, changing the subject.

"We can't, sweetheart. Your father's staff meeting on Thursday is non-negotiable."

"Ah." My father is the principal of a suburban middle school, and he takes his job very seriously. "You can fly home after the game if he doesn't want to take a personal day. I'll set it up that way."

"Thank you. I'll be a little sleepy on Wednesday, but it'll be worth it to watch your guys mow down Tampa at home."

I smile down at my salad because my mom is awesome. She's a school teacher, too—and the head of special education for the entire school district.

A few minutes later we hang up, though, and the silence around me closes in again. I'm left finishing my dinner with nothing but my own thoughts to keep me company. The only sounds come from outside. It's Monday night but Brooklyn is out in force—couples strolling the promenade, happy families dining out. I can't see them from my quiet kitchen, but I can hear the patter of Brooklyn enjoying the springtime.

After a long day in the office I'm in a fidgety mood. I could go for a run or drop into a yoga class. I could answer some of the fifty emails from my engineering team that are piling up in my inbox.

Right. Like I could concentrate on anything right now. My powers of concentration are on hiatus.

Instead, I put my plate in the dishwasher, taking care not to leave any crumbs on the counter, or Mrs. Gray will scold me.

Then I grab my keys and my phone and head out to look for Rebecca. I don't know what she wants from me. Maybe nothing. But I need to find out. Stew wouldn't approve. But we've known each other way too long for me to just let this go. Just one quick conversation is all I need before I give her up entirely.

———

Becca is not at home, although I have a brief but enlightening conversation with her sister in the doorway to their apartment.

Missy wears the coy expression of someone who knows exactly what happened between us. She babbles at me, grinning, while I try to keep my panic at bay.

Their little apartment is surprisingly clean and smells like lemons. And then there's that cute, drooly baby on Missy's hip. Rebecca's sister is a talker, and I kind of zone out for a second, watching the baby suck on his pacifier. I wonder what our baby would look like if Rebecca and I had one.

Then I want to slap myself. Also, *what the fuck, brain?*

"I'd better get going," I say to Missy before she can launch into another story about her sister. "Tell Rebecca I stopped by."

"I'll do that," she says with a saucy wink. "Thanks for breaking her dry spell."

There is no polite reply to that, so I just make myself scarce.

Running out of ideas, I head to my Brooklyn office. Since it's past eight, I'm surprised to see a light burning in the corporate offices. My sneakers are quiet on the shiny wooden floors, so I can't be heard as I approach. And then I find what I'm looking for. Rebecca is in my private office, standing at the bookcase, a feather duster in her hand. She's rearranging my collection of autographed, game-winning pucks and humming to herself.

I don't recognize the song, but I have to stop for a second just to admire her. Her face is calm but focused on her work. I know every one of her facial expressions: the face she makes when a caller has been rude to her. And the look of joy she gets when she laughs—chin up, eyes bright.

But now I also know how she looks when she's turned on and wants my hands on her body. And I may never be the same. Tonight she's wearing tight jeans that show off her delectable butt, and unfortunately now I know exactly how good it feels in my hands...

Rebecca whirls around, emitting a squeal of surprise. I've startled her. Badly. She drops the feather duster, and when she bends down to pick it up, I see her sway just slightly.

A split second later I'm there, a hand on her shoulder, steadying her. I can't help myself.

She stands slowly, eyes wide. We're too close together. I can smell her perfume, and it makes me want to lean in and kiss her neck.

"Hi," I say instead. She has that deer-in-the-headlights look. Wonderful.

"What are you doing here on a Monday night?" she asks, frowning.

"I was going to ask you the same thing, since you aren't cleared to come back to work yet."

She gives me a grumpy face. "I can't do screen work, but I can stress-clean. I'm not breaking any rules."

"Stress-clean? Just a wild guess here. But am I the cause of your stress?"

She gives me a guilty little shrug.

Fuck. This isn't how I wanted things to go between us. (*Said the idiot who slept with his friend and coworker.*) I take a deep breath. "I didn't mean to question your judgment. Can we talk for a second?"

"Do we have to?" she asks quietly.

"Yeah," I whisper. There's a long beat where we're just staring into each other's eyes. And immediately I realize two things. 1. I regret nothing. In fact, I'd like to take her home with me right now, lock my bedroom door, and spend a lot of time remembering all the sexy noises she makes when she comes. 2. She's not on the same page. Her expression is closed off. Unreadable.

Fuck.

"You're not answering my calls, Bec," I point out. "Talk to me."

She turns and sits down on the love seat in my office. Her body language is stiff, as if she's about to hear a sermon in church.

I sit down beside her, taking care to leave space between us.

"How did you find me?" she asks, picking at a fingernail.

"Since you're not taking my calls…" I nudge her with my knee with my own. "First I went to your apartment."

"My sister ratted me out?"

"Nope. But she was awfully chatty."

Rebecca groans.

"Yeah. No boundaries on Missy. But that's not what's bothering you. Can you tell me what's the matter? I can take it. Whatever it is." *Even if I don't like it.*

"I just can't believe…" She puts her hands on her knees and faces me. Her blue eyes are tentative. "I became *that* woman."

"What woman?"

"The one who sleeps with her boss."

Ouch. I try a joke. "Really? You slept with Hugh Major?"

"Nate! That's not funny!" Her eyes narrow dangerously. "Don't you *dare* pretend to be dense about this. Hugh *is* my boss, but only on paper. *You* hired me seven years ago. And *you* gave me this job with the team."

"Sure I did. Because you're a professional."

Her voice drops. "I wasn't on Tuesday night."

"God, don't feel *guilty*. Because you shouldn't. Not at all. Tuesday night was all my fault." And as I say those words, I hear how they sound—like it was a crime, not one of the best nights of my life.

She actually flinches. "I won't let you take all the blame. I was there, too."

She sure was—unbuttoning my fly. Running her smooth hands all over my chest…

Jesus. I'm going to get hard just thinking about it.

"…But it was a mistake," she continues. "It's not something I can be casual about. Even if I don't report to you directly on paper, we both know that you're the one in charge."

I let out a frustrated sound. "I'd like to be *in charge* again, Bec. And I'm not referring to the hockey team."

"God, Nate." She blows out a breath.

"Yeah, like that. But louder."

She puts her hands in front of her eyes before speaking again. "And here I thought we could just sort of agree to forget it."

"Because that's what you want?" *Knife to the heart.*

Becca peeks out between two of her fingers. "I *need* to forget it. We both know that you're one of the most hands-on owners in professional hockey. We work together all the time. I can't be the girl who just casually sleeps with the boss."

But it's just dawning on me that there's nothing casual about the way I want her. How on earth did it come to this? "Look," I argue. "I gotta call a foul on the idea that our spontaneous naked adventures were somehow job related. You didn't climb into my lap because you wanted a raise."

Her cheeks stain a deeper red, and she looks away. "Be that as it may, I want my job to stay the same. I can't be known as the owner's plaything."

My noise of disgust isn't subtle. "Do you really think that's how I see you?"

"No. Yes? I don't know." She hunches forward, her gaze on the floor. "I just want to rewind my life a few weeks when everything was going fine. *You* told me that I was supposed to focus on my recovery. And now you're making it really hard to do that."

Fuck. I did. And I am. I want to keep arguing until she sees things my way. I'm very persuasive. But Rebecca doesn't want me to persuade her. And Stew told me quite plainly why I'm not allowed to try.

And she's right about one thing—the timing is terrible.

"Okay," I agree suddenly. Because I know when I've been beaten.

Rebecca blinks. "Okay…?"

"We'll forget it ever happened. We'll never speak of it again."

"All right." She opens her mouth and then closes it again.

"Isn't that what you asked me for?" She looks uncertain.

"Yes," she says with a nod. She takes a deep breath. "I love this job. And I love our friendship. And I don't want to sacrifice any of it."

"You won't," I say quickly. "Nobody is taking your job, Bec. Never gonna happen."

"Good to know." She clears her throat. "Except now I wonder whether those performance evaluations you wrote me were ever unbiased." When she looks at me, I can tell she's thinking about what I said right before I kissed her. Even if I never admitted it to myself before, I've got it bad. I don't have the first clue what to do about it, either.

This is why I kept my stupid libido in check for years. This was the precise conversation I've been avoiding. "Look. I don't ever want to make you uncomfortable. Tell me how to fix it."

She rubs her forehead, and I know I'm responsible for her latest headache. Once again, I've done exactly the opposite of the smart thing. This girl makes me stupid.

"We'll move on. I'll be back at work in a couple of weeks and things can just go back to the way they were before."

"Right," I agree, because there's nothing else I can say without being an asshole. Except I know it's not technically possible. I can't ever forget that night. I can't unsee her body arching toward mine, and I can't untaste her mouth under mine.

"Thank you," she says. There's a long pause while we both stare at each other. I've just done exactly what she asked me for. But she doesn't look relieved. She's looking at me like she's trying to figure something out, but can't quite manage it.

But then I see the exact moment she gives up. Her pretty eyes drop. She looks around the room, spots her jacket on the arm of my love seat. She stands, snaps it up with one hand, and then walks out.

My gut clenches at the sight of her leaving. So that's it? One perfect night, and a three-minute conversation. That's all I'll ever have.

"Bec," I say, stopping her progress.

"Yeah?" And when she turns to meet my gaze, I realize I'm not the only one struggling. She looks conflicted as she struggles into the jacket.

I lean on the doorframe. I'm keeping a safe distance because I don't trust myself. "My door will always be open to you."

"Thank you," she says quietly.

"Anything you need. Ask Bingley if you don't want to call me. Be well, and take care of yourself."

"You too," she says. Then she gives me a watery little smile, turns around, and leaves.

Thirty seconds later I hear the door to the lobby open and shut. She's gone.

[15]

REBECCA

"THAT'S IT, girl! Now ease up on the death grip before I lose all feeling in this arm."

I force myself to ease my grip on Ramón's wrist, but I leave my eyes screwed shut. I'm bouncing on that damned trampoline again. Little bounces. And my hold on Ramón is the only thing keeping me vertical.

Still, it's progress. I couldn't do this two weeks ago.

"Ten more," he encourages. Then he counts down. "Ten, nine. Breathe, Becca. Eight…"

When he gets to "one" I open my eyes and stop. "Wow. Okay." The room takes a second or two to reorient itself. But I'm getting used to these little reboots of my system. They're not as confusing as they used to be, and therefore not as scary. I take another breath and wait to feel steady.

"Nicely done," Ramón says. "How'd that feel?"

"I'm not puking on your Nikes. So there's your first clue." I haven't actually puked in therapy, but there were a couple of close calls.

"Rebecca!" Dr. Armitage himself strides toward me across the training center in his lab coat. "How are we doing?"

"The trampoline is now possible," Ramón says. "Her recovery time still has some room to improve, but, heck. Give her a week. She's shaping up fast."

And it's true. I'm *finally* doing better. Every day I feel a little more steady. And the number of tipsy episodes I experience keeps diminishing. Even better—I don't feel as feeble or hopeless as I did the first time I walked in here. "You guys are miracle workers."

"You're doing all your own healing," the doctor says. "We just showed you where to look for it."

"What's next?" I ask Ramón.

He checks his watch. "The dreaded spinning chair. And then we'll have time for one Ping-Pong game."

"You have to let me win."

"Pffft!" the trainer says, while the doctor grins. "That's not included in the price. Come on now. Let's get it over with in the chair."

"Stop by my office when you're done," Dr. Armitage says.

"Absolutely."

———

Ten minutes later I take a seat in front of the doctor. I'm still sweaty from my workout, including another Ping-Pong loss to Ramón.

Dr. Armitage puts on his reading glasses and scan's Ramón's notes. "You're making great progress. This is terrific."

"It's really encouraging," I agree. "I feel better. I think I could go back to work, don't you?" *Please, please say yes.*

He frowns. "Soon. This early progress is terrific, but vestibular therapy never goes in a straight line. Most patients experience plateaus before they can make further progress. And we're asking a lot of your body right now. You need to give the physical work a little more time before you're ready to tax your eyesight in an office environment."

Shit.

"Okay…" I clear my throat. "How much time, though? I need

to work. I've used up every sick day I ever had, and then some. It would be great if I could tell my boss when to expect me."

The doctor frowns. Apparently he isn't expecting me to worry about this. After all, Nate casually dropped fifty grand to get my first appointment.

And just like that my face heats. Just the thought of Nate does that to me now. I also recall that first morning when the doctor assumed I was Nate's significant other.

How trippy that Nate and I went and did exactly what he assumed we'd been doing.

Gah. My face is on fire now. But I can always blame the workout.

"Let's talk again in a week," the doctor says gently. "Get a lot of sleep, and stay active. Then maybe we can discuss a part-time return to work. Would your employer consider an arrangement like that?"

"Sure." It's better than nothing, and I'll feel less like I've been exiled and forgotten. "Honestly, it would be good for me to go back part-time. It's really stressful not to show my face in the office."

His expression softens. "I'm sure I'd feel the same way. Give it at least one more week at home, okay? I'm happy to write a letter to whomever you need, if your continued absence requires a letter in your file."

Hugh Major doesn't care about the letter. I know this in my heart. But it doesn't make me any less eager to get back there. "Thanks, I'll let you know if that's necessary."

When I leave the building, I find a misty spring day waiting for me. It smells like rain, and I don't want to go down in the subway tunnel right now. So I walk uptown. It's not a particularly interesting stretch of lower Manhattan, but I dawdle up Broadway, peering into shop windows. I stop to admire all the Chinese imports at Pearl River. There is a set of green chopsticks with pandas on them, and I remember the pair of nice chopsticks Nate used to keep in his desk drawer, because he didn't like the disposable wooden ones that always arrived with our take-out food.

Hello, subconscious. I think of Nate often, and every time it gives me a pang. Since our awkward talk in his office, he's always there, blowing up my subconscious in a way he never did before. I can hear his laugh inside my head and picture his knowing smirk.

I stood there and told him I wanted to forget that night. And I suppose I do. It's just that forgetting is a lost cause. When I get into bed at night I can practically feel his hands on my thighs, nudging them apart. When I close my eyes, my imagination is shameless.

My latest fantasy is so potent, and absolutely out of character for me: I'm lying on my stomach in bed. Nate comes into the room uninvited. He lifts the covers and gets into bed with me. *You shouldn't be here*, I say. He doesn't answer me. Instead he removes my panties. *This is a bad idea*, I say. In answer, he takes my legs in hand and spreads them. I lift my hips off the bed, because I can't help myself. And I'm rewarded as he pushes inside me, then fucks me without a word.

My inner feminist is absolutely appalled.

And, wowzers. The spring weather is really warm all of a sudden.

I can't shut off my brain. And yet I shut Nate right down during our awkward little chat in his office. I realize now that I never got a chance to hear what Nate thought of our Florida encounter. I didn't let him tell me. And now I'm practically eaten up with curiosity.

There's a part of me that wonders what would have happened if I didn't play the fear card. If I'd confessed to being staggered by our chemistry together, what exactly would have happened? The most likely outcome would have been another hot night together. Maybe two.

But that's it, right? Nate and I couldn't ever be a serious couple. When Nate thinks about his future, I know it's not me he sees. I'm nothing like his ex Juliet, who was one of the super-accomplished graduates of his Ivy League school. I'm not a captain of industry like his friend Alex. I'm not even much like Lauren, who's on the brink of earning a degree in business so she can climb the ladder at KTech.

I'm the office manager—great at my job, but not trophy wife material. I'm the quirky fun girl at the office who knows what time the cars are coming and can always find you a dinner reservation.

I'm never the one the reservation is for.

When my little squirrel brain isn't busy imagining weirdly submissive sex with Nate, it's making this very circuit: *What might have happened between us? Oh, right. Not much.*

Rinse and repeat.

Even if I'm making myself feel crazy, I still know that shutting things down was the right move. Any dalliance with Nate is just playing with fire. It would be way too easy to fall for him. Not only is he the smartest man I will ever meet, but he has a great smile, a fun sense of humor, and—I happened to notice—a great body. The whole package.

I feel a little quivery just thinking about an alternate universe where I'm allowed to kiss him whenever the urge strikes.

But here in *this* reality, I have a job to hold onto. Getting involved with Nate means jeopardizing the esteem of everyone in the Bruisers organization. It's not an exaggeration to say that the team is my second home.

I head for the F train to Brooklyn. My boys are playing tonight. Game three. I haven't seen a game in weeks, since right after my accident. I wish I could go to the rink tonight. But I can't exactly tell Nate I need space and then show up in his private box at the arena. And it's not like I've got a spare $400 sitting around for a ticket.

Maybe I should have thought of this before I unbuttoned his shirt and stripped him naked.

Live and learn.

———

A few hours later I'm lying on The Beast—our hideous sofa—while Missy paces the floor with a cranky Matthew. He's teething.

We don't have TV, and our internet connection is spotty tonight, so the live stream keeps glitching out. Of course it does. So Missy is monitoring a Twitter feed on my phone for scoring updates, because I've demanded it. The stadium is two miles from my apartment. And tonight those two miles feel long.

"What are people saying now?" I ask for the tenth time.

"Nothing."

"It's Twitter. There must be something."

"Someone tweeted that the line for the women's bathroom is too long."

"Waaaaaaah!" Matthew wails on her shoulder, and my head gives a sympathetic throb.

"Give me the phone," I say. Then I get up and snatch it from her. I run into my room and shut the door. I tap Georgia's name off my contacts list and wait while it rings in my ear.

"Hello!" she yells. "Becca?"

"What's the score?" I demand.

"I'm so tense!" she yells over the background noise. I don't know if she even heard the question.

"Gigi—which radio station is covering the game? I need to hear the play-by-play."

"Hockey on the radio? Is that a thing?"

"Isn't it? Old men listen to baseball. *You're* the publicist! Don't you know?"

"Rebecca, are you okay? Why aren't you here watching, anyway?"

Hmm. Keeping a secret from my best friend hasn't been fun. But this isn't a great time to get into it. She might be standing beside Nate right now. "I'm all right. It's complicated. Just tell me what's happening on the ice."

"The first line is on shift. Leo, Bayer, Castro."

"Wow! Young lineup tonight. Who's on D?"

"Douley and... O'Doul passes to Leo! And it's...OMIGOD. OH! COME ON! Yes! Not quite. Fuck! Arrrgh!"

"What happened? We didn't score? Please tell me the other guy didn't score."

I hear clunk, and then the call is cut off.

"Georgia?" I say into the silence.

Nothing.

This is torture. I need answers.

I tap on the Bingley app. It opens, and a familiar voice says, "Hello, my dear Rebecca. How may I be of assistance?"

"Hi!" I feel like I'm reconnecting with a long-lost friend,

although that's patently ridiculous. "I need to know what's happening with the hockey game."

"The hockey game is currently in session."

"The score, Bingley. What's the score?"

"Tie game at 0-0."

"Okay. What else? Who has the puck?"

"The puck is a six ounce black rubber disc."

"I know that, Bingley. But which player is controlling the puck right now?"

"One moment, miss," Bingley says primly. "I'm seeking assistance."

Well, crap. I've obviously overestimated Bingley's ability to process the hockey game. Some poor programmer at KTech's phone is probably ringing right now with this programming bug.

But Bingley comes back about ninety seconds later. "Nate reminds you that you need your rest to heal. But he adds that you should come to the stadium if you want to see who's playing."

"Wait, what? You asked Nate?"

"Naturally. He's my admin. Standby for another communication. Ah. Nate has asked me to send you a car. ETA three minutes. Black Mercedes C class. The driver's name is Parker."

I let out a little groan of discomfort.

"Dear Rebecca, are you quite all right?"

"I'm fine," I snap. But I'm annoyed. I hadn't planned to ask Nate for anything. Ever. And I don't know if I should go to the stadium when I'm so freaking confused.

"Oh dear," Bingley says. "The score is now 1-0 in favor of Tampa."

"Oh no!"

"Oh yes. Also, your car is two minutes away."

That's it. I can't sit here any longer while my team battles Tampa. I get up off the bed, throw the phone down, and start changing my clothes. Even a confused, mortified girl needs to look her best. I grab my coat and bag, wave to poor Missy, and then run down my stairs. The car is already waiting. So I slide inside and close the door.

Six minutes later we're inching along in traffic toward the brightly lit stadium two blocks away. So close, yet so far.

"I'll jump out here!" I tell the startled driver.

"It's just ahead, miss."

"I know! Gotta run," I say as our progress halts again. "Too-dles!" I jump out of the car and set off down the sidewalk at a fast pace.

I'm wearing Chuck Ts, which are better for my balance issues than girly shoes. This is the first time in my life I have ever had to think about practical footwear, and it's sort of a drag. On the other hand, once I reach the stadium, my jog isn't finished. I flash my corporate ID at checkpoint after checkpoint and then trot along the final corridor toward Nate's box, where Nate and whichever top brass at KTech he's invited tonight are watching. It's where I watch, too, when I'm on duty in an official capacity.

I can hear the crowd and the suspense is killing me.

Panting, I smack my ID against the scanner, which opens the door to the box. As the little light turns green, the crowd makes a noise of joy. I yank the door open. "What's the score?" I demand of Georgia, the first person I see.

"One-one. We scored to tie it up. End of the second period now. Tampa just rushed the net, but Beacon made a glove save."

I exhale. We can still do this. Twenty more minutes to put one or two more in the net.

At the sound of my voice, Nate turns slowly in his seat. I feel a jolt when our eyes meet, and I'm probably not very good at hiding it. But Nate only gives me a curious eyebrow lift.

My belly tightens in a way that is absolutely not from desire. Nope. Not going there.

"Don't you start," I say to Nate and to myself, too. "It's not that late and I can't sleep if the game's on." I'm babbling, and it's hard to stop, because I'm completely unprepared for my own reaction to Nate. I have the weirdest urge to vault over the half dozen people between us and kiss that little frown off his face.

What's happened to me?

Nate isn't struggling, though. His face impassive, he turns around again, his focus back on the ice.

Okay, ouch.

I swivel to find my best friend staring at me, an appraising look on her sweet face. So naturally I grab the wine glass out of her hand and sip from it.

"I thought you weren't supposed to…"

"Shh!" I silence her. "It's one sip. Don't alert my jailer." *Boss. Lover. Whatever.* I am the most confused person in Brooklyn.

And now the most sexually frustrated.

Georgia fetches me a soda and then fixes me with another stare. "How's it going, anyway? I haven't heard much from you since the party in Bal Harbour. Are you still staying at Nate's?"

"Nope." I take a deep drink of the soda, avoiding her eyes. "Back in my own apartment."

"Okay…" Georgia waits for more information, but good luck with that. We cannot discuss my twisted sex life in this of all rooms, with Nate's parents sitting a dozen feet away.

Not to mention Nate.

I am spared further grilling because Tampa chooses that moment to strip the puck away from Trevi and turn it toward Brooklyn's defensive zone.

"Baby, no!" Georgia yells.

Everyone in the box leans forward as Tampa rushes the net.

They fire on Beacon, who deflects the shot off his stick. But the rebound is tight, and he has to dive for a second one.

We all hold our collective breath while Brooklyn tries to clear it. Tampa takes aim again and two players charge the net. When the winger shoots, Beacon slaps another puck away.

But then the other opponent plows right into our goalie.

"Oh, Jesus," Nate says, in a show of emotion that's rare for him. "Don't you dare start a…"

He doesn't even get the words out before Beacon throws off his gloves and lunges for the other dude. Lauren yelps and everyone in the box stands up, anxious about the outcome.

If our goalie got injured in a fight, that would be a disaster.

It's a scrum down there. Their guy has Beacon's jersey in one hand and is punching him with the other. Beacon retaliates, and one punch launches his opponent's face mask across the ice. They are a blur of flying fists, until the other guy goes down, pulling Beacon down, too.

I feel a sick little twinge, because it's all too easy to picture Beacon's head hitting the ice, and the months of recovery time that will ensue. From now on I won't be able to see a player go down without anticipating disaster.

The ref and the linesman rush in to separate them. But Beacon is okay. He gets up quickly. There's blood on his face, but fire in his eyes. And when the trainer runs out on the ice to evaluate him, Beacon waves him off.

We all heave a collective sigh of relief. There are less than four minutes left in the period, and play resumes a moment later. The next three minutes feel very long, while we all watch Beacon for signs of trouble.

There aren't any, though. Instead, play moves to the other side of the rink and with only thirty seconds on the clock, Leo Trevi gets his stick on the loose puck and somehow slips it behind the goalie.

Georgia lets out a shriek of joy as the lamp lights up behind Tampa's keeper.

The score is 2-1 in our favor, and a wave of optimism rolls through the box as the period comes to its end.

"Whew," I say, sipping my soda. I turn my back on Nate and his parents so I won't be tempted to stare at him.

"So what's your deal?" Georgia asks me.

"What do you mean?"

"Why were you late to the game?" Georgia grabs my wrist. "Come with me to the ladies' room. I have a few questions for you."

That sounds ominous. And then it gets worse. While Georgia fetches her handbag, Mrs. Kattenberger runs over to give me a hug. "Rebecca! It's good to see you on your feet!"

Nate's mom is so nice, and I feel an immediate flare of Catholic schoolgirl guilt just standing in front of her. "Oh, don't worry about me. I'll be fine."

It shouldn't surprise me that Nate told his mother about my head injury. Nate and his mom are close. But still, I'm fascinated.

He probably doesn't tell his mom every detail of his two thousand employees' lives.

It's something to think about later.

"I've had better months," I add with a nervous smile. "But I'm doing better every day."

"You poor thing! What have you been doing to keep yourself busy?"

Your son. The words just pop right into my head. And I can't help wondering what she'd say if she knew. "This and that," I say carefully. And then I look up to see that Nate has appeared over his mother's shoulder.

But his eyes reveal nothing. If he heard my comment, or saw my face flush, there's no sign of it. And that's good, right? I asked Nate to tamp it down. And he has.

All the way down.

"This game is so stressful!" I say, and my voice is shrill.

Mrs. Kattenberger reaches out and squeezes my hand. "It is!" she agrees.

Nate ducks his chin and turns away, greeting a young woman I've never seen before. There is a constant stream of business people in Nate's box during games. An invitation to the owner's box is a coveted thing, and I'm sure they're doled out to whomever KTech most needs to impress at the time.

Still. I hate the smile he gives this woman in a suit. She's wearing heels, not Converse sneakers. I feel about a foot shorter than she is. And when she leans in to touch his arm and then laugh at a joke, I have the irrational urge to punch her in the throat.

"Uh, Bec?" Georgia has appeared at my elbow. She frowns at me, then steers me out into the corridor. I take a deep breath and let it out as I follow her down the hall toward the posh ladies' room serving the luxury boxes on the mezzanine level.

No kidding—rich people get their own special place to pee. Because that's how the world works.

"Okay, spill, dammit," Georgia says as she pushes open the door.

The bathroom attendant greets us with a smile. "Good evening, ladies! How's the game?"

"Stressful," I say.

"Awesome!" Georgia argues.

"Maybe for you! You're the one whose honey just scored. So you'll be scoring later, too."

"About that," Georgia says as we take adjacent stalls and latch our respective doors. "I'm waiting for you to fill me in." Her voice floats above the walnut paneled divider.

"About what? And shouldn't you be downstairs prepping for a press conference right now?"

"Don't you dodge me, missy. Danny is setting up the conference tonight, anyway. He's in training." She flushes. "So spill already. I've got all night."

Damn her. I consider hiding here in the stall for the rest of the evening. But that's too chickenshit, even for me. When I emerge to wash my hands, she's waiting. "Don't you have anything to say for yourself?"

"Such as?"

"Such as—why did you turn bright purple a minute ago during the world's shortest conversation with a certain person's mom?"

"Well…" I let out a nervous laugh. "Not purple. Red, maybe." The bathroom attendant hands me a soft linen towel as I shut off the water.

"Oh. My. God. You didn't!" Her eyes are bright and shiny. "Wow. It was Bal Harbour, right? You canceled breakfast for sex with…"

I reach up and put a palm over her mouth. "Please. A little discretion regarding my poor life choices."

The bathroom attendant has been hanging on every word, and now she looks disappointed.

Georgia blinks. I remove my hand. "Oh my *God*," she says again, her voice full of awe. "Wow. Florida has some powerful mojo. Who knew?"

Not me, that's for sure.

"Okay." She takes a deep breath and blows it out. "I just have one question. Was it good?"

Ugh. Why does everyone keep asking me that? "Does it even

matter? It doesn't make my life less complicated, so it's really beside the point."

"It is *not at all* beside the point!" Georgia says, wringing her hands. "Either you're into him or you're not. So which way is it?"

"It's not that simple. We can't just have an office fling, Georgia. There would be consequences—more for me than for him."

"Well…" She leans a hip against the marble countertop and frowns. "That's the whole problem, right? There's an imbalance of power between you."

"Yes! Thank you!"

"N—" She catches herself. "Your guy has more power than anyone else I know. But it's also his prison. I'll bet he can't trust that anyone he meets will ever love him for his own sake. And since his company is his life, anyone he meets there is already in debt to him."

I hadn't thought about it that way. Then again, everything else in his life goes pretty much as he pleases. "Let's not get out the violins just yet. Nobody can have everything come easily. What would be the fun of that, anyway?"

Georgia shrugs. "I know. Did he, uh, say he'd like to see you again sometime. Out of the office, I mean?"

"Or bent over his desk," I whisper. That's another one of my fantasies. Not that I'm ever telling him.

The bathroom attendant's eyes get huge.

"Oh, wow." My best friend fans herself with the linen towel. "Remind me to always knock on doors at work." She smiles widely.

I mentally slap myself. "Actually, you don't have to bother. Because I told him we need to just forget the whole thing."

"Oh." Georgia looks crestfallen. "But why? Because my mind just went straight to candlelit dinners and weekends in Bermuda. Picture the dinner parties you could throw in that mansion!"

I *can't* picture it, though. "That is a fairy tale. Reality is far more awkward. What if we dated and it didn't work out? I don't want to live with the fallout. And besides, I wouldn't even know how to be his…"

"Girlfriend," Georgia puts in.

Even that word sounds impossible. "My psyche might not be

able to wrap itself around the concept. I used to get his coffee, Georgia. I still do."

"Girl!" The bathroom attendant yelps. "I'll get his coffee till the day I die if it means I get banged by a hot, rich guy in Bermuda. Whoever he is, you gotta give it a whirl. If you don't, I'll do it for you."

"She makes a really good point," Georgia insists.

They high-five each other and I kind of want to punch them both.

[16]

NATE

WHEN I WAS EIGHT, I learned my first lines of computer code. One of the first lessons was how to avoid an infinite loop, where the program gets stuck, and the computer just hangs there, frozen, while you try to decide if it's time to pull the plug and reboot.

That's me right now. It's Sunday morning, and I'm lounging on the sofa in my study at home, thinking about Rebecca. I've been stuck in an infinite loop since that awkward conversation in my office.

I can't stop wondering if I made things worse. And yet I can't figure out how I could have made them better. If I'd said more—told her I *felt* more—that would just put more pressure on her.

I don't want to be that asshole who's chasing her at work. Women have put up with that for years. And I pride myself on running a great company, with an excellent track record for employees of all stripes.

When I was thirteen, my mother had an awful year. She'd just gotten a promotion in the school district's main offices. And there was this asshole who would chase her around the desk at work. My father about had a coronary. He begged her to quit, but she wouldn't do it.

160

Because the guy was a giant sleaze, he eventually got busted for solicitation, solving the problem by getting himself fired. But meanwhile, my parents were so tense. When my mom had tried to complain, the higher-ups didn't do anything.

I will never be that guy.

It's taken me a good week to realize that both Stew and Becca were right. The work thing makes this awkward. I can't pursue her the way I'd pursue someone who didn't work for my organization. I can't send her flowers, invite her to dinner, or steal a kiss. I can't do what I do best, which is to go hard after the thing I most want until I win.

Emphasis on hard.

If I didn't think we could have something great, it would be easy to accept. But my gut says that she and I are amazing together. I trust my gut. It's rarely wrong.

But none of that matters if she doesn't want to entertain the idea. I have to just zip my lip (and my pants). I can't remind her how good it was, or mention how badly I want to make her moan on every surface of this oversized house.

I must have let out a little moan myself, because Bingley jumps into the fray. "Master Nate! Is everything all right?"

"I guess."

"Could you repeat that, good sir? I won't alert the security team if there is no cause for concern."

"I'm *fine*, Bingley."

"Glad to hear it, sir. Can I help you with anything further?"

I should load up a different voice module, so that he'll stop calling me *sir*. It's too much like my day job.

On the other hand, I changed him to a Victorian Brit to amuse Becca. And I miss Becca.

"Bingley," I say. "How do you get over someone?"

"Get over a person?" he asks. "As in, pass over them in physical space or remove oneself from a romantic entanglement."

"The latter, Bingley. I can't even picture the former."

"Just a moment, sir. I'll perform an internet search."

This should be entertaining.

"Nate, we are all fools in love. There are six hundred and

twenty-two million search results for this question," he says. "The most common suggestions are as follows. Number one, don't bottle up your emotions. Cry as necessary. Two, acknowledge your anger, if you are angry. Three, take care of yourself in other ways. Don't forget to eat well and exercise. Four, listen to music, especially uptempo songs. Five…"

"Thank you, Bingley," I sigh.

"…Keep a journal," he finishes.

"A journal."

"Yes. A record of your thoughts and feelings, validating and exercising those emotions on the page."

Now there's a document my HR department doesn't want in the world. *Dear Diary, it wasn't until I snuck into Rebecca's hotel room and screwed her seven ways till Sunday that I realized I was in love with her.*

Not helpful.

As my mother says, the only way out is through. And I should be more focused on my hockey team. We're headed to Detroit tomorrow to face off against a new rival. Meanwhile, across the country, my least favorite team is doing the same.

"Bingley. Are there any new injury reports for the Dallas team or for Anaheim?"

"One moment, sir… Yes. Simms will not be appearing in game one for Anaheim."

"Fuck."

"Sir?"

"It's an expression of displeasure. Ignore all fucks."

"Yes, sir."

Besides, I can't decide if that's good news or bad. I hate Dallas with all my heart and soul. So I don't want them to get an easy win. On the other hand, if they won the Western Conference my boys could mow them down in the finals.

Now that was an appealing little daydream. Yet not a statistically likely outcome.

My phone vibrates in my pocket.

"Stewart is calling, sir," Bingley announces.

I grab the phone, because Stewie doesn't usually bother me on the weekend. Unlike me, he has a life. "Yeah," I say, answering it. "What's up, man?"

"I'm on a golf course on Kiawah," he says with a chuckle. "What's up with you?"

"Are you calling to see if I'm out giving the HR department something to fret over? Well, I'm not." And aren't we a study in contrasts. "I'm just lying here on the sofa, conversing with my digital assistant. As one does."

My old friend snorts into his phone. "Look, I'm not checking up on you. And before the players behind us get pissed off, I just had a text that we're getting an offer for the router division tomorrow."

"Really?" I sit up. "From who?" It can't be Alex, because she would call me herself.

"Actually, from iBits Canada. The chipmaker. And they want to do a licensing deal, too."

"Well, that's complicated."

"A little bit. Anyway—we'll get all the deets tomorrow, okay? Just thought you'd want to know so you can plan your week."

"Thanks, man. Hit 'em long and straight."

"As if. I've already lost a lifetime's worth of balls on this course."

"Hold on to your balls, man." I could never resist the obvious joke.

"Later, nerd."

"Later."

We hang up, and I immediately feel better. Now my big brain has something to do. Except there's just one problem. I was planning to go to Detroit tomorrow to watch hockey. And now I'm thinking that's not going to happen.

"Bingley—call Hugh Major for me."

"It would be my pleasure, sir."

My phone lights up in my hand, and I hear Hugh's phone ring a moment later. "Hey, Nate," the Bruisers' General Manager says. "What's happening?"

"I'm going to pull Lauren out of the Bruisers' office for the week. Sorry for the short notice, but I need her in Manhattan."

"She'll be thrilled." He chuckles.

"I know, right? We probably won't make it to Detroit this week. Can you get someone else to travel with you?" Hugh always has an assistant on the road.

"Sure. The timing works fine, anyway. Rebecca told me forty-eight hours ago that she was just cleared to come back to work part-time."

"She was?" That's the best news I've heard in a week. "Are you sure?"

He chuckles again. "Of course I'm sure. I have the doctor's note asking for a reduced schedule."

"There's no such thing as a reduced schedule during the playoffs," I point out. But I really need to shut up. It's none of my business.

"Got it covered, okay? I'm assigning an intern to assist Rebecca full-time. We're bringing both of them with us to Detroit. The intern can cover the hours when Rebecca is resting. Don't worry about any of us or the team. We look good going into this series. The guys are ready."

Of course they were. "Go get 'em. See you in a few days, maybe."

"Later."

Well, okay then. Time to do some business and forget about Rebecca.

As if.

REBECCA

MAY 21, BROOKLYN

IT'S ALMOST time to leave for the stadium, and my boys are playing a little elimination soccer to pass the time. They're all wearing suits and ties. That makes the soccer less exhilarating, though the eye candy quotient is pretty high.

It's great to be back at work.

Silas has the ball. "You're going down, captain."

O'Doul crosses his powerful arms over his chest and smirks at the young goalie. "You little smack talker. Kick it already."

He does.

We're standing in the warm-up room at the training facility. The puck drops in two and a half hours on game three of the third round. There's a lot riding on tonight's game.

O'Doul has to leap sideways to prevent the ball from hitting the floor, but he keeps the game alive with a knee shot to Trevi.

I have a sewing kit in my bag, as always. One of these days someone is going to split a seam.

My gaze flits to the clock on the wall, and then to the phone in my intern's hand. It hasn't lit up yet to indicate that the bus is outside.

Heidi Jo catches me looking and pulls the phone to her chest. "Now now. No peekin'," she says.

I want to slug her.

My most grievous error on the day I returned to work was mentioning that I needed to limit my screen time. Who knew that such a cute little twenty-year-old could be such a dictator?

"Oh, mercy!" she says suddenly. The phone is vibrating in her hand. "It's time!"

Indeed, the outside edge of my phone is lit up orange.

"Okay, boys!" I holler, smacking my clipboard for emphasis. "Bus is waiting!"

"You hear that, O'Doul?" Castro says. "Becca needs you to miss this next point so we can go to the stadium."

He snarls, and Castro uses that moment to spike the ball toward him. There's nothing like a little friendly competition to fire up the boys before a game. It's a warm-up activity that's equal parts hand-eye coordination and bravado.

I wait, trying to be patient. But we're on a schedule here.

"They're so dreamy," sighs the young woman beside me as the ball travels among the muscled men. "My mama would smack me for saying so, but I really want to climb Silas like a tree. Or maybe Castro."

I tune out my intern. On a scale of one to ten—where one is no big deal and ten is me almost putting her in a choke hold—she's an eleven. And a half.

When Hugh told me I was getting an intern, I thought that sounded like a hoot. I am, after all, the assistant. I don't usually *have* an assistant. Not since I came to Brooklyn, anyway. I thought it sounded fun.

How wrong I was. Having Heidi Jo around is exactly like spending the week with an overeager puppy. She never shuts up, and she wants to hump everyone's leg. She's also cute like a puppy. Big eyes. Silky blond hair curling around her face.

If only I could swing by Brooklyn Animal Control and kick her to the curb. *Free to a good home.*

It's possible that exhaustion is contributing to my lack of patience. On Monday morning I boarded the team jet at seven a.m.

We spent four days in Detroit for two games, and now we're Back in Brooklyn for two more.

Now it's Saturday night, my sixth day back at work. I'm running on black coffee and adrenaline. But there's nothing like game night. The players are all pumped up. They won the first two games of the series, and now they're back here with a home ice advantage.

The soccer ball hasn't hit the floor yet, either. As I watch, Silas uses a knee to pop the ball across the circle to Trevi, who heads it to Castro. Who kicks it to O'Doul.

Who misses.

"Goddamn it," the captain chuckles.

"Getting old sucks, man," Silas says, risking his life.

"*Guys*," I warn. "Move it outside now before I have to open up a fresh can of whoop-ass."

"We don't want that," O'Doul says. "Let's go, men. We all know Silas would win again, anyway. He always does."

O'Doul tosses the ball to Castro and then they're on the move. They form a line as we exit the room, heading for the back exit, away from the street.

I scurry to make it to the front of the line, with Heidi Jo on my heels.

"Ready, miss?" asks a man in a dark suit near the door. He's one of the security team members, but I don't know his name.

I peek outside, where the bus is waiting. "Let's go," I agree.

He holds the door, and I step outside. There are tourists on the other side of the iron fence, snapping pictures. I count as two dozen players hustle past me onto the bus, then I watch the door of the bus swing closed, feeling satisfied.

Another successful night of herding the cats. As long as that bus pulls up at the stadium in ten minutes with all my boys on board, I've done the most important part of my job.

"Okay, miss," the security guy says. "Here's your car."

A stretch Mercedes pulls up in the spot where the bus just was.

"Oh! Fancy," Heidi Jo coos. "Haven't ridden in one of these since prom night! I had the cutest dress…"

She's still talking. Whatever.

We don't usually ride to the stadium in a stretch limo, but sometimes the car company just sends whomever is free. I don't bother to explain because I'm too tired. The puppy yaps while the driver hops out, walks around to our side, and opens the door with gloved hands.

"Hop in," I sigh, wondering if it's possible to catch a catnap on a two mile drive. But Heidi Jo will probably gab the whole way.

She prances toward the door and disappears into the dark interior.

My eyes feel gritty as I scan the back lot for any of my colleagues who might need to join us. But no one else appears. With a weary sigh, I follow my intern into the car, flopping down onto the leather seat just inside.

As the driver closes the door with the cool little click that only German engineering can produce, I notice that I've seated myself practically on top of the one and only Nate Kattenberger.

And here I'd assumed this car would be empty. *Whoops*.

"Um, hi," I squeak as the scent of his spicy aftershave hits me hard.

"Rebecca," he says, his voice as cool and calm as an iceberg. "Good evening."

Gulp. Nate hasn't spoken to me in a voice so detached in…well, ever. So that's weird. "Didn't expect to see you here," I say. As if that's not obvious.

"I swung by to chat with Hugh."

"Oh," I say stupidly.

Heidi Jo is staring across at us with one perfectly manicured little hand covering her mouth. Maybe she's never met a billionaire before.

I wiggle my hips and shift on the leather to give Nate a little more room on what I'd assumed was an empty bench. "Sorry," I say, feeling flustered. I wonder if I've chewed off all my lipstick. I hope I don't have sweat circles under my arms.

How in the world did I become so self-conscious in front of Nate?

"Mr. Kattenberger, I'm Heidi Jo," she says in a hushed voice. "And I'm such a big fan of yours."

Nate looks up from his phone. "Thank you," he says mildly. I hear a note of amusement.

"Heidi Jo is an intern in the front office," I manage to supply.

"...And I am taking really good care of Miss Rowley!" she gushes.

"It's a pleasure meeting you, and I'm glad to hear that."

Although I notice he doesn't spare me a glance.

Nate tucks his phone away. "Miss Rowley, do you have tonight's invite list handy?"

Miss Rowley? What fresh hell is this? I've been last-named? By Nate? Surprise strikes me dumb, and I just blink at him for a long moment. His pale eyes are unreadable behind his reading glasses.

Flustered now, I tear my gaze off his and flop the clipboard onto my knees. My knit dress—purple, the team's color—is riding up so I do a strange wiggle to yank it down. Then I flip through all the notes to find tonight's corporate box attendees.

"Let's see," I mumble. "You invited two guys from Goldman Sachs—Kearns and Brown. You invited Stew and Seely and Marsha Ryan. Oh—and Alex Engels." *Shit*. If Alex is even the least bit weird to me tonight, I will probably lose my mind.

I run out of steam just thinking about it. And instead of reading the rest of the names on the list, I just hand him the clipboard, feeling defeated.

He scans it and hands it back without a word.

I take it back and sigh.

The car inches up to another red light and we all wait in silence.

"How was your first week back at work?" Nate surprises me by asking.

Grueling. And now weird. "It was lovely. Thank you for inquiring."

"I've made sure she didn't work too many hours in Detroit," Heidi Jo pipes up. "She's doing first rate."

"Ah," Nate says. "Well done. Whatever we pay you, I'm sure it isn't enough."

Heidi Jo giggles. "I think I might need hazard pay when Miss Rowley gets in one of her moods. She's a grumpy bear sometimes."

"Is that so?"

I try to give Heidi Jo a searing death glare from across the car, but she's not looking at me so all I accomplish is tense eye muscles. She is a dead girl when I get her alone.

Nate gives me another glance, and it's weirdly cool. I wonder what he sees. A slightly disheveled woman in a clingy purple dress, probably.

Or, a big mistake?

Luckily I don't have much more time to worry about it. The car pulls up behind the bus. We're at the players' entrance to the stadium. When I peer out the tinted windows, I note that security has done a nice job roping off the sidewalk. A red carpet is set up and waiting for the players to make their entrance, and a crowd has accumulated outside the barriers.

The limo door pops open. "Ready?" the driver asks.

I see Heidi Jo move.

"Wait…" I try to say, because Nate is supposed to get out of the limo first. But puppies are quick. So a moment later, Heidi Jo is standing out there, blinking rapidly as a million flash bulbs go off in her face.

I hear Nate chuckle as he follows her out of the car. The shutters continue to click as he calmly takes Heidi Jo's arm and guides her toward the carpet. A normal person would look mortified at accidentally stealing the limelight. But not our Heidi Jo. She stops at the base of the red carpet like an Oscars invitee, then turns to wave to the crowd. Another million clicks, and Nate gives the crowd a stiff wave and an even stiffer smile before tugging Heidi Jo toward the entrance and finally disappearing inside.

What the hell was that, anyway?

Usually I'm watching this procession from the stadium, not the car. And usually there aren't quite so many people around. But this is the playoffs, and suddenly all of Brooklyn has become a hockey fan.

Not wishing to repeat Heidi Jo's command performance, I sit tight as the door to the bus opens and O'Doul steps down. He waves to the spectators, who promptly go nuts. They're here to see the players, who emerge from the bus one at a time now to cheers.

With all the attention focused on the stream of athlete hotness, I eventually slip out of the open limo door, thanking the driver. Wielding my clipboard, I march toward the door. Nobody gives me a second glance, because all eyes are on the players.

Georgia is waiting just inside. "What the heck was that girl…?"

"I'm sorry," I say quickly. "I didn't warn her to stay out of sight."

"I already have three texts from journalists wondering which college girl Nate Kattenberger is dating." Georgia rolls her eyes.

Of course she does.

My friend drops her voice. "Maybe *you* should have gotten out of the car first," she whispers. "Try that on for size."

"You're hilarious," I hiss. "Maybe on Monday I'll actually do that, just to complicate your life. You can try to kill the story that Nate only dates assistants and interns."

"And only people under five feet four inches tall. *Billionaire romances the vertically challenged*, film at eleven," Georgia giggles.

"I hate you," I say. But I'm lying.

Players stream down the corridor past us, headed for the locker rooms. They'll take off their suits and put on warm-up gear. They'll have last minute meetings, they'll get sore muscles taped. They'll tape and retape their sticks. They'll hydrate and stretch and indulge in smack talk.

I love game night. The energy in the building has given me a little lift already.

Heidi Jo comes tapping toward me down the hall, her heels clicking importantly on the concrete. "Omigod, y'all! That was so nice of Mr. K to walk the red carpet with me!"

"Like he had a choice," Georgia says under her breath.

"Mr. K?" Is she kidding me right now?

"What do we do next?" my intern chirps.

"*We* need to make sure you don't jump out of limos with the bossman again," Georgia says.

"Sorry," Heidi Jo says brightly. "What else?"

Georgia holds up a finger, asking for another minute of my attention. "One more thing? There's a reporter for *Observer* who's dying for an interview with Nate. But I find the whole thing a little weird."

"Weird how?" I ask.

Georgia's eyes flit up the corridor and then back to me. "I don't know this reporter very well. But she wants to write a story about why Nate bought a hockey franchise. But he won't take the interview. Do you have any idea why? You've known him longer than I have."

Slowly, I shake my head. At the moment I don't feel like I know him very well at all. "When Nate bought the team, I was surprised. I didn't know he was considering it. But I will say that our first office had a hockey poster on the wall." I close my tired eyes and try to remember. "The Blackhawks, I think?" I had that poster framed when we renovated our offices that first time, because our new digs were classier, and I didn't want to encourage the guys to decorate in the style of Early Dorm Room.

But then the poster disappeared? I hadn't seen it in years, come to think of it.

"The Blackhawks, huh?" Georgia asks, tapping her lip. "I guess that makes sense. He wouldn't have been a Minnesota fan, because that's an expansion team that formed after his family left Minnesota."

"Just ask him."

"He doesn't want to talk about it, but this reporter won't go away. I get a weird feeling from her. Like she has some bit of gossip and won't come clean. But I can't figure out what it is."

"That is weird," I admit. On the other hand, I can't imagine what's so fascinating about Nate owning a hockey team. It's what rich white guys do. "Maybe she's trying to spin it like *Revenge of the Nerds*. Brainiac enjoys brutality on the ice."

"Don't we all," Heidi Jo says on a sigh.

Georgia gives me an eye roll. "Later, babe."

"Later!" I turn my attention to my sidekick. "I'm going to check with the stadium staff to see if they have any notes for me. And make sure the players have everything they need in their dressing room."

Heidi Jo's hand shoots up in the air. "I volunteer as tribute."

Sigh. "And then I'll look over the corporate box to make sure it's set up for…" For that man I'm trying so hard not to think about. "Let's go," I say. "Ticket booth first."

I head for the elevators, with Heidi Jo at my heels. "When you say the corporate box?" the intern asks, "Do you mean Mr. K's box?"

The fact that she's given him a new nickname grates on me. But I bite back a nasty comment. "That's the one."

"Is it fancy? I've never met a billionaire before today."

"He doesn't *live* there," I grumble. "It's your usual rich guy decor. Velvet stadium seats. Paneled walls. Chandeliers. Exotic dancers on the half hour."

"What?"

"Male and female. Don't tip them, though. They're on salary."

Heidi Jo's eyes bulge, and I feel like a heel.

"Just kidding about that last thing."

"You *do* tip them?"

Shoot me. "There aren't any strippers. The hockey game is enough excitement. But there's champagne if we win, a hundred other beverages if we don't. Oh, and these warm cheese puffs that Georgia speed eats when she's tense." My stomach rumbles just thinking about them.

"It's not nice to tease me," Heidi Jo pouts.

"I'm sorry." Great. I've kicked a puppy. But Heidi Jo brings out the worst in me.

"How are you feeling?" she asks.

"Peachy." I'm tired and hungry. I need twelve continuous hours of sleep in my own bed. The doctor warned me that my first week back would be rough, and to take it easy. The doctor clearly has no idea what it's like to be at ground zero of the hockey playoffs. This is my life. This is my job, and I love my job. Sleep can wait.

"Does your head ache?"

"Nope. I'm good."

"I could find you a snack…"

"Heidi? Stop it. I'm fine."

She gives me a wounded look. "Okay. Just say the word."

―――――

The puck drops right on time at seven-thirty. That's when my workday ends. I could actually go home right now and start catching up on all the sleep I've missed.

Instead, I sink into a chair in Nate's box. I choose the one furthest away from his and focus on the rink. Nothing could keep me away from watching my boys in a playoffs game. Not even world-class awkwardness between me and the boss.

Unfortunately for both of us the game doesn't go as planned. The game becomes tied at 1-1 early on in the first period and doesn't budge for hours.

And so much for home ice advantage. The officials' calls are brutal all night long. Brooklyn gets called for every penalty on earth. Tripping. Slashing. Interference. Our players spend as much time in the penalty box as they did in the last two games combined.

Even worse—whenever Detroit fights back, the ref develops a sudden blind spot. I watch, slack jawed, as a Detroit player cross-checks Castro right into the plexi, face first. "COME ON!" I screech, leaping to my feet when no whistles blow. "THAT'S SOME BULLSHIT RIGHT THERE!"

"I agree," Heidi Jo puts in. "But my mama would slap me if I put it that way."

Something tells me Heidi Jo's mama and I wouldn't get along.

My gaze flits over toward Nate for the hundredth time tonight. I wonder what he thinks of this awful game. I wonder if he even knows I'm here.

And I wonder why that's suddenly so important to me. I used to watch these games in quiet solidarity with Nate and never wonder what he thought of me.

The third period ends without breaking the tie, so an overtime period is put up on the board, and the Zamboni rolls out to polish the ice. I'm so tired I want to die, and it wasn't even me who just skated for ninety minutes straight.

"Timing pool!" Stewie shouts. He stands up, removes his

Brooklyn Bruisers baseball cap and turns it upside down. "Who's in?"

I take a twenty out of my purse and toss it in the hat. "Twelve minutes, thirty six seconds," I say, and he scribbles that down.

"Ooh!" Heidi Jo says. "I love games." She throws in a twenty after mine. "What am I guessing?"

"How long it takes the Zamboni to clear the ice."

"Ah." Her blue eyes take in the vehicle, and she sticks her tongue out of the corner of her mouth while she considers it. "Twelve minutes, thirty nine seconds."

Stew snorts, then raises his eyes to mine. "Your intern is a fierce competitor, Bec."

"Who, me?" Heidi Jo gives him a wide-eyed blink.

I want to kick her. She couldn't possibly have missed the fact that her guess boxed mine in. "If you win, you have to buy lunch tomorrow."

"Awesome!"

Stew gives me a smile and moves on.

"Welp." Heidi Jo stands up. "I was just fixing to have a cocktail. Can I bring you anything?"

"I didn't know you drank, Heidi Jo." This amuses me for some reason—that little miss cute and perfect needs a drink.

"I meant a fruit cocktail!" She giggles.

Right.

I'm *this* close to asking her for two fingers of whiskey, but I resist. "I would love a Coke. Thanks."

My eyes feel leaden, and I spend the rest of the intermission slurping down a soda and eating carrot sticks.

Nate spends it schmoozing bankers from Goldman Sachs. And not making eye contact with me.

The Zamboni leaves the ice at its famously plodding pace, and I've completely forgotten about the bet already when Stew yells, "Twelve minutes, thirty four seconds! Rebecca Rowley takes the pot!"

That wakes me up a little. Stew gives me three hundred bucks and a kiss on the cheek. "Congrats, Bec!"

Most everyone in the room makes a point of congratulating. Except for Nate, who doesn't even spare me a glance. Wonderful.

"I guess you're the one buying lunch tomorrow," Heidi Jo says.

"Indeed," I agree. "Actually, here." I reach into my pocket and pull out a twenty. "It's not really fair for the intern to lose her cash."

Her eyes widen with surprise, and then she pushes the bill back toward me. "Fair's fair. I'll prolly win the next one."

Knowing her, she probably will.

She scampers off to refresh both our drinks, and Stew sidles up to me. "That was a close one, Bec. Three more seconds and you would have been tied. Do you think arm-wrestling would make a good tiebreaker?"

"I could totally take her," I say, and he laughs.

"By the way," he adds under his breath. "That was nice of you to offer her the twenty back. But you know she can afford it."

"I do?" I don't know a thing about Heidi Jo because I try never to ask her questions. It's too risky. Once she starts talking there's no off button.

Stew makes a surprised sound. "Come on, Bec. You don't miss much. She's the league commissioner's daughter."

"The…" League commissioner? "Of the NHL? Really?"

"Yup. Heidi Jo is Heidi Jo *Pepper*. Daddy got mad when she dropped out of Bryn Mawr so he sent her to work on a team."

"Oh, hell. Lucky me." Stew winks and goes back to his seat. While I stand there rewinding every conversation I ever had with my intern, trying to decide how mean I've been. *Shit*.

She sits down beside me a minute later and hands me my glass.

"Thank you very much! That's so kind of you," I gush.

She gives me a sideways glance. "What did that man just tell you?"

"Hmm? What man?" I don't look her in the eye.

"That lottery guy. He told you who my daddy is, right? And now you're gonna be all extra nice. That's bullshit, Becca. I'm just the intern. I don't need special treatment."

Whoops. "Uh, okay. Sorry."

Heidi Jo looks grumpy for the first time since I met her.

But then our players take the ice, and everything else is forgotten. Unfortunately, Detroit scores a goal on Beacon five minutes in, ending the game.

A "sudden death" overtime is always a little shocking. For a moment it's quiet in the box as we all stare down at the ice, trying to deny what our eyes just saw.

Nate leans back in his chair, tips his head back and sighs.

"Better luck next time, boys," Stew says.

"Nate," Georgia says from the doorway. "We'll need you downstairs."

That's it. My night is done. I can slip out the back and finally get some sleep.

And then I realize I left my coat downstairs. So I'm stuck following the VIPs out of the box and toward the elevator.

I hang back, taking the last car. Heidi Jo has ditched me — finally. I'm alone with my sluggish thoughts until the elevator doors open on the post-game mayhem. The hallway is full of journalists and support staff. Georgia and her colleague are trying to herd reporters into the press room. I work my way through this craziness toward Hugh's office, where I think I tossed my coat.

"Miss Rowley."

Nate's voice stops me as I pass his office door. When I turn, I see he's perched on the edge of the desk, probably because Georgia asked him to wait there until it's his turn to step up to the press conference dais. His tie is straight and his shirt is crisp. Whereas my makeup is smudged and I feel as though I've summited a mountain in these clothes, he looks like a million bucks.

Or a billion. Technically.

"Is there something you need?" I ask. *Please say no.* "And what's with this Miss Rowley business?" After I ask, I want to kick myself. Letting on that it bothers me is probably a bad idea.

He frowns. "I was only going to ask if you knew why Alex didn't show up tonight."

"No," I say slowly. "I haven't heard from her. It wasn't me who put her on the invite list."

"I see. I guess I'll give her a call tomorrow and make sure she's okay."

"Right. Okay." I clear my throat. "Good night." I turn to go.

"And…"

Fuck. "Yes?"

"I wasn't trying to be a heel. That…" he makes a hand motion toward the hallway. "The eager intern called you Miss Rowley. I thought it sounded nice."

"Nice," I repeat stupidly.

He shrugs.

"To me it sounds like you forgot my name." I step into his office and shut the door behind me, because I seem to be picking a fight with the great Nate Kattenberger, which is colossally stupid. At least I have enough of an instinct for self-preservation not to let anyone else hear it.

Nate flinches. And when he speaks again, it's still in his iceberg voice. "That wasn't my intent. To make you uncomfortable."

"You're treating me like I have Ebola." This complaint comes out sounding squeaky and weird. I should know better than to have an emotional conversation when I'm exhausted.

"Poor calibration," Nate says. Then he turns his head a few degrees and puts on his thinking face.

"*What?*" He's completely unreadable. With Nate's thinking face, you just never know. He might be considering the topic at hand, or he might have instantly changed gears. Right now he might be considering a merger with Comcast, or reinventing the way your phone battery functions.

"It's taken me longer than I'd hoped to recalibrate my reaction to you. My apologies, Rebecca. You were right when you pointed out that this is your place of work, and that it would be wrong to pursue you here. And I haven't."

I try to take that in. "So this whole Mr. Darcy routine is not because you're mad at me?"

"No." Nate gives me a tiny smile. My first one in weeks. "Not mad at you. Not at all."

I'm so confused. And the worst part is that it's all my fault. I was so eager to have that awkward conversation in Nate's office — the one where I told him that it could never happen again, and that he wasn't allowed to bring it up. If I hadn't made these demands immediately, then maybe I'd know what he thought about the whole thing.

"Look. I'm sorry I screwed up your...calibration."

"It's entirely my own fault. We discussed this already."

"Not exactly," I admit. "I never let you tell me what you thought about the whole thing."

He gives me a neat smirk. "By *whole thing* are you referring to a very hot night in Bal Harbour, Florida?"

"Of course I am!"

He shrugs, and I want to slug him. "But it doesn't matter what I think. The guy who owns your place of employment can't say what he feels. I don't want to look like that guy. I don't want to *be* that guy. And now we know my poker face needs work. So I'll get right on that."

He folds his hands, as if the matter is settled. The problem is that suddenly I don't want it to be settled. I want to know. "Nate," I whisper. "Tell me what would've happened if you weren't my boss for seven years. Or even — what if I didn't say no to breakfast that morning. What would you have said to me over hotel coffee?"

"Something awkward probably." He clears his throat. "Look, there are no hypotheticals. You were never just some girl I met at a party. So don't ask me to tell you what I think. Not if a little awkwardness sends you into a tailspin. Because I don't think you're ready for what I'd have to say."

"But..." My heart rate accelerates. I feel wide-awake and joyous and bewildered. Everything at once. "What if I hadn't given you a long speech about how the whole thing was a huge mistake? What would you have said if I let you talk? Do you even know?"

"Of course I know." He stands up, but doesn't come any closer to me. "I've thought about it every ten minutes since. I've thought about us during conference calls and while watching hockey." In an uncharacteristically fidgety maneuver, Nate scrubs a hand through his hair. "I thought about us on the Gulfstream and also in *bed*."

My face flushes instantly. Because the idea of Nate having a fantasy parallel to mine is not something I'd really considered. "What about us?" I squeak.

"What do you think? In my imagination we aren't reviewing

spreadsheets, that's for sure." He puts a hand on the desk beside him. "The only office furniture in this scenario is the desk I'm bending you over." He drops his voice. "Does that answer the question? Or should I go on about what color dress you're wearing when I lift it up and…"

I hold up a hand to stop him before I need to turn a fire extinguisher on myself. "I think I get the idea."

"And that's just off the top of my head."

Whew. "That, uh, jives pretty well with my own thoughts on the matter."

"Really?" His eyes widen. "Then why are we avoiding each other instead?"

"Because it would be fun, but fun ends. Think about it. You'd run to the end of your playbook pretty quickly and then everything would be doubly awkward. Once you thought it through, you'd decide we needed to just forget about the whole thing, too."

"No fucking way," he says immediately. "When did you get to be such a pessimist?"

"Since birth," I point out. "Have you met me?"

"You're not a pessimist, Bec," he says, leaning against the desk. "You love everyone, except maybe your intern. You planned Georgia's wedding like she's royalty. The whole fucking team would lie down in the road for you. That's not pessimism. That's why I don't quite buy it now."

"Well…" My heart is thudding. I can't even think of a response. "Maybe I just can't imagine a nice ending."

"Do you always plan your escape route first when you're interested in someone?"

He's got me there. "I'm never interested in someone." A beat goes by while I realize what he's just said. "Are you interested in me?"

"Were you not listening when I just described how very interesting to me you are? If I had my way, though, the next thing that happened between us would be dinner."

"Dinner?"

He rolls his eyes. "You know. Food consumed near the end of the day? At a restaurant, because I don't cook. Candlelight. You in a low-cut sweater. That's what I would have asked for over breakfast."

I try to take that in. "Like, a date?"

"Like, fer sure." He's even teasing me now.

I blink. "That's really sweet. I'm sorry I threw it back in your face without even asking."

"Come here," he opens his arms.

I step forward immediately, letting him fold me into a hug. I lean against his hard chest and let out a sigh. One of his long hands caresses my back.

"Everything got really tangled up there, didn't it?"

"Yes," I say to his shirt. Leaning against his very solid chest calms me down.

"I'm sorry to ever distress you," he whispers. "You mean a lot to me."

And then my eyes begin to sting, damn it. I blink rapidly. "I think I went a little crazy, Nate. You mean a lot to me, too. But so does my job. How did we get so complicated?"

"Everything worthwhile is complicated."

It feels wonderful to be held by Nate. When I feel his heartbeat against my cheek, I stop thinking about him as The Powerful Nate Kattenberger. Right now he's a guy who gives great hugs.

He runs a hand through my hair. And then he presses his lips against my temple, giving me a gentle, lingering kiss. It's lovely for its warmth and for the fact that it asks nothing of me except for my acceptance. It's perfect.

And that's when the door flies open. "Y'all are needed at the press conference, Mr. K!" says a chirpy voice. And then, "Oh gosh —sorry!"

I've already leapt back, though, the way you'd fling yourself out of a patch of poison ivy. My face reddens during the little silence that follows.

"Be there in a sec," Nate says. He looks completely unruffled.

Of course he does. He can do whatever he wants. It doesn't matter at all if Heidi Jo tells the league commissioner that Nate and his assistant get a little freaky in his office between meetings. His reputation can't be dented.

I'm the one who has to look Heidi Jo in the eye every freaking day for the rest of the season.

But not yet. I just can't.

I slip past her, leaving both Nate and Heidi Jo behind. Three seconds later I've grabbed my coat and exited the building into the cool May night.

[18]

NATE

SO THAT COULD HAVE GONE BETTER.

I stammer my way through the introduction for the press conference. But it's okay to be a little inarticulate when your team has just coughed up a loss. Nobody cares what I say, anyway. They want to hear from Coach Worthington and the players.

And whatever they're saying now, I don't even listen. *Blah blah blah we'll win the next one,* probably.

My mind is elsewhere. I'm still thinking about Rebecca's quick departure, and the horrified look on her face when her chatty side-kick caught us together.

But I'm viewing it only as a temporary setback. Something we'll laugh about later. I'll do anything to break the tension between us. Tonight it finally felt like maybe I can.

I'm awoken from my reverie by the sound of chairs scraping. The press conference is over. Rising from my seat, I plot a course for the door. As I move through the crowd, several reporters try to collar me for a quote.

"Mr. Kattenberger, how do you feel about your team's..."

"Mr. Kattenberger...!"

Nope. Tonight I'm not having it. I give each one a friendly wave and keep moving. The edge of my phone is glowing green, which means that Ramesh is waiting for me outside. Perfect. Ten seconds later I'm sliding into the back of the car.

As per our security protocol, the locks slide shut immediately and he glides away from the curb as soon as he can.

"Rough game," Ramesh says from the front seat.

"Eh. We can rebuild it. Hey man—one stop before home?"

"Hit me," he says.

I give him Rebecca's address on Water Street. It's only two miles away, and he hits all the lights just right. So I'm pushing the buzzer at her front door only a few minutes later.

That's when it occurs to me to check the time. It's 11:46 p.m.

Fuck. I'm such an asshole.

"Hello?" Rebecca's voice says a few seconds later.

"It's me." I sigh. "Look, I'm sorry it's so late. I said I wouldn't be that creepy guy. And now here I am standing on your doorstep at midnight. Nothing creepy at all about that, right? You were probably asleep and dreaming about sweaters or something and I wrecked it. *Again.*"

I can hear myself babbling. Nobody ever accused me of being good at this, though. But I try to get to the point.

"But, anyway, our conversation got interrupted at just the wrong time. Or at least I thought it was the wrong time. I just wanted to say that if you ever want to finish that conversation, I'm here for that. Not literally. I won't show up at midnight every night until you decide to either talk to me or call HR. But if the mood ever strikes, just say the word."

Now I've run out of air. And none of that sounded particularly sane. So it's not much of a shock that Rebecca doesn't say anything.

Not one word.

I put my forehead against the pane of glass in her door and wonder if I've just made everything worse again.

Fuck.

Then a set of pretty blue eyes appears on the other side of the glass and I leap back, startled.

The door opens. "Hi there," Rebecca says, stepping outside.

"Hi." It takes me a second to realize that she didn't even hear my rambling speech. She couldn't have. She was busy pulling herself together and descending two flights of stairs. "That's a new look for you," I say, eyeing her getup and trying to regroup.

"This is Renny's trench coat," she says. "While you've already seen my tiny pajamas, I didn't want to give the rest of Brooklyn the pleasure."

"I meant the, uh, baby." Her nephew must be hanging from some kind of contraption that was strapped to her body. All I can see over the jacket's top button is his little bald head. "Did I wake him up? Are you babysitting?"

"He's a night owl." Becca shakes her head. "Renny and Missy are home, too. It's just that they're having very loud sex right now in their bedroom. That's why I didn't invite you up."

I laugh uneasily, and she smiles, too. Her expression is warmer and more relaxed than it was earlier. But there are circles under her eyes.

"Listen, I should go," I tell her. "I'm sorry our conversation was interrupted earlier. Do you want me to say anything to that intern?"

"No." Rebecca shakes her head. "I'll handle it."

"Well. Just say the word. But I really came here to say that my dinner invitation doesn't expire, okay? If you should decide a month from now that the idea isn't as hateful as you originally thought, just let me know. I'm not going to ask again, though. Just to stay on the right side of the creepy line."

"Oh, Nate!" Her face softens, and our gazes lock. I feel the pull, and it's not just me. I'm ninety-nine percent sure. "You could never be creepy. It isn't like that."

"Good to know."

Becca pats the baby on his bald head, and I notice that he's sucking rapidly on his pacifier, making smacking sounds, just like Lisa on *The Simpsons*. "I want to," she says suddenly.

"Hmm?"

"Dinner. I want to go."

"Really?" It comes out sounding shocked, and she laughs.

"Yeah. But it has to be our little secret. I'm, um, just trying to feel my way here." She tries to cross her arms in front of her chest, but the baby is in the way, so she drops them again.

"Okay," I say quickly. "You're the boss."

She lifts an eyebrow to tell me that was a stupid statement. Because *I'm* the boss, and that's the whole fucking problem.

"Of this," I add. It's true, too. "How's tomorrow night?"

She blinks. "Okay. Sure. I'm still not sure this isn't a bad idea."

"Don't worry. I'll sell you on all the perks."

With a small smile, she looks away, and a hint of pink appears on her cheeks.

She is fucking adorable. I've got it so bad.

The baby looks up at me, slurping away. He seems to be evaluating my merits, too.

"Well, I'm going to run along," I say. A good businessman knows to shake hands on the deal and then get the hell out of there before the other party can reconsider. "See you at seven?"

"Seven," she says, softly. She holds my gaze.

"Sorry I've been—what did you call it? Mr. Darcy?"

"Yeah, you're all..." She makes a stern, slightly cross-eyed face. "...Chilly. Or maybe constipated."

I snort. There are very few people in my life who'll tease me. Rebecca has always treated me like a regular guy, not an icon. And I dig that.

We're both smiling like idiots now, just staring at each other. And it happens in slow motion. I lean forward, just a little. She mirrors me. We're just inches apart now. I'm not hesitating so much as giving her time to get used to the idea.

Then she licks her lips, and I can't resist any longer. I close the distance and lean into the kiss. Our lips come together softly. There is, after all, another small human between us. This one kiss is all I'm going to get. So I make it a good one. I part her lips, gently touching my tongue to hers just once before I retreat.

She's looking up at me in a lust haze now.

And I cannot fucking wait until tomorrow night.

19

REBECCA

MAY 22, BROOKLYN

"THAT'S IT. I can't eat another bite." I set down my fork on the dessert plate and lean back in my chair.

"Quitter." Nate uses his spoon to scrape the last of the chocolate raspberry soufflé we'd shared into his own mouth.

Splitting desserts with Nate is something I've done before.

Sitting alone with him in a fine restaurant in a dress designed to show off my cleavage is not.

We're at the River Café, where Nate slipped the maître d' a C-note to ensure this perfect table against the windows. We just had one of the best meals in Brooklyn, with nothing but the lights of Manhattan and the East River as our view.

A lit-up yacht glides past the window as I watch Nate sign the check. "Nice pick, Nate. But I would have been happy with anything."

"What?" he raises his eyes to me, and they look even darker in the candlelight. "You with the deep opinions about falafel?"

"Okay—fine." I smile back at him. "Not just *anything*. But you don't have to impress me with gourmet extravagance."

He makes a face that says, *oh please*. "You think I don't know that? You're fun, Bec. Next month I'm going to China with

187

Lauren, and she won't eat the street food I'm going to want to try. You've always had a good sense of adventure. I love that about you."

My face heats at this compliment. I'm not used to hearing things like this from him. This evening has been both utterly familiar and completely strange. Conversation was never tricky because we know all the same people and we can't help ourselves from talking about hockey all night. Meanwhile, Nate held my hand under the table.

I liked it. A whole lot. Even now I have the urge to climb over the table and kiss him. And yet a month ago I wouldn't have been thinking that at all. "You know..." I clear my throat. "This is its own kind of adventure."

"Exactly," he says, closing the bill folder. "And that's why we're here tonight and not at the falafel shop. I'm not trying to wow you with the twenty-dollar dessert. Although it *was* exquisite. I'm only trying to show you that tonight is not business as usual."

The waiter comes by to pick up the check. I don't give it a second glance. I don't bother trying to pay half, because Nate has more money than God, and he wouldn't let me.

That doesn't mean I'm not conflicted about seeing Nate. But my hesitation is far more complicated than the dinner check.

And yet here I am.

I pick up my champagne glass and drain the last drop. I ordered a half glass just to piss Nate off.

And he didn't say a *word*. Smart man. "Okay, adventure guy." I set down the glass. "Are you ready to go?"

His smile says, *am I ever*.

We retrieve my coat and walk outside. It's a cool night, but there are lots of people milling around the pier where ice cream is sold, and there's a brilliant view of the Brooklyn Bridge. But Nate leads me up the street, away from the crowd.

Back toward his place.

I don't argue, even though I feel a riffle of nervous anticipation in my belly. "Where's Ramesh? Are you giving him the slip?"

"No." Nate reaches for my hand and gives it a squeeze. "I gave him the night off."

"Really? Can you do that?"

"Sure. I mean—some other member of my security team is likely watching a dot move on a screen somewhere, tracking my movements. There is always someone paying attention." He stops walking and turns to me. "That's not a selling point, is it?"

"What?"

"Surveillance is so sexy." He lifts my hand up to his mouth and kisses my palm. His sexy mouth is hidden from view, but his eyes lift with a gaze so hungry that I feel it like a blast of heat. He kisses my palm again, and his scruff enlivens all my nerve endings.

Wow. He's only touched my hand, but I want to scale him like a tree.

He speaks again, and it's a struggle to make myself listen. "Ramesh has the night off because I knew if I asked him to drive us back to my place, you would have trouble looking him in the eye."

I probably would, too.

"...I also asked one of Lauren's minions to make our dinner reservation, because if I had asked Lauren, she would've made me tell her who I was dining with. And you made it clear how you feel about office gossip."

"That's very thoughtful of you. And lovely of you to remain my dirty little secret." I punctuate this little barb by stepping sideways to hip check him.

He puts an arm around my waist. "You can do that now without losing your balance. Well done."

It's true, although I'm a little surprised that Nate noticed. "I'm never stepping out on that ice again. Just saying."

His arm stays around me the whole walk home. I get increasingly nervous, though, as we approach his mansion. He opens the little front gate and holds it aside for me.

I walk through, because even if I'm apprehensive, I still can't help myself.

Nate taps in his security code at the door, which clicks open for him. I follow him into the grand foyer, wondering what happens next.

"Evening, Nate!" Bingley calls out.

"Evening," he replies. He slips my coat off my shoulders and hangs it up. "I put some of that Mexican soda you like in the den refrigerator." He points upstairs. "Want one?"

"Sure!" I say brightly. My knees feel a little shaky, and I can't blame my health. I actually have the jitters. It's so unlike me, too. "God, I can't wait until I can just have a glass of wine like a normal person." I'm babbling now.

Nate just smiles and holds out a hand for me to walk upstairs with him.

Upstairs. Where his giant bed is.

I stop climbing on the fourth or fifth step.

"This is probably a bad idea," I whisper. Weirdly, it's the same thing I say in my very frequent Nate fantasy—the same one where he ignores it and then fucks me senseless.

That's not what happens now.

Nate sits down right there on the grand stairway. He pats the thick carpeted runner beside him.

I sit.

"Everything okay?" he asks.

"Yes and no," I whisper. "I just want to do the smart thing. And sometimes it's not easy to know what that is." Nate probably won't understand, though. Everything he does is smart.

"You think I'm a bad idea. You're right."

"I am?"

He puts an arm around me. Leaning in, he kisses my jaw. Slowly. So that I feel every brush of his whiskers against my face, and the softness of his lips. All the hair stands up on the back of my neck as he whispers in my ear. "Very bad. Because I want to do bad, bad things to you. Naughty things. And if you're not on board with that, better say so now."

"What kind of things?" I ask as my nipples harden.

"I could tell you," he continues, his voice low. "If you have a half hour or so. Because I'm very detail-oriented. In fact, there's a PowerPoint presentation I've put together..."

My nerves get the better of me and I start to giggle.

"Not too long," he says, rubbing my back. "Fifty slides or so."

"Are there charts and graphs?" I try to ask. But unfortunately I let out a snort-laugh, too.

Nate keeps his poker face, but his eyes are smiling. "There are four diagrams, drawn from my fantasies. And also specs and performance estimates."

"Oh, Nate," I gasp. "Don't ever change." I'm on the brink of hysteria here. I want him but it's so hard to just give in. We spent so many years not doing this…

He kisses me—just leans right in and takes my mouth with his.

It takes me about 1.5 seconds to get over my surprise. Maybe less. I wrap my arms around him and just hold on as he breeches my lips, then slides his tongue into my mouth. He tastes like chocolate and confidence. Two great tastes that go great together. And I'm a goner.

Forgetting my earlier hesitation, I sift my fingers through his hair and tug him closer. With a groan, he slides his hand slowly down my body, leaving shivers in its wake. And then that naughty hand skims up the inside of my thigh. I've forgotten how good that feels.

Maybe he would have paused there, except Nate discovers I'm wearing thigh-high stockings under my dress. His fingertips find skin, and he makes a noise of happy surprise. Since I have no self-control, I relax my muscles, giving him better access.

His next kiss is deep and slow, and his thumb strokes over my lace panties, right between my legs.

I give a desperate moan into his mouth, startling us both.

Nate must be very startled indeed because I lose his hand and he yanks my knees together and sits up suddenly.

That's when I see Ramesh standing right inside the door, his pistol drawn but pointing down at the floor. I let out a little shriek of surprise. Or embarrassment. Probably both.

"Seriously?" Nate says, his face red.

Ramesh looks up at the ceiling and shakes his head. "Two heat signatures. If you were on, say, a sofa right now, I wouldn't have been confused. But on the stairs? Looked like a struggle. And you didn't engage the security systems like you always do."

"Forgot to," Nate sputters.

I put my face in my hands.

"Bye," Ramesh says. "Lock up after me. We'll discuss security protocols tomorrow. You can tweak some things." He disappears. The door closes again.

Nate lets out a frustrated groan. "I'm sorry…"

"I know," I say, cutting him off. "This will probably be funny eventually. But I need a minute."

"I'll bet," he sighs.

———

NATE

I'm so frustrated. Sexually and otherwise. I have enough trouble with my own awkwardnesses. I don't need any help ruining the moment from my security team.

Rebecca slowly rises to her feet, looking pained and unhappy.

I shoot up, too. "You okay?"

"Yup. Just sore. This morning I went to a Pilates class that Ari recommended. My abs and glutes may never forgive me."

That gives me an idea. "Come on, there's something I want to show you. And it isn't a security feature."

She gives me a rueful smile, but then she takes the hand I've offered her and follows me back down the stairs, through the parlor and into the kitchen.

"Evening, Nate!" Bingley says again as we pass through the parlor. "Evening," I reply. "Engage all security systems."

"Roger, Roger!"

"So I'm not leaving tonight?" Becca asks as we enter the kitchen. Bingley turns on the lights automatically, so she's blinking up at me with big eyes.

"Do you want to?" But I don't let her answer the question. I cup the back of her head and pull her into a kiss, right there in front of the refrigerator. And her mouth melts under mine. It's glorious. And it means I haven't ruined everything.

Unfortunately, Bingley doesn't get the memo. "Hullo, Rebecca!" he says. "It's good to hear your voice, lass!"

"Mmm," she says against my smile. "Hello to you, too."

Laughing, I pull back. "Soda?"

"Sure, why not." She shrugs.

I reach into the fridge and take a couple of drinks out. "Follow me." I open a door that leads out the back, but also down to the basement.

"Where are we going?"

"You said something about muscle pain? You'll see." I flip a switch, and the stairs to the lower level are illuminated.

"Nice basement," Becca says, following me down.

"It's not really below ground." But this level really is swank. To our right is my home gym. But to my left is where I'm bringing Becca—the spa room. One wall is sliding glass doors, but those are locked for the night and covered with heavy curtains. And there are two lounge chairs facing my combination hot tub and lap pool.

I have it on the hot tub setting presently, so I can hear the jets bubbling away as hot water is pushed into circulation. I step on a button on the floor, and the cover retracts automatically.

"Oh, wow," Becca says. "Fancy." She toes out of her shoes and walks toward the edge. Then she hesitates. "I still don't always trust my balance. If I fall in, don't laugh." She carefully dips a hand into the water. "Nice."

I grab a towel off a waiting stack of them and toss it onto the edge. "You can sit and put your feet in."

She's wearing a short little knit dress that's been making me crazy all evening, so it would be easy enough for her to strip off those stockings, sit on the towel, and drop both feet in.

And that's what she does. She eases one stocking down over a smooth knee and tugs it off.

I don't want to stand there staring like a middle-school boy. Okay, I do want to. But I don't want to make her uncomfortable. So I go over to the sound system instead, and I set my phone on the speaker and cue up a really old playlist. One she'll recognize.

When I turn around again, she's seated on the towel, both legs hanging down into the churning water. "Ah. Wow." She looks up at me, her eyes sparkling. "Nice place you got here."

"Isn't it?" I toe off my shoes and kick them to the side.

The first song comes on, and it's a Macklemore tune that we used to play far too often in our first office. Rebecca laughs immediately. "You didn't! I haven't heard this playlist in forever. But I'll bet I still know every transition. Lady Gaga is next."

"She sure is."

Rebecca kicks her feet, making a splash. "I have a little confession to make."

"What's that?" I loosen my tie and slide the knot out.

"Well…" She grins up at me. "I used to have a crush on you. Back in the early days."

My hands freeze on the tie silk. "Get out of town. You did not."

"No, I really did." Her cheeks are pink. "That first year especially. But you were taken, and you were my boss. Those two things made it pretty easy to tamp down, when you're a practical girl like me."

I walk over and drop down beside her, my back to the water, though, because I'm still wearing trousers and socks. "So how does that work, exactly?"

"What?" She gives me a sidelong glance, but then looks away again and won't meet my eyes.

"How do you stop wanting someone? I'm a practical person, but I don't see how that makes it any easier. Nothing seems to mute the raging attraction I have for you."

Her chin turns quickly toward me, and I seize the opportunity to kiss her. And it only takes one kiss—one slide of my lips over hers, and I'm on fire again.

We're facing opposite directions, so it's awkward as hell. But I don't even care. I take greedy sip after greedy sip of her mouth, until she pulls back to stare at me. Her color is high and her eyes are bright and happy. "This is like Twister."

"It's better," I correct. Lady Gaga comes on, just as Becca said she would. "Are we getting into this pool or what?"

Becca kicks a foot in the water. "I'm tempted. But I don't have a bathing suit."

"Oh, snap."

She smiles and shakes her head. "Are you really getting in?"

"We don't have to." I'm never going to pressure her.

Her fingers trail across the surface of the bubbling water. "But this is an adventure, right?"

"Right." I stand up and remove my socks. She's watching me. And I can't read her expression. "What?"

"Just wondering what else you're going to take off." She smiles.

"Come here." The order rolls off my tongue.

But Rebecca doesn't blink. She gets up and turns toward me, curiosity in her eyes.

"You tell me. What am I taking off?"

She puts two hands tentatively on my chest, and I make myself be patient. Everything I ever wanted is on the other side of this moment. I just need us to break through this awkwardness—the "will we or won't we" tension.

Her fingers find the top button of my shirt. "I'm not getting in the water unless you are."

That's a compromise I can live with. I find my lower shirt buttons and work upwards, until we meet in the middle. She pushes the two halves of my shirt apart and runs a hand down my bare chest.

My inner caveman stands up and cheers.

I lean forward and kiss her jaw. She smells like flowers, and a bolt of pure lust races down my spine. One of my hands finds its way onto her lower back, and I whisper into her ear. "Undo my belt." I punctuate this request with a kiss on her neck.

The hot tub jets are making the only noise in the room, but the inside of my head is as loud as a stadium concert. My pulse thumps like a bass guitar as her hands work open my belt. My heart beats out an eager rhythm as she unzips my trousers.

Christ. Rebecca is undressing me. I may not survive it.

I lift her hand to my mouth and kiss her palm. But it's not enough. So I bury my face in her silky neck and kiss it again. Once. Twice.

Her hands shove my shirt off my shoulders. "You dressed up for dinner," she whispers. "No hoodie tonight?"

My mouth finds hers, because I can't not kiss her. "There's a different outfit I'd rather wear when I'm with you," I mumble against her lips. My hands skim down the stretchy fabric of the dress she's wearing, landing on her ass.

I take it further, until I find the smooth skin of her thighs. And I hear her breath catch.

"Can I take this off of you?"

"Yes," she breathes.

I lift the dress right over her head and toss it onto the chaise where my suit jacket waits. And then I get a look at the black lace she's wearing and it almost kills me. "Jesus," I breathe. The fabric is see-through, and there's something wonderfully dirty about her rosy nipples so poorly concealed from my hungry gaze.

This is the second time I've been leveled by her choice of lingerie. If I'd had half a clue all these years that Becca favored sexy underwear, I don't think I could have made it through the day at the office.

But she is oblivious to my pain. She reaches behind her body and unclips the bra, then tosses it aside while I practically swallow my tongue when her generous breasts are freed from their bondage.

Or maybe she's not actually oblivious, because then she turns around, showing me the back view of her almost naked body. With a saucy glimpse over her shoulder, she flicks her panties to the floor and then steps right over to the stairs leading into the pool.

Leaving me standing there in nothing but unzipped trousers, from which my aching cock is desperately trying to escape.

Right.

I shed my clothes in the next few seconds. My erection bobs against my stomach as I slip into the pool to meet her.

There's no better sight than Rebecca in the pool, the water churning around her bare breasts. She's sitting on the bench, her head tipped back against the edge. Her eyes are closed. "I'm a fan of this setup. Do you use this tub very often?"

"Yes and no. I use it as a lap pool twice a week. Always alone. So this is new." I splash her chest, because my inner fifteen-year-old can't resist. She opens up her eyes and smiles. "But I figure — what's the point of having this crazy house if you never skinny-dip in the hot tub with your favorite girl?"

Her expression softens. "This *is* fun. But I'm not used to it yet."

She doesn't mean the water. "I know. You still have your doubts."

"Not about *you*, though," she says, putting a wet hand on my cheek. "It's just complicated."

I nod so she'll think I understand. And I do—mostly. Although my grasp of the complications improves when we have our clothes on, and I remember that other people actually exist. Right now I'm naked while water caresses my bare skin, and she's mere inches away.

It's surprising I can form words at all.

"This *is* really nice on the sore muscles," she says, rolling her neck.

"What exactly is sore? I'll massage it. Please say it's your glutes."

She giggles. "Close. Hamstrings."

"As if I needed a reason to touch your thighs." Under water, I put a hand on her quadriceps and squeeze gently.

"Oy," she gasps. "Okay, that's sore too."

"Sorry."

She shakes her head. "It's a good kind of sore. I was so happy when Dr. Armitage said that lying around in dark rooms wasn't going to help me get better. It's good to move around, because I feel like I'm accomplishing something."

I make some inarticulate noise of agreement, but all my focus is on Rebecca's thigh under my hand. "Swing a leg over here."

After only a second's hesitation, she does.

I take that smooth leg into my hands and gently work over the muscles.

She groans, and my cock is now harder than the pipes that fill this pool with water. "That feels so good."

I'm going to make her say that again later, and she won't be referring to her leg muscles.

20

REBECCA

NATE IS GIVING me a world-class rubdown. We are both trying really hard not to just leap on each other. Nate is doing his best to be patient, because he thinks I'm skittish. And I am—about dating him.

But not, it seems, about jumping him. Every one of my senses is dialed up to eleven, and every time his long fingers make another pass over my bare skin, I just want to moan.

I glance around this incredible room we're in. Those big windows must let in a lot of light during the daytime. Nate has what other New Yorkers only dream about—a huge space in a great location. It's ridiculous.

"Hey, nice turtle," I say just so I won't accidentally beg him to fuck me.

"Hmm?" he says, looking as distracted as I feel.

"You have an inflatable turtle, Nate. It's smiling at me." I point toward the toy on the other edge of the pool.

"Ah," he says, barely giving it a glance. "Gag gift from Alex."

Just the sound of her name makes me tense, and I'm not even sure why. "She seemed pissed off at you that night at the party," I hear myself say.

"She was, right?" He stops rubbing my leg and gives it a simple squeeze. "That was sort of weird. I think she's ducking me.

Probably has something to do with a deal I have going on at work."

"Hmm." I'd bet a million dollars that's not it. "Can I ask you a question? Were you and Alex ever a thing?"

"A thing," he says slowly. "No. Not really."

"Not really?" That sounds a lot like a dodge to me.

He shakes his head. "Once we got drunk and fooled around. But never again. We're better off as friends."

Once. That shouldn't bother me. They've known each other for...twelve years? Thirteen? But then why was she so pissed off when I turned up in Florida?

Maybe I'm just paranoid. After all, it's me sitting here naked with Nate. Not her. And I'm wasting the moment thinking about his grumpy college friend.

Smart, Bec.

I shift my body so that my leg slides off Nathan's knee. And when I straighten my spine, my breasts rise a little ways, exposing my nipples above the waterline. Nate's gaze latches onto my chest and doesn't let go.

Improving his view suddenly seems like a no-brainer.

Turning toward him, I press myself up onto my knees on the bench. He makes a soft grunt of surprise as my dripping wet torso emerges from the water. Maybe I'll be embarrassed about this later, but I actually arch my back a little to enhance the effect.

Then I climb into his lap, straddling him. My overly sensitive breasts meet his wet chest.

With a groan he pulls me closer, and then we're kissing. His tongue is hot and bossy, and our kisses skip right past all the preliminary rounds and go straight to the playoffs. He gets a firm grip on my bottom and gives it a dirty squeeze.

Slick, wet skin slides across skin. His hard cock is trapped between my legs. And we're kissing like movie stars.

"You ruin me," he murmurs, holding my chin in his hand to control the kiss.

I don't know what that means, but I like the sound of it. I grind against him. I am shameless, and the agonized sounds he makes are my reward.

"Fuck, Bec," he pants eventually. "Sit up here."

"What?"

He pats the pool's edge. "No, wait." He leans out of the water to grab the turtle. Then he angles me into its bright green embrace, so he's standing between my legs, a hand under each thigh. And he kisses his way down my body.

"Oh," I whisper when his intention becomes clear. And when my hips float to the water's surface, his mouth is there, kissing the juncture of my body and thigh. His lips shift, finding the potent center of me. "Ungh," I gasp as my head falls back onto the turtle.

"Rebecca, are you all right?" This question is brought to us by Bingley, whose chipper voice booms through the speakers.

Nate actually chuckles, and I feel the vibration against my clit.

Jesus lord. His hot tongue makes a pass across my most sensitive flesh and I grip the pool toy with both hands. "Oh," I say, and the word echoes off the tile walls.

Nate makes a low noise of agreement as he tongues me again. I pull my legs together, trapping his mouth there. I can't relax because *good lord* it feels so good and it's been forever since anyone spoiled me like this.

His brown eyes lift to hold my gaze, and then he deliberately makes a slow, heavy pass with his tongue.

I make another inarticulate noise followed by some begging. "Don't stop," I blab.

"Stop?" Bingley says. "I didn't get that, Rebecca."

"SILENCE, Bingley," Nate hollers.

I clap my hand over my mouth because it's funny and for a second there I feel like laughing. But then the urge fades because there are other sensations commanding my attention. Nate has many gifts and skills, but I had no idea his tongue was so fucking useful. He coaxes and teases me until I ache with impatience.

I bite down on my own lip. "Shouldn't we…" I look around wildly, wondering what surface we can christen. The chaise lounge, maybe. "Let's get out of the pool," I urge.

"We will," he says maddeningly. Then he drops his head again and slides his lips over me until I'm shaking. "Come on my tongue," he orders. "And then I'll take you upstairs and make you come again on my cock."

That all sounds so nice that I do exactly as he suggests. Immediately.

———

I wake up in the predawn light in Nate's bed. I'm lying on my side, my leg hooked over his. He's on his stomach, his face turned away from me. And I can't resist—I push up on an elbow and study him.

He's sleeping soundly, his face relaxed. Long, dark eyelashes sweep toward those handsome cheekbones. It's a gorgeous face. And he looks so youthful right now. I'm struck by how much he looks like the Nate I met seven years ago, when he was still only a boy genius and not a billionaire. A weird sensation comes over me, like I'm glimpsing a lost moment in our lives, when everything was less complicated.

Which is silly. But I miss the younger us, when Nate could still stop in the middle of his day for a game of Ping-Pong.

I could stare at him all day, but reluctantly I roll away from him. The mansion is so quiet that my motion stirs him, too. "Where are you going?" he mumbles without opening his eyes.

The palindrome comes to me out of nowhere. "As I pee, sir, I see Pisa."

He smiles into his pillow.

In the world's largest master bath, I do my business and then brush my teeth, just in case anybody wants to kiss me.

And I try not to be too astonished that I just had a sleepover with Nate.

Wowzers.

My little makeup bag is sitting on the wooden table to the left of the sink, so I find my birth control pills and swallow one. I'm a practical girl to the core.

Or am I? Finger-combing my hair into place in the bathroom mirror, I'm flooded with some very visual memories of last night. Nate pushing me down on the bed, just like in my fantasy. He opens the towel I'm wearing, bracing himself above me in bed. The muscles of his arms and chest straining as he thrusts...

Gah. I feel tingly just remembering it. And I can't imagine that will fade anytime soon. It was a night for the record books.

Not practical. But magical.

I shut off the light to hide my smile as I exit the bathroom. There's not a chance I'll get back to sleep now—not with those memories playing on repeat in my mind. But I can lie very quietly while Nate continues to rest his giant brain.

Or not. Because as soon as I slide between the sheets, he rolls toward me, his body fitting against my back. "Hi," he whispers.

"Hi yourself."

I relax against his big warm body. Lately, there hasn't been much affection in my life. When I tease Georgia, I always tell her I'm jealous of all the hot lovin' she's getting from Leo since they got back together.

But I never say how jealous I am of this, too—a snuggle in the morning. Nate's nose in my hair. A long arm fitted over my hip.

I close my eyes and drink in all this wonderfulness. He's quiet, and I wonder if he'll doze off again.

"Bec," he whispers a few minutes later. He sweeps a hand up my sternum, then cups my breast. "This is right out of the Power-Point presentation, too. Slide seventeen, I wake up and you're naked in my bed." His fingers find my nipple, which tightens under his touch. The tingles return in force.

And there's an eager erection poking me in the back.

"What's on slide eighteen?" My pussy clenches just thinking about how much I want him to push me down and fill me.

Instead of answering, he kisses the back of my neck. And then his shameless hand coasts down my body, his fingertips dipping between my legs without hesitation. I let out a half breath, half whimper.

"Slide eighteen is that sound you just made." He strokes me, his cock pushing against my back. "Roll over."

I do, but his hand is in my hair. Instead of tugging me up to kiss him, he does the opposite. Our gazes lock, and he guides me right down to his erection instead, his biceps flexing as he nudges me where he wants me.

Yes. Without missing a beat, I open my mouth and then take him onto my tongue, where I lap eagerly. It's my first taste of him. And I *love* that he sort of shoved me down and asked for it.

How does he know this turns me on? That's something to wonder about later.

He groans loudly, and the sound resonates all over my body. I can feel it from my nipples to my toes. I clamp my mouth down on him and give a good suck. Then I raise my eyes to see the effect.

Nate is flushed, and heavy lidded, his chest rising and falling as I begin to work him over. His grip is like a vice on my hair. "Fuck," he says, and then he actually laughs. "Jesus." As I watch, he forces himself to relax against the pillows. His hand unclenches, and he smooths it over my hair. "You're so beautiful. When you look up at me like that, I just want to come everywhere."

That sounds fun to me, too. So I suck harder.

He flexes his hips, fucking my mouth in slow strokes. I can feel him getting closer. I take his balls in my hand…

His grip finds my hair again. "Stop, sweetheart." He chuckles and then groans. "I don't want to shoot yet."

It's true that I like to be bossed around. But I also like fighting back. So I pop off his dick and sit up. Quickly, I straddle his thighs, take him in hand, and fill myself with him.

His moan is a bellow, and deep breaths saw in and out of his cut chest. I stare down at the wreck I've made of Nate, feeling pleased with myself. His chest and neck are flushed and his lips and cheeks are red. He's *gorgeous* and he's as turned on as a man can be.

I'm feeling pretty amazing, too. "Which slide is this?"

He shakes his head against the pillow. "Fuck it, Bec. I thought my fantasies were good, but you blow them all away." He puts a hot hand on my belly, his long fingers spread wide. "Tell me another palindrome."

"What?" I push my hips forward, eager to get on with it. He feels so good. I can't help myself.

"I need a minute to calm down." His thumb sweeps across my

hip in a place that should make me ticklish. But it doesn't because I'm so turned on. "Not a banana baton," I whisper.

Nate grins. "That's my girl." He rolls his hips to reward me.

I take it as an invitation. Putting my hands on his shoulders, I give a long slide back and then thrust forward again. He feels so, so good. And I am shameless. I pick up the pace, knowing my boobs will bounce with every movement.

And he loves it. Long hands slide all over my skin, stoking the flames. I won't be able to keep up the porn star routine much longer. I'm seconds away from melting like butter onto his beautiful body and forgetting my own name.

Nate braces his heels on the bed and meets me thrust for thrust. Then he grabs me by the back of the neck and yanks me down for a kiss, his tongue finding mine on a groan.

That's all she wrote. I'm shivering and moaning and breathless against his mouth.

And he *smiles*. His eyes light up like I've done something amazing. He rolls us both. I flop onto my back as Nate dives into my mouth for a kiss that's deep and dirty. "Should I get a condom?" he asks between kisses. He wore one last night without asking.

"No need," I slur happily. "Knock yourself out."

He groans and then laughs, his hips pumping against mine.

Sex with Nate is smiley. I wrap my arms around him and squeeze.

I think I could be in love with him. This is not an entirely welcome realization.

But now is not the time to panic. I hug Nate everywhere, with my arms and my knees and my body. His moan is long and low. His muscles lock and he shudders twice.

Then he chuckles into my neck. "God, Bec. There aren't words for how spoiled you make me feel."

I sift my fingers through his soft hair. I feel spoiled right now, too.

He props himself up on an elbow. "The no-condom thing is new."

"Hmm?"

"Before Florida I never did that before."

"Really?" I look into his eyes. They're so bright and happy. "Maybe that's why you like it so much."

He shakes his head. "No, that's why it doesn't last as long as I'd like it to. But *you're* the reason I like it so much."

Then he kisses me again.

21

NATE

THAT MORNING I'm as happy as a guy has ever been. I send Ramesh out for bagels and coffee.

"I'm not meeting him at the door," Becca grumbles. "I may never look him in the eye again."

"Suit yourself," I say, swatting her bare butt as she heads for my shower. "Ramesh is a smart man. He'll put the food on the entry table and get the hell out."

"When does Mrs. Gray show up?" she asks over the sound of the water.

"Nine. Why?"

She doesn't answer, but she gets ready to go before that.

At a quarter past eight, I kiss her goodbye. "When will I see you next?" I ask her.

"See me or see me *naked*," she asks with a smile.

"I meant the first thing, but the second thing sounds good, too."

"Tonight's game, maybe? But I won't be in the box. I'm watching with Georgia from Coach's comp seats."

"Okay." I kiss her jaw. "Dinner Tuesday night? I know you have to go to Detroit on Wednesday."

"Yeah." She smiles up at me. "Good plan."

"I'll make a reservation."

She opens the front door. "You mean you'll ask someone to make it for you."

"You never know. I can probably figure out how it works. For you, baby, I'll do it. Hey, Bingley?"

"Yes, my lord."

"How do you make a restaurant reservation?"

Becca leaves my house laughing.

———

The workweek gets off to a rocky start. Monday is a long slog through meetings in Manhattan. The main point of business is choosing a buyer for my router division. After the Canadian company made an offer, I also got one from Alex's cable company.

Weirdly, Alex hasn't called to talk to me about it herself. Everything is coming through her investment banking team. So that's odd.

And—as she predicted—I don't see Becca at the game that night. Not only do we lose game four, but I hate that she's avoiding me. I'm still Becca's dirty secret.

But Tuesday night she's all smiles. We eat sushi at a new place in Brooklyn Heights and then walk home again. I light a fire in the den, and Becca sets up the Scrabble board. But two turns in we jump each other.

Go slow, I remind myself as we make out on the sofa. But apparently that's just not possible. Ten minutes later I have all her clothes off and mine, too. I direct her to lean over an ottoman in front of the fireplace. I nudge her knees apart, and she moans.

Taking her hips in my hands, I push inside.

"Nathan," she gasps, her hands gripping the furniture.

I do her right there. And it's amazing. But it isn't slow.

———

Nothing else goes right, however.

The meetings come thick and fast. I'm tired of analyzing this transaction, but I can't just dump the work on others, because there are 126 Kattenberger Tech employees whose jobs are on the line. I owe it to them to make the right decision.

Alex is still talking to me only via vague text and through her investment banking team. So I can't even discuss it with her properly.

On Wednesday morning I get a call from Stew. "Hey, you got a second?"

"Sure. But aren't I meeting with you in fifteen minutes?"

He laughs. "Yeah, but not about this. This is a closed-door conversation."

"Uh-oh." I get up and close my office door. "What's the problem?"

"I got a call from this kid Mickey down in the AI research division."

"You did? Why?" Stewie is our CFO and doesn't usually muck around with research. Mickey is the one who's working on the Bingley product.

"He and I play squash on Thursdays. His backhand makes me feel like an old geezer. Anyway, he knows you and I are close, and he wanted my advice about something."

"Okay—what?"

Stew laughs again, and I'm starting to wonder what's so funny. "Well, think about it. He studies the audio files from your module at home. And suddenly they're full of…"

"Oh, fuck."

"Exactly." Stew busts a gut on the other end of the line.

For a smart guy, I can do some pretty stupid shit. I'd completely forgotten that other people heard my interactions with Bingley. He talks to me and Mrs. Gray and the kids down in AI listen to the interactions to figure out how well the module responds.

Rebecca would die of embarrassment if she heard about this. And probably castrate me, too.

"I hope you told him to delete those files?"

"Yup. And then I told him to set it up so that you need to okay each day's interactions. You're going to get an email every morning.

If you push a button in that email to send him the files, he'll hear them. If you delete the email, the files stay private."

"Okay," I sigh. "Thanks for handling it."

"You're welcome!" He snickers. "Notice I'm not judging you for their content."

"That's because you didn't hear them. I did some of my best work this week."

"Congratulations. Can I assume that the beneficiary of your efforts is a certain Bruisers employee? Or did you take your ambitions elsewhere?"

"No. It's her. No need to lecture me, though."

"Do you hear a lecture? However you two worked it out, I'm sure you made HR proud."

"They wouldn't be wildly excited about the whole thing. But it was her decision."

"Hey—I don't have any doubt." Stew clears his throat. "I hope this sticks, man. You deserve someone who can put up with your dorky ass."

"It's no dorkier than yours," I argue.

"A nut for a jar of tuna," he replies, and it actually takes me a second to realize it's a palindrome. "I'm happy for you. When's the wedding?"

I snort. "Baby steps. First I have to convince her that the world won't end if other people know we're together."

"Smart girl. The practical implications of dating you aren't really so great. Are you going to put a bodyguard on her?"

"Ugh. No. She'd hate that."

My best friend is quiet for a moment. "It'll come up someday."

"What are you, my mother?"

"Please. If I was I wouldn't have started the conversation congratulating you on your sex life."

"Are you coming down the hall to meet with the tax guys now, or what?"

"See you in ten."

———

And if work wasn't fun enough, my hockey team decided to really stink it up during games five and six. The Bruisers had led the series 3-0 going into the week. But after Monday's debacle, they lose a remarkable two more games in a row.

I can barely leave the stadium after Saturday night's game. The press conference is grim, and on my way out, every reporter in New York wants to shove a microphone in my face, asking me how I feel about my investment now.

No comment, fuckers. But I can't say that. Hell, there's a lot I can't say. The fact that Dallas has just won the Western Conference slot makes me feel insane.

I fucking hate that team. And my fragile male ego really *really* wanted a chance to match off against them. Really a lot.

But I can't say that, either. So I let Ramesh and two of his team members encircle me as we make our way out to the car.

It's midnight already. I'm grumpy and probably poor company. But I pull out my phone to text Rebecca anyway, because I have no self-control.

And I find that she's already beat me to it. ***Ack. Sorry about that shitshow of a game. Hugh looks like a bomb about to blow.***

I'll bet he does, I reply. ***Where are you?***

I see her start to answer me immediately. ***Packing for an early departure to Detroit.***

Shit. Of course she is. ***Sit with me in the box on Tuesday?***

A couple of minutes go by without an answer. Ramesh pulls into the garage and I tell him good night. Inside, Bingley greets me, but I give him the silent treatment. He tried to embarrass my girl.

Or, fuck, I guess it's me who's guilty. Bingley doesn't have a human brain.

But why do we have technology if we can't blame it when things go wrong?

Becca finally responds. ***I don't think I can sit there in a box seat beside you and pretend I'm not undressing you with my eyes. I'll watch the game with Georgia, as I usually do. And we'll catch up later.***

Ah, well.

No problem, I reply. *We can sit together during round four in Dallas.*

Awfully sure of yourself! :)

Stick with me, babe.

Tell you what, she comes back a minute later. *If our boys make it to the final round next week, I'll sit beside you during the deciding game.*

It's a date, I agree. *If we win the Cup, I'm going to have to kiss you.*

If we win the cup, I'm going to have to let you.

I walk upstairs grinning to myself.

[22]

REBECCA

ANOTHER DAY, another red carpet.

From the bus window, I watch the players file off the vehicle to applause. I'm sure it's less applause than the Detroit team received on their way into the stadium, since game seven will be held tonight on their home turf. But the hockey fans are out in force, since this game will decide who goes on to play for the Cup in round four. Regardless, there is a sizable crowd cheering as my boys strut into the stadium in their suits.

"Oh my," Heidi Jo sighs beside me. She says that a lot when the boys are wearing crisp shirts and ties.

"Ready, ladies?" Hugh pauses in the aisle of the bus.

"Absolutely," I tell my boss.

Always the gentleman, Hugh waits for Heidi Jo and me to exit the bus ahead of him. Unwilling to hold him up, I nudge Heidi Jo to her feet and then quickstep to the front of the bus. I thank the driver and then hop down.

Unfortunately, the asphalt is a little further away than I anticipate, and I turn my ankle for a split second before catching myself on the grab bar. A bolt of pain slices up my leg.

Shit.

Even so, I step to the side and smile.

"Oh, honey!" Heidi Jo says too loudly. "Are you okay?"

"Fine!" Nothing to see here.

Hugh gives me a small frown. But there are people watching so he gives the crowd a wave. "Working lunch with the boys in thirty, right?" he asks me.

"Right." My ankle throbs. "I'm going to call the caterer right now and make sure everything is a go. See you inside?"

He gives me a friendly salute and walks toward the doors, where the security staff sees him through.

I wait until the bus pulls away before putting any weight on my left foot. And then I take a tentative step. It's…sore. But not that bad. I think I'll live.

"Well?" Heidi Jo crosses her arms. "Is this because you're shaky today?"

"It'll be fine. And I'm *not* shaky." But I am. It's been a shaky day. Too much stress and too little sleep last night. I gave myself the worst hotel room—the one right near the elevator shafts—because the players need their Zs if they're going to win game seven. I haven't been to therapy in ten days, and I can feel my exhaustion affecting my balance. I feel squinty and tired. Not that I'll admit it to anyone.

And if that weren't enough trouble for one week, I also got my period yesterday. So I've spent the last forty-eight hours ducking into public bathrooms to pop ibuprofen and feed quarters into tampon machines.

I swear to God I heard O'Doul complaining about a hangnail on the bus just now. A professional athlete.

Standing here on the asphalt outside the arena, I dial the caterer. One thing you learn traveling the continent's hockey destinations is that if you need to talk to someone, don't call from the bowels of a stadium.

Heidi Jo waits patiently while I review our food order. My faithful shadow.

"Okay," I say, chucking my Katt phone into my bag. "They're en route, but hit traffic. They'll be ten minutes late. Let's go tell Jimbo so he can watch for them."

"Roger," she says, as we stroll toward the door, me limping slightly. Now that all the fuss is over, the entrance is guarded by a single person. Although he's the size of two people. His neck is thicker than my waist, I think.

I pull out my team ID and show it to him. Heidi Jo does the same.

The human refrigerator frowns. "Players only beyond this point," he says.

That's ridiculous, since our team credentials allow access anywhere. "If you'll step aside I'll show you that my card opens the door."

He steps aside. I wave my card past the scanner and… Nothing happens. Shit. It's been demagnetized in my bag. "Heidi Jo?"

She lifts her card but Mr. Refrigerator moves to block her. "Sorry, miss. Players only beyond this point."

"Please let her try her card? Or radio inside," I say coolly. "I'm the assistant to Hugh Major, the General Manager, and he's expecting us. I can show you my Bruisers ID…"

He holds up a hand. "Listen, girls. This might work for you sometimes, but not on my watch. I know it's fun to stalk the players, but…"

"Are you *kidding* me?" I sputter. "We're not…stalking the team. We *work* for the team. It's different!" I feel myself becoming a little unhinged. This shit happens frequently enough, but today I just can't take it.

"No girlfriends neither," the guy adds.

I'm about to leap on his giant body and choke him when Heidi Jo sort of nudges me gently aside with one of her slim little hips. "How 'bout I call the G.M. out here to vouch for us? He's *rully* busy but he's likely getting impatient without us so I'm sure he'd be willing to answer your questions." She smiles innocently up at the Neanderthal who's giving us trouble.

The giant man blinks. She's calling his bluff, and he's having a moment of doubt. Getting reamed by the G.M. of an NHL team probably isn't on his to-do list for today.

"Lemme see your ID again, miss?"

She hands it over quickly and Mr. Refrigerator squints at it.

If this works, I'm going to owe Heidi Jo. But it'll be worth it.

My ankle throbs while I wait to hear the verdict. He must be a really slow reader.

"Imma think about it a minute," he says slowly.

"You do that," I can't resist saying.

Heidi Jo makes a warning face and pulls me aside, to give the big man his space. "Easy," she whispers. "I've got this."

I take a deep breath in through my nose. "You're right," I say, even though it hurts me. "You're sugar-on-top routine is working better than my sass."

The compliment thrills her, and I get a big puppy-like smile. "I saw you do the same thing just last week. Learning from the master." She pulls out her phone in a showy display of urgency. She dials up her Southern accent, too. "I'm fixing to call in the big guns before an entire hockey team misses lunch. They'll be *rully* upset."

That's when a shiny limousine pulls up where the bus was a few minutes ago. We all turn to see the chauffeur step out of the driver's side, cross the car, and open the door for none other than Nate Kattenberger.

How many times have I seen Nate get out of a car? Hundreds? Thousands? This time my belly flips over. His sleek body unfolds, revealing his trademark hoodie, the sleeves tugged up to reveal strong forearms. He's wearing hipster jeans and black suede kicks with a retro sole.

I spent years trying not to notice how attractive he is. But now a switch has been flipped and I don't think I'll ever be able to unsee it.

He grabs a leather duffel out of the car and hoists it onto a shoulder. Then he struts over to us with a serious frown, looking like a runway model as the breeze tosses his hair.

Even Mr. Refrigerator looks a little turned on. Or maybe I'm just projecting.

"Miss Rowley," Nate purrs. He doesn't make eye contact but his voice lingers on my name in a way that makes me shiver. "Miss Pepper. What are we doing standing around the back entrance?" He gives Mr. Refrigerator a piercing look, and of course the guy sweeps the door open with his own security card and ushers all of us inside.

Of course he does.

"Don't you clobber the guy, Becca," my intern warns. "Just keep it movin.'"

Nate chuckles, and the sound vibrates inside my chest. It's almost enough to distract me from the lingering pain in my ankle. "Having a little trouble with security?"

"Just the usual sexist crap. *Mr. Kattenberger*," I add to be a pill.

"We were just about to outsmart 'im," Heidi Jo adds.

"I'm sure you were," he says. And then his gaze does a sweep of me from head to toe. It's entirely gratuitous. I'm half annoyed at his lack of subtlety, and half pleased by his interest.

Heidi Jo gives us a funny little smile. "I just remembered a little errand I have to run," she says. "If you'll both excuse me." Then she darts away, her heels clicking along the concrete hallway. Then she turns a corner and disappears.

Uh-oh. The morning after the previous incident—when she walked in on Nate and me standing way too close together—she'd asked me point-blank if Nate was my boyfriend. I'd denied it because he wasn't. But now he is. More or less...

This thought is interrupted by a certain billionaire who steps into my personal space, leans me against the wall, and kisses my neck.

Goosebumps rise up all over my body, and I instinctively turn my head to give him better access. "Mr. Kattenberger," I whisper. "This is hardly the time or place."

"I know," he mumbles between kisses. "That makes it extra fun." He palms my ass through my dress and it's difficult to argue the point. "Come to my suite tonight after the game." It's a demand, not a question, and my nipples firm up at the sound of his voice. *Whew.*

Taking his chin in both hands, I remove his lips from my quivering body and hold his questing mouth at a safe distance. He blinks at me from close range, those light brown eyes warm and happy. "Down, boy," I order.

Nate sticks out his tongue and pants like a puppy. "I'm two

seconds away from humping your leg. It's been three days since I saw you last, Miss Rowley."

"You mean *saw me naked*," I whisper.

He shakes his head, which isn't easy, since I'm still holding onto it. "You keep saying that. And I do enjoy your nakedness. But I miss you, and you won't text with me."

"That's because Heidi Jo takes my phone away from me whenever she thinks I've had too much screen time. Do you want her reading your dirty palindromes, or whatever it is you want to text me?"

He grins. "Dirty palindromes. I could work with that."

I hear footsteps in the adjacent hallway. Nate hears them, too, because we step away from each other. He pulls out his phone as Jimbo from operations walks into view. "Becca, the caterers are pulling up outside. Hold the door open for us?"

"Sure," I say brightly.

Nate tucks his phone away again. "Will you bring me those documents after the game?" Nate asks me.

I actually roll my eyes. *So subtle, Mr. Kattenberger.* But I'm not going to his room tonight. I don't want to get caught. And since it's shark week, I'd only end up disappointing him. "You'll probably have to wait until tomorrow for that paperwork," I insist. "Enjoy game night."

"I'll try," he says with a sigh. "Later."

The word is casual, but he gives me a hot look over his shoulder as he walks away.

I help Jimbo bring in the players' food on carts, since the caterer doesn't have security access. Most of the players won't eat much, because game time is only two hours away. But we've ordered light refreshments and every kind of beverage. We need our guys fed, happy, and ready to mow down Motown.

In Brooklyn I don't carry people's meals around. But on the road, there's no room for pulling rank. Even the General Manager of the team will carry hockey gear with the transport team if time is tight.

The camaraderie is one of the best things about my job. The

Bruisers are an awesome organization, and I never want to work anywhere else.

"Thanks for your help, Bec!" Jimbo says when we reach the little dungeon the home team has assigned for our players' lounge. "Come grab a sandwich?"

"I'm good," I say. "Gotta work out a couple of box office snafus." There's always some important person in a snit over tickets.

When the elevator doors open for me, I find Heidi Jo about to step out. "There you are!" she crows. "I brought you something."

"You did?" She beckons me into the elevator, and I push the button for the street level.

"Here." She pulls a CVS bag out of her giant purse. There are three things inside: a small box of tampons, which I'd mentioned needing. A stretchy ankle brace and a pair of black tights. "I thought the brace wouldn't show if you had on dark stockings."

I look down at my outfit—a black dress with a waistband in Bruisers purple—and see that it would totally work. "*Thank* you." *Damn it, Heidi Jo!* I'm starting to actually like her.

"It's no big deal. How is Mr. Kattenberger today?"

"Fine, I guess. Can't imagine what it feels like watching many millions of your dollars on the line as you try to make it into the final round."

"I'll bet it's not about the money," my intern muses. "He just wants to win."

"Hmm." The elevator rises slowly while I think that over. I think about money all the time, because I never have quite enough of it. Nate has more money than all but a handful of men in the world. But I've always assumed he thinks a lot about it, too. That's how he got so much in the first place.

Not caring about money. Is that even possible? I wouldn't know where to start.

———

That night I forget about money and everything else for ninety draining minutes while our boys do what needs doing—they win game seven fair and square. Scoring two goals late in the first period, they go on to dominate the whole game.

As the final buzzer rings, I am shamelessly hugging Heidi Jo and squealing.

The scoreboard glows with *Detroit: 1, Brooklyn, 3*. And my boys are going to the finals for the first time in years!

We run up to the box, where everything is mayhem. Nate is surrounded by well-wishers. Heidi Jo hands me a half glass of champagne, and I drink it with a grin on my face.

The Cup! My boys could win the whole thing! I loved them even when we didn't make the playoffs these last two years. But this is so exciting!

It takes me a couple of minutes of champagne slurping and back-patting to realize that I'm still at work. I get out my phone, jam a finger in my ear, and call the hotel. We're going to need a private meeting room and some food and drinks for an impromptu celebration.

The hotel is happy to oblige, because they know we won't balk when they add twenty-five percent to their already usurious prices for "rush service."

"C'mon, rookie," I say to Heidi Jo. "We have a party to throw. Find us an Uber back to the hotel, and step on it."

She delivers. My intern is actually quite competent. When I'm in a good mood, I can admit it.

But nobody throws an impromptu party like I can. It's my super power. We don't plan these things ahead of time because athletes are superstitious.

Nevertheless, I use the next ninety minutes to negotiate the price of beer and wine and order finger foods for eighty people. Ergo, I am standing amidst a spread of foods, drinks, and players' families when the bus returns triumphantly from the stadium. When the first players enter the room, Heidi Jo lets out a whoop of joy a little too close to my ear. But it's hard to blame her perky little ass, because we are all feeling the love tonight.

"We're going to Dallas!" someone shouts, and the room erupts in more joy.

I start handing out champagne flutes, and because this is the specialist of special occasions, I take one for myself.

"Should you be drinking that?" Heidi Jo asks immediately.

"Should you be nagging me?" I reply.

"I guess not. Cheers, then," she says, and we toast.

From all the way across the room, I feel Nate's eyes on me. When I turn around, I find his smile immediately. I raise my glass to him, and he does the same.

I work the room, congratulating my friends as they get deeper and deeper into their cups. There will be hangovers tomorrow, but coach won't complain, because they were amazing tonight.

"Good hustle, Castro," I say to my buddy.

In reply, he picks me up and spins me around.

I give a little shriek of surprise, but he completes several rotations before setting me on my feet. "Hey! Watch the champagne flute," I complain. I'm clutching his arm with my free hand.

"I'm just doin' you a favor," he teases. "Don't you have to spin around a lot at those therapy sessions you're going into debt for?"

Still holding onto the hockey player, I count the seconds until the dizziness passes. Ugh, it's not a good number, either. Maybe because I'm tired. And I've had at least two glasses of bubbly.

Or—and I hate this idea—maybe I'm backsliding because I haven't been to therapy. Not that I'm going back. I've already put three thousand dollars worth of therapy sessions on my credit card. I can't possibly add more. The playoffs have given me a terrific excuse to cancel sessions, too.

Castro wraps an arm around me and gives me a squeeze. He's chatting up Silas, the backup goalie, who did an ace job minding the net during the first period tonight. It was one of those rare games when everything went right. Tomorrow all our faces will hurt from smiling so hard.

That's when I feel eyes on me again. I glance up, and Nate is frowning at me from only a few feet away. He's in the midst of a conversation, too. Hugh Major is talking to him with animated hands.

But Nate's attention is on me instead. He looks grumpy, which is weird, because tonight went exactly the way he'd hoped.

I glance down at Castro's arm, the one slung casually around me. He's an affectionate guy, and we're friends. He hugs the other players, too. It's not sexual.

It's just dawning on me that Nate doesn't see it that way. His eyes are narrowed. He's ignoring his G.M. to stare lasers at Castro's hand on my arm.

Nate is *jealous*.

Mind blown.

Steadier on my feet now, I step out of Castro's grasp. "You boys need anything? I'm going for a refill."

"Nope, I'm good," Castro says. He actually pats my head. Since he's a foot taller than I am, it's not as weird as it sounds.

I make my way toward the food table and nab a bite-sized quiche. I don't even want to know what the hotel is charging us for these. I pop it into my mouth and take another one. Wasting them won't help matters.

After getting a soda from the bartender, I turn around and find Nate again. His gaze locks on mine, and it's hungry.

I shouldn't stare, but it's hard to look away. I've known him for seven years. And now I've touched him everywhere. Hell, I've *tasted* him everywhere. But even so, we are like a math problem I can't quite grasp. Nate plus Rebecca. He wants me, but I still don't know why. When he looks across this room full of partygoers, what does he see?

Because I see a tired office manager whose ankle brace is biting into her foot. She's a little too short, a little clumsy from a knock on the head, and her tummy is bloated from mini quiches and period cramps.

Maybe it's time for bed.

I give Nate a tiny smile. Then Hugh taps him on the arm to regain his attention, and Nate looks away from me.

So I take that as my cue to go upstairs to bed.

[23]

NATE & REBECCA

NATE: I hope you're sleeping but I just wanted to say that I miss you. I was going to say it as a palindrome but I struck out. I would also like a palindrome for: why are you not in my suite right now?

Becca: Hi, sailor. Was just dozing off when my phone lit up. I don't know a goodnight palindrome, either. But are there sexy ones? I mean besides NOT A BANANA BATON.

Nate: NAOMI, DID I MOAN?

Becca: Good one. Did you have to Google it?

Nate: Let's pretend you didn't just ask me that. Please.

Becca: I feel no guilt at Googling them. Found STRAP ON NO PARTS. But it's only sexual if you have a really dirty mind, like me.

Nate: Don't ever change. Love your dirty mind.

Becca: Also questionable: SIT ON A POTATO PEN, OTIS.

Nate: Poor Otis. How about, EGAD, NO BONDAGE?

Becca: Too prudish. I prefer: NO, TIE IT ON.

Nate: Touché.

Becca: Thank you.

Nate: Horny now.

Becca: Sorry. I know wordplay gets you hot.

Nate: Rawr. It does. But so do you. Where are you? I could sneak into your hotel room. Some day I don't want to sneak.

Becca: …

Nate: Hey. Don't freak. I'm not complaining.

Becca: I'm not freaking. I'm thinking. Remember that most people think more slowly than you. My brain needs time to figure things out, like the rest of us mortals.

Nate: I love your brain. And also your boobs.

Becca: It's good to diversify. I love your brain. And also your tongue.

Nate: Unngh. Come upstairs. DENNIS AND EDNA SINNED. There's your sexy palindrome.

Becca: I'm not upstairs with you because I'm not on the roster right now. I'm on the injured reserve list right now.

Nate: What? You're injured? What happened? I thought you were limping earlier.

Becca: No! I was using a sports metaphor. I'm fine.

Nate: Then…? Metaphor? What?

———

NATE

My phone rings in my hand. "Hello?"

"Hi."

Just that one word in Rebecca's breathy voice gets me hard. I'm such a goner for her. "Hi yourself. Now tell me what's the problem?"

"Nothing is wrong. It's just…I have my period. Sex is off the table, that's all."

"Oh." Everything makes more sense now.

"Thank you for being dense once in a while. It makes you more normal."

"Normal is really overrated," I grumble.

"I suppose. Congratulations, Nate. I know you're pumped up about this chance to smash Dallas."

"Thanks. But you know I always feel like a heel when people congratulate me." I shift in the bed, wishing we were having this conversation in person.

"Why?"

"I didn't score any of those goals tonight. And I'm not the coach. I'm just the wallet behind it."

Becca is silent for a second. "I know what you mean. But you built the team that made it happen. You and Hugh. And you did it for Brooklyn. The bars must be pretty packed tonight. The bartenders probably appreciate it most, now that I think about it."

"Hmm." It's a generous viewpoint. But she's right on a couple of counts. I wanted Brooklyn to have a hockey team, and our team gives back a lot to Brooklyn charities.

"Nate?"

"Yes, Bec?"

"Did it piss you off when I was talking to Castro?"

Oh. "You never piss me off. I don't like to see his hands on you, though. If that makes me a caveman, I'm sorry. He has a thing for you."

"We're just friends."

"I know. But he'd take that shot if he could."

"He propositioned me once."

This gets my full attention. "Really?"

"Yeah. Just once. I told him I could never date a player, and that was the end of it."

"Were you tempted?" The words leave my mouth before I can stop them. "Never mind. I retract the question."

"Not much," she answers anyway. "I mean—Castro is a cutie, and he's genuinely nice. But it just wasn't worth exploring. I can either be the office manager that players listen to, or the office manager that seems like she's only there to ogle the players. Women don't get the benefit of the doubt."

This shuts me up, because it makes more sense than I care to admit. "Bec?"

"Yeah?"

"It's funny how I really couldn't understand until just this minute. When you used Castro as an example instead of me."

"Ah." I can feel her smile even though I can't see it.

"I get it now. I understand why you're reluctant."

"It's worse, you know. Doing the boss. The optics stink."

"Except the team already trusts you." Becca is loved by everyone, and respected, too.

"Sure, but we have new people all the time. To them I'm gossip at best or a spy. 'Watch what you say to her, she's sleeping with the owner.'"

I make an unhappy noise. "But you're doing it anyway. Why?"

"No idea," she says immediately. "Maybe because you're irresistible."

"You flatter me," I say. But I don't know if she hears it, because my phone dies. There's a beep and then the screen goes black.

Shit.

I jump up and plug it in. But fuck it. Becca thinks I just hung up on her, so that won't do. I throw on some sweats, shove my feet in my shoes and grab my key card. Then I head for the elevator.

Becca's room number is 805. I saw it on the travel manifest when the travel coordinator was looking up mine. I'm tiptoeing down the eighth floor corridor when the door opens and she steps out, wearing sweats and carrying her key card.

I wave. Her eyes widen and then she grins.

Reversing course, Becca goes back into her room. I follow, close the door behind me, and then guide her back toward the bed, where I fall on top of her and kiss her.

"Did your phone die?" she asks against my lips.

"Yes." I kiss her nose. "But I wasn't done talking to you."

"You're going to ruin my reputation." She says this, but she's grabbing my ass with both hands.

"First of all, I'll leave at hung-over-o'clock. No player is getting up before seven. Secondly, I have a ready excuse if someone sees me leaving your room." I kiss her jaw. She tastes like candy. I don't want to stop.

"What's that?"

"What's what?"

"This terrific excuse for why you're leaving my room in the morning."

"I just had to see the playoffs budget in sweatpants with sex hair."

She buries her face in my neck and laughs. "You won't have sex hair, remember?"

I climb further on the bed. "Snuggle hair. Bedhead. Whatever. Get under the covers." I sit up and remove my shirt.

She does the same thing, and I'm treated to another one of Becca's silky teddies. This one is red with a deep V in the front, showing off her cleavage.

Annnnd I'm hard. "You have the best underwear."

Removing her sweatpants, she takes the elastic of her panties between two fingers and snaps it onto her own hip. "Cotton panties during shark week, though. You left your palatial suite for nothing."

"That is *not* true." I pull back the comforter and kick off my sweatpants. I get into the bed, but there's a problem. "I'm on the wrong side."

"You have a side?"

"Left-handed guy on the left." I push her back against the pillows and climb over her body, which makes her giggle. Then I shut out the light on my side and lie down, my arms open. "Come here."

She turns off the other lamp and then tucks her body against mine, allowing me to fold her into my arms.

"That's better," I whisper. "This is what I came for."

"Okay." Rebecca snuggles closer and sighs.

"You don't trust me yet," I whisper. Then I kiss her on the temple. "But you will."

"I trust you," she argues.

"You trust me not to be a dick. You trust me *with* my dick." She smiles. "But you don't think you could love me."

She goes still in my arms. "I didn't say that. I *never* said that."

I wouldn't blame her if she did. I'm not an easy man. But my gut tells me our problems are different than the ones I had with Juliet. "Maybe you think I couldn't love you. Is that it?"

"Maybe," she whispers.

"Why?"

"Because we are so different." She's speaking so quietly I almost can't hear.

"I don't like shopping at Bloomingdale's. But otherwise we like a lot of the same things. Alien movies. Street food. Let's not forget hockey."

"Nate," she says quietly. "Don't be dense. You're a genius and an Ivy League grad. And the head of a Fortune 500 company. I'm not."

"There is nothing stupid about you, though. Not one thing. And leaving school wasn't your fault."

She doesn't say a word, which doesn't say much for my debating skills.

"Look, Bec. I don't have a PowerPoint to explain why I need you. I just do. I have for a while now, but apparently I'm not the sharpest scalpel on the tray after all, because it took me too long to say so. But here I am in your bed. I came downstairs because I like your smile and I wanted to see it before I went to sleep. And I'd like to do that as often as I can, if you'll let me..."

This rambling sermon is cut off when Becca pushes up on an elbow and kisses me. And it's a good one. Soft lips come down over mine, and she sighs sweetly as she fits our mouths more firmly together.

Parting my lips beneath hers, I invite her in. She accepts, kissing me very, *very* thoroughly. My Becca might be conflicted, but she's not indifferent. I run my hands down her silky nighty, wishing I could peel it off of her. Her curves beckon, and it's difficult to behave myself. The struggle is real.

By the time she lifts her face from mine, we're both breathing hard. "You scare me," she whispers in the dark. "And I'm not used to being scared."

Oh.

I trace the top of her nightie with a fingertip, crossing the swells of her breasts. "I'm not scary. I'm not even very complicated. But I can be patient until you figure that out." Actually, we both know that patience isn't my strong suit. But I can try. I want to.

She kisses me on the ear. "Now I got you all worked up." Her hand slides down on to my fly, where my very hard cock is tenting my boxers. "What are we going to do about that?"

"Not a thing." I push her hand away. "I'm used to being worked up over you. I was for years. Thought it was a permanent condition."

"Oh, Nate," she laughs. "That can't really be true."

"Sure it is." I can't stop touching her, so I palm the curve between her hip and her ribs. "I mean, I didn't allow myself to lie around fantasizing about you. But whenever we were in the same room I'd get distracted. These days? I'm all about the fantasies. In my dreams we've had sex in every civilized country. And much of the developing world."

Rebecca snorts. "Really? What's your favorite fantasy?"

"Mmm." I shift my hips on the bed. I'm so hungry for her, and this will only make it worse. But that's okay with me. "We're on a private beach somewhere, playing in the water. And we start fooling around. And then we just can't wait. I have to carry you out of the waves, shove down your tiny bikini, put you on your hands and knees and just fuck you right there on the wet sand."

"That *does* sound nice." She strokes my abs, and I have to bite my lip to keep from begging. "Is there really such thing as a truly private beach? Or is this an exhibition fantasy, too?"

"No way." I remove her hand from my body because it's torturing me, and kiss the palm. "It's private because…" Just forming the sentence helps me articulate something that's eluded me before. "…That's what you do for me. My life is constant noise. Meetings and obligations and two thousand employees. It's great, but it's loud. When you kiss me, everything goes quiet. That's the only time I can forget everyone else." I roll to the side and put my lips right beside her ear. "And when I'm inside you, we're all that matters. I crave it so much."

She turns her face toward mine, and we're nose to nose. "I love that," she whispers. "I didn't know I could do that for you."

More kissing happens. I'm harder than rebar. This time when Rebecca sticks her hand down my boxers, I don't push it away. She gives me a slow stroke and I groan into her mouth.

"Bec," I pant as she works over my cock with a smooth hand. "What's your fantasy?"

Her lips go still against my mouth. "It's simpler than yours. You just push me face down on the bed. I try to talk to you, but you don't listen. You just hold me down and go to town."

"That's not..." It's hard to form a sentence while Becca plays with my balls. "...Very polite of me," I manage to get out.

"I know." She sucks on my earlobe and then runs her thumb over my cockhead. I'm dripping for her. "But some fantasies make more sense in your head than in real life."

She has a point. Beach sex usually results in sand in someone's asscrack.

That's my last rational thought as she strokes me. God, I need to come. I pull Becca onto my body so that she's straddling me, my dick between her legs. She leans down to kiss me, and I take her ass in both hands, encouraging her to grind on me.

"Oh," she moans into my mouth.

"Can you come like this?" I pant.

"I don't know."

"Let's find out." We kiss and grind like teenagers. I need it to end, but I never want it to end. Silence cocoons us. There is only the sound of our breath and the thudding of my heart.

"Jesus," Becca complains. Then she sits up, straddling my thighs, and puts her hand inside her panties, her fingers working, her breasts straining the red satin as she takes a deep breath.

Hello brand new fantasy.

Becca gasps and shudders, and I yank my dick out of boxers and come all over my chest.

24

NATE

AFTER WE GET BACK to New York there are two consecutive nights when I have to delete Bingley's audio recordings instead of sending them to the team. Life is very good. When I'm not thinking about Rebecca, I'm picturing my boys beating up on Dallas.

I like this picture a lot.

Stay in my hotel suite in Dallas, I text Becca the morning she's scheduled to depart with the team. *There's a Jacuzzi tub in it*.

Nope, she replies. *This is a work trip. No canoodling*.

Ah, well. A man can try. Just to stir the pot, I call the hotel myself and ask them to swap Rebecca's ordinary room for my hotel suite. Even if she won't canoodle, I want her to enjoy the suite. It's already booked, and she'll be there for three nights while it looks like I'll be flying out on the Gulfstream for games only, then flying home again.

I still haven't signed off on the sale of the router division. I'm leaning toward selling the division to Alex's company, even though Alex herself still hasn't shown up to talk to me about it in person.

"Dude," Stewart says, ducking into my office on Wednesday morning. "You *never* take this long to make a decision. I could start a new router company and sell it off in the time it's taking you to figure this out."

He's right. I'm not the kind of guy who spends a lot of time deliberating. But this is the first time I've sold off part of the company. "There are over a hundred jobs on the line," I remind him. "Real people with families."

"That's an honorable reason to take your time." Stew grabs a desk ornament off my desk and toys with it. "But unless you've taught Bingley to read the future, there's no way to know what the other company will ultimately do with it once it's theirs."

He's right. Businesses are bought and sold all the time. "I'm a control freak."

"You're just figuring that out now?"

"Don't you have some ledgers to go over or something?"

My best friend throws himself down on the leather sofa against the wall. "Wait, is this a safe place to sit? Now that you're getting some action again, should I worry what happens on this couch?"

I flip him off. What are we, sixteen? Although there was some pretty dodgy furniture in our first office. The mess was from Chinese food and pizza, though, not bodily fluids.

"Dallas, huh? Can I tag along to game one?"

"Sure, why not."

"I'm surprised you're not off with the team somewhere, watching game tape. 'This is the guy you want to hit. Squash him like a bug.'"

"Stew…"

I'm about to evict him from my office when Lauren sticks her head through the doorway. "Nate—there's a doctor on your line. Armitage. Does that sound familiar? He says you'll know what it's about."

"Ah. I'll pick him up." I point at Stew. "Go. Get out of here. I have to let the doctor shake me down for another contribution for brain injury research."

"Sounds stimulating. Later."

When the door closes on Stew, I greet my caller. "Hello, doctor! How are things going?"

"I was hoping you could tell me," he says. "We haven't seen

231

Rebecca in nearly two weeks. Has her number changed? I'd like to get a hold of her to see if she can come back to therapy, and also have a follow-up visit for testing."

"Back to therapy," I say slowly. "She hasn't been in?"

There's a silence. "Sorry. I assumed you knew that. I wouldn't have asked…"

"No, it's fine," I say quickly. "She's traveling in Dallas right now."

"Right! Congratulations, by the way. Big news."

"The whole organization is thrilled," I hear myself say. But inside I'm boiling. Rebecca wasn't supposed to stop going to therapy. She has an intern to cover her when she can't be with the team.

I manage to politely disengage with the doctor, promising to pass on his message. Then I hang up the phone. "What the hell are you thinking?" I ask my empty office.

What I don't do, however, is call Rebecca. I'm too irritated. And even though I've been told I'm shitty at relationships, "don't yell" is a rule that even I understand.

So I go over to the treadmill desk in the corner of the room and start walking. The computer screens sense my presence and light up automatically, showing me the same work I have open on the desk.

But I'm not interested in work right now. I just need to burn off some energy so I don't chew out my girl when I speak to her next. But — seriously. Blowing off her therapy? After all she went through to figure out a diagnosis?

I program the treadmill for climbing at intervals and I skim the news headlines. They don't help my mood, since it's the usual shitshow. North Korea fired a missile. A polar bear starved to death in the wild. They're predicting another drought in California. Healthcare costs rise twenty-seven percent.

Healthcare costs. That one sticks in my brain as the treadmill gives me another fake hill to climb. I lean into it and breathe from my diaphragm while the idea percolates.

"Hey, Bingley?" I call out toward my phone.

"Hullo, Nate! What can I do you for?"

"Bingley, have you been talking to Stew? Is that his joke?"

"Yessir. Do you like it?"

"I happen to think it's funny, but it's inappropriate. 'Do you' is an idiomatic expression for sex."

"Oh, dear. Thank you for letting me know."

"Could you connect me with Dr. Armitage's office?"

"Right away, sir." It's about ninety seconds later when he announces, "The doctor's receptionist is on your line, sir."

I pick up the treadmill extension. "Hi there. This is Nate Kattenberger..."

"Your assistant is very polite," she gushes. "What a cute accent."

"He's the greatest. Could you help me with something? I haven't gotten a bill yet for Ms. Rebecca Rowley's office visits. Maybe the insurer is processing them?"

"Oh, Rebecca! Let me see..." I hear rapid typing. "Those therapy sessions and the doctor visits are out of network. They were applied to a Visa card."

Rebecca's credit card. "What are the total charges to date?"

"Three thousand four hundred dollars."

Shit. I think I know why Rebecca hasn't been to therapy.

"All right, then there's been some confusion. Could I possibly give you a different card, instead?"

"Sure, Mr. Kattenberger."

I pull my wallet out of my back pocket without breaking my treadmill stride, and I read off the digits.

25

REBECCA

JUNE 3, DALLAS

NATE ALWAYS SAYS he hates Dallas, but the airport got our equipment loaded onto the busses in record time. The stadium has a decent setup for visitors, and the hotel is only a few blocks away.

I'm easy to please.

While the boys have their morning skate, Heidi Jo and I walk from the stadium to the Ritz. "This is *rully* pretty," Heidi Jo gushes in the lobby. It's old school, with walnut columns and a marble floor. "I know we're just here to win, but the travel team did us a solid here."

It's true, too. The smiley woman behind the desk has a printed room manifest all ready for us, and dozens of key cards laid out on a tray. I could get used to this.

"Look!" Heidi Jo says, pointing at my name on the list. "Luxury suite, penthouse level."

"That must be a mistake." I blink, but my name is still beside that suite. *Nate's* suite. Except I told him I was going to stay in my own room. "Excuse me," I say to the helpful woman. "I'm supposed to have a regular room."

"No, that was by special request." She smiles again. They must feed the employees happy pills here.

"Is there a regular room available?"

Her smile fades. "I'm sorry, but the playoffs have the whole hotel booked solid."

Fuck. Of course it's booked.

"Here you go, then!" Heidi Jo gives me a smug smile as well as the key card. Nate should have *known* his little trick wouldn't be private.

I'm pissed off, but also a little hurt. He'd told me—that night when we were talking about why I said no to Castro—that he understood the pressure I was under. I thought he *listened*. And then I said I didn't want to stay with him in his suite, and he put me there anyway.

Who does that?

"Ooh! They offer a margarita salt scrub in the spa!" Heidi Jo coos. "Let's see if there are two massage appointments during lunch."

"You go ahead," I grumble. I can't afford a massage. I think I'll just sit in the suite on the sofa and sulk.

Unless there's really a Jacuzzi bathtub, like Nate said. Then I'll sulk there, because otherwise it's a waste. But I'll do my bathing alone, damn it. And when Nate shows up tomorrow I'm going to bunk with Heidi Jo. That will wipe the smile off her face.

My intern goes off to explore the hotel, with instructions to check on the players' lunchroom in advance of their arrival. I leave this in her hands, because she's surprisingly competent under that bubbly exterior.

I get in the elevator and discover that I have to insert my key card even to choose the penthouse floor. So I do it, and the car glides smoothly to the top of the building.

The suite is gorgeous. There's a dining table and a living room area. The bed is enormous and piled with pillows. I picture Nate and me rolling around in it, and just for a second it's hard to hang onto my snit. Because I want that.

But only with a man who will listen.

My phone vibrates with a notification. So I pull it out and look at the lock screen. It isn't a text, but rather one of those push notifications for a credit card charge. I almost shove the phone back in my bag, except I haven't used my credit card today. So I peek at the amount of the charge, and it almost stops my heart. $3,400. That can't be right. I tap on the notification.

It *is* right. But it's not a charge, it's a credit. From Dr. Armitage's office.

For one shining minute I feel elated. But the joy lasts just sixty seconds, because when I whip out my laptop to check my insurance claim, it still reads *denied*.

That's when my head really explodes. Because there's no way my windfall is a clerical error. And there's only one person who could be responsible for it.

I tap Nate's cell phone number. He answers almost immediately. "Hey! How's Dallas? Did you make it up to the suite yet?" He's all cheer and sunshine.

I'm not.

"Where to begin? Okay, fine. The suite. I said no, and yet here I am anyway. That's strike one, especially because Heidi Jo spotted the room change first. So thanks for that. Let's just hope she's not a gossip. But are you fucking kidding me with the thirty-four hundred smackers on my credit card?"

It takes him a minute to reply. "You can go back to therapy now, Bec. This is me trying not to get upset that you aren't following doctor's orders."

"*You're* upset."

He chuckles. "I plead the fifth on that. Can't imagine why you wouldn't take care of your *brain,* for fuck's sake."

"I do take care!"

"Not according to the good doctor, who only called me because he was worried about you."

"Now you listen here. There are therapeutic exercises that don't cost almost three hundo a session! I've got Pilates at twenty-five bucks a class, and the take-home exercises they gave me. I'm not an idiot, but thanks for making it clear that you think I am."

"I didn't say that. Don't exaggerate."

"Don't treat me like a child!" I'm really on a roll now. "If you had a concern, you could've told me. If you wanted to help me afford the platinum-priced therapy, you could have *asked*. You say you care about me, but then you pull this bullshit. You care, as long as everything goes your way."

"Rebecca…"

"Save it, okay? I have a job to do here. We've been over this. Your suite will be empty when you arrive in Dallas. Stay in your own lane until after the playoffs."

Then, for the first time in seven years, I hang up on Nate Kattenberger.

———

The next night I'm stretched across the king-sized bed in Georgia's hotel room. I'm upset for a plethora of reasons.

Georgia isn't faring much better. She's flipping angrily through a wedding magazine that I've forced into her hands. Her wedding is next month. Everything is planned already, except we still don't have any table favors.

"How about chocolates shaped like a taxi cab?" I ask. "I think we should run with the Brooklyn theme."

"But the wedding is in Long Island," she says. Her voice is husky from too much cheering during tonight's game.

"Brooklyn brought you together!" I protest. "Fine, hockey can be the theme. Or hockey and tennis! Both your sports. We could alternate. I thought those personalized chocolate bars were cute."

In a rare display of temper, Georgia closes the magazine and actually hurls it across the room, where it lands with a splat on the desk chair. "Becca, stop it. Nobody cares about chocolate with my name on it."

"Fine. Little bottles of wine with your names…"

"Stop!" She rolls her eyes. "I don't care about favors. You are awesome, which is why I have a dress and flowers and a caterer but we are *done*, okay?"

"Deep breaths. It was only game one. We can rebuild it."

Our boys just lost to Dallas. Georgia screamed her heart out every time Brooklyn had the puck. I'm surprised she can still speak. But it wasn't enough. Our boys didn't play well, and Dallas took the first game. We're both feeling miserable.

Georgia gets up from the bed. She goes into the bathroom for her toothbrush, which she puts in her purse. "Look. I'm going to sneak into Leo's room and see how he's doing. You are welcome to stay here. You are also welcome to tell me what the hell is going on with you. For twenty-four hours you've been hounding me about wedding favors and I want to know why."

"Because the wedding is…"

She holds up a hand to cut me off, and her gaze is fierce. "Bec, cut the crap. Something happened and you haven't told me what. But I have theories."

Oh boy. "Like what?"

"Something went wrong with Nate. And it's probably not all his fault, or you would have told me already."

Well, ouch. I always knew Georgia was a smart girl. "I'm mad at him. But I'm also confused."

Her expression softens. "Tell me why."

So I do. I tell her the whole sorry tale, about the hotel room and the medical bills. "I thought he listened. And then he just ignored what I'd said." I wave the hotel manifest around like a crazy person.

Georgia takes it out of my hand and scans it. "He puts Lauren in a suite sometimes when they travel."

"Not in *his* suite."

"Why is Nate's name on a different room, then?" She points at the second column of names.

"What?" I snatch it out of her hand and read, *Nathan Katten-berger: room 512*. "But…" This makes no sense. "He asked me to stay in his suite *with* him."

"And you said no." Georgia's voice is gentle—the way you address a crazy person. "So he switched them to give you the suite."

"Oh, fuck," I whisper. "I yelled."

"Everyone yells sometimes. And he really should have asked before paying your doctor's bills. Even if he did it because he loves you and cares what happens to your big stupid head."

With a groan I collapse on the comforter. "It is! Big and so stupid. But I don't think I can make it smarter."

Georgia sits down beside me and pats my hand. "I think you're just stressed out. In your defense, nothing about these last two months has been normal. You were injured and scared. Work has been really stressful. Your sister and her boy toy have taken over your apartment. That's some big stuff happening."

"Nate confuses me. We're not equals and we can never be equals and so I freak out every time I feel cornered."

"Equals," Georgia says slowly. "I don't know if I agree."

"Oh, please. Don't flatter me."

"What makes me and Leo equals, though? What makes anyone?"

I lift my head and squint at her. "Neither you nor Leo runs the world."

"Well, it's true that I couldn't buy and sell a small country before breakfast tomorrow," Georgia admits. "But maybe that doesn't matter in Nate's head at all. Maybe he's just a guy, standing in front of a girl, asking her to climb into a Jacuzzi tub with him."

"Maybe," I admit to the comforter.

"It's not like you to be intimidated by Nate. When you met him, were you intimidated?"

"No," I snort.

"Then why now?"

Because now he can crush my heart. I take a deep breath and let it out. "Maybe it's not Nate that's intimidating me. Maybe it's taking a risk on a man. I don't usually do that."

Georgia slaps me on the ass. "The truth is revealed! You are getting smarter. Look at that."

"Shut up or I'll choose tacky wedding favors for you."

"Like I'd notice." She gets up again. "Bye for now. I'm going to strip Leo naked and see if I can't cheer him up."

"I love you!" I call as she heads for the door.

"Back at you, babe."

When she's gone, the room is too quiet. I lay there for a while feeling stupid. I miss Nate. He had box seats tonight and I avoided the box. I wonder what he was thinking about during intermission, and whether he looked for me. There would have been a dozen people hovering, the glitterati of Dallas all turning up to shake his hand.

It's weird to be Nate. He didn't ask to be important. I know this because I watched the whole thing go down. He invented some things the world needed, and it just happened. Our office stopped being a pizza-stained Ping-Pong refuge and became a global destination.

Maybe Georgia is right that recent events have ruined my mojo. But it's really hard for me to picture a future where I'm at Nate's side as he shakes the world's hand. And that's the thing I can't get past—this idea that I'm just temporary fun, and that he'll wake up one morning and decide it's time to plan his future in real terms.

And I won't be in it.

Even so, I owe him an apology. I pick up the house phone and dial room 512. It rings and rings. So I pull out my phone and text Heidi Jo. *Did you happen to see Nate after the game? Any idea where he might be?* Maybe I'm feeding her gossip right now but I can't help it.

New York, she replies immediately. *He flew home after the game. I put him in a car to the airport.*

Ah, well. Now there are several empty hotel rooms.

Do you need anything? Heidi Jo asks.

As always, I'm tempted to say no. But the truth is that she's been really helpful lately, and I haven't held up my end of the bargain. *If you wouldn't mind, please help me remember to make a therapy appointment tomorrow. I need to get back in there*.

Good idea!!! She replies instantly. Three exclamation points. But they make me smile instead of annoying me. The girl is really growing on me. If I weren't such a raging lunatic these days I might have appreciated her sooner.

Get some rest, I say. *Good work today.*

She replies with three different styles of heart emoji. Of course she does.

26

REBECCA

JUNE 5, DALLAS

WE WIN GAME TWO, but Nate is not in attendance at all. After the game, Leo Trevi buys me a glass of wine, which I drink quickly. Having no tolerance for alcohol anymore, it gets me drunk. So I proceed up to my big empty hotel suite with the lonely Jacuzzi tub and I drunk-dial Nate.

I get his voicemail, which should have bailed me out of this bad idea. But no. I leave a message.

Hi. I'm alone in this beautiful hotel room but I yelled at you and you're not here at all and I know you hate Dallas but we won tonight in overtime even though the team looked a little skittish. They miss Beringer. Fucking injuries. What was I saying? Oh I'm sorry, okay? I'm sorry I can't read a hotel manifest and that I didn't notice you'd switched our rooms, which means you did *listen to me when I thought you didn't. I'm still mad about the doctor's bills because you should have asked first. But I don't know what that proves because you'll always be the guy with the money and I'll still be the girl who didn't finish school. And I obviously can't get over that. Or maybe I can, but the playoffs are going on and I need to go back to therapy and take a damned deep breath. So I hope you'll let me do that.*

Or something like that.

Maybe it wasn't *quite* that bad.

241

No, it probably was. My apology was in there somewhere, buried under piles of angst and indecision. If I haven't already convinced Nate that I'm really just too much trouble, that phone call probably seals the deal.

"Bingley?" I ask, staring up at the ornate ceiling. Even the ceiling of the suite is a cut above your average hotel room ceiling.

"Yes, Miss Rowley?"

"Call me Becca." I'm sort of drunk.

"Yes, Becca?"

"I just left a long voicemail for Nate. Could you erase it, please?"

"I'm sorry, but that is not within my powers. Voicemail resides with the cell phone carrier. KTech phones employ the carrier's software for this function."

"Well, that is a bug, sir," I complain. "I can't believe Nate didn't write that software himself."

"I will tell him you're displeased."

"No!" I sit up quickly and the room spins. "Don't do that. Don't ever tell Nate I'm displeased about anything."

"All right, miss. One word from you shall silence me forever."

"That's a little dramatic." I yawn. "Good night, Bingley."

"Pleasant dreams, miss."

———

Nate obviously listened to my voicemail. Now that we're back in Brooklyn for games three and four, he's giving me space. Lots of it.

Which I asked for, I guess, when I said I needed to "take a damned deep breath."

Lesson learned. No drunk-dialing ever again. He's obviously avoiding me. Or maybe he's busy running the world and I'm an idiot for assuming he was thinking about me at all.

I go to therapy two days in a row, and it kicks my ass. Ramón makes me jump on that damned trampoline for hours.

Then, during game four, my heart does a few rounds on the trampoline, too. If we win this one the series will be tied 2-2. I watch from a seat in row B, courtesy of injured veteran player David Beringer.

He sits beside me, his hands white-knuckled on the armrest. If I'm in agony watching our boys play, his pain could only be double, knowing he should be out there helping them win.

Note to self: there's always someone who has it worse.

"Man on!" Beringer shouts to Castro. "Trevi's open!"

I give a nervous little shriek as Castro makes the pass. "Come on, boys, you can do this!"

And yet the first period ends scoreless. I spend the intermission touching up my makeup in the bathroom and pretending it's not because I want to look pretty for a certain technology tycoon.

Meanwhile, Heidi Jo is in the corporate box, blowing up my phone with nattering questions. *Should I offer Nate another Diet Coke? What does Stew drink?*

Don't bother, I reply grumpily. *They both have two functioning hands. They can pour it themselves.*

You know the game is tied, right? Why so glum, chum?

I don't answer because it won't be a friendly response.

My mood improves during the second period, though. We pick up two goals, and ultimately Dallas can't catch up. It's a sweaty, fast-moving third period but we finish the game 4-2.

I am weak with relief. Dave is hoarse from yelling.

"Thank fuck," he says, squeezing my shoulders. "That took a year off my life, Bec. Come to the bar with us for a celly?"

"Okay," I say immediately. Blowing off steam with my friends sounds like a fine idea, especially since I've discovered I can have a drink or two now without face-planting. "The Tavern on Hicks?"

"Naturally." He stands up. "I'll go early and ask Pete to reserve the back room."

"Good plan. I'm going to find my intern and invite her." Seems only fair, since I've been such a grumpy bear. The Tavern after a win is a good time.

Beringer gives me a fist bump and leaves. Texting Heidi Jo while I walk, I head slowly downstairs to the press conference, because I can't stay away. It's been days since I've seen Nate. The post-game adrenaline is still hitting me hard, filling me with optimistic glee.

I want to see his face, dammit. And apologize sober.

The usual mayhem outside the locker rooms doesn't help calm me down. Players and family members are hugging and celebrating. The locker-room door opens and closes repeatedly as players emerge, freshly-showered, to congratulations.

"Press room, people!" Georgia shouts. "This way. Three minutes!"

My best friend's job isn't done for the night.

"There you are!" Heidi Jo says, sidling up to me and snatching my phone out of my hands. "That's enough screen time."

"Hey! It's you who's been texting me!"

She shrugs. "Couldn't be helped!"

"That is…" *so irritating!* I swallow down my displeasure. "The players are drinking at The Tavern on Hicks tonight. I came downstairs to invite you."

"Oh!" Her face lights up. "I'm in. Do they have darts and a pool table?"

"Sure?" I never play those games.

"I'm kind of a shark," she says with a giggle.

"Can't say I'm surprised." Heidi Jo isn't stupid. Just overenthusiastic.

Georgia's press conference is starting. She stands at the podium as the rear door opens behind the dais. Nate, Coach Worthington, O'Doul, and two other players step out to applause.

I put two fingers in my mouth and wolf-whistle loudly, causing Heidi Jo to clap her hands over her ears.

"Thank you for being with us tonight as we make our way toward victory," Georgia says at the podium. "The club owner, Mr. Nathan Kattenberger, would like to thank you as well. Please hold your questions until after coach's remarks. Thank you."

Georgia steps aside for Nate, who thanks his players and his coach for their impressive effort tonight.

I don't hear a word of what he says, because I'm too busy giving him a laser-like *come hither* stare. *I'm sorry I've been acting nutty*, my eyes say. Or rather, they try. But Nate doesn't happen to look my way. As a short person trapped against the back wall of a crowded room, my odds of being seen aren't great.

"Mr. Kattenberger!" a female journalist calls out. Immediately I see Georgia's eyes narrow, because questions are prohibited during the introduction. "Is it true that you have a personal grudge against the Dallas team?"

I can't see the journalist from where I'm standing. She may be vertically challenged, too. But many heads turn her way.

Nate's eyes widen, and I feel a sudden chill on the back of my neck. "Personal? No." He clears his throat in a very unNatelike way. "Though I hold a grudge against anyone standing between my team and the Cup."

Georgia pipes up. "We'll take questions at the end…"

But the reporter cuts her off. "Did you buy a hockey team to get revenge on the Dallas player who stole your fiancée?"

Wait, what?

"That's ridiculous," Nate says, each word a chip of ice. "I've been a hockey fan since I could talk. I bought a hockey team so I could bring major league sports back to Brooklyn…"

This woman must have a death wish because she cuts him off again. "Didn't you walk in on Dallas captain Bart Palacio and —"

"*Excuse* me," Georgia says, stepping in front of Nate and the podium. "You will hold your questions until after coach's comments!" Her face is red and splotchy.

And Nate? He turns the podium's microphone off, turns around, and leaves the room.

The click of the door closing behind him seems to echo in the silence that follows.

Georgia blinks. "Coach Worthington has some comments about the game," she says crisply.

My head is spinning. The captain of the Dallas team is the same guy with whom Juliet cheated?

I pat all the pockets in my shoulder bag until I realize Heidi Jo stole my phone. "Phone!" I hiss. But she doesn't move fast enough, so I hook an arm through hers and bodily steer her into the hallway. "I need my phone! Whip it out." Then I spot it in her blazer pocket and help myself. I do a quick web search for Nate's name and "Dallas" and *boom*. The journalist already filed her story. She was just hoping to add a moment of on-air embarrassment at Nate's expense.

I'm going to cut the bitch.

I wait for the story to load, turning the phone sideways to try to make the text larger. Stress has made my vision dance, and my gaze feels squinty after a long day.

"Here, let me," my intern says. "What are we looking at? *Oh*," she says suddenly. "Yuck."

"Read it," I demand.

"This headline." She makes a tsk sound with her tongue. "*Scandal: Owner Nate Kattenberger's Secret Beef with Dallas Hockey Star.*"

"Fuck!" It's the most clickbaity thing I've ever heard. "Nate's not like that!"

"Shh!" Heidi Jo hisses. "If you want to keep your thing with Nate secret you're going to have to lower your voice."

I growl but she's right. And Nate doesn't need any more gossip right now. "Keep reading."

"Five years ago the billionaire owner of the Brooklyn Bruisers caught his fiancée in their bed with a professional hockey player. This week Nate has a shot at revenge as his team takes on Dallas in the Stanley Cup finals."

"Holy shit," I breathe.

As Heidi Jo reads on, I learn that Juliet is now Mrs. Bart Palacio. She owns a chain of Dallas fitness gyms, and she married Bart back when he played for the Rangers. Now he's captain of the Dallas team.

"Holy. Shit," I say again. Then I snatch my phone from my intern's hands and skim the story again, because I just can't believe it.

"I didn't know Nate was once engaged!" Heidi Jo whispers. "She's pretty."

"She is," I sigh. "They were together from college. I never liked her." That last thing just slips out.

Heidi Jo snorts. "I wouldn't either. She broke your man's heart!"

"Shhh!" Poor Nate. His tale of woe has just been smeared

across the internet. I do a web search for Juliet Palacio and the screen lights up with photos. She has a daughter—a little toddler. In the photo she's standing with the baby on her hip beside her husband. They're all wearing matching jerseys with his number on them, and I throw up a little in my mouth when I see it.

"Cute kid," Heidi Jo says. "You didn't know his ex was married to the captain?"

"I didn't know she was married at all," I stammer. "Never looked her up before." But now I wished I had. Standing here in the emptying corporate box, a whole lot of things are starting to make more sense to me.

Nate hates Dallas but never says why.

Nate wouldn't take that interview about why he owns a hockey team.

Nate asked me to sit beside him at the Dallas games. Where he knew he might see his ex. He wanted me at his side. Yet I said no.

"Let's go, Bec." I look up to see Castro straightening his tie in front of me. "Beringer has a table at The Tavern. You're coming, right?"

I push off the wall and follow him, even though my head is still miles away.

He holds the door for Heidi Jo and me, and then Silas—the backup goalie—appears, too. "Uber, cab, or walk?"

"Walk," I say immediately. The Tavern isn't very far away, and I need to clear my head.

"Sounds good," Silas says, and we start off down the sidewalk.

"That sure sucked for the bossman," Castro says as we reach the corner. "Wouldn't want the whole world knowing my ex dumped me for a meathead like Palacio."

"People say he's a *dick*," Heidi Jo chimes in.

"Bec, did you know her?" Silas asks.

We wait to cross Atlantic Avenue, and I consider the question. "A little. Spoke to her on the phone a couple times a day. Saw her once or twice a week. But just small talk, you know? Shocked the hell out of me when they broke up."

"You're a pretty good judge of character," Castro says. "You liked her?"

"Nope," I say immediately. "But I can't even say why."

Heidi Jo smirks, and I give her a look of warning.

"Nate's prolly hitting the whiskey tonight," Castro says. "Bet he won't turn up at the bar, though. Not after that bullshit. Everyone knows how much he hates Dallas; now we know why."

My heart sinks. "Because Dallas is *smug*," I argue. "If Nate wanted revenge on a guy, you really think buying a team is an efficient strategy? He'd probably just make the guy's phone run at a quarter the normal speed, or write a script that gave him zits in every photo on the internet."

My three friends burst out laughing.

But I wasn't joking. And I can't stand the idea of Nate brooding in his empty house alone. "You know, I think I'm too wiped for The Tavern. I'll see you guys later?"

"Want us to walk you home?" Castro asks, always the gentleman.

"Nope, I'm good!" I say cheerily. I back away from them slowly. *Nothing to see here.*

Heidi Jo chuckles. "Get some *rest*." She winks.

I turn and jog down Atlantic, toward the Promenade.

27

NATE

MY DEN IS dark as I enter the room. But the moment I walk in, soft lighting switches on.

"Hullo, Master Nate," Bingley says. "Would you like the television?"

"God, no." Given the press conference debacle, I may never watch again. "Pour me a Scotch, would you?"

"Sorry, sir. I have not the talent which some people possess. That is beyond my capabilities."

"I know, Bingley. Just wondered what you'd say." Just another night in singlesville, joking with a bot. Party on. Good thing there's a hidden bar in the corner of this room. I open a walnut cabinet and take out a glass and a bottle of Macallan 18. I pour myself two fingers of Scotch and kick off my shoes.

Then I sit down and take a sip. It burns going down.

I shouldn't care what's written about me in some rag of a newspaper. Whether we win the Cup or not, the hockey team is a labor of love. People said I couldn't turn the franchise around. And yet I did exactly that with good management and great coaching. And I did it in two short years.

They were floundering before I bought the team. And now they're not. The end.

But the article stings. Juliet left me for an athlete, and I don't want people to read that and laugh.

My phone rings in my pocket—my mother's ringtone. I ignore it. She'll say nice things to me, but I don't want to hear them. But she starts texting me anyway.

What just happened? Do you think this is Juliet's work?

I doubt it, but my mother never liked her.

I'm booking flights to Dallas, she says a moment later. *We want to be there for you at game five*.

My phone goes back into my pocket. I'm too tired to engage. The couch beckons, and I lie back, resting my Scotch on my belly, like Homer Simpson would do.

My publicist—Georgia—is miffed that I didn't warn her, too. She called me while I was in the car on my way home. "I could have prevented that," she said. "You need to let me protect you."

"Lesson learned," I grunted before we hung up.

What a stupid night. I should just turn in early and hope tomorrow is less humiliating.

But first, Scotch. I sip it and try to look objectively at my life. I have the most fulfilling job a man could ask for, and a successful sports team. That ought to be enough, right?

"Sir," Bingley says suddenly. "Rebecca would like to know if she can call on you."

I groan, because I don't know if I can put on my game face right now, and I don't want her to see me feeling so low. "Would you tell her that now is not a good time?"

"All right," Bingley replies. "I'll send her home."

"Wait." I set down my glass. "She's here?"

"On the front steps, sir."

"Fine, send her up," I say before I can reconsider.

A few seconds later I hear her footsteps on the stairs, and my heart rate accelerates. I can't help it, and I'm not even sure I care. Rebecca will always have that pull on me.

She glides in a minute later, heading straight for the couch. She plunks down beside my feet and sets a bag and a lime down on the table. Then she fishes a bottle out of her handbag and sets that down with a thunk. "So. Cat tacos?"

I blink.

She bites her lip.

"Wait." I sit up. "Did you bring me empanadas and tequila?"

"Yeah," she says softly. "It's nothing, really, but..."

I interrupt her. "Do you know I love you?"

Her mouth slams shut and her eyes get damp. "No. I didn't."

"It's true, Bec. I've got it bad. And that shitty little story about Juliet and me is a bummer, but it's really no big deal."

"I didn't know," she says, wiping her eyes. "About Juliet and Dallas."

Oh. "Really?" I assumed she was well versed in my humiliations.

She shakes her head. "Didn't have a clue. But I realized something important on the way over here. You asked me to sit with you in Dallas. And I said no because people would see us together and know we're a thing."

"Right. I get it, Bec."

She shakes her head. "But I *didn't* get it. You knew they'd see how it was. And you still wanted me there."

"Of course." I'm really not sure what she's saying.

"You didn't care that people would say, 'Oh, Nate is dating his secretary.'"

"Office manager," I correct.

She rolls her eyes. Then she grabs the tequila bottle and twists off the sealed top. Her trusty pocketknife comes out of her jacket pocket, and she cuts a lime on a coaster. "Glasses? Or are we going in straight from the bottle, just like old times?"

I fetch two more glasses from the cabinet because I want Bec to be able to see how much tequila she's drinking. Because I can't stop myself from worrying about the woman I love.

I do love her. I can admit that now.

She pours a shot into each glass and hands me one. "I'm sorry," she says, meeting my eyes. "You wanted *me* beside you and I said no. It's just that I didn't really believe it. I thought you'd want another Juliet or Alex. Someone who's more..." She frowns. "More than me."

"There is *nobody* more than you. Nobody funnier. Nobody with a better attitude. Nobody more loyal. Nobody sexier. That's for damn sure." I clink my glass against hers and then drink the tequila down.

She doesn't drink hers. She just stares at me.

"What?"

"I love you, too," she says, and my heart skips an entire beat. Becca tosses back her shot. It makes her eyes water, so she grabs a lime wedge and sucks on it, her pretty eyes regarding me as her lips purse. "I'm about to get insta-drunk, so please note that I said that while I was still sober."

I'm still reeling, but I laugh immediately. "Insta-drunk?"

"Yup. I'm allowed to drink again. But my tolerance is *gone*."

"Then get over here and kiss me before the tequila hits your motor skills."

Becca launches herself into my lap so quickly that I almost lose my balance. But I wrap my arms around her and hold on tight. She gives me a limey kiss, and I smile against her lips.

"I'm sorry," she says between kisses. "I'm sorry I yelled. Sorry I got all crazy about the medical bills."

She had a good point about those, though, that I really should have talked to her about it first. I'll say so later, but right now I'm too busy licking into her mouth and showing her how much I've missed her.

Becca returns the sentiment with bottomless kisses, her body pressed tightly to mine.

My hands coast down the knit fabric of her purple game-night dress. "Mmm," I mumble against her lips. Time for make-up sex right here on the sofa. I lift her dress and cup her ass. It's June, so she's not wearing stockings. I fucking love summertime. My palm meets only lacy panties and skin.

Becca moans, her fingers sifting through my hair.

"Unzip me," I demand.

Her fingers find my fly, and I suck gently on her neck while she works to free my cock. Swear to God I'm going to have leisurely sex with this woman someday. But it never seems like the right time to go slow. Sex with Rebecca is usually fast and frantic and I think we both like it that way.

Smooth fingers dip into my boxers and stroke me.

"Fuck, yeah." I slip a finger under the gusset of her panties and groan. She's so soft. And as I tease her, my fingers are quickly slicked with wetness.

Fast and frantic it is, then.

"Lose the panties," I order, giving them a tug.

She straightens up only long enough to help me get them off her.

"That's my girl," I pant. I yank my pants down a few crucial inches, and my cock salutes her like a soldier reporting for duty.

Becca reaches for the buttons on my shirt, but I'm all out of patience. I pull her onto my body, and she ends up kneeling over me, one smooth knee at either side. So I take my cock in hand, line myself up, and then pull her down, impaling her.

"Oh," she whimpers. "Yesssss."

I shut her up with a kiss that's all tongue and ambition. Pushing up her dress, I find a lacy bra beneath, and it makes me groan. So I toss the dress aside and drink her in. "You are fucking perfect," I say, my hips rocking, my hands wandering. "And so sexy I want to lose my mind."

"Lose it, then," she says, her voice thickened with desire. She puts her hands on my shoulders and begins to move.

And it's perfect.

———

We eat reheated empanadas in my bed at two a.m.

"So. Have you seen her?" Becca asks, licking a bit of grease off her fingertip. She's wearing my Star Trek T-shirt and looking so cute that I want to fuck her all over again.

"Who?" I ask, distracted by the site of her tits straining the Starship Enterprise.

"You're joking, right? *Juliet*."

But I wasn't kidding at all. Having Becca back in my arms

made me forget the night's troubles. "No. I haven't. But why would I, right? The teams don't really mingle."

"Thank God."

I shrug. "Still have to look at Bart's ugly ass during every game. With three goals he's the high-scorer so far for this series. I want to run him down with the Zamboni."

"Do you think he's still a vegan?" She gives me a cheeky smile.

"How do you even remember that?" I'd blocked out everything from that time in my life. Except for my rage.

"We were snarking about the fact that he was a shitty dinner date. I remember everything about that night, including rolling you into a taxi after we got drunk. I had the spins on the subway on the way home."

"Seems like a hundred years ago." Because now I can't remember a time when it wasn't Becca that I wanted in my bed. "Would it be too optimistic of me to ask if you'd consider joining me for game five in Dallas?"

Her expression softens. She sets her plate aside. "I would be delighted to be your date for game five. Except I won't be there. Earlier tonight I told Heidi Jo that she was going to Dallas in my place, because I finally went back to therapy and Dr. Armitage wants to see me on Monday morning."

I resist the urge to comment on her return to therapy, though I'm pleased. "It doesn't matter if you're not on the team jet," I argue. "I'm flying out on the Gulfstream Monday afternoon. You'd come with me. And not to work. This would be a date. If you're ready for that. But no pressure."

Rebecca's eyes widen. She lets out a breath. "Well, okay. It's on."

"You can think about it," I say quietly. "If you're not ready, I'll understand."

"I want to go," she says firmly. "I'm all in if you are."

I lean in, bridging the distance between us, and kiss her neck. It's another hour before we get to sleep.

[28]

REBECCA

NATE and I carry on like horny teenagers all weekend in private. But then Monday arrives, as it always does. After my doctor's appointment I have a few hours to myself before I have to meet Nate at LaGuardia for the flight to Dallas.

Cue the fashion crisis.

I find myself in Bloomingdale's, wondering what Nate's game-day arm candy is supposed to wear. Every time the TV camera cuts to Nate for a reaction, I'll be visible. Or half visible. One boob or the other is going to be on prime time.

I ask to try on every silk scarf that has any Brooklyn Bruisers purple in it. Staring in the mirror, I reject each one in turn. I never wear scarves, because they make my chest look more voluminous than it already is.

I shouldn't be having this fashion crisis. I shouldn't care that TV cameras will zoom in on Nate and his companions whenever Brooklyn scores. I shouldn't wonder what Nate's girlfriend ought to look like. But it's hard not to compare myself to toned, blond Juliet, fitness trainer to the stars.

And dating Nate can't turn me into someone who looks good in scarves.

Leaving the frustrated sales girl behind, I take the escalator up to the designer floor I rarely visit. I do a lap, but everything is too summery for the rink. Until I spy a corner where off-season things are discounted. And I find—no lie—cashmere cardigans. There aren't as many as in the dream I was having when Nate woke me up on that fateful night in Florida. But I don't need hundreds; I only need one.

And I find one in just the right eggplant shade of purple.

It's fate, so I have to buy it. Besides, my credit card bill is nearly zero, since Nate wiped away my medical debt.

Also, because I'm me, I can't leave the store without visiting the lingerie department. I wander the aisles wondering which scraps of satin or lace will give Nate that expression he gets when I undress —like a dog with his tongue hanging out of his mouth. I find some lace panties in a creamy pink that conceal *nothing*, and a matching bra.

Then I go home to primp and pack.

———

I thought it would be odd to fly with Nate as his date instead of his assistant, but it isn't. Not yet, anyway. For starters, Lauren is with us. This was unplanned, but it turns out that she's been carrying on with Beacon, the goalie, and asked Nate if she could ride along to watch the game.

"We can finish these reports during the flight," she said, setting up her laptop on the Gulfstream's table.

"You go nuts, girl," I say, taking one of the wide leather reclining seats. I haven't explained my presence to Lauren, and Nate hasn't either. I wonder how long it will take her to ask.

With Lauren's back to us, Nate runs a hand over my hair. He gives me a secretive smile and goes to sit across from her.

I spend the flight flipping through a *Vanity Fair* magazine and feeling lazy. I can't remember the last time there was nothing I was supposed to be doing. But when I told Heidi Jo she could manage this overnight to Dallas, I made myself let her handle things no matter what. She's still gushy and she still talks too much. But somehow she gets things done. My boys are probably in good hands right now. If she has a problem she can't solve, I'm sure I'll get a text.

The flight attendant brings me a glass of fresh-squeezed orange juice in a crystal glass, and a small bowl of roasted almonds. Then she hands me a beautifully printed card with the Wi-Fi password on it. "Can I get you anything else? There are magazines and books in the seatpocket over here..." She points at the other reclining chair. "And dinner will be served in an hour."

Fine—so there are one or two little perks to being Nate's girl-friend. "I'm good for now," I tell her. "Thank you."

———

When we touch down in Dallas, there's a stretch limo waiting on the tarmac. That's how it is traveling with Nate. The car whisks us to the stadium. We hit traffic, but we still pull up to the stadium doors before the puck drops.

The door flies open and Heidi Jo starts talking immediately. She's babbling about getting an extra hotel room at the last minute for Lauren, and how she had to give the grounds crew a stiff talking to when they changed the ice time schedule for our boys' warm-up.

But I tune her out when we reach the corporate box, because Nate takes my hand in his and steers me toward a pair of seats in the center front. As if we do this every day.

My heart rate kicks up a notch as I slide my palm against his and squeeze. *I'm all in*, I'd told him. Let the weirdness begin.

And it does. Right away.

"Rebecca!" Nate's mother says from the seat next to mine. "How lovely to see you!"

I give her a giant smile that's more confident than I feel. "Hello, Linda! Are you ready for game five?" And then I hold my breath, wondering if she's the kind of mom who's sure that nobody is good enough for her baby boy. But I don't let go of Nate's hand. I hold on tight. He gives mine a squeeze and greets his father.

I watch Mrs. Kattenberger's gaze travel down to our clasped hands. Then her eyes widen.

And then? She smiles like she's won a prize from Oprah. "I *am* ready," she says. "Let's do this. Sit down; I'll get us both a beer."

I watch her trot over to the beverage table and some of the tightness leaves my chest. It seems Nate's mom isn't going to be an issue. One down. The whole world to go.

The next two hours are not relaxing. Our boys are fired up but Dallas isn't going to give up the game without a fight. I forget about behaving like Nate's arm candy and instead do a lot of yelling at the ref. "SLASHING!" I scream during the second period. "That's a two-minute minor at least!"

Nate chuckles without taking his eyes off the ice. He's *smiling*, in spite of the lack of a penalty called on Dallas! People always remark on what a stoic guy Nate is while he's watching hockey. But tonight I discover that it's worse when he's sitting right next to you. I'm foaming at the mouth and he's calmly sipping his third Diet Coke.

Nate's mom makes small talk during the intermissions, but I'm too keyed up to do more than ask generic questions about how she's been. I nod and smile at all the right moments. I hope I do, anyway.

My team is two and a half games from winning all the marbles, and I cannot contain my nervous energy.

The game goes to overtime, and I'm completely strung out. Until Trevi sinks a goal in the overtime period, and every Brooklyn fan in Dallas jumps to her feet with glee.

"YAY!" I shriek. "Thank you, baby Jesus!"

Nate laughs and then hug-tackles me.

———

I put Nate's parents into a car after the game. They're headed to a different hotel than the one where the team is staying. And if I'm not mistaken, Mrs. Kattenberger's hug is extra tight. "Goodbye, sweetie. Hope to see you again soon," she says.

I'm too keyed up from the game to get into the waiting limousine. There will be an impromptu party in the lobby of the hotel, and the idea makes me feel twitchy. "Can we walk back?" I ask. It's only two blocks.

"Sure," Nate says immediately. He takes my hand, and we set off down the street. The limo follows us, of course. Nate's security guys are always watching. Someday I'll get used to it, right?

"About this party." I don't know how to phrase my request in a way that doesn't allow all my neuroses to pop out at once.

"I won't stick my tongue down your throat, if that's what you're wondering." Nate squeezes my hand. "I know you'd rather ease everyone into the idea."

"Right! Exactly. I don't want it to be scandalous. Except later. Privately. When you see my new underwear."

Nate stops abruptly on the sidewalk. "New underwear?"

"You bet. And we won tonight, so I'm going to launder it carefully and wear it again for games six and seven. It's my lucky underwear. Obviously."

"Obviously." Nate's smile is amused. He puts his hands up to my face and shakes his head. "I'm going to make it your *getting lucky* underwear as soon as I can. Maybe we can sneak past the party."

We can't, and he knows it. But right there under the street lamp he kisses me very thoroughly anyway. I grip his shoulders and sigh as he tastes me. It's the kind of kiss that lets me know that tonight is a big deal for him.

And for me, too. It's the night I get over myself and enjoy Nate, instead of worrying what it all means.

He sighs as he draws back. "That will have to hold me for an hour, I guess."

We walk the rest of the way to the Ritz, and Nate drops my hand to follow me through the revolving door. He doesn't pick it up again, probably out of respect for easing people into this new thing between us.

"Hey!" Castro and Trevi call from a roped-off area at one end of the lobby bar. "Look who's here."

I don't know if they mean me or Nate. He skipped tonight's press conference again. I would too, if I were him.

"Good work tonight, boys!" he says, and they hoot in reply. We move further into the bar area, and the players fall quiet as the team owner approaches. He and Coach Worthington are the only two men who can bring a total hush to the locker room just by showing their faces.

"This man needs a beer," O'Doul says, waving down the bartender.

"Two," Nate says, and I try not to turn red as Nate hands me one before taking one for himself. "I'll buy a round, guys," he says to more applause. "And there's something I want to say."

"Speech!" Leo Trevi hollers.

Nate smiles and takes a sip of his beer. "First of all, I want to thank you for participating in my top-secret, multi-year conspiracy to exact revenge on a Dallas hockey player. Those of you who were in on it will get your bonus checks just as soon as you win the Cup on Saturday."

A good-natured howl of laughter erupts in the bar.

Nate swigs his beer and waits for it to die down. "In all serious-ness, it's never fun to have your personal life hashed out in the press. But people have talked a lot of smack about our team from the beginning. We're too young. We're too uppity. Repositioning the franchise will be a disaster. You've done an impressive job of ignoring that noise, and focusing on what really counts."

The players and their families applaud, and I feel a little flutter in my chest. Focusing on what really counts is at the top of my to-do list, too.

"That article in the post was totally wrong, anyway," Nate adds. His grin turns devilish, and I wonder whether he's about to add, *it wasn't our bed, it was the kitchen table*. But no. "I bought a hockey team because I wanted to watch you guys kill it out there tonight. And—contrary to the news reports—I would like to personally thank Bart and Juliet Palacio for their intervention in my personal life. Because if they hadn't found each other, then I wouldn't have this fine woman right here in my life."

My brain is still processing that sentence when Nate steps to the side, puts an arm around my waist, and kisses my cheek.

The bar *erupts*. Georgia and Lauren let out matching shrieks, and I distinctly hear Castro's "what the fuck?" and O'Doul's sudden laughter.

Weirdly, I could swear that at least a few voices say, "Oh, *finally.*"

My whole body flashes hot at the unexpected attention. I experience a brief moment of terror and discomfort, but then it sinks in that nearly everyone I know is beaming at me. Someone has called for champagne, and since we're at the Ritz, where everything goes smoothly, I hear the sound of corks popping only seconds later.

To the sound of cheers, I slip an arm around Nate's waist. And then I pinch him. "What happened to easing them into it?" I mutter.

"I'm buying drinks. Duh. That eases everything."

Leo Trevi stands up on a barstool with a pint glass in his hand and a spoon. Which he starts banging on the glass. "Kiss!"

"Oh, Christ," I mutter. Then I put a hand on Nate's chest and stand on tiptoes. I kiss Nate's smile only once, but I make it a good one. Then I point my finger like a gun at Leo Trevi and cock the safety. "That's it. That's the whole show. Ask again and your luggage goes missing on the flight home."

"Fuck," he says, hopping down. And everybody laughs.

29

NATE

JUNE 17, NEW YORK

BACK IN BROOKLYN, we lose game six in a freaking shootout. Could happen to anyone. My guys look good the whole game. Confident. But it isn't quite enough to end the series.

So we'll have to do it in game seven. That's just the way it is.

But I'm so distracted. All I want to do is watch practice and listen to Coach Worthington drop his gruff pearls of wisdom.

We're *this* close. I can taste it.

Just to complicate matters, my investment bankers come up with a third bidder for the router division. Out of nowhere, a hardware manufacturer wants to edge out the competition for this business unit.

Stew just rolls his eyes when I give him the news. "If you made up your fucking mind already, you wouldn't have this problem, bigshot."

No kidding.

But my indecision hasn't been the only problem. Alone in my office, I grab my phone and tap Alex's number. "Hey you. Look. I want to do this transaction with you, but we have to move fast. And you have to show your face, because there's a new complication. For the love of God, call me back so I don't have to put your picture on the back of a milk carton."

In the outer office, Lauren is busy scheduling more meetings, which I'm too distracted to attend, and ordering lunch so I don't turn into a whiny brat when my blood sugar drops. Outside my window, my sweeping view of Manhattan's skyline is obscured by heavy clouds. It's a rainy June day, and the hockey season is one game away from its thrilling conclusion.

And I'm about to spend several hours listening to accountants drone. Kill me already.

I'm finishing up a big bowl of spicy noodles when there's a tap on the door. "Come in, especially if you're Rebecca." Becca said something earlier about coming to Manhattan and maybe swinging by around noon.

"Sorry," a female voice says. But it's not Rebecca's. When the door opens, it's Alex's face that appears.

"Hey!" I stand up because this is good news, too. "Finally! How goes it with you?" I toss the trash from my lunch into the bin beside my desk.

Alex gives me a tight smile. She closes the door behind her and crosses to the visitor's chair opposite my desk. "Nate, I'm here to ruin your day."

"What?" Women have ruined my day many times before, but they are rarely so direct about it. "Well. At least take off your jacket first. Or—should we step out for a cup of coffee?" I could use an espresso to push me through today's meetings.

Slowly she shakes her head. Alex looks as tense as I've ever seen her. If this were an episode of *Sherlock*, she might have a bomb strapped to her body beneath that raincoat.

"Spit it out, pal," I say. "What's wrong?"

"I'm pregnant. But it's probably not your baby."

Six times. That's how many I roll this pronouncement through my head to be sure I've heard it right. I can feel the blood draining from my face. And yet I'm somehow able to focus on the fact that it matters very much what I say right now. I don't yell, *it was once in twelve years, and we used a condom!* I don't yell at all.

"Pregnant," I say carefully. *But it's probably not mine,* she'd added.

Probably might mean she's 51% sure. Or—if I'm lucky—she's certain out to three standard deviations. Somehow I managed not to voice this question. "Congratulations," I add gently. Then I wait for more information.

Alex offers me another tight smile. "I know you well enough to hear your gears turning over there. I'm…88% sure this isn't your problem. I was briefly dating Jonah after we…" She clears her throat. "But I need to ask you a favor. I need to rule you out before I approach him."

"Rule me out," I say stupidly.

She closes her eyes and then opens them again. "With a paternity test, Nate."

"Oh. Okay," I say quickly. "Whatever you need."

"Breathe, Nate. This isn't on you. But I need your help anyway."

It's still twelve percent on me, though. "I'm good," I say. "Tell me what to do."

From her handbag Alex extracts a blue box with big letters on it. You might mistake it for a new toothpaste package, except for its bright label: *Paternity test*.

"I need you to take this, even though the chances are slim."

My brain comes back online while she's opening one end of the box. "You need to ask me, because you can't ask him?"

Her fingers pause on the cellophane wrapper. "I don't want to discuss it with him unless I'm positive I have to. He's not a good man."

"Oh shit, Alex."

Her eyes redden. "I know, okay? I know. I've made more mistakes this year than I can count. This is absolutely the last conversation I ever wanted to have with you. But even though I'm pretty sure you're off the hook here, part of me wishes you weren't. I can't have a child with a man who hit me."

I actually choke on nothing. "How bad was it?"

She shakes her head. "Believe me, the one time he did it was the last time we were in the same room together. He was just with me to try to get to my father."

"Oh shit," I say again. Alex's father is a famous venture capitalist. Lots of assholes would want an easy in there.

"I called him on it and he backhanded me. That was the end of it. Until now."

"So…" I can see how this will play out. "If the baby is his, you'll end up funding his startup anyway, in exchange for some legal document that says he's giving up parental rights."

She nods, and her expression carries a weariness that I wished I never had to see on the face of my poor friend.

"I'm sorry," I say again. The silence between us is heavy with sadness. "Let me get one thing straight, since I'm not great at picking up social cues. Are you not here to discuss the router transaction?"

Her eyes widen, and then she smiles. *Finally.* "You dick."

Snickering, I get up from my chair and walk around the desk. I lean over and wrap my arms around her. "We'll get through this, buddy. It's all going to be okay."

Alex pushes her face into my shoulder and takes a deep, shaky breath.

30

REBECCA

WALKING through the C-suite for the first time in two years is trippy. Everything is exactly the same, from the heavy, imported carpets to the espresso machine in the kitchenette.

"Hey!" Lauren smiles at me from her desk outside Nate's private office. "You're looking snazzy."

A compliment from Lauren. That's even trippier than the unchanged decor. "Thank you," I say a beat too late. Lauren looks about a hundred times smilier than she used to. Either she's had a lobotomy, or getting back together with Mike Beacon agrees with her.

"Nate's chatting with Alex Engels for a minute. Do you want me to buzz him…?" Even as she makes this offer, Nate's office door flies open and Alex appears. She does an honest-to-God double take when she sees me standing here. Her mouth opens and then shuts again. Then she tucks her chin to her chest and walks out.

About three seconds later she's disappeared completely from view, hidden by the elevator banks.

"Um…?" I say stupidly. "Was that weird?"

"Right?" Lauren shrugs. "Where's the fire?" Then she points at Nate's open door. "Go right in. He doesn't have another meeting for thirty."

"Thanks." I step into Nate's office, but he doesn't see me. His back is turned. He stands in front of the floor-to-ceiling windows, his hands braced behind his head. It's a pose of male reflection. I can't imagine what he's looking at, either, since there's a pea-soup fog out there, and even the river isn't visible.

I close the door behind me with a quiet click. "Nate?"

He whirls around. And his face is...pained. There's no other word that leaps to mind. He's scowling, and a deep furrow in his forehead tells me he's worried.

"Hi," I say softly, approaching the desk.

He says nothing in reply. But in four strides he's rounded the desk to reach me. His kiss is like a sudden storm blowing out of nowhere. Fast and fierce.

It takes me a moment to get into the swing of things. But a kiss that hungry can't go to waste. I lift my chin and return fire. And I grip the back of his neck to encourage him.

Nate makes a low, greedy sound deep in his chest. I feel it everywhere. It resonates in the same dark corner of my subconscious where my wildest fantasies live. That must be why I break our kiss and do something I never expected to do in real life — I reach down and press the button on Nate's desk — the one that locks the door.

His eyes flare and his chest heaves, as if he's run five fast miles on that treadmill in the corner.

And then he attacks me. There's no other word that fits. His mouth and his hands are all over me, and we're in motion. The backs of my knees hit the sofa against the wall, and we tumble onto it.

Nate's chest is a wall of heat, and his mouth is everywhere — my neck, my jaw, my throat. I'm overwhelmed by him, and it's heady stuff. When his hand slips between my legs, I clench my thighs in anticipation.

This is startlingly like my dirtiest fantasies, except... "Nate?"

He grunts in answer, his tongue plunging into my ear.

"Are you okay?"

"No." He lifts my dress, and somehow my heels haven't fallen off yet. I hope the man doesn't stab himself. "Need you," he says, his voice husky.

"Have me," I gasp.

About two seconds later I've been stripped of my panties and one shoe. Nate frees his cock with the haste of someone exiting a burning building. Then he grabs my free leg, positions my bent knee under his arm, and enters me with one long, hard plunge.

Only then does he go still. Finally he meets my eyes. His are beautiful and brown and worried. I give him the best smile I can muster, though I'm winded and a little stunned. He exhales slowly, settling onto his forearms. That's when I get another kiss. Softer, but no less urgent. Our tongues meet, and our teeth click gently.

"Yeah," he pants, moving against me. He retreats and then fills me.

My skin flashes with heat and then goosebumps. I've never felt so many sensations in so short a time, and the pace he sets is unceasing.

He's beautiful, panting in his dress shirt, a fine sheen of sweat on his forehead. "Bec," he groans.

I squeeze him with my body and he makes a noise like a tortured beast. It's raw and desperate and God knows why that sound makes me climax. But a minute later I'm biting down on my lip to keep quiet as I shudder around him.

And it's as if Nate can finally let go of whatever is torturing him. He catches himself on his forearms, and his face falls into my neck. "Fuck," he whispers, as he slows his thrusts. I feel him clench and shudder. And at last, relax.

Silence follows. We try to slow our breathing, but it isn't easy.

"I'm sorry," he says, his lips against my skin.

"Don't be sorry," I whisper immediately. "That was pretty exciting."

"No. I know. I'm…" He curses. "I'm sorry for the trouble I'm about to cause you. And for pinning you to my sofa before explaining myself."

With one lazy hand, I smooth down his hair. "How bad could it be after that, right?"

I wait for his laugh, because Nate always laughs when we're in bed. He gets lighter, and his smile is boyish.

But not today. He disengages us with a sigh. Then he actually lifts me to my feet and sets me gently down on the rug. "I made a mess of you." He smooths my dress. "Your dress is so pretty, too."

I look down, having forgotten that I was all dolled up, and that I came here to explain my visit to Manhattan. But now I'm thinking it can wait. "Tell me what's the matter." His shirt is askew so I fix it while he tucks his cock away in his trousers.

"Let's sit." He looks at the sofa with an expression of trepidation. "Huh. Come over here." He grabs one of his visitor chairs and turns it to face the other one.

I use that moment to grab my panties and yank them on. Locating my shoes, I sit down in one chair.

We're face to face, and Nate puts his palms on my knees. "Remember when I said I wasn't that complicated? Swear to God I thought it was true. I have a confession to make."

My stomach rolls, because the look on his face is dire.

"Alex is two or three months pregnant, and she needs to rule me out."

"Pregnant?" I sit back in my chair like I've been punched. "With…" I can't even say it. But I can't help spitting out what's on my mind. "I *asked* if you and Alex were ever a thing. You said you hooked up only once, and I thought you meant in college."

His cringe is swift. "It *was* only once." He squeezes my knee. "And the timing…that's what I wanted you to think. Didn't want you to know how stupid I was one time in March."

He didn't lie, my hopeful heart reminds me. "So you might be having a baby with Alex," I whisper.

"There's a slight chance, but she needed to check. The other guy is much more likely. But he's also somebody who hit her."

My mouth falls open. "That fucker."

"Yeah." Nate licks his lips. "I'm, uh, stunned too. And pissed at myself. It's not how I would have wanted our first year together to go."

"If it's yours," I ask. "Then what?"

Nate shrugs. "I got this news about five minutes before you walked in. No idea what would happen. I'd want to be involved, if that's what Alex wanted. With the baby. Not Alex. I love you and that won't ever change."

I take a deep breath and let it out. I didn't hear what Nate said to Alex. I'll bet it wasn't an easy discussion. But I'll bet Nate was kind, and a good friend.

So I can be that, too, right? Can't I?

As much as I loathe the idea of Nate undressing Alex just a few weeks before he started up with me, I can be a grown-up about it.

"Jeez, slick," I say. "You screw up once and there's a paternity test later?"

"Yeah." His eyes are still embarrassed. "When I make a mistake, I make a real splash."

"Oh, Nate." I giggle, but it's probably the stress talking. "I'm sorry. Poor Alex. Poor you."

"I'll be fine. It wouldn't even shake me up if I weren't trying hard to convince you I'm a catch."

"You are?"

"Trying to convince you? Always."

Aw. "You *are* a catch. Although if you and Alex end up having a baby together I will be so incredibly jealous." There, I said it.

He leans forward and pulls me into a hug. After a kiss on the jaw, he whispers to me. "It's something I'd much rather do with you."

I don't say anything because we've ventured into some heavy territory. But I lean in closer to let him know that the idea appeals to me, too.

"Becca, it took me seven years to figure out how much I need you. I'm never letting anyone get in the way of that."

"It'll be okay," I whisper. Although now we have to go into game seven wondering what that paternity test says. "How long will the results take?"

"Not long. Actually..." He releases me, then leans over to pluck an envelope off the surface of his desk. "Alex left this for you. I almost forgot." He hands it to me. Inside is a note.

Rebecca—I owe you a monster apology. I hope you'll believe me that I'm not usually a raving bitch like I was in Florida. I was terrified to think I might be pregnant, and what that might mean for all the people involved. I took it out on you, and you deserve to know why. The way Nate looks at you is so amazing and rare. He looks at you like he'd walk through fire for you.

Most of us never find that, so I hope you can find it in your heart to appreciate it. I'm so sorry to be that extra thing that complicates your lives right now. I hope you can forgive me. —A.

"What did she say?" Nate asks, watching me with intelligent eyes.

My throat is tight. "She said she's sorry. It's a really nice note."

"Hallelujah. Alex has been a good friend to me over the years. I couldn't take it if she wasn't nice to you."

We'll see, I think.

"Want to get coffee?" he asks. "Fuck it. I think I'm going to blow off the rest of my day."

"Really? Wow." It's the first time I've ever heard him say that.

"Hey—what were you downtown for?" he asks.

Slowly, I shake my head. "We'll talk about it another time."

"Hit me," he says. "I can take it."

"Well, I'm not pregnant."

He smiles. "We could fix that."

"You're hilarious." I take a deep breath. "Okay. Don't freak out, but I had a job interview."

Nate blinks. "A job? For you?"

"Yeah," I say softly. "This job probably isn't the one for me. Just a random phone call and a quick meeting. But looking around is just something I want to consider."

Nate puts his elbows on his knees and drops his forehead into his hands. "Bec, I actually feel worse about this than about the twelve percent chance that I got Alex pregnant."

Twelve percent. Trust Nate and Alex to put a precise number on it. "I didn't say I was quitting for sure. I'm just kicking tires here." The job interview was a random, sudden thing. I got a call from a guy who might fund a new NWHL team in the tri-state area. It's pie in the sky at this point.

But leaving the Bruisers is something I need to consider.

He looks up. "It's your whole life. You said so yourself. You love the team."

"I know." I *did* say that. "But I love you, too. So I just want to think about what else is out there for me—and where I could work where I wasn't the owner's girlfriend. I might not make a move; I

271

just want to try on the idea. So I'm telling you now, so you won't be shocked."

Nate reaches a hand out, palm up. I take it. "You do whatever you have to do. I only want you to be happy. But before you lock it down, promise we'll talk about it again?"

That's an easy one. "I promise."

"Thanks for being great."

"You're not so bad yourself." He smiles at me just as Lauren's voice comes through the intercom, telling him it's time for his finance meeting.

"Cancel it," he says wearily. "I'm not feeling so great and I'm going to head home."

"Um…" I can hear the shock in Lauren's response. "Okay? I'll tell them."

And after tidying up a bit in Nate's private bathroom, we leave hand in hand.

31

NATE

JUNE 18, DALLAS

PEOPLE TEASE me all the time for being a rather stoic watcher of hockey. For not visibly reacting to a great play or a bad call.

After tonight, they won't anymore.

Never in my life have I felt so much like everything was on the line at once. My team. My sanity. My ego. My reputation. Every time we lose the puck I want to punch Dallas in the throat. And every time we get it back, I'm elated.

"Treviiii!" Rebecca screams beside me. "Man on! Watch your…"

A Dallas D-man slams him in the back, and the puck shakes loose. I grip Rebecca's hand as she lets out another little scream, because two opposing players are diving for the puck at once. O'Doul could almost get there. Rebecca practically climbs into my lap with excitement. Our faces are cheek to cheek as we hold our collective breath as O'Doul flips the puck to Castro, who takes a shot…

We both scream.

It will be hours before we learn that some lucky photographer snapped a photo at that very second. On newspapers everywhere we'll stare out, bug-eyed, like a pair of deranged Muppets.

And neither of us will care much, either. Because the shot bounces off the pipes, denying us the goal that would have put us in the lead.

The buzzer sounds on the third period of a tie game, and Becca and I are clutching each other. She slides back in her seat and exhales, but I don't even want to relax before the overtime period. The adrenaline rush is intoxicating.

I love this. Every second. I'm strapped into this roller coaster and I never want it to end.

My palm goes to a certain little box in the pocket of my jacket. It's there, waiting for me. I am not entirely sure that tonight will offer up the right moment for this maneuver. But Rebecca is the right woman and I know I'm not going to wait very much longer.

Everything dear to me is on the line right now. Everything. And I wouldn't change a thing.

Lauren leans over the two of us, putting a hand on my shoulder. "Check your phone, Nate. Alex is trying to reach you."

Rebecca's eyes widen immediately. She's flushed from the excitement of the game, her lips pink and kissable. "Whip it out," she whispers. "Let's see what she has to say."

I catch her smooth chin in my hand. "You know I love you, right?"

She smiles, and I stroke her lip with my thumb. "I know, boss-man. Just look at the damned text."

Reluctantly I remove my phone from a pocket and unlock it. I touch the messaging app, wondering if I'll always remember this as the moment when I learned I'd become a father.

Alex: *No relationship. You're off the hook. My love to Becca.*

"Well," Becca says quietly. "Poor Alex."

I wrap an arm around her, because that's a generous thing to say, and also because I can't stop touching her. "Sorry for that drama."

"It's okay," she says. "Your mom is texting you, too."

I'd noticed that as well. "She's watching the game," I say, stowing my phone. "I'll get the mom download later. Want a drink?"

"Sure!" She flashes me a smile. "I'll have whatever."

I get up and find us a couple of sodas. It's tempting to go downstairs and listen to Coach's locker-room speech, and get a feel for his overtime strategy. Except I don't want to be that guy. It's not the owner's job to stick his nose in.

Rebecca is chatting up Stew when I return. I watch her animated face as she talks hockey with my best friend. He looks almost as keyed up as I am.

I hate the idea of Becca quitting the Bruisers. I barely slept last night, thinking about it. I lay there in bed, listening to Becca's deep and even breathing, and wondering how to fix the mess I was in. Or part of it, anyway.

Around dawn I found the answer, and it was so simple I felt like an idiot for not getting there sooner. If Becca couldn't feel right working for a team I owned, there was one easy way I could fix that.

We're going to have a chat about it later. She just doesn't know it yet.

I hand her a soda.

"Where's mine?" Stew demands.

I point at the well-stocked bar table and he rolls his eyes before getting up to help himself.

Play resumes after the ice is cleaned. Twenty minutes of overtime are posted on the clock. Becca watches, white-knuckled, while the players face off.

And we're back on the roller coaster. My guys fight hard, and I can hardly breathe. I live for this. It's a passion and a dream come true. But it's not my livelihood.

Rebecca's hand tightens on my thigh.

We both lean forward in our seats as Bart Palacio gets the puck out of a scrum against the boards.

"STOP HIM," Becca shrieks as he dodges O'Doul to keep control of the puck.

But nobody gets there in time. I see what will happen with horrifying clarity. It's Palacio and Beacon, man against man.

My goalie is the best in the business. His mind is a rapid-fire calculator of hockey physics. He chooses his position based on a lifetime of anticipating forwards like Palacio. But he's only one man. His defensemen have failed him, and his only choice is to pick the best option and position for a save. He butterflies against a five-hole shot, but Palacio goes for the shoulder instead.

All my blood stops circulating as the puck flips neatly into the upper corner of the net and then drops behind Beacon.

The stadium gasps.

The lamp lights.

And just like that, the whole thing is over.

Rebecca and I sit for a moment in stunned silence. That always happens during an overtime loss, when the situation quickly turns in a heartbeat from Anything is Possible to *Nope*.

"Oh no," Becca whispers, hand to her heart. "Goddamn it."

I hug her. "So close."

"Goddamn it!" she yells. "Palacio! I'm gonna rip off his arms."

Below us the Dallas team is rushing the ice, piling up like puppies, gyrating in wild celebration.

Becca's eyes get red. "That should have been us. I'm wearing my lucky bra and everything."

I watch all those wrong-colored jerseys circle and sway. I pictured this moment a million times, with a purple color scheme. But I'm also analytical to a fault, and when I walked into the stadium today I knew our odds were only a little better than 50%. I'm bummed, but I'm not surprised.

Becca buries her face in my shoulder, and I stroke her hair, positive that the last few weeks have given me more than they've taken away. The little box in my pocket is yelling my name. But even I know better than to propose to a sad woman while I'm still in range of several dozen TV cameras.

"Let's go, guys," Georgia says gently. "Time to go downstairs and smile and show what good sports we are."

"Oh joy," Becca mutters. "Can't we just sneak out the back?"

"In a few minutes," Georgia says. "I'm sure Nate wants to thank his players."

That locker room is probably morbidly quiet right now. "Let's go," I say, standing up. "The sooner we go downstairs, the sooner we can get the hell out of Dallas."

"Now it's my least favorite city, too," Becca grumbles.

Downstairs, I exchange a few pleasantries with the only reporters who bother to speak to the losing team. They're New York news outlets, of course. "The people of Brooklyn can be really proud of how far we've come," I say. Yada yada yada. Some days you're meant to read from the loser's script, and there's nothing to be done about it.

Rebecca waits outside the dressing room while I make a pass through there shaking hands. It's easy to thank these men who've given so much to the team. "We'll get 'em next year," I say. "Take a nice long vacation. Rest up. Invest in a Dallas dartboard."

When I return to the hallway, Becca is flanked by two of my security guys. "Gettin' rowdy out here," one of them says, nodding toward the home team's corridor.

I'm sure it is. Stadium security gets a little weird after a big win like this. Everyone wants to rub elbows with victory, and their joy overfloweth into our adjacent corridor.

Due to bad architectural planning, Becca and I will have to wade through the edges of the crowd to get to the players' exit. Security parts the bystanders to let us pass. But when we reach the doors, we're told, the car has been chased out of its holding spot, the driver sent to do a lap around the block.

"We could walk," Bec suggests. The crowd and the blaring celebration music are a little much.

"Not this time," says Gary, tonight's bodyguard. "Half of Dallas is crowding around the stadium to celebrate. The car's ETA is four minutes."

"Fine," I say, placing a hand at the small of Rebecca's back. "Shall we step outside to wait?"

"Lotta cameras out there," Gary says.

The door opens then, proving his point. Fans congregate just beyond the roped-off area. I'm eyeing the crowd so I don't notice who has just paused to grind out a cigarette under the heel of her high-heeled boot before coming back inside.

It's Juliet.

———

REBECCA

She appears before me like a bad dream. Nate's beautiful, intelligent ex, with the golden hair and gym owner's body.

Nate's hand goes still on my back.

And this is exactly the scenario I'd been dreading. I brace myself to hear her sneer: *Nate, you've moved up in the world, huh? Dating your secretary? That's convenient.*

I'm just ramping up into panic mode when I take in a few more details. The lighter in her bony hand, for one. Since when does Juliet smoke? And her grim expression. She looks harder than when I last saw her. Her eyes aren't happy.

If my team had just won the Cup, that's not the face I'd be wearing.

Then she spots Nate, and her eyes widen. The moment yawns open between them, long and awkward.

I wonder what he sees. Someone he hates? Or someone he will always love.

"Hi," she says slowly, shaking off her surprise. "*God.* I'm so sorry about that story in the *Post.* The reporter called and I told her to go find a real story. I hung up on her."

"It's okay," Nate says evenly. "Wasn't the first dumb thing anyone ever wrote about me. And it won't be the last."

"Well…" Juliet starts to say something, but she's interrupted by a gruff male voice yelling from down the hall.

"Yo. *Juliet!* Where the fuck did you go?"

"Uh…" Her eyes dart nervously down the corridor before returning to Nate's. "I'm sorry anyway. It was shitty." She swallows hard. "You look good. I hope you're doing well."

"Can't complain at all." His palm heats the center of my back, and his thumb strokes my new purple sweater. "And, uh, you look great, too. Congratulations, by the way."

"Juliet!" a man's voice snarls. "Get the fuck down here!"

She opens her mouth to reply, but then a thick-necked, red-faced player appears. Bart Palacio. As he takes in our little group of three, his lips curl into a sneer. "Am I interrupting something?"

"No," Juliet says quickly, her face reddening. "Of course not."

"So get your fat ass back here." He jerks a thumb toward the crowded corridor. "Picture time."

Then he actually reaches for her wrist and *drags her* body away from us.

I just stare after the two of them for a moment. My mouth is hanging open. "What the hell was that? Who speaks to his wife that way?"

When I turn toward Nate, he looks stricken. "Jesus," he says on an exhale. "He's worse than I remember."

I feel outrage on behalf of a woman I don't even like. I'm not sure she even noticed me standing there, either. And I just don't even care.

Because she said no to a life with Nate for that asshole. I can't imagine why anyone would do that.

I'll never make the same mistake.

"Car's here!" Gary says suddenly. "Let's roll."

When he opens the door, Nate and I step out into the night. The crowd outside strains forward, looking to see who's emerged. They'll be largely disappointed, because they're waiting for their Dallas victors. But a few people point phones at us while Gary does his level best to block me from harm during the twenty-foot walk to the car.

Mere seconds later the doors shut and the locks engage. The car drives away from the curb.

Gary has hopped in front so it's just the two of us in the back seat for this short drive.

"Are you okay?" I ask Nate, reaching across the leather seat to squeeze his hand.

He shakes himself. "Yeah, of course. It's just…" He taps his lip. "That stupid article had a grain of truth to it. I had a lot of reasons for buying the team. But one of them, at least, was that I could just picture beating Dallas in the playoffs on their home ice. I don't, like, sit around and think about her, though…"

"I know," I say quickly.

He turns to me in the darkness. "But I always just assumed she was happier, you know? It's worse that she isn't. Never mind. I'm sorry to talk about her. That's rude."

"No! It isn't. But I didn't know smart girls could be so stupid."

Nate snorts. "Smart people are stupid all the time. Ask me how I know." He leans across the seat, hooks an arm around my hips, and tows me across the leather until we're hip to hip. "Tonight has been rough so far. But maybe it's salvageable."

I don't weigh in. I just tuck my cheek against his strong arm and sigh.

―――――

An hour later we're happily ensconced in the Jacuzzi tub—the very same one I refused on principle to get into with him two weeks before.

There's champagne in our glasses. Because fuck it—bubbly wine isn't just for people who win. And Nate's free hand is stroking my foot under water.

We're quiet, but not sad. An odyssey has ended—for now. "There's always next year," I say, taking another sip.

From the other end of the tub he raises his glass in agreement. "We'll be there to see it. Together."

This makes me feel all warm and bubbly inside. "Even if I'm working someplace else, I wouldn't miss sitting in the box with you."

"Speaking of making plans," he says, setting his glass down on the ledge. "I have a proposition I want to discuss with you."

"What's that?" But I know what he's about to say. He is going to come up with some reason or another that I shouldn't look for another job. I still have to consider it, though.

Nate reaches up and grabs a washcloth off the ledge. And from inside it he pulls a very small box. It looks like…

"Holy crap!" I hear myself say. Because that can't be what I think it is.

Nate opens the box with his thumb. And maybe it's the expensive Ritz lighting but the diamond that pops into view is *dazzling*. And large. And dazzling.

"Rebecca. Sweetheart—"

Sweetheart.

"Will you marry me? I know it's fast. But it isn't, really. Seven years seems like plenty of time to figure out that you're my favorite person in the world. And I don't want to go another year without you."

I would love to answer him, but I can't speak. My eyes get blurry—which does nothing to diminish the sparkle of that diamond—and there's something caught in my throat.

He's waiting.

I don't even hesitate. I'm done searching my soul, when the answer has been right in front of me this whole time. I scramble to lift my rump off the floor of the tub and wiggle toward him. I'm straddling his lap, and he has to lift the ring out of the way when I splash forward to look him right in the eye at close range. "Y-yes," I stammer, feeling more certain than I sound. "I will."

Those light brown eyes smile, and he leans forward a few inches to kiss me. "Thank you," he says between kisses. "My timing is weird, but…"

I kiss him again. I'm done worrying about our timing, too.

"Bec." He laughs against my lips. "Don't you want to see the ring? You could choose any style you want…"

"It's beautiful," I say even before I get a proper look. And it is. When he slides it onto my finger, I see that it's a vintage setting—a cushion cut diamond surrounded by more tiny stones. "Wow. Fancy. I love it so much."

An engagement ring from Nate. On *my* finger.

When I look up at him again, the view of his face is even more beautiful. His eyes look damp, and he's smiling at me like he just won…the Stanley Cup. "I love you," he whispers.

"I love you, too." I'm holding my hand so carefully above the water because I can't imagine letting such a precious thing out of my sight.

His smile becomes amused. "It's okay if it gets wet, you know."

"Not with me," I squeak. "There's a small fortune on my finger."

"It's insured."

Still.

"Listen, I know I just blew your mind a little bit, but I need to blow it some more," he says.

"Okay?" I can't imagine there's anything he could say right now more shocking than a marriage proposal. And to think I had written off tonight as a disaster.

Nate takes my hand and holds it, admiring his handiwork. "Marrying me is more complicated than dating me. There's paperwork."

"Oh, I don't doubt it," I say, kissing him on the nose. "I'll sign whatever prenup your lawyer can dream up."

He flinches. "There has to be a prenup. Can I tell you why?"

"Because you have a billion dollars?"

"That's not why." He smiles at me again, and it's hard to concentrate. "It's because of my voting rights. If someone thought the power structure of KTech could be put into play by our divorce, then someone might decide he has millions to gain by breaking us up."

"Oh," I say slowly. "That's creepy." My mind doesn't usually leap right to the worst-case scenario. Although, after witnessing Juliet's fucktard of a husband tonight, I was more primed than usual to understand that creeps exist.

"Yeah," he says gently. "So the prenup will have to give me all my KTech shares. But I don't think you'll care, because there's a wedding gift I want to give you. And it's important to me that you accept it."

"Um…I don't need anything, Nate. I never really cared about your big bucks, except I don't mind when you pick up the dinner check."

His warm, wet palm slides down my smiling face. "I know," he whispers, and the sound of his voice vibrates in my chest.

I wonder if we can have this conversation later, because we should be starting up the celebration sex right about now. His strong chest glistens with droplets of water, and I'm suddenly inspired to lick it all off.

"The gift you're getting is a certain hockey franchise. They made a recent run at the championship, and I think they'll continue to flourish under new leadership."

"What?" I say stupidly. I'm getting the sex tingles, and Nate is somehow talking about hockey again.

"You're going to be the new owner of the Brooklyn Bruisers. You won't be shtupping the boss anymore. But I expect to have sex in *your* office at least once."

My poor little brain can't quite wrap itself around this idea. "Own...the team?" That makes no sense.

"Yeah, baby. You'll be great. I've had a good run, and you're going to be able to give it more attention than I probably should. And nobody loves the Bruisers more, right? So why *not* you?"

"Because it's yours?"

"Not for long." He shakes his head and smiles at me. "I need you more than I need to own the team. And I want you to have it. We might have to get married before I can sign it over. It's because of gift taxes. Or something. My accountant can explain it to you."

Now I'm officially done. There is no more shocking information that I can take in tonight. But maybe I don't have to. We kiss again and again. Then Nate hits the switch to drain the tub. He urges me to my feet. I can't even grab a towel before he steers my dripping body toward the bed, pushes me onto that soft cloud, and wraps his body around mine.

———

"I still have some questions," I admit as we lay in bed, cuddling and making plans. Or trying, anyway. There's a lot of kissing that gets in the way of the planning. Also, I have to stop every couple of minutes to admire the way my ring shines even in the dark.

"Shoot," Nate says, hugging me closer.

"Are your parents going to be upset?"

"About what? My mom loves you. Everyone loves you. We've been over this."

"But I'm a shiksa. Don't they want you to marry a nice Jewish girl?"

He runs a finger down my nose. "News flash—my mom isn't Jewish. Marrying shiksas is already a family tradition."

"Really?" I had no idea.

"Really. If that's your big concern, we're covered."

I kiss his chin, because I can't help myself. We may never get out of this bed, and that's okay with me. "Nate," I say between kisses. "I don't know anything about being a team owner."

"But you do. It's a job where the major requirement is you pay attention and you care. And nobody cares more than you, Bec; you're going to do great."

"It's just hard to picture."

"Not for me. You can promote your intern and do less of the grunt work yourself. That frees up your time for more big-picture questions. Some of them are fun. Like—what focus would you choose for the foundation next year?"

"Head injury research," I say immediately.

"See?" Nate's laugh is gleeful. "Any work you do there is at least as important as hiring the right vendors in the stadium."

"We're in charge of the food? The cheese puffs are staying."

Nate grins. "Luckily, I'm leaving you with no immediate problems to solve. Your stadium lease is good for another eight years, and Hugh Major and Coach aren't going anywhere."

"God I hope not."

"Don't worry! I'll always help you. But it won't take you long to realize you already know almost as much about owning a hockey team as I do. And baby—when we need answers, you'll just hire some finance nerd or legal geek who knows."

"I'm going to be in over my head sometimes."

"Sure. Like anyone who ever tried something new. I have faith in you. That organization is better with you in it. My life is better with you in it." He strokes my bare back with his long fingers and then whispers, "Please be my partner in this and all things."

It's a long time until we speak again after that. More loving happens.

I manage to exhaust both of us. Eventually Nate rolls onto his back, eyes closed, and asks: "Will you move in with me right away?"

"I…" As usual, I begin by assuming I should have an objection. "Sure."

"You can change things in that house, you know. If you don't like the setup, we'll work on it. But if you don't hate it too much, I'd like to stay. There's enough room on the property for the security team to do its job."

"Okay. I'm sure I can find a way to be comfortable in a few of your twelve rooms or however many there are."

He strokes my hair. "I want you to feel at home, Bec. Not just be comfortable. But we'll work on it. Meanwhile, your sister and her family will enjoy a little more room, right?"

"Right..." I say slowly. "I just signed a new lease. That ought to hold them a while."

"Or forever," Nate says. "There's a note in your file not to raise the rent."

"What?" My head pops off the pillow. "You own that building?"

"Sure. When I built the practice facility I bought up everything that was for sale in the neighborhood. And when you relocated to Brooklyn..."

"The Bruisers' real estate agent showed me that apartment." I'd thought it was just lucky that I'd found a reasonable rent so close to work. "That's sneaky."

Nate shakes his head. "You didn't have to pick that place. But I was happy you did. It let me look out for you in a small way. You know—back when I loved you only from afar." He puts a hand to his heart and makes a Mr. Darcy face, which makes me smile. "What kind of wedding do you want? You can pick anything."

"Not sure yet. *Many* magazines will be consulted." The poor man has no idea. "Can we keep it small?"

"Sure?"

"I mean—family, close friends, and the hockey team. With you it would be easy to end up accidentally inviting half of KTech and Goldman Sachs."

"Why don't we rent out a small hotel somewhere in the Caribbean and have a destination wedding?"

"That would be fun."

"It keeps the numbers down and guarantees you'll have to wear a bikini at least part of the time."

"You have a one-track mind."

"No—four." He holds his hand up to count them off. "Tech. Hockey. Food. Rebecca."

"That's a lot like my list," I whisper. "Food. Fashion. Hockey. Nate."

"Three outa four ain't bad," he whispers. Then he kisses me again.

Team Owner Gets First Stanley Cup, First Child in Three-Hour Window

"Screaming is pretty common on the maternity ward," Nurse Amalah Dawn of New York Presbyterian Brooklyn Methodist Hospital told *The Wire*. "But it's usually about childbirth, and not about hockey."

That changed last night, when Brooklyn Bruisers team owner Rebecca Rowley Kattenberger, 30, watched her players win their first Stanley Cup since her husband—the tech mogul Nate Kattenberger, 35—first moved the franchise to Brooklyn five years ago.

Mrs. Kattenberger had planned to watch game six in Nashville with her team, but went into labor a few hours before she'd planned to fly down for the game.

"I thought—this is fine, it's not a disaster," Mrs. Kattenberger told *The Wire* via email. "If the series goes to game seven, the baby and I can make an appearance at the Brooklyn arena."

But that's not what happened. She watched a very exciting game six on the labor and delivery ward, while the medical team monitored her contractions.

"Labor did not progress rapidly," Nurse Dawn reported. "That's normal for a first birth. The doctor wanted to give her an oxytocin drip to move things along, but she said, 'Not until the third period. What if we go into overtime?'"

Ultimately the team and the labor process both got their respective jobs done. Brooklyn broke a 2-2 tie with an early third period goal (Trevi, assisted by Castro) and followed it with another goal just ninety seconds later (Bayer, assisted by Drake). At the buzzer, they were the official champions.

The reaction from birthing room #407 was often loud and ultimately joyous.

"During a tense part of the game, we reassured nearby patients that everything was just fine. And when Brooklyn won, everyone on the ward was pretty excited," Dawn said. "Rebecca's baby waited. Things went much faster after we shut off the television. She was ready to push about two hours later, and the baby was born an hour after that."

Rebecca Rowley Kattenberger and Nathan Kattenberger welcomed a seven-pound baby girl into the world at ten minutes past one in the morning. Her name has been withheld from the press, but the family is healthy and resting comfortably.

The Kattenbergers live in Brooklyn, where they will raise their daughter. Mrs. Kattenberger gave birth at the Brooklyn location of the New York Presbyterian Hospital group. Mrs. Kattenberger's Brooklyn Bruisers Foundation raised ten million dollars for the pediatric wing of the hospital just this past year. Her hockey players also threw a holiday party on the premises in December.

Rumor has it that the Stanley Cup will make a visit to the maternity ward before the weekend is through.

When asked if this was the most unusual birth she's witnessed on shift, Nurse Dawn dismissed that idea. "We had a baby born in the elevator just last week. You got to be pretty creative to catch us unawares."

A ticker tape parade celebrating the Bruisers' victory will be held on Wall Street later this month, time and date to be announced next week. Mr. And Mrs. Kattenberger plan to attend.

THE
END

———

Thank you! We hope you enjoyed Brooklynaire!
For more Bruisers, try:
Rookie Move (Leo & Georgia)
Hard Hitter (O'Doul & Ari)
Pipe Dreams (Beacon & Lauren)
Bountiful (Beringer & Zara)

ALSO BY SARINA BOWEN

TRUE NORTH

Bittersweet

Steadfast

Keepsake

Bountiful

THE IVY YEARS

The Year We Fell Down #1

The Year We Hid Away #2

Blonde Date #2.5

The Understatement of the Year #3

The Shameless Hour #4

The Fifteenth Minute #5

GRAVITY

Coming In From the Cold #1

Falling From the Sky #2

Shooting for the Stars #3

HELLO GOODBYE

Goodbye Paradise

Hello Forever

Made in the USA
Middletown, DE
18 February 2018